ISHBEL
AND THE
EMPIRE

A Biography of Lady Aberdeen

DORIS FRENCH

Design and Production:Andy Tong
Printing and Binding:Gagné Printing Ltd., Louiseville, Quebec, Canada

The writing of this manuscript and the publication of this book were made possible by support from several sources. The publisher wishes to acknowledge the generous assistance and ongoing support of **The Canada Council, The Book Publishing Industry Development Programme** of the **Department of Communications** and **The Ontario Arts Council.**

Care has been taken to trace the ownership of copyright material used in the text (including the illustrations). The author and publisher welcome any information enabling them to rectify any reference or credit in subsequent editions.

J. Kirk Howard, Publisher

Cataloguing in Publication

Shackleton, Doris French, 1918-
  Ishbel and the Empire

Bibliography: p.
Includes index.
ISBN 1-55002-036-6 (bound) ISBN 1-55002-038-2 (pbk.)

1. Aberdeen and Temair, Ishbel Gordon, Marchioness of, 1857-1939. 2. Governors general - Canada - Spouses - Biography. 3. Women in politics - Canada - Biography. 4. Social reformers - Canada - Biography. 5. Canada - Politics and government - 1878-1896.* 6. Aberdeen and Temair, John Campbell Gordon, Marquis of, 1847-1934. I. Title.

DA816.A23S48 1988   941.081'092'4   C88-093809-9

Dundurn Press Limited
2181 Queen Street East, Suite 301
Toronto, Canada
M4E 1E5

Dundurn Distribution Limited
Athol Brose, School Hill,
Wargrave, Reading, England
RG10 8DY

ISHBEL

AND THE

EMPIRE

A Biography of Lady Aberdeen

D ORIS F RENCH

Toronto and Oxford
Dundurn Press
1988

CONTENTS

Preface

A governor-general, the representative of the queen, presides over the country at an uncontaminated level, above the corridors of political power. So says the constitution. In reality, most governors-general and their wives carry the usual baggage of political bias. To decontaminate them for the duration of a viceregal term is an easier task in some instances than in others.

The appointment is, after all, made by politicians. In the case of the Earl of Aberdeen, Canada's seventh post-Confederation Governor-General, the honour was bestowed by William Ewart Gladstone, the prime minister who had given the Liberal party of Britain form and substance. The Aberdeens, and particularly Lady Aberdeen, were his devout admirers. He had chosen them first to represent the crown and government in Ireland, during a heady six-month term in 1886 when the first Home Rule Bill lent unprecedented glamour to their appointment. The defeat of the Bill and the government had abruptly ended their term amid wildly protesting and adoring throngs of Irish nationalists.

Lady Aberdeen, a mere 29 years of age, had absorbed that adoration like a thirsty sponge. She had set afoot all manner of Irish nationalist projects, both practical and symbolic, from introducing the Irish jig at Dublin Castle, to dressing her small children in Paddy green coats, to lobbying furiously for the sale of Irish laces in the world markets. So strongly identified had she become with Home Rule, that the Aberdeens in fact became a political liability to Gladstone. When he was next called to office, in 1892, Home Rule had become the most contentious issue in Britain and to hold factions together the new Liberal government had to lay out a very delicate course. The path might lead to Home Rule, but only by treading lightly on eggshells all the way. A figurehead of a Viceroy, not an activist, was needed. A partisan wife would be truly embarrassing.

So it came about that Lady Ishbel, Countess of Aberdeen, was dealt the rudest blow of her young life. She was convinced that she was right for Ireland; she could use her boundless energy and high position to accomplish miracles. She had hundreds of loyal Irish followers. While the Liberals were out of office she had remained engaged, from London, in untiring efforts to keep alive her Irish associations and projects. When she reappeared in Ireland she succumbed to the flattery of those who called her their "Irish queen." She was overwhelmed and shattered when Gladstone, a weekend guest at the Aberdeen's Dollis Hill villa on the edge of London, informed them that they might take any viceregal post they wished, but not Ireland.

It was her husband who chose Canada. They had already made two extended trips to the senior Dominion, rattling across the land in a special car on the glorious CPR. Lord Aberdeen had a keen interest in railways. He had also become a landowner, with hundreds of acres of ranch-land and new orchards in the Okanagan Valley. He was pleased at the prospect of going to Ottawa, and he assured the nervous Colonial Secretary, Lord Ripon, that there would be "no whisper of complaint" on partisan political grounds.

But Lady Aberdeen accepted the post with downcast resentment of those advisors of Gladstone who had kept her from Ireland. She had been interested in Canada and Canadian politics, particularly vis-à-vis the United States. But it was a terribly Tory place. The Conservatives were in power — Macdonald had just died — and it seemed everyone of wealth and position was a Tory.

And she was not at all sure that there would be much for her to *do* in Canada. It was her belief that one is called to high office in order to serve. Her concept of "serving" would not have been amiss on a tennis court, where a powerful wham, if well directed, wins the set. She saw the Canadians, overall, as a tediously parochial population, far too close in sentiment to their republican neighbours, suspicious of *lords* and *ladies*, lacking Celtic charm. It would be hard to love them, very hard to be loved. She proceeded to Canada reluctantly.

Yet nowhere else over a long and fruitful career did this remarkable woman, attractive, ardent, intelligent, loyal to a fault, effect so much or leave so strong an imprint. Quite the opposite of the prototype Victorian lady, she dominated, energized, antagonized, battled and won over whole battalions of Canadians who remember her today in some awe as "Canada's Governess-General."

Acknowledgements

It would be churlish not to acknowledge the continued help I have received in the writing of this biography. I hesitate only because so much time has elapsed since I began that I run the risk of overlooking many who made real contributions along the way. But some few at least must be mentioned. Others I hope will simply accept my unacknowledged thanks.

Originally, Dr. R.H. Hubbard, cultural advisor at Government House, Ottawa, provoked my interest in the subject through his excellent 1967 book on Rideau Hall and its successive residents. Dr. Hubbard was good enough to encourage me, believing that the time had indeed come for a full-length biography of Lady Aberdeen.

Much more time went by before the work was begun, and completed. Assistance in the cost of travel for research was received through a Canada Council Explorations grant. A supplementary grant was received at a later date from the Ontario Arts Council.

Family descendants of Lord and Lady Aberdeen have been very generous, showing considerable interest in the project and taking the trouble to clear many ambiguous points. The fifth Marquess of Aberdeen and Temair, Archie Aberdeen, was especially helpful on the two occasions when I interviewed him in London, and through our correspondence. I much regret that his death occurred before publication. I was courteously received by Lady June Gordon, Marchionness of Aberdeen and Temair, at Haddo House in Aberdeenshire, and allowed valuable weeks of time searching the records and copying photographs and paintings. Other family members were equally generous: Alistair Gordon, the sixth Marquess; John Sinclair, Lord Pentland, of New York and his daughter, Mary Rothenburg, who is "Ishbel's" great-grand daughter. I was also pleased to meet in Kelowna John and Ursula Surtees, Canadians related to the same family.

I am grateful for the extensive help given me by several archival institutions: the Public Archives of Canada, who helped over a long period of time; the Archives of Ontario, with particular thanks to Allan J. MacDonald and Hugh

MacMillan; the Provincial Archives of British Columbia; the City Archives of Metro Toronto, Perth, Ontario, and Vernon, B.C., and the Historical Association of Kelowna, B.C.

In Britain I received friendly assistance at the National Library of Scotland, Edinburgh; the Bodleian Library, Oxford; the University of Birmingham Library; Somerset House, London; the Record Office, the House of Lords, Westminster; the Public Record Office, Kew.

In Britain I also had worthwhile conversations with Thomas Michie, Haddo House; Mr. and Mrs. James Drummond, Aberdeen; the Reverend M.W. Burgess SSC, Church of the Annunciation (formerly Quebec Chapel), London, and others.

I would like to thank Elizabeth Harvor of Toronto for good advice at an earlier stage of writing. My thanks also for their interest and support go to representatives of three Canadian organizations founded by Lady Aberdeen: to Pearl Dobson, executive secretary of the National Council of Women, Jean Leask of the Victorian Order of Nurses, and Gertrude Holt of the May Court Club of Ottawa.

Finally let me thank Kirk Howard, publisher at Dundurn Press for his faith in the book, and the people who worked with him in its production, especially Leslie Derbecker, editor, for her warm support and expert judgment.

Not singled out are the dozens of people whom I have consulted in a variety of ways over the past dozen years. It is my hope that, imperfect as it is, this biography will be read by them — and others — with interest. May it focus attention once more on the multi-coloured past, making it seem less long ago and its inhabitants less dead, so that we catch the breath of their nostrils and the warmth of their fingers as we pass them on the stairs.

Doris (Shackleton) French
October 1988

PART 1
MAYFAIR

Chapter 1
Cradle and Child

When one remembers that Ishbel, born Ishbel Maria Marjoribanks (pronounced Marchbanks), lived until March 1939 she seems a person of modern times, in touch with events still well known. Indeed she was. But her birthdate in 1857 puts her in a different light. We go back to a time when men described young women as "fair ones" with "silly little heads." The hoopskirt had reached enormous proportions, a woman proceeding down the street seemed to inhabit a large birdcage, and took up the whole sidewalk, so that ungallant men complained of having to walk in the gutter. Opinions were expressed that make most of us shudder now. A radical sociologist, Henry Fawcett, described an ideal England "of well-fed, well-educated citizens, with skilled artisans and peasant proprietors at the base, scavenged for and waited on by Negroes and Chinese."[1]

The year of Ishbel's birth was the year of the Indian Mutiny, blazing in violence and ruthlessly suppressed. The northern reaches of Canada were also in the news. In Aberdeen harbour that year the *Fox* was being outfitted by Lady Franklin for one more voyage in search of a lost husband. The Conservatives were in power, but the Whig-Liberals were shaping a party that would soon attract William Gladstone as its leader. The palace announced the engagement of Queen Victoria's oldest daughter to Prince Frederic William of Prussia, who would father the Kaiser of the First World War. It would be two years before Darwin published *On the Origin of Species*, ten before Karl Marx' *Das Kapital*. It was 1857. England was entering its time of greatest glory. It saw itself and was seen as master of the world. Decline would begin before the century ended, but brilliant decades, a "plenitude of power"[2] lay between decline and the year 1857. Ishbel Marjoribanks was born on the crest of the nation's fortune, in London's Mayfair. Her father was Dudley Coutts Marjoribanks, wealthy owner of Meux Brewery. His investments included large shares in the Hudson's Bay Company, and his wealth poured into the home bank.

The family claimed descent from Robert Bruce, who in 1315 settled on his daughter Marjorie the lands along the River Annan, which became known as Terre de Marjoribankis. Ishbel's favourite ancestor was of course a Scot, "a tall handsome girl of eighteen," Grizel Cochrane, who saved her father, a follower of the Duke of Argyll, from execution as a traitor to James II. She disguised herself as a boy, and robbed a messenger who was on his way to Edinburgh with the death warrant in his pouch.[3]

A later Grizel, Ishbel's great grandmother, married Edward Marjoribanks; their home was still in the Border country, in Lees, Berwickshire. While their oldest son was off to Edinburgh, the second, another Edward, made for London. There, trading on an obscure family connection, he joined Thomas Coutts, founder of Coutts Bank at 59 the Strand. Edward Marjoribanks progressed to senior partner, remaining in that position until his death in 1868. Members of the royal family relied on his good judgment. He was Queen Victoria's banker. He became an extremely wealthy man.

The Marjoribanks fortunes were thus linked to the prestigious bank. Thomas Coutts had made it a family institution, strictly regulating the number and selection of partners, so that although Edward Marjoribanks was highly regarded only one of his sons could also be taken into partnership. It was a prize that had to go to the oldest, another Edward. Ishbel's father, Dudley Coutts Marjoribanks, was left to scramble for a suitable position. For many years he tried to open the magic door to a partnership at Coutts'. He even considered marrying the eccentric lady who in 1837 succeeded to all the Coutts wealth, Baroness Angela Burdett-Coutts. She was one of the richest women in the world, of whom many strange tales were told, including the belief that her blotched skin produced body lice. From that fable derived the word "cooties", slang for the pests that bedeviled Britain's infantry in the first World War.[4] The Baroness was Ishbel's godmother. However she coldly denied Dudley his hope of a partnership, perhaps believing his somewhat tempestuous nature made him unsuitable to be a banker.

She grew even colder towards the Marjoribanks family when in 1877 the brother Edward, partner in the bank, was found to have dissipated his own considerable fortune, and to be on the verge of personal bankruptcy. This was letting down the bank's reputation. The partnership was quickly dissolved and reconstituted without Edward. It was the snubbed younger brother Dudley, who had angrily announced to Angela that he had received "a far better offer, pecuniarily speaking" from the brewer Sir Henry Mieux,[5] who came to Edward's rescue and paid off his debts.

Dudley had prospered, aside from the benefit he received on his father's death when he was made principal heir, supposedly in compensation for missing the Coutts partnership. He acquired large properties and even turned his admiration for works of art to profitable dealing. Like every rising young Londoner he had taken the Grand Tour of Italy, and his letters to relatives reveal a robust nature that refused to echo the pious conventional praise of cathedrals, seeing in them not the glory of God but the uncommon cleverness of his fellow men. At Milan he wrote:

> But oh ye gods and little fishes what shall I say about the Cathedral here, it beggars all description, what avail is it to tell you that it is an enormous Gothic building of white marble of the most splendid workmanship... It raised my opinion of [man]. I had no idea before that he could have planned much less executed such a noble temple.[6]

He wrote also to his sister Annie that he was keeping in touch with British politics from abroad:

> You will be surprised to hear that I approve of the Income Tax although of course there are many and grave objections to it as regards Professional men, Merchants and others, perhaps a Property Tax would have been better, but some tax of the sort was quite necessary but it is decided [sic] better than resuming the beer tax or imposing other taxes that would affect the poor and not the rich. I do hope they will lay it on the Irish Absentees.[7]

With such views Dudley was obviously destined for the Liberal party, and it was as a Liberal that he was elected in the family's Berwick-on-Tweed seat. He was made a baronet in 1866. He lost out in the 1868 election, but regained the seat in 1874. A stalwart of the Liberals, his role was not in the front benches. He failed to master the scholarly oratory expected of parliamentarians; he was said to have made only one speech in the House in his entire career. In 1881 he was raised to the peerage as Baron Tweedmouth.

Dudley married Isabella Hogg in 1848. Her pale intensity and genteel airs attracted him and they were well suited in ambition, although their personalities clashed and led to continual marital discord. Isabella taught her children that her bloodline was exceptionally pure, with a sprinkling of refugee French aristocrats and "an unbroken descent from Edward I, the first Plantagenet King of England."[8] She was the oldest daughter in a family of seven daughters and seven sons whose father was Sir James Hogg, originally from County Antrim in northern Ireland, a skilled lawyer and senior official of the East India Company, and a Tory member of parliament. Hogg and his large family were devoted adherents to the evangelical wing of the Church of England. Lord Hailsham (Quintin Hogg), Lord Chancellor in the cabinet of Margaret Thatcher in the 1980's, was of this family. He has described the "great spiritual crisis" in the life of the earlier Quintin Hogg, his grandfather and Isabella's brother, on reading Darwin's *On the Origin of Species*.[9] The challenge to Holy Scripture was an intolerable shock. Piety and social success seemed to have equal weight in Isabella's scale of values. She pursued both with relentless vigor. Recalling her in later years, Lord Hailsham, her great-nephew, described her as "an old dragon." To the child Ishbel, her mother was a goddess, a presiding queen in the glittering drawing rooms of her home and her social circle. Behind the glitter was an unnerving ambition. The Marjoribanks' crest was an eagle's claw. Their motto was "Advance with Courage."

Dudley, Ishbel's father, had sent a curiously candid letter to his bride's mother after their wedding night. It suggests how bluntly he expressed his feelings, a trait that would lead to violently overbearing outbursts of behaviour in later years:

> I felt almost as if I were doing a wrong action in taking such a loving devoted daughter and sister from her own happy home to one that she did not know, where she might, possibly, not find everything congenial with her own pure and exalted ideas of what is right and good... Isabel, though pale and tired this morning, is better than I ventured to hope for.[10]

Isabella, pale and tired, followed the usual course of the Victorian wife in submission to her husband's demands. Her revenge was to develop to a high degree a martyr complex, which would deeply affect her sensitive young daughter. On their eighteenth wedding anniversary Isabella gave her husband a watch, along with some excruciating verse:

> And as I strive soon may I be
> More worthy of my s'poso;
> Earnest in duty let me see
> God's will and his also.[11]

She was a woman who would say she "gave her husband" sons and daughters, and apologize to him for their misconduct. In later years the widowed Lady Tweedmouth would show considerable spirit and a dominating will of her own.

Ishbel was the third of five surviving children. The house in Mayfair where she had been born was soon replaced by a handsome mansion, continuing the name of the original Brook House. It stood on one of the choicest sites in London (hence, in the world), at the corner of Upper Brook Street facing on Hyde Park. From her bedroom window Ishbel could look down on the Park where the Prince of Wales and his

"Brook House", Ishbel's family home in Mayfair, Park Lane, London. Architects Drawing, 1870.

friends rode, and she could canter there on her own pony, the purchase of fine horses being a particular obsession of her father's.

The properties were leased to select persons and built to the Duke of Westminster, Lord Grosvenor's guidelines. The Select Committee of the House of Commons on Town Holdings was told in 1887 by Mr. Boodle, the Duke's agent, of his grace's instructions: "to have wide thoroughfares instead of narrow, to set back the houses in rebuilding so as to obtain broad areas and good basements for servants... He is a great lover of architecture and likes a handsome town..."[12]

In today's much changed London, a dignified red brick "Brook House", containing the offices of several commercial enterprises, perpetuates the name of Ishbel's childhood home on that corner of Park Lane and Upper Brook Street. The rest of the block at the upper end of Park Lane has been taken up with large Arabian-owned banking establishments.

In addition to his town house, Marjoribanks acquired a pretty and elegant "farm" property with choice dairy cows and a strawberry field just out of London at Dollis Hill. Next he looked for a shooting domain in Scotland, and in 1856 bought up a vast stretch of forest, hills and lakes near Inverness, called Glen Affaric. The big house, Guisachan, "place of the firs", was added to and refurbished in the "Adam style" which he especially admired. Ishbel found Guisachan highly preferable to London. There she was free to run about, and to ride along forest trails surrounded by the quiet beauty of lake and mountain. She was proud of her name, a Gaelic version of her mother's "Isabella".

The move each year to the Highlands in late summer or fall was the greatest excitement in her life. Making the transfer from London was in fact an exercise in logistics; it was like a regiment on the move, with coaches, horses, and coachmen going first; servants to open the house sent second with bales and boxes; and mother, children, ladies' maids and governesses following by train as far as the town of Beauly and over the last twenty miles in a bouncing omnibus. Sèvres china and fine silver were part of the baggage. Last of all, when the fuss and clatter were over, the master of the place arrived, often with guests. It had all to be done in reverse before Easter, when Marjoribanks must be back in London for the opening of parliament and his wife and older daughter for The Season.

"Guisachan" near Inverness. Water colour by N.E. Green. Country Estate in the Scottish Highlands built by Ishbel's Father.

In Guisachan it was part of Ishbel's duty to visit the tenants in the small granite village of Tomich which Marjoribanks had built for them, having removed them from their homes in thatched cottages throughout the surrounding hills and valleys. He had provided them with a school, shops, a mill, a smithy and a brewery. They could no longer hunt in his forests, so Ishbel brought them surplus game from her father's shooting parties, as well as gifts of stockings and medicine dispensed by Isabella. Ishbel made her rounds by pony or in a little dogcart, observing the curious lives of these Gaelic-speaking people, and going sometimes to the school to preside over recitations by the children there. Marjoribanks employed many of the Tomich men to look after his horses and farm, and as ghillies, keepers and stalkers, while in the off seasons many of them found work building bridges and roads on the estate. It was in his terms magnanimous, yet the eviction of the crofters tugged at Ishbel's conscience. Her first interest in Canada was as the destination of immigrants from among these people; she hoped it was cheerful and bountiful with churches nearby to keep them good.

Ishbel's oldest brother Edward and sister Mary (called Polly) were considerably older than herself. She had two younger brothers, Coutts and Archie, whom she patronized and did not care to play with. Thus, except during vacations when Harry Mieux, the child of Marjoribanks' deceased partner came to visit, she had few playmates. Her memoirs recall a Sèvres china dinner set for her dolls, blue with a border of pink roses, and the "blackness of despair" when one of her many aunts swept by the low table where the dishes had been set out, and caused "irretrievable ruin" with her wide-swinging crinoline.[13] The picture is of a child who played alone with lavish toys.

Before she was four she had taught herself to read a book of fairy tales by pestering the servants for help. But formal lessons, when they began, were not meant to be enjoyable, and the fairy tales were put on a high shelf, out of reach. She was placed in a high chair with a straight back and taught to knit and to sit correctly. From there she progressed to spelling and sums, and there was rigorous French instruction which made her fluent in that language.

As a child, Ishbel was not shy with guests; when gallant men said they intended to marry her when she grew up she believed them, and felt betrayed when they went off and married someone else. She would have liked things to be what they seemed, and the process of learning this was not so, made childhood difficult.

At the age of six Ishbel carried on a clandestine correspondence (without governess supervision) with "My Darling Papa," insisting, "I can't get on without you," and longing to see "a galoping coach come up with you and my brothers," while he teased her by replying that he had a nursery ready at Guisachan for the pony, Filbert, and a stall in the stable for her.

Papa took her with him to a Whitehall balcony when she was seven to see Guiseppe Garibaldi, the Italian "Liberator" adored by England, riding through throngs to receive the freedom of the city. The hero wore a rather sad expression except when ladies leaned against the barriers to reach out to him, when "his countenance at once changed, as with the most winning courtesy he turned to press their hands and always had for each fair partisan a word or two of English."[14]

Ishbel at the age of three, painted by Eden Upton Eddis, from the Haddo House Collection.

Garibaldi wore his usual uniform which had inspired a London fashion, a plain grey capote over a red tunic. And Ishbel, on the balcony, was beside herself with joy because she had on a yellow tunic of identical cut, over a blue skirt, and she hoped everyone would see her and know they were her father's campaign colours in Berwickshire.

The close attachment to Papa lasted only a year or two longer. By that time she had become aware of the mysterious and dreadful rift between her parents, she sensed that her mother was being bullied, and she threw all her childish love to the aggrieved parent.

A picture emerges from Ishbel's own recollections [15] of a little girl commissioned, as she believes, by supernatural command, to guard and protect her mother by performing certain mystic rites without revealing her secret to anyone. The solemn youngster annoys everyone by refusing to descend the staircase properly, by practicing only piano scales of her own choice and these incessantly, every contrary act accompanied by a scowl and a refusal to obey. If she could keep it up until the age of twelve, she was convinced that Mama would be saved. Outwardly, however, the precocious child had become an unattractive brat, and in no time impatient older people were finding fault and deploring her size and awkwardness.

As an adult Ishbel was convinced she had suffered a wretched childhood. The discipline imposed on an impulsive, outgoing nature, to whom it was a punishment to sit still and erect for any length of time, no doubt coloured her memories. There is reference in one of her father's letters to her four-year-old exuberance when her grandfather bent to kiss her, and she locked her arms around his neck and nearly toppled him, to peals of boisterous joy. The relatives were shocked.

She was sensitive about her size. Children in those days were expected to stand mutely while adults frankly appraised them, and adults invariably decided that she was too large for a girl. Someone had also told her she had a "potato nose"; she carried this hurt through life, though her nose, if not classically Roman, was quite unremarkable. As for Papa, he called her a "great Brobdingnagian."[16] In her diary she attributed the fact that she weighed over nine stone (close to 129 pounds) at the age of thirteen to "all my linsey petticoats."[17]

Her father was undoubtedly a tyrant. Marjoribanks expected his children to compete in the world, and do well. Their cherished wishes were most often dismissed as too absurd to bother with. There was no appeal. Ishbel records that she sometimes would stand by her father's Wedgwood mantelpiece staring balefully at a row of almost priceless Derby vases, and enjoy the fearful urge to bash them, with one fierce sweep of her fist, and bring down ruin and damnation.

At the age of thirteen Ishbel was given a diary, subject no doubt to Mama's supervision. Her long habit of recording her life, a source of constant fascination, began. Discretion, regrettably, caused her daughter Marjorie, Lady Pentland, to destroy the private accounts of later particular events, after a selection had been used in the Pentland biography, *A Bonnie Fechter* (a doughty fighter).

Some series of the journals remain. The earliest ones have been kept at Haddo House, her home after her marriage to Lord Aberdeen. There, also, is a rich store of family papers of all kinds. A record of the formative years of a woman of influence, who came to play a conspicuous role in Canada in the 1890's, is generously available to visitors.

Chapter 2
Advance with Courage

On Christmas Day when Ishbel was fourteen she received from Mama three books: *Light and Truth, Sacred Allegories,* and a book of prayer. Some months later she took communion for the first time in the Church of England, and a long letter of admonishment from her mother (Ishbel was at Folkestone with her nurse, convalescing after a serious illness) guided her through the ordeal:

> ...*Satan* is ever at hand to snatch what he can of blessed privilege from us. Therefore fail not to fill up every smallest interval of time with prayer and holy meditation...You know you must take off the glove from your right hand as you approach the altar...[1]

Sunday religious instruction in Mama's boudoir was a cherished hour of intimacy during childhood. On a table in that room was a framed picture of a dead infant sister who had become a little angel in Paradise. Such little angels were considered especially effective intermediaries at the throne of grace.

Backing her mother were Ishbel's numerous Hogg uncles and aunts, a formidable phalanx moving in and out of the young girl's journal. She called them, especially her young uncle Quintin Hogg, "a source of Christian inspiration." For contrast she had her father's sisters, two Marjoribanks ladies who gave her very different gifts —a "beautiful coral bracelet" on one occasion, a gold locket on another, and her first glimpse of opera (*William Tell*) from their box at Covent Garden.[2] Somehow she reconciled these matters, explaining cheerily that, "The person who prays can have as many wishes as he likes."[3]

But her close attachment to her mother became dominant as she moved into adolescence. A particular moment in time is mentioned in her daughter's biography as a traumatic

Lady Marjoribanks, later Lady Tweedmouth.

experience. The summer before her illness Ishbel was at Brighton with her mother and the other children for a brief mid-summer holiday. As Marjorie Pentland describes it, Lady Marjoribanks took her daughter in her arms, swore her to secrecy, and then confided that she had never previously dared to show affection because "Papa would be jealous."[4] It was an experience both profound and corrosive. It bound Ishbel to her mother with a commitment that continued into adulthood. Her father was seen as her rival. She professed to hate her father (even at his death in 1897 she was unforgiving). Mama continued to confide in her and took her into her bed at night when Papa was away. Ishbel eulogized her mother as the most elegant of women, above reproach, her "best friend."

Marjoribanks' crimes against his wife are not clear, though he appears to have had a raging temper. Still, if he was harsh he also sought the affection of his children, and a letter he wrote to Ishbel at Folkestone is in marked contrast to the one in which his wife, on the same day, wrote of Holy Communion.

> When are you coming back?—*They* are behaving to me worse than ever, always gadding, not content with dinners, theatricals, concerts and balls, *They* have taken to garden croquet, cricket, archery and Punch — you see by this that *They* have commenced their second childhood.
>
> There are two dances, I call them *balls*, but *They* say no, on the 18th and 22nd — do you mean to be back for the second of these, if you do we will have a dance all to ourselves and march the others right out of the window into the lane..."[5]

To reject such overtures in loyalty to her mother must have been deeply disturbing. The illness could have had emotional overtones; it was lengthy and debilitating and was diagnosed as rheumatic fever. That summer Ishbel found solace at Guisachan, losing herself in the beauty of hills and sky where she sensed "a great wave of Divine power which sometimes seemed to make one's physical body quiver all over," as she recalled it much later.[6]

There was little to engage her mind. She tried to paint the Highland landscape and was quickly disillusioned; she only "made a mess of it." Back in London there were piano lessons, dancing lessons and singing lessons— though as to the third of these she said, "I can't see it is much use." Later, with

Sir Dudley Coutts Marjoribanks, later Lord Tweedmouth.

instruction, she would learn to paint rather well; a large collection of water colours and oils is still to be found. Her habit of self-criticism persisted, however, so that though she was widely admired as a platform speaker she could still report that she "spoke badly."

For two years she was allowed to attend a weekly class conducted in French and covering history and geography. Each girl student was accompanied to class by her governess, who supervised the memorizing of correct answers for the next class. It was highly competitive and rigidly structured. Ishbel captured top honours; her father rewarded her with "the most lovely old locket and ear-rings to match."[7]

At this point her formal schooling ended. A year or two later she went (again with her governess) to a few lessons in English literature with a more inspiring teacher, J.M. Meiklejohn, who was impressed with the quality of her compositions and tried without success to persuade her father to let her enrol at Girton, the new women's college at Cambridge. Meiklejohn wrote her sadly:

Now you labour under the disadvantages of being totally — well no, not quite — uneducated; on the other hand, you are well worth educating. But the fact is, you must do this for yourself.[8]

One phase of education was hers from an early age: the ever fascinating world of politics. Gladstone and other prominent Liberals gathered frequently at their house; by the time she was eighteen she was reading Edmund Burke and Thomas Macauley. At dinner one night in her late teens the elderly John Bright instructed her in the principles of making a public speech. He thought she might begin by reading his own, along with, for poetic utterance, the book *Earthly Paradise* by William Morris. And he added that one must always have one's peroration ready "to which you can have a quick recourse if you think your audience is beginning to weary."[9]

Lady Marjoribanks had been careful not to relinquish the Conservative ties of the Hogg family and once had Disraeli to dinner. Ishbel had become so staunch a Liberal after conversations with Gladstone and Bright, that she recoiled in some horror at the thought of giving Mr. Disraeli her hand. Good manners instiled by her mother carried her through.

Ishbel Marjoribanks, at about the age of 18.

The social invitation to Disraeli was prompted by Lady Marjoribanks' desire to further the career of her new son-in-law. She had managed a marriage for her older daughter Polly to Matthew White Ridley, wealthy and eligible and the son of a viscount who happened to be a Conservative. Matthew was also destined for parliament. In memoirs Polly has been praised in qualified terms as a "prominent *Conservative* hostess."

London was a bright and shining world for young ladies from Mayfair. Ishbel and Polly would often canter through the town on beautiful ponies, quite aware of how charming they looked in their neat-fitting riding habits as they passed the Household Cavalry Barracks on the way to escort Sir Dudley home from the House of Commons. Ishbel wrote about the state visit of the Shah of Persia, his diamond-studded dress, the stories of his abysmal table manners, and the delight of seeing his magnificent white horse, with its tail dyed red, led out to exercise in Hyde Park. She attended the concert that opened the Royal Albert Hall, when the queen came out of mourning long enough to say a few words to the packed assemblage.

The excitement when first Edward (Teddy), and then Polly were married was enough to fill pages of her journal. Teddy had won the hand of lovely and intelligent Fanny Churchill, daughter of the Duke of Marlborough and aunt to Winston. Papa picked out presents for each of his children to give to the bride, a cascade of jewels: Polly was to give a diamond and ruby locket, Ishbel "a chatelaine with a watch set with pearls," young Coutts a "big gold locket," and Archie "a diamond ring."[10]

When Polly also left home Ishbel was elevated in status to "Miss Marjoribanks." On her seventeenth birthday on 14 March 1874 she had her pocket allowance increased to a hundred pounds a year, and she had her own German personal maid. That day for the first time she "put on a chimney-top hat to go out riding. Papa gave me a lovely set of pearls and turquoises: necklaces, ear-rings and studs — quite too good."[11]

Yet, a month later at Guisachan, she was writing in her journal:

The deep calm and peacefulness that reign here are far beyond description and make one's whole being thrill with enjoyment of life. The sounds we catch in letters, of all the London excitement and gaiety are certainly anything but inviting and make me feel as if I would fly to the very depths of the woods to hide myself from all that turmoil and false pleasure, when my turn comes. [When she would be eighteen, presented to society and eligible for marriage.] It is so delightful to gaze on all the exquisite loveliness around and to think that it is my own Lord who has made it all—. And yet so much darkness![12]

But if Ishbel was dreading the ritual pre-marriage social whirl, her mother was giving the landing of a husband her full attention. A proper match for this tall, solemn and deep-passioned child was not the easiest to arrange. She had already made the choice, and fortunately Ishbel had met the man and been favourably impressed. They were aiming very high. The quarry was an earl, heir to one of the oldest titles in the Scottish peerage, John Gordon, Earl of Aberdeen. He was ten years older than Ishbel, a handsome boyish twenty-four when they first met while riding in the Park. His companion knew Polly and galloped off with her, leaving Aberdeen to trail behind with the younger sister, making solemn conversation which Ishbel found most flattering. The encounter was of course reported to her mother, and the wheels began to turn.

One of the first moves was to change from the church they had been attending, Grosvenor Chapel, to the smaller Quebec Chapel near Marble Arch, which Aberdeen and his sister attended. This church had been built in 1859 and named to commemorate Wolfe's victory in Canada. Its site today is the Church of the Annunciation at a corner of Old Quebec Street. In the 1870's a very popular chaplain, Francis Holland, was in charge, widely famed as a speaker who addressed social problems. When Ishbel first heard him preach she was somewhat shocked and told her journal that he "missed the point of the sermon entirely." Soon she was under Holland's spell, and entered joyfully into Sunday School work, teaching a class of small boys.

Lord Aberdeen was apparently also impressed by Francis Holland. He had a desire to work among the poor in the East End, in the manner of Lord Shaftsbury, and influenced by the moral stance of his own father. Aberdeen was a slight, dark-haired, rather nervous young man, not very good with people, fascinated by the new railways that were transforming indus-

Ishbel Maria Marjoribanks, about 1875.

trial England. He lived a good part of the year in London with his mother and sisters. The great estate in Aberdeenshire had been neglected. He carried the burden of an unhappy past, though the origins of his family were romantic and colourful.

The Gordons can be traced back to 1315 when the family was given lands in the barren north-east of Scotland. A few generations later it split in two, the legitimate Gordons moving on to power and position as Marquesses and then as Dukes. The other branch, descended from an oldest brother who made the error of entering into a union known as "handfasting" with a Scottish lass, fared nearly as well, acquiring vast lands and much wealth, and eventually a title as Earl of Aberdeen. Buffeted between Royalists and Calvinists, the first Earl settled down at Haddo House, a bleak, massive stone structure which he built in 1731. His most famous successor was the fourth Earl of Aberdeen who became foreign secretary of Britain under Wellington and Peel, when he presided over the giving away to the United States of a large part of Maine ("Pine Swamp!")[13] followed by an even more generous gift, Oregon, which had up to that time flown the British flag. Aberdeen was Prime Minister of Britain from 1852 to 1855.

Luckily for his successors, this fourth Earl undertook to improve the estate, though he left the house pretty much as it was. He drained the swamps, planted thousands of trees, built roads, and developed a finely landscaped garden; he improved the farming methods, conducting relations with his tenants in a style that visiting François Pierre Guizot once described as "cette grande existence féodal!"[14]

Young "Johnnie" remembered a visit to his grandfather when Queen Victoria and Prince Albert were there as guests. In their honour two *sequoia gigantea,* the conifer that grows to such magnificent heights in California and is known in Britain as *Wellingtonia,* were planted near the house, where their dark spires still rise high above the roofs, commemorating not only her young majesty but, as it turned out, the birth in London that same year, 1857, of a child called Ishbel.

One of the fourth Earl's younger sons, Arthur, was Governor of New Brunswick in the crucial period before Confederation. But the oldest son, George, Johnnie's father, remained in the shadows, a serious disappointment to the prime minister. (George, from birth, assumed the hereditary title, Lord Haddo.) He was inhibited and neurotic, and fell ill whenever

John Campbell Gordon, seventh Earl of Aberdeen, about 1877.

an election loomed and his illustrious father attempted to buy him a Commons seat. The father also rebuked his manners, telling him to: "endeavour to feel that it is always indispensable to be civil and attentive to a woman, be she old or young, ugly or pretty. A savage and morose manner to anyone is a real misfortune, to a woman it is barbarous."[15]

Lord Haddo did the right thing in his father's eyes by marrying Mary Baillie, said to be descended from John Knox, and sister of the Earl of Haddington. But he chose to live in personal austerity, giving away most of his yearly allowance of £3000. In London there were ragged crowds of unfed urchins, stinking slums, illiteracy and crime. Haddo felt a strong Christian obligation to work among the poor, though he preferred not to go in person but to send agents, who were instructed to read the Bible and pray for the salvation of souls as they distributed coal and food.

Haddo had no aptitude for the life of a nobleman. He was tempted to give it up, to disappear under an assumed name, going perhaps to Australia. Instead, he eventually made it into parliament, where he remained as inconspicuous as possible. From 1853 on he was an extremely ill man, gaunt and weary, and found relief only in sun-lapped voyages by barge down the Nile River, a popular diversion among the British. He justified his travels by handing out Bibles and tracts to the Egyptians.

In 1859 he wrote to his wife:

> I have no doubt that I have an incurable wound in the stomach and that all that can be done is to avoid as much as possible exertion of mind or body, to pay attention to diet, and to eat as little as possible.[16]

One motion, originating from his deep sense of imperative Christian duty, Lord Haddo himself made in the first Session of the new Parliament, July 25, 1859, on a subject peculiarly trying to his sensitive delicacy of feeling. It was for discontinuing the Government grant of £100 to schools of art where unclothed models were employed. The report in the *Times* of July 26 is as follows:

> Lord Haddo called attention to the exhibition of nude living models in the Government schools of art. He had on one occasion been accidently a witness of the mode of study

pursued in the Government schools of art, and he felt bound to say that he had never witnessed a more painful or scandalous exhibition.[17]

Haddo paid close attention to the morals of his own children. There were three daughters and three sons. Johnnie, the youngest, was born in 1847. They were not allowed toys except those they could fashion for themselves, and Johnnie recalls his delight when his grandfather brought him the gift he had requested, a little wheelbarrow. Theatricals were forbidden. So were any jokes related to drinking, which eliminated a good deal of Scottish humour.

In 1860 the fourth Earl died, and with the greatest reluctance his melancholy oldest son took up his responsibilities. He spent more time at Haddo House. The daily routine there had never been on a more parsimonious scale. He put some effort into building better homes for his tenants, though his motive was largely concern for the immoral sexual habits pursued within crowded hovels. He screened the recipients of his new cottages to admit "none but those whose character was free from that blot which he so anxiously wished to see removed from the face of society in the district."[18] Since he also increased the rent for new cottages he was not exactly hailed as a benefactor.

He was Earl for three years; he died when only 47. He had just arranged for the printing of a lugubrious leaflet: "Death May Be Near".

The tragedy of the fifth Earl's sickly ways had predictable consequences. His oldest son George, now the sixth Earl, could not face the complexities of running the ancestral estate. After barely two years he took off for America, where he assumed the name of George Osborne and signed on as first mate on a schooner out of Boston — an Earl in hiding. His infrequent letters to his mother were signed only "George", with no clue to his whereabouts. Meanwhile James, the second son, athletically gifted and in many ways an attractive young man, was equally unprepared to shoulder responsibility. He let himself be persuaded to run for parliament, and a fortnight later shot himself in his rooms at Cambridge.

At that point the family began a frantic search for the runaway Earl, whose letters had mysteriously stopped. A former tutor was sent to America to find him, but five months passed before George Osborne was traced, and it was discovered that he had been swept overboard in a storm and had drowned.

Long judicial proceedings were required to confirm his death and settle the title and estate on the third brother, John.

And by this tragic route — as John Campbell Hamilton Gordon would tell his wife Ishbel, "through this dark portal" — the seventh Earl of Aberdeen, presently to be Lord Lieutenant of Ireland, then Governor General of Canada, came into his inheritance.

At 24 Lord Aberdeen was frequently attracted to girls, but shy and nervous. He accepted that he must take a wife, but procrastinated. No doubt the battery of determined mothers of London's debutantes appalled him. He avoided dances — but he did go to church. And it was on walks to and from Quebec Chapel that his acquaintance with Ishbel Marjoribanks blossomed.

Chapter 3
Victorian Courtship

Ishbel was not personally averse to marriage; it was only the preliminaries that discouraged her. She knew she was not cut out for spinsterhood. Her mother's example did nothing to deter her. She knew she had faults, for her mother reminded her of them, and must try to curb the wilfulness that would surely seem unattractive to a man. But once she had settled on her choice of husband she expected to marry him; it was inconceivable that it might turn out otherwise.

The choice was apparently made sometime during her seventeenth year, three years after their first meeting in the Park. The journals began to mention Aberdeen's name, a guest for tea or dinner, obviously at her mother's invitation. Once he appeared at Guisachan: "Most delightful day — rode with Matt, Lord Aberdeen, Mr. and Mrs. Peel..." said the journal.[1]

In the fall of 1874 there were allusions to late-night confidences between Ishbel and her mother. Then in January 1875, the year when she would be eighteen and would "come out," the journal began to unfold the progress of love.

> This new year promises to be an eventful one for me. Mama and I were praying together when it began...I must surrender myself entirely to Him, who knows the desires, hopes and fears of my heart concerning my earthly life... How changed from last year! To have been allowed to come under Mr. Holland's ministry and teach in the schools, and then to have *as a friend* (at least) one whom I could love so intensely!... Papa has been kind enough to give me an allowance of £200 on my coming out.[2]

Ten days later, some conflict arose between Christian devotion and her pounding heart:

A very mechanical and unsatisfactory Sunday, at least from the moment I caught sight of *him* at the 8:30 sacrament service — from that moment my whole being began to be in a whirl and it seemed literally impossible to fix my mind on anything I was doing, saying, hearing, or reading — least of all could I truly pray. I know not how to alter this state of things.[3]

Next Sunday her turbulent feelings again confused her.

Having run into *him* on the way from church to her class, she couldn't settle down to teach, and left the "Expression" stop out on the harmonium, causing a frightful row. But Lord Aberdeen "came to tea about six. I let him in ... He was so nice, so warm — oh, can it be..?"[4]

Unfortunately Lord Aberdeen was strictly observing Lent during February and Ishbel's first appearance at a formal dance was no pleasure at all, for *he* was not there.

I got on well enough but did not find where the wonderful enjoyment lay, hopping around the room and talking about the floor, the weather and such-like. I went wishing not to be carried away by it all but without the slightest notion I should think it so stupid.[5]

The following week Aberdeen came to luncheon after morning service, and "is going to dine with us on Saturday week. D.V. [God willing]"[6] At that dinner party Ishbel was instructed by her mother to play the piano for most of the evening, but Lord Aberdeen "sat by the side of me and talked and chatted so warmly between the pieces."[7]

Then it was March. She would be eighteen on the fourteenth of the month, she was like a kettle on the boil; ready to fly apart. She could no longer contain the uncertainty. She asked God for a sign: if she was to have "this wondrous blessing," she would expect "some particular civility" from Aberdeen within the next two days. The day before her birthday, a Saturday, they met in the Park. Lord Aberdeen was accompanied by a friend, Lord Gurvagh, whom he introduced to Ishbel. He chatted then about the evangelical preachers from the United States, Moody and Sankey, who had come to London. Ishbel managed to turn the conversation to another dinner invitation from her mother — next Tuesday or

Thursday? But Aberdeen declined; he was engaged. Ishbel's faith fluttered wildly.

Seeing her strange agitation Aberdeen left his friend and rode back to her side. He apologized if he had seemed rude? Ishbel burst forth: she would be eighteen next day. Would he please think of her as "a Christian friend?" That seemed reasonable enough and Aberdeen agreed. But obviously the seeds of apprehension had been sown. In the evening they met again at a party. Ishbel was "in a violent fidget, and showed it too, I am afraid."[8] Aberdeen bowed to her, but confined his attention to Mary Gladstone and other young ladies on the opposite side of the room. When he approached Ishbel and her mother it was only to exchange courtesies and again to apologize if he had seemed rude that day — perhaps she had not wished an introduction to his friend? Events were *not* signalling Divine intention.

The supremely important eighteenth birthday arrived. She wrote: "The *agony* ..." Her feelings had been too clearly shown, she had not set about this in the right way. "Papa and Mama worry themselves about it too. It has not been a very joyful birthday. Papa gave me a most beautiful suite in pearls and diamonds: necklace, locket, ear-rings and bracelet..."[9]

The young lord's behaviour was erratic. He was warm and chatty on Monday. Her mother called on *his* mother and reported that Lady A. was "also most warm." Two more afternoon calls and a meeting in the Park, Aberdeen acting "constrained" each time. Or seeming, unaccountably, "shy and confused."

Meanwhile there were complicated preparations for her presentation to the Queen on March 19. The dancing instructor came to teach her the ritual of curtsies. A beautiful gown was designed and jewels chosen.

On the 19th she spent the entire morning being dressed. She wore a white satin gown embroidered with a pattern of white thistles, the skirt round as a bell, a wide décolletage with lace, a misty veil secured with jewels, and a train, ruffled, three yards in length. She carried a fan, and had to manage this as well as the train, with as much grace as possible. When she finally stepped forward to begin her measured approach to the seated royalty, an official of the court gathered up her train and looped it over her arm. Thus encumbered she made seven curtsies to various members of the royal family, managing without mishap, back straight, head slightly bowed. To the queen she lifted a hand as she knelt, presenting it palm up to meet the queen's hand. At that moment Victoria unexpectedly leaned forward to kiss her rosy, intent face. A very faint sigh passed through the gathering. All seemed to have gone exceedingly well except that, as Ishbel hurried down the staircase, she stumbled and fell. Her beautiful fan was broken and her face bruised. But what mattered more than any of this was that, leaving Windsor Castle, "who should we see on our way back but dear Lord Aberdeen in a hansom but he did not see us."[10]

She heard Aberdeen was leaving London for four weeks, an incredible turn of events. "For a few days I have scarcely ever felt so ill and *done* in body, and as to mind and soul a sort of agony swept over, almost more than I could bear."[11] Her mother comforted her. Lord Aberdeen's departure without speaking of marriage was a trial of faith. The Lord would answer their prayers, but Ishbel must try even harder to be submissive to His will. Ishbel sought to obey, but knew she was now unable to suppress "waves of contradiction and rebellion that are washing over me."[12] Never noted for patience, she had expected a whirlwind romance and was devastated by delay.

In this, Ishbel had been utterly transparent. Mr. Holland, the minister, saw what was going on, and had a sympathetic little talk with her. He would join in prayers for her happiness. Half London seemed to know. When she and Aberdeen turned up at Lady Katherine Bannerman's party to welcome the Prince of Wales back from India, Lady Bannerman "was so kind, putting us together in a little room upstairs with a few others."[13] Nothing came of it. Lord Aberdeen journeyed back and forth from London, sometimes accepting, sometimes declining invitations, sometimes aloof and sometimes "warm."

Gradually Ishbel resigned herself to waiting, to a period of preparation, as she saw it. Her best course seemed to be to "get hard at work at things." She read, and critically analyzed what she read, she was a conscientious teacher to her Sunday class of boys, seeking to bring them to the light of truth. When at Guisachan she worked on a simplified catechism. The stern Scots wouldn't allow a harmonium in their Sunday School, but she managed the singing with the aid of a pitch pipe.

So an entire year of waiting passed. Then a serious blow — a letter to Lady Marjoribanks from the Duchess of Marlborough, who had been told by Lady Aberdeen that Johnnie did

Ishbel in presentation gown, early 1880's.

of course intend to marry, but definitely would not choose a wife from among his London acquaintances. He would prefer a girl of the sensible, homely type, not a society girl, according to his mother. Ishbel felt a rush of anger. What a dull and stupid approach to marriage!

She turned then to her former English tutor, J.M. Meiklejohn, telling him she was considering writing as a vocation, and asking advice. Did she have the ability to "write a book which would last and which would have the power of influencing others for good?" The teacher replied that "with patient thought, study, and observation, [Ishbel] should be able to do something that would be useful to the country."[14] It was an ambiguous reply, yet an encouraging one. She had not been told that the mounting ambition in her heart was foolish or impracticable. Someone had recognized that she had the ability to make an impact on the world! She resolved "to keep that aim in view and work as hard as possible."

Meanwhile, when in London, there were "calls and balls and excitements and bothers," none of which she really despised. Half a century later when she was a revered grandmother she liked to recall the etiquette of those days, and she admitted that, "in spite of being thus hedged about, and despite my qualms, I really had a very good time during my two and a half years of 'being out.'"[15] Illustrious neighbours, the Duke of Westminster and Lord and Lady Dudley, gave balls for her; she was considered a fortunately situated young lady. She went with her parents to country house parties, which were mostly a matter of changing from one elaborate costume to the next. A woman wore to breakfast a smart dress with a train, coiffed hair, and kid gloves, and proceeded through various changes of wardrobe to the bare-throated radiance of a dinner gown worn with all the jewels that could be hung on the female person. Ishbel had trouble with kid gloves; hers were always splitting. Hoopskirts had passed out of fashion. Now it was the "pin back" dress, figure fitting in front, and most of the eleven or twelve yards of material gathered in the great bustle and train behind. Young ladies must appear slim, and Ishbel's curves were constrained within tight corsets so that she was always uncomfortable and thus reminded of society's inexorable demands. Because she was tall she avoided high coiffures; her brown hair curled over a broad forehead; she had brightly attractive wide-set eyes and a pleasing smile. One of her assets was a melodious, sweet-timbred voice, which would appeal strongly to audiences when she later appeared on platforms.

During these two and a half years, as Ishbel proceeded from seventeen to twenty, Lord Aberdeen was avoiding London society as much as possible, although he came to the capital regularly to attend the House of Lords. He was at that time a Conservative. He was delighted when in 1874 he was appointed by Disraeli chairman of a Royal Commission on Railway Accidents; he found the evidence on braking systems a fascinating study. He had been enamoured of railways since the age of twelve when Sir James Elphinstone, a guest at Haddo House, presented him with a written letter of permission to ride the engines anywhere on the Great North of Scotland Railway. He had learned to imitate vocally the distinctive whistles used by engineers on various runs, and gave renditions for the entertainment of his friends. Getting married seemed to be very far from his mind.

By 1877 Ishbel was ready to concede that a proposal from Lord Aberdeen had become remote. For the first time she considered "other Christian gentlemen." She told her journal she must either "be married or die"[16] — and she didn't want to die until she had known the joys of "love on earth." There were apparently some offers. A letter from Sir Dudley about this time responded with relief to the news that she had turned down one proposal, since in the father's opinion: "The man, though nice enough, estimable enough and rich enough is not of sufficient weight and calibre to suit."[17] The family had set their hearts on the young Earl.

As the social season opened in February 1877, the ambiguous courtship was renewed. Lord Aberdeen and his mother gave a concert in the house he had taken for the season at Grosvenor Square. Ishbel and her mother attended, and on this occasion roused the old feelings again, even more hotly. Aberdeen, to be sure, was "nervous and fidgeting about a good deal," yet at the same time "very nice;" Ishbel had only to look at his "dear face" and her feelings were obvious to all. The consequent gossip was a great worry — "how people will talk *as if it was going to be* between us! Ethel Cardogan asked me yesterday if it were true, she heard so much about it."[18] But after only a few pleasant encounters the elusive man was off to Scotland again!

So it continued to the middle of May. By that time Ishbel was out of patience and determined to make a new move. She attended a tea party, a romantic setting held occasionally in those days at the Foreign Office at Westminster. There she met again the man she now called "Johnnie". Lady Aberdeen discreetly turned her back on the pair, engaging Lady Marjoribanks in conversation. Ishbel suddenly poured out her feelings to Johnnie, but this time, she thought, very cleverly. She said she was just as annoyed as he was at all the foolish gossip. They must just ignore it and be friends. He could think of her as another Jo March (the tomboyish sister in *Little Women*) who had no intention of marrying. As a matter of fact she might be off to Australia in a year or so, with her young brother Coutts. Couldn't they, therefore, resume their friendship?

Lord Aberdeen, stumbling a little, responded that he would indeed like to be able to speak to her without being misunderstood. They talked then about such safe subjects as Sunday services, the music going on around them, the weather in Scotland. This conversation seemed to glow with hidden warmth, and Ishbel returned from the party with her head in a whirl of joy. "I could dance and skip!" She wrote in her journal. And surely she had not been *very* deceitful: "I told him nothing untrue; although he may have understood me to mean that I didn't care for him and wouldn't have him if he wanted me I never *said* so..."[19]

Again nothing came of it, except that Aberdeen was more skittish than ever. They met frequently, but he was by turns warm towards her and downright rude. In July came the final blow. "The one dream of my life for the past six years has dissolved into nothing and I must face life without him."[20] They had met by appointment on Sunday after the service at Quebec Chapel. He had told her bluntly he felt only friendship — nothing more. Next day he called at Brook House to make this clear to Lady Marjoribanks, remaining for an hour. There appears to have been a polite argument before he was allowed to leave. He had first to promise to "propose himself to Guisachan" (send a note proposing a visit) if he should change his mind.

Gossip, meanwhile, had got out of hand. "People don't believe it when I deny it. The Queen wrote to the Duchess of Roxburghe [sic] to tell her to find out whether it was true. Papa was so angry."[21] It was more than Lady Marjoribanks could endure. She sent a letter flying after Lord Aberdeen.

She told him of the annoyance they had endured and ended:

> In conclusion I venture to tell you that I am sure you are
> deceiving yourself. What is the evidence of love but the
> seeking of companionship? Continual introspection is a fatal
> error. For your own sake I would not have you throw away
> a priceless blessing.[22]

At Haddo House, Lord Aberdeen received this stern
message. He carried it in his pocket to Edinburgh. He was
troubled; no gentleman trifles with the affections of a young
girl and what if Ishbel turned out to be a priceless blessing
after all? Then, of course, he did have an obligation to marry,
and no one else in view. So he answered Lady Marjoribanks'
letter. He said he wished to return to London immediately —
by Wednesday next. On consideration, his feelings were not
merely friendship after all. Would he be permitted to call?

It was late in the evening when he took his letter to post.
Once it was dropped in the box he tried to pull it out again. He
became frantic. He thought of his friend the postmaster
general and rushed a message to his house: would he mind
very much having the pillar box opened? The postmaster
general was not at home. The letter went on its way to Brook
House.[23]

A week later Lord Aberdeen walked into Sir Dudley's
office to put the ceremonial question to him. He then proposed
marriage to Ishbel. It was three weeks before she could trust
herself to confide in her journal. She wrote that Aberdeen's
love was "deep, holy, deferential, tender, heavenly." The
waiting had not been "a scrap too long as a preparation for
such Paradisical happenings."[24]

Everyone in their two large family circles was delighted at
the announcement. Congratulations poured in. Mr. Gladstone sent his photograph. Queen Victoria asked for a photograph of Ishbel. Extravagant gifts arrived. Johnnie came to
lunch and afterwards decked her in the Gordon family jewels
of amethysts and gold. The tenants at Guisachan sent gifts,
with a deputation to convey their flowery good wishes; a
celebration with food and music was prepared for them and
Sir Dudley warmly thanked them all. At Haddo House on the
other side of Scotland there were fire-works and a banquet for
Aberdeen's tenants.

Ishbel married Lord Aberdeen on 7 November 1877, at fashionable St. George's Church in Hanover Square.[25] The ceremony was performed by the Archbishop of Canterbury, assisted by Aberdeen's cousin, Canon Douglas H. Gordon, chaplain in ordinary to the queen, and by the Reverend Francis J. Holland. Arthur Balfour was best man.

Ishbel wrote: "Very composed during the service and forgot all about the people." She wore a dress as rounded, frosted and frilled as the wedding cake itself, of white duchess satin trimmed with yards of Brussels lace and orange blossoms: "a full trail of the flowers was laid between the plisses of satin on the train," said the London *Times*. Above the wide décolletage an insert of soft tulle covered her shoulders and throat. Her veil was held by a tiara with seven diamond stars, a gift from her father. She wore Lord Aberdeen's gifts, a necklace and earrings of diamond and pearls and a diamond locket with a large sapphire centre, and she had on jeweled bracelets given to her by the tenants of Haddo House.

The list of wedding presents occupied most of a column in the *Times*. It began with the gift of His Royal Highness Prince Leopold, a Cellini cup, and ranked the largesse from dukes, marquesses, earls, lords, ladies and common folk.

Two hundred guests went to Brook House for a wedding breakfast and the cutting of the "bride-cake from Gunters of Berkeley Square." Ishbel wore a traveling dress and bonnet of sapphire velvet trimmed with fox as she stepped into another of her father's gifts, an open barouche pulled by four horses, for their drive to Seven Oaks. Halstead Place had been lent to them for their honeymoon by her Marjoribanks aunts.

She wrote: "Arches erected for us and a band playing as we arrived. We had a few words of prayer before we went to bed. Went to bed at 12 o'clock."[26]

Lord and Lady Aberdeen took up married life at 37 Grosvenor Street in London. In December they set off on a wedding trip, traveling up the Nile. They met Johnnie's cousin, General Gordon, Governor of Sudan, who gave them silver coffee holders of Egyptian filigree. Ishbel was favourably impressed by his soldierly bearing, his constant reference to the Bible, and his determination to wipe out slavery in the Sudan. He, however, merely commented unpleasantly to his sister Augusta that Aberdeen had married "a great fat girl."[27]

In Cairo, Ishbel to her own dismay snapped "rather impatiently" at Johnnie. She was annoyed because tea was

Ishbel Marjoribanks in her wedding gown, 1877.

late. But how could she have been so irritable? "I used to think that if only J. was given to me, all would be right... The last half-hour of the Old Year is flying away and I cling to it..." She wondered sadly if perhaps the days on the Nile were too idle, and she vowed to consider the journey as preparation — once again! — for the future, "an opportunity to prepare for the *active* life we have begun together."[28]

Chapter 4
"Onward and Upward"

Ishbel proposed one morning that they put the persistent rumours of slavery to the test. Aberdeen was to approach their sailing ship's captain and discreetly suggest an interest in black servants. When they pulled into port near Aswan the captain obligingly paraded before them "a slave merchant with three little boys of eight, nine and eleven, to be looked at, and another man who wanted to part with his boy of about sixteen."[1] The Aberdeens listened incredulously as the boys' serviceability was extoled and a tentative price put forward. Through their interpreter they learned that the boys were kidnapped near their home in a Sudanese village. Lord Aberdeen was inspired to proclaim them free, by virtue of their appearing on board a vessel flying the Union Jack (in his honour). The crew in high spirits hustled the slave dealers off deck, though not before soft-hearted Aberdeen had slipped them a few coins "for their trouble."

Ishbel soon had the boys dressed in red shirts and blue pants and installed in a position of privilege on board. She commissioned the interpreter to teach them English, while she and her husband took pains to calm their fears. In March, on her twenty-first birthday, she wrote to her father:

> Don't be shocked! ... I fear you would not think that I had arrived at years of discretion if you saw Johnnie and me romping about teaching our little Arabs to play ball.[2]

A Christian education was to be provided. They paused at Asyut where there was a Presbyterian mission school. Red tape had to be cleared away: the boys were to be baptized, a legal guardian must give permission. The Aberdeens adopted all four, first at the office of local legal officers and again in celebration at the school, where the boys were given new names: Campbell, Aberdeen, Gordon and Haddo.

A letter signed by Campbell, the oldest, followed them back to Scotland:

> To His Excellency our Revered and Honoured Parent Lord Aberdeen, may he be continually preserved. I cease not to feel grateful for your kindness in placing me in school-orchards to pluck the fruit of knowledge and good breeding under the care of virtuous Christian people. As to our news, we — thank God — are happy to the highest degree and are progressing in our studies, save that owing to the change of weather I have been sick but am now better.[3]

Regrettably two of the younger ones died of respiratory illness. Only one, Gordon, pursued his new educational opportunities and became in time a teacher at Gordon College in Khartoum.

Though they were married in November, Aberdeen waited until the following June to conduct Ishbel to her new home. There was a brief stay in London, the Nile trip, then a pause in the Italian Alps and lastly a visit to the Paris International Exhibition. His devious delay was to let her see the place at its best. Even so, a raw wind from the North Sea welcomed them, and the twenty-mile drive over bare untreed land was in marked contrast to Ishbel's childhood memories of the western highlands. The Haddo tenants turned out lustily, escorting them over the last mile and drawing up to cheer them at the door.

Ishbel surveyed her domain. The 1700 acres of estate land were spacious, the house was large, but admiration ended there. Little had been done to relieve the discomfort of eighteenth century origins. On the east side were the broad steps and formal parterre which were the prime minister's only improvement to the house, but Johnnie's father had done nothing at all to make it more habitable.

Practical, fond of comfort, expansive, Ishbel proceeded to spend Aberdeen's money and her own in a Victorian re-doing of the house from top to bottom. It took two years. Before she ever set foot inside she declared the entrance impossible. It was on the second floor, approached by narrow stone staircases. "Distinctly unsuitable," said Ishbel, and tending moreover to cause confusion to guests arriving from a distance, who suddenly found themselves ushered into the room with all their wraps, through what appeared to be a window."[4]

Below at ground level behind five-foot-thick stone walls, were the kitchens and servants' quarters. The north wing, originally stables, had been used in Johnnie's time as the children's bedrooms.

Ishbel hired the most renowned architect in Scotland, C.E. Wardrop, and London's best interior designers, Wright and Mansfield, who specialized in the "Adam style" recommended by her father. Presently a new doorway led into a foyer with pink pilasters and pastel murals. Beyond, a great open staircase led to the principal rooms on the second-floor balcony supported by pillars, and ornamental sweeping stairs to the area below. It was a stroke that did much to modify the austere design, though when all was done Haddo House would remain a "massively plain building" to the approaching visitor.[5]

With bathrooms and bow windows, a new rear wing with nurseries and sitting-rooms, a new large library, and completion of a small chapel which Aberdeen had begun, Victorian comfort was added to the historic house which has become an attraction to tourists.[6]

Studio Morgan, Aberdeen, Scotland.

Haddo House, Aberdeenshire, home of the Earls of Aberdeen.

Tall portraits of Ishbel by James Sant and of Lord Aberdeen in academic robes (LL.D., McGill) by Canadian painter Robert Harris, now hang above library mantelpieces inlaid with eighteenth century green and white Wedgwood Jasperware. Fine paintings have survived the gradual selling-off of the art collection as times dictated. A variety of other treasures includes a cabinet of Doulton porcelain dinnerware painted by the woman artists of Canada as a farewell gift to Ishbel in 1898.

Ishbel said that the cost of the 1879-80 renovations was "scandalously high."[7] And despite the improvements Haddo House was never as dearly loved as their second estate, Cromar, south on the river Dee, in a kinder landscape. Here Ishbel early decided to have a prettier home, and eventually one was built, a turreted castle of pink stone for their retirement. Not far off lies Balmoral Castle, favourite holiday home of royalty. It was one of Aberdeen's functions when he became Lord Lieutenant of Aberdeenshire to preside over the queen's arrivals and departures.

Aberdeen did nothing to restrain his wife's enthusiasms. The homecoming celebration went on for a week, ending with a banquet for over 900 tenants and their wives, and cost them £7,500. Now that she was a countess, Ishbel resolved to be "firm but kind" to the many people in their employ. For staff members like the laundress Mrs. Stevens and her husband, the reform was drastic:

> I trust I have acted rightly in this matter — we cannot but give some belief to the united chorus of all the people that they are a disgrace to the country and yet no one will bring a positive proof of their guilt. Anyhow they swear and that is enough to let them go.[8]...Had a talk with Jemima and Bella Helman this morning and dismissed them also.[9]

Meanwhile she saw to it that the servants had a "hop" now and then in their own quarters, and lavish holiday meals followed by such treats as a magic lantern show. Her untoward interest in the household staff was ridiculed in high places, and the Aberdeens had to contend with persistent reports that they "ate with the servants." Queen Victoria once asked Lord Rosebery to find out if it was true. It is certainly true that one day in 1879 a wedding breakfast was prepared in the servants' hall in honour of a kitchen maid named

Elizabeth Harris. Lord and Lady Aberdeen were both present, and his lordship proposed Miss Harris' health.[10] J.M. Barrie's play, *The Admirable Crichton*, was popularly believed to reflect the Aberdeens' radical notions and Lord Aberdeen, publicly humiliated, asked for and got an apologetic denial from Barrie.[11]

The servants were invited to join a Household Club and one or both the Aberdeens usually attended its meetings. There was an annual membership fee of one shilling. It was established because charity must begin at home or, as Ishbel explained, from:

> an uneasy feeling on our part that we were doing nothing for the members of our own household ... to bring all into human relations with each other and ourselves, beyond our daily gathering in the Haddo House Chapel for family worship day by day, and on Sunday evenings.[12]

The workings of the Club included "a singing class led by our head forester; a carving class led by our governess; a drawing class led by our nurse, and a home reading circle led by a neighbouring schoolmaster," with social evenings fortnightly, when "one played a melodeon, another a concertina, another the piano or violin; many could sing or recite; others gave readings or short lectures. It was surprising to learn how much home talent there was."[13]

All this under their own roof, but reflecting similar benevolence among the tenantry. The Aberdeens endowed a cottage hospital with resident nurse in their village of Tarves, an "institute" of education for young men in their village of Methlick, and a program of hot penny lunches for school children. Such charity was only the beginning. Ishbel organized and took part in "working parties" where farmers' wives and daughters met to sew for the destitute, have tea, and listen while a worthwhile book was read aloud.

The Onward and Upward Association[14] grew out of their Household Club, on similar uplifting lines. (A reporter once asked, "Why 'Onward and Upward'?" Ishbel answered, "Better than 'Backward and Downward'.") It was designed for servant girls in the houses of their mistresses, eventually comprising 115 branches and 8,280 members across the Scottish countryside, and absorbed at last into the Scottish Mothers' Union. The farm wives supervised as their maidservants took courses by mail in "Bible topics, history, geography, literature, domestic science, needlework, knitting, etc." with prizes and certificates awarded annually. These activities took place in the farm homes because, as Ishbel noted in a letter to her mother, the women were much against their female servants being allowed out to meetings lest their morals be put at risk:

> They one and all agree that they cannot think of allowing their girls to get into mischief. Of course this is carried a great deal too far and they are very hard on their girls. But then the morality of the girls is something terrible.[15]

At Ishbel's suggestion the annual Games Day for the two villages of Methlick and Tarves that lay within the estate was moved to the grounds of Haddo House. No liquor was allowed, but there was tea and lemonade, and a flower show was added to the program. About 8,000 people turned out.[16]

Small wonder Gladstone told Ishbel's mother he admired the Aberdeens as "an edifying couple". Such intervention in the lives of the tenants and servants was appreciated in a community that had few opportunities for sociability except church on Sunday. The farm homes were bare of entertainment and transportation was lacking. In 1898 when the Aberdeens returned from Canada they noticed how the life of the countryside had changed with the advent of the bicycle.

Although so much of her time was given to what she saw as the responsibilities of her position, she had also to contend with society, and their place in it. Ishbel seems to have found this a less enjoyable duty.

Teas and balls and parties were more bearable because they could be put to use "influencing for good" the people of wealth and power in Britain. Ever the moralist, Ishbel saw some benefit also to her own character, noting that "the disciplines of society and ... the necessity of suppressing personal likes and dislikes are not experiences to be despised."[17]

It would be some decades before Ishbel could look back and say with amusement that she and her husband must have been dreadful prigs in their young years. Aberdeen, strongly influenced by the example of his neurotic father, equaled her in piety if not in generalship. He was given to generous and impractical schemes. He soon learned to leave the management of the estate to his factor, embarrassed by an early incident when he found himself unable to deny the plea of a young tenant to set up on a relative's small acreage which, as a matter of good economics, should have been added to the next farm to make a more viable unit. The factor stepped in to settle the matter by persuading the young man to emigrate to America. Aberdeen gave him some guineas, regretting that they were not enough to set him up in the new world. "It is inevitable, owing to the business element in the relations between landlord and tenant, that such cannot always be of the roseleaf sort," he sighed.[18]

His biggest gaffe was his grand plan in the first year of their marriage to build a branch railway line through the properties. Things had advanced to the point of staking out a right-of-way, with white flag markers fluttering in the oat fields, when their Edinburgh lawyer, Mr. Jamieson, made a trip to Haddo House to lay bare the financial realities. As Ishbel reported it, the line would have to be paid for within twenty-five years, at a cost of £4,000 a year. That meant the Aberdeens would have an income of £16,000 annually after deducting operating expenses on their properties, with such items already committed as an annual £2,000 toward tenants' cottages. Another prior claim was a regular annual allowance for Ishbel's young brother Coutts, who was out of favour with Sir Dudley. Coutts would, in fact, become a constant charge on Aberdeen's generosity. Their proposed spending included another £500 a year for charity, most of it already pledged. Ishbel, noting it all down in her journal, added, "Out of the rest [we are] to save as much as possible, but there will be no saving for the next two or three years, as long as these alterations on the house are going on.[19]

The railway indeed had to go. Aberdeen gave his tenants a half-year's rebate on their rents to ease their disappointment.

In January 1879 Ishbel gave birth to their first child, a sickly boy. He was named George, and as eldest son was called by the hereditary title of Lord Haddo. In December 1880 they had a daughter, Marjorie (later Lady Pentland); a second daughter lived only a few months; a second son, Dudley Gladstone, was born in May 1883 (and became in 1965 the heir to titles and estates, passing them on to his sons); a third son, Ian Archibald, was born in October 1884. Along with all the other demands on her time, Ishbel was a conscientious

The Earl and Countess of Aberdeen, shortly after their marriage.

Ishbel with her three older children, Marjorie, George (Lord Haddo) and Dudley, early in 1884.

and loving mother, less severe and remote than her own mother or indeed than most mothers of her class.

Incredibly, Ishbel regarded these years as "a tranquil time" in her life. She reflected:

> All the foundations of the society in which we moved seemed so stable, that there was a kind of assumption that as things had been, so would they continue. Changes of Government between the Tory and Liberal parties appeared to us to be the most violent form of upheaval which we could contemplate.[20]

Politics provided the excitement and drama she needed. It was to her the most fascinating of all pursuits. It was theatre and arena, playing field and high moral endeavour, brawl and contest. Committed to the Liberal party, which she believed had a monopoly of admirable men and sound argument, she listened passionately as Gladstone and his colleagues sought in the early '80's to gain power again. Her first contribution was of course to move the Earl of Aberdeen, nobleman of considerable rank, from the Tory benches to the better side.

Shortly after their marriage, late in 1878, Disraeli launched a punitive expedition into Afghanistan, the traditional buffer state between Russia and British India. Gladstone opposed the military invasion, resisting the high wave of Tory imperialism that would engulf the closing years of Victoria's reign. Ishbel urged her husband to take Gladstone's view, and joyfully reported in her journal that on one occasion he in fact "spoke on Afghanistan against the government" at a public gathering where he was presiding.[21] They were visiting in Edinburgh when they learned that Aberdeen's party was in fact divided on the issue. Lord Derby and Lord Carnarvon were opposed to Disraeli's policy. Ishbel persuaded Aberdeen to send a wire adding his name to a list of these dissenters.

Unluckily for him, the issue soon came to a vote in parliament. He had to declare himself. He had gone down to London just as the vote was brought to the second chamber. A Tory friend, sensing Aberdeen's distress, advised him not to turn up. But Aberdeen knew that to absent himself would be seen as cowardly — and there was Ishbel wrapped in a great cloak to conceal her advanced pregnancy, enduring the long debate on the straight-backed visitors' benches.

"I never spent a more miserable five hours. I felt like an outcast," Aberdeen recalled.[22] He spoke briefly to support his "No" (leaning on the memory of his prime minister grandfather). Afterwards he got rid of his agitation by going off to skate, in elegant sweeping circles, on the frozen Serpentine.

It required other "talks with Johnnie" to complete the conversion. Ishbel invited the grand old radical, John Bright, to Haddo House in October 1879. The father of the Anti-Corn Laws, who in the interest of Liberal free trade took off the tariffs from imported grain and lowered the price of bread for Britain's millions, was invited to defend his position with the indignant farmers of Aberdeenshire. Several of them came to Haddo House to discuss with him the problem of cheap imported American beef, selling at ten percent less than their own. Bright took the high road of free trade while the farmers "grumbled fairly." Haddo House added to its reputation as a hotbed of liberalism at a dinner for twenty-one the same evening. The guests invited to meet Bright included the Lord Provost of Aberdeen city, the Huntlys and others of consequence — a largely Conservative company. Ishbel recorded: "Animated discussion. I lost my temper."[23] She felt all was saved and equanimity restored when Bright read aloud the First Canto of *Paradise Regained* "most splendidly" after dinner.

Rumour of these events reached the ear of Lord Rosebery in Edinburgh, probably the most influential Scotsman in the Liberal party. He was at that time developing a plan for a bold and unprecedented public campaign for Gladstone, aimed at the next election. Gladstone was to sweep through Midlothian speaking to the common people — such a tour by a political leader had never before been attempted. Largely through Rosebery's planning, the Midlothian Campaign made history as a magnificent success. Gladstone "set the heather on fire", touching the hands of hundreds, touching their hearts with a resounding moral appeal to maintain abroad Britain's high image of justice for all. There at Dalmeny, Rosebery's home near Edinburgh (a household that pleased Ishbel with its moral "tone"), the campaign was hatched in late November 1879. An assembly of top-rank supporters included the still officially Conservative Earl of Aberdeen, obviously wavering in his affiliation, and his wife the Countess Ishbel.

Dinner at Haddo House by artist A. E. Emslie (with Gladstone seated on Lady Aberdeen's right and Lord Rosebery on her left)

Ladies had no part in these affairs. Only six women, including Mrs. Gladstone and her daughter Mary, Lady Rosebery, and Ishbel, were at Dalmeny that weekend. At an initial dinner for forty people the women dined separately in an upstairs room, and only caught the after dinner speeches by Rosebery and Gladstone by slipping quietly down to listen behind a door. Ishbel wasted no energy protesting the burden of her petticoats. Her role was to make a Liberal of Johnnie, and she was succeeding. She also occupied her time profitably, she believed, in intimate conversation with Rosebery's Jewish wife, the former Hannah Rothchild, who impressed her as very religious-minded; surely in time she would "be brought to Jesus."[24]

Her hopes for Johnnie were raised by the more active role he was playing in public affairs, when he spoke very creditably to a gathering, giving a "splendid lecture on Railways and Locomotives," she was beside herself with delight. She appraised his performance: "quite splendid in every respect — voice, manner and matter and the way of putting it — I was proud of my Johnnie."[25] He gave another fine lecture on Egypt at the Methlick Institute. But the real test was still to come. In January he received an invitation to attend and move the resolution of support to Gladstone at a Liberal rally in

Aberdeen. He accepted, "not without searchings of the heart."
On January 30 they drove into the city, Aberdeen rehearsing
his speech on the way. He went alone to a gentlemen's dinner,
then picked up Ishbel and other ladies — four females were
this time to sit on the platform as special guests. The Music
Hall was crowded with an audience of three thousand men,
mostly staunch Liberals delighted to welcome the young Earl
as a convert to their ranks.

> Lord Fife gave an excellent address and was well received.
> But Johnnie was quite as enthusiastically received and all
> the audience rising involuntarily to their feet when he stood
> up and waving hats and handkerchiefs they cheered lustily.
> He was quite overcome and looked straight down, blushing,
> and it rather put him out at first and he lost his place in his
> notes and forgot to put the allusion to himself as speaking
> from a Liberal platform for the first time, at the right place.
> But he put it at the end and it did very well and he spoke well
> and fluently and looked very well. My own darling! He was
> extremely nervous beforehand and so was I, sickeningly so.[26]

In March Disraeli called parliament into session, and the
Aberdeens went down again to London. Aberdeen was now
committed. He had written to Lord Granville, the Liberal
leader in the House of Lords, stating his decision, and had of
course been cordially welcomed. He took his seat on the
Liberal benches on the day Disraeli dissolved parliament for
the election.

Gladstone swept back into power. There had been correspondence between Ishbel and her mother: Sir Dudley had
put in a claim on Aberdeen's behalf, and he received his first
public appointment as Lord Lieutenant of Aberdeenshire. It
was followed a year later by a second honour. Lord Rosebery
negotiated this one, and wrote to Ishbel:

> It appears to me that Aberdeen would make a most excellent
> Lord High Commissioner to the Church of Scotland: not the
> least of his qualifications being the Lady High Commis-
> sioner.[27]

With much pomp and pageantry, Aberdeen was to represent the British government in Edinburgh at the Church
Assembly, which in its sturdy independent character and
tradition preserved some of the elements of the old national

parliament of Scotland. In addition to ceremonial duties Aberdeen must entertain frequently. Ishbel's inclination, abetted by Rosebery, was to expand their guest lists to many influential people outside church circles. She even made a personal overture to the Free Church Assembly, going boldly to listen to that rival group debate a topic in which she felt an interest. Official frowns cut short that overture. The Aberdeens found the government allowance of £2,000 (plus lodging at Holyrood Palace) not nearly adequate for their expenditure, and when Gladstone proposed a second term in 1885 they accepted under protest. Gladstone heartlessly advised them to "restrain the free and large current of your hospitable entertainments," though he at the same time noted with approval that the position had become a "different office," and "a channel of much influence, most munificently conceived by yourself and Lady Aberdeen," and urged them to stay on.[28]

Meanwhile during the parliamentary season they liberally entertained the Liberals at 27 Grosvenor Square. And at this period they acquired first a suburban house called Littleberries, and then Dollis Hill, taken over from Sir Dudley. It was delightfully remote from the city. The Gladstones' biographer, Joyce Marlowe, says that Gladstone severely inconvenienced cabinet business when he insisted on driving there for a relaxing Sunday in any kind of weather. In 1883 Gladstone walked out of a cabinet meeting to attend the christening of Aberdeen's son Dudley, for whom he stood godfather, presenting the child with a Greek Testament. In 1894 there was a visit by the Gladstones to Haddo House. It took on all the glamour of a state visit, with torchlight processions and mounted escorts.

Even in Gladstone's own day the most intense interest in this prime minister centred on his "night walks", his dealings with London prostitutes with the stated purpose of rehabilitating them. Prime Minister Mackenzie King in Ottawa, only a short time later, took up the same pursuit, with the same wild surmise and wise assumptions on the part of those who, in the style of the times, politely refrained from mentioning anything but the public version of his activities. Ishbel knew all about it, like everyone else. She probably convinced herself that Gladstone's behaviour was eccentric but morally correct. She took the singular course of associating herself with his endeavours. Down she went herself to the Strand Rescue Mission, every Friday evening, and out into the dim alleys to speak to the women of the streets. Her approach was to invite them into a nearby shop for a warm cup of tea. If she could, she drew from them their tales of woe, and urged them to seek religion and a respectable way of life. How successful she was is uncertain, though letters remain from these women who spoke of Ishbel's "sweet face" and their talks together.

In any case, Ishbel's rigidity in moral matters had by now (1884) been changed. She had come under the spell of the handsome and electrifying young man who would open her heart to "The Greatest Thing in the World."

PART II
TRANSITION

Chapter 5
Henry Drummond

When illustrious visitors were present at Haddo House on a Sunday they were often pressed in to delivering a sermon, or a reading if they were not quite up to a sermon, in the family chapel. This small pleasant place glowed with the mellow warmth of polished oak in the light of a beautiful east window by one of Victorian England's favourite artists, Burne-Jones. A west window of stained glass also, was designed by the chapel's architect, George Edmund Street. The building was Street's last work, an intimate modification of his more impressive achievements in the cathedrals of Britain. This was a place for friends.

Here on a Sunday evening in August 1884, Ishbel took her place with her husband, household staff, and a few guests, to listen to Henry Drummond. Drummond was more than usually inspired. He was more than usually eloquent. He spoke of love. Out of the sermon came a religious booklet that had a phenomenal sale and world-wide circulation, and is still sold wherever the Church of Scotland vends its wares. Love is greater than faith — what a revelation! Faith had seemed sufficient to earn one's passage to heaven. This man said there must be love. He told them how to recognize it:

> Something more than the sum of its ingredients, a glowing, dazzling, tremulous ether. A palpitating, quivering, sensitive living thing... You will be changed from tenderness to tenderness. It is better not to have lived than not to love.[1]

Henry Drummond was born at Stirling in August 1851. From a family of Free Church believers engaged in the seed and garden nursery trade, he followed the obvious course through common school. But he was not a common boy. Classmates detected in him a special grace, a standout in the usual group of "clumsy, unformed awkward Scottish lads."[2] Friends called him the"the Prince" He had hypnotic powers which he used as a game until, while still a student, he began to feel ashamed of this petty kind of domination, and gave up playing with the skill he knew he possessed. At 17, at Edinburgh University, he published an essay on "Mesmerism and Animal Magnetism", asserting that hypnotism, which some men were then discussing as "electro-biology", and which others ridiculed, was indeed a demonstrable and useful practice for those endowed with the ability to exercise it.

Five years later when the evangelical American team, Dwight L. Moody and Ira D. Sankey, swept through Britain, Drummond joined their entourage, sometimes preaching, sometimes putting to use his ability to draw forth confession and gently heal, in the personal conversion sessions which were called "inquiries".

He was not given to confession. He passed off any invitation to disclose his personal problems with a charming light-heartedness that once more set him apart — his acquaintances saw him as free from care and from temptation, an angelic sort of chap. He had skipped erratically through university courses in philosophy, but was much more interested in natural science. This led him to Darwin. Into the raging controversy he introduced unruffled faith; to Christian belief he added a singular rejoicing in scientific discovery. "The absence of all trace of revolt is characteristic", said his biographer; Drummond merely ignored what was "hostile or superfluous".[3] Instead of the agony of soul-searching he began to devise a happy creed of his own, encompassing everything, and in particular melding Darwin's natural laws with man's spiritual Ascension, in argument that glided neatly over disparity. It was in essence a message of hope, to make people happier and more comfortable with themselves and their world.

In appearance Henry Drummond was slim and tall, lithe in movement, handsome, with red-brown hair and compelling dark eyes, fastidious in dress. He got on beautifully with his own family, his sisters, his brother James, his father (though there were some irritations), and especially his mother, who was his life long confidante. With other ladies too he entered into charming and exhilarating correspondence. His manner with them was circumspect on the whole, but there were

Henry H. Drummond, miniature by Miss E.M. Ross, from the Haddo House Collection.

possibly indiscreet associations. To one lady, Mrs. Stuart of Altrincham, he wrote of a decision he was sure she would understand, that he was not inclined to take up ministry in the church and would hold back from ordination at the end of his studies, because of his aversion to "Mrs. Grundy".[4]

Instead he took up a post as lecturer at Free Church College in Glasgow. He was to lecture on Natural Science, not an incongruence at a theological college because Darwin had provoked a burning desire in scholars to justify Christian faith in "scientific" terms. He soon had devoted classes of students, not only in Glasgow but in a specially arranged lecture series in Edinburgh as well. He believed in what he was doing for the young; he considered this ministry his true life's work. His main effort seemed to be to soothe their chaotic young emotions and strengthen their resolution to be good, law-abiding fellows. Contemporary theologians found fault with him because he seemed unaware of the concept of sin.

Drummond traveled when he could on geological expeditions that took him to America's Rocky Mountains and the Mediterranean, delighted with everything he saw, and adding to these experiences the lasting pleasure of several months' study at the University of Tübingen in the German mountain regions. It was no doubt in that nobly romantic setting, where theological dispute resounded among philosophers like Friedrich Strauss over the possibility that at least part of the Bible was more fable than truth, that Drummond fashioned his own open-ended faith.

When Sankey and Moody came to Britain a second time in late 1882 Drummond joined their missionary tour again, and it was apparently at this time that he came to the attention of Ishbel's uncle, Quintin Hogg, who was helping to sponsor the tour. Hogg recommended Drummond to the Aberdeens. At that time Drummond was deep in the process of writing the book that would make him famous, *Natural Law in the Spiritual World*. It was translated widely and sold 119,000 copies, an amazing popular success.

Ishbel and Henry Drummond met at about this period, but the precise date is obscure. There is a curious inaccuracy in her account of it in the Aberdeens' memoirs. It is curious because the impact of the meeting was so great, and the subsequent friendship so freely acknowledged. Though she had both letters and journals to work from in compiling her memoirs, she puts the first meeting in May 1884, which is out by a year, according to Drummond's papers. She advanced the date of the second Sankey-Moody tour by one year. She errs in a reference to Drummond's year of travel just prior to May 1884, when in fact according to his travel notebook he was out of the country for only six months and had been back since January.

The significance of this error is hard to judge. At least, it was an odd mistake, since she described in a long and fanciful passage the coming together at Holyrood that spring, and the instant attraction between the Aberdeens and the distinguished young theologian, world traveller, and popular author. There is a possibility that the advanced date obscured a romantic involvement that resulted in the birth of Ishbel's youngest and best-loved son, Ian Archibald, in the fall of 1884. lshbel's journals from 1883 on have been destroyed.

Whatever the truth of the matter, Ishbel could not bring herself to extinguish all evidence of their long and intense relationship. The letters from Henry were reduced to typed copies with many deletions and no doubt some omissions. This typed volume is preserved at Haddo House. It covers the years from 1885 to 1895, ending not long before Drummond's death when Ishbel was in Canada. It is a large collection — many hundreds of letters — showing the writer as a lover, attentive, playful and teasing, anxious to meet, lonely in absence, torn when his work interfered with their pleasure. What emerges also from the letters is a sense of their object as a desirable and intensely loving woman. For poignancy, one finds among the pages an elegant small envelope bearing Ishbel's crest and a penciled "Henry"; inside the envelope is a curled lock of reddish brown silky hair that springs from the thread that ties it in a rather unnerving way.

Ishbel left behind also, a gold-framed miniature of Henry Drummond, looking decidedly Byronesque, sharing place at Haddo House with miniatures of her husband and parents.

The letters she wrote to Henry do not survive. They must have been a large part of the papers that were turned over to his brother James after his death. James returned them to Ishbel in two batches. The first lot apparently was to help the Aberdeens in writing We Twa. In February 1924 a second lot was returned and Ishbel then wrote to James to thank him especially for the discretion he had used in holding them back and mailing them later to her:

You have correctly diagnosed the situation ... We do indeed
greatly appreciate the consideration and delicacy with which
you have parceled these poor old letters of ours.[5]

When Lady Pentland wrote a biography of her mother in
the 1950's, she used some extracts from letters from Ishbel to
Drummond, as well as what were described as Ishbel's journals, after 1884. Having been used in this way, the letters and
journals alike vanished. The daughter, not unnaturally, had
trouble coping with this aspect of her mother's life and wrote,
gingerly:

Ishbel's youngest son, Archie.

Although regarded as a leader among women, Ishbel herself had always been most at ease with men friends; objectively, constructively, discussing things and plans rather than emotions and acquaintances.[6]

Lady Pentland selected one passage said to be from a journal to expand on this delicate subject:

...our first great friendship with a contemporary was with Henry Drummond, and in more recent years too, some of our men friends have become real comrades and have taught me more about 'the joy of living' than ever I knew in my youth. I do not suppose that any woman can have enjoyed the satisfaction of such friendships more fully than I have; I am sorry for those who have no such opportunities. A. has rejoiced so much in this that for me all has been plain sailing. Of course, I owe it to the blessed lack of jealousy in his composition, and I believe that he too has reaped benefit from his generosity.[7]

It was perhaps inevitable that Ishbel should find a lover, despite her youthful shocked reaction to the endless flirtations and liaisons pursued in Britain's great houses. Her marriage far from satisfied her highly charged, romantic and ambitious nature. Nor could her ardent spirit easily submit to the rigors of evangelical religion. It was for her an extraordinary release to be set free of its more negative limitations. When it happened, her natural affection broke all bounds. Her love for the shining messenger was part of her liberation. After the first euphoria there followed years of doubt and turmoil, for the dictates of the church had been sincerely followed, the devil ever at her elbow, and so great a change was not easy to resolve. The later journals must have been a story of much emotional chaos.

Drummond visited Haddo House first in the summer of 1884, writing to his mother of the expanse of parks and lakes and the "magnificent" house, "quite the finest thing I have ever seen."[8] In this letter he told his mother that Ishbel already "has three youngsters, including a son and heir, " besides the child expected in October. From then on there were many visits, including several to Dollis Hill where Henry was thrilled to meet "The Grand Old Man" (Gladstone) and also Robert Browning, who is quite unlike a poet, and talks plain prose. To meet him you would think the man an elderly but well preserved and smart French banker. Harcourt, Lord Bute and a crowd of other notables were also here."[9] Ishbel saw to it that he was also invited to Guisachan, thus opening new doors for him. She tried to put herself on Henry's social level by deploring "that stupid handle to one's name," adding, "The abolition of titles will be one blessing of the Radical programme!"[10] Henry was thrown into a great commotion when Ishbel proposed that she and her husband "come to you in Glasgow". He worried that his house at No. 3 Park Circus would not pass muster.

> I am getting all ready for the Aberdeens who come at 6 tonight. I think the house is *clean,* at least, if not gaudy. We dine tonight with John Burns, and they leave on Wednesday evening... Now I must run away and buy a counterpane...[11]

Ishbel jealously frowned when Henry accepted an invitation to proceed from Haddo House to Aboyne Castle, where the Huntlys, Aberdeen's impious cousins, lived. She apparently told him that he could do very little in the religious line with them, and he deferred to her opinion and cut short his visit.

But she did enlarge his acquaintance in other directions. She personally canvassed Liberal Members of Parliament with his writings. (He wrote: "How you *are* badgering all those young M.P.'s. I am sure they must hate me cordially."[12]) Next to London high society. She boldly resolved to transport Henry, who was such a hit among students, to the Duke of Westminster's drawing room to instruct titled gentlemen. Henry was startled and reluctant, but she persuaded him, saying, "you may think I am making too much fuss about such people, but many of them are centres of influence both in London and in their own country districts."[13] She set up three Sunday afternoons at Grosvenor House, advertising discreetly in the *Times* that tickets could be had from the Earl of Aberdeen. The series of meetings was a notable success.

> To be able to collect, even under a ducal roof, on four [sic] successive Sunday afternoons, four or five hundred people, many of them of the highest distinction, is a triumph of ingenious ingenuity. Mr. Drummond has invented a new gospel... He does not consign to perdition all who fail to lead highly spiritual life here... Mr. Drummond has, in fact produced upon his hearers the impression that the teachings of

science are, upon the whole, in favour of revealed religion...
The audience has departed profoundly impressed by the
words of wisdom and solemnity issuing from the lips of a
young man with a good manner, a not ill-favoured face, a
broad Scotch accent, clad in a remarkably well-fitting frock
coat, and reciting, after his prelection, the Lord's Prayer in
a tone of devout humility...[14]

Ishbel sought to sustain the impetus of these meetings.
With Lady Tavistock (later Duchess of Bedford) she organized the Associated Workers' League, to co-ordinate the
charitable efforts of London ladies and draw in new volunteers. Drummond was to inspire and assist. Somewhat more
nonchalant after his first success, he fell in with this plan to
activate "the unemployed of the West End" as he called them,
and wrote to his brother James that he seemed to be spending
a great deal of time in drawing-rooms.

Ishbel developed a sudden interest in science. She enrolled in a correspondence course in biology under Professor
Edward Poulton at Oxford. Made aware of her own ignorance,
she took up the cause of admitting women to universities,
becoming president of lobby groups in Edinburgh and Aberdeen, and pressing letters on Mr. Gladstone for changes in the
Universities Bill of 1885. Drummond was consulted in this
project as in all others and gave support, writing: "The main
thing surely is that the Higher Education be *real*, and not a
mere accretion of further 'accomplishments'."[15] When the
British Association (of scientists) met in Aberdeen she had
her husband engage a house there for the entire week of its
deliberations, to be in the thick of things. She had the leading
speakers to Haddo House, along with Henry Drummond.

Henry was contrite when Ishbel reproached him for argu-
ing with the great, not-to-be-questioned Gladstone, in the
pages of *Nineteenth Century*. Gladstone had attacked Thomas H. Huxley for a scientific view of creation; Gladstone,
author of *The Impregnable Rock of Holy Scripture,* would
have none of it. Drummond, as usual, had moved in softly,
assuring them that both were right, though Huxley had an
edge. When *Genesis* was written, Drummond explained, there
was no scientific practice, so *Genesis* was only splendid
poetry, "a presentation of one or two elementary truths to the
childhood of the world." Huxley and Gladstone were not,
apparently, swayed.

The Aberdeens and Henry had a brief holiday boating on the Thames. It was Henry's idea: "... a Bohemian expedition, rail to Oxford then in a skiff for a couple of days returning on Thursday next. The Aberdeens never have any such adventures and they are looking forward to this..."[16] Henry was their guest at Dollis Hill, at Haddo House, at Holyrood. There in Edinburgh in 1885 Ishbel attempted to bring Free Church leaders face to face with the leaders of the Church Assembly. She had them all to breakfast. Rosebery, fascinated by the prospect, wrote to her:

> Your breakfast is most thrilling. I hope they won't fight. Feed them on boiled eggs which do not admit of poison.[17]

Henry expressed mock horror at what she might take into her head to do next; Ishbel glowed with confidence, spun new schemes by the dozen. Aberdeen, on the other hand, was in less than radiant health. Rosebery admonished him: "You are looking thin and pallid and should take a restorative holiday."[18] Ishbel had diverted so much attention to Henry that the husband must indeed have felt chilled, while her impetuosity must have kept him in a state of alarm. Yet he and Henry got on well enough, and Aberdeen staunchly upheld the image of Henry as a family friend. The children, encouraged by Ishbel, adored him and called him "Uncle Hen." Occasionally he visited the frail oldest son, Haddo, once he had gone off to school, and managed to inject reassurance in his reports to Ishbel.

Once in the course of these busy years, in September 1888, Aberdeen proposed joining Henry on vacation in the Swiss Alps, and Henry agreed without a great deal of enthusiasm, asking Ishbel:

> And you? It would be ever so nice if you could come and join us. I would promise to pick you an absolute solitude, somewhere among the pines and glaciers where you could dream and paint, and read poetry, and be at rest. I do long for you to get that, wherever you get it.[19]

But Ishbel had a heavy program of meetings scheduled for those autumn weeks. Henry wrote from Lucerne to reproach her for taking on yet another project, a conference for women platform speakers:

My dear Eisdrubail [a German variant of her name, used after 'Lady Aberdeen' came to seem too formal]... I am half delighted and half disgusted to see you running so many new things. But you are incorrigible and it is a waste of breath trying to scold you...[20]... I liked your Perth address *much*, and have been hearing about it from the Barbours. You will now be on the threshold of the Aberdeen one. Oh weh weh. Why can't you eat, drink and be merry just for one month?[21]

In Aberdeen's company he suffered "an epidemic of cousins", even though he drew the line at anyone not surnamed Gordon. He wrote to Ishbel that Aberdeen had a knack for sneaking off and leaving Drummond to arrange their entertainment. Somewhat disgruntled, his letter to Ishbel on their arrival back in England announced that he would deliver "your Great Parcel" to Haddo House the next Saturday morning.

In the pattern made familiar by the philandering of the Prince of Wales, the existence of the extramarital lover was both concealed and acknowledged. Who gained and who lost? It is difficult not to conclude that the Aberdeens and Drummond gained, all three.

Chapter 6
Ireland and Aftermath

Ishbel was not at all pleased when she learned of the Irish viceregal appointment in 1886. She had quite enough to do in London and Edinburgh, and she had Henry. She was probably happier than she had ever been before. Then in February 1886, after the election in which Gladstone announced his intention to introduce Home rule to Ireland, Aberdeen was requested to take the post. Ishbel was on a visit to Lady Rosebery at the time. Aberdeen met her at Euston Station on her return: Gladstone had called him in that afternoon, requesting an immediate answer because the new government members must visit the Queen for the "kissing of hands" next day. (The Irish Lord-Lieutenant, or Viceroy, was sworn in as a member of the government, unlike the arrangement with the dominions overseas.) Aberdeen, assuming his wife's concurrence, had accepted. Ishbel's chief emotion at that moment, however, was a restlessness for Henry's company: she was cherishing the latest letter she had had from him:

> Writing is such a miserable thing after talking...I suppose that is why I have been so long silent...[1]

The silence had in fact been one week long, after a visit by the Aberdeens to Glasgow. Now she wrote to Henry of her anxiety and annoyance at the sudden turn of events:

> Don't you think I ought to be very offended at not being consulted, I who have registered a solemn vow never to set foot in Ireland? [We are] plunging into the unknown. We are not dwelling on the danger [four years earlier the Irish Secretary, Sir Frederick Cavendish, husband of Gladstone's niece, had been murdered in Phoenix Park], — we do not think of it — but it all seems dark ahead and I just feel overwhelmed. Perhaps it is partly because of the perpetual

gloomy fog and the poor mobs of unemployed rioters, and my having been maddened with neuralgia yet having to go on with crushing correspondence, and interviews! The house has been filled with applicants for the ADC-ships...[2]

The panic passed. She got Aberdeen's consent to offer Drummond an official post at Dublin Castle. Drummond cautiously declined "a post of such honour and publicity" which he felt, in view of his "real work and mission in life", would leave a wrong impression on the public mind. He begged Ishbel to think of such an appointment "in relation to my friends, and my *audience,* past and future. For Mrs. Grundy I do not care, I hope, but for the others, for the students, and for those to whom one may yet speak of a Spiritual World, one would like to avoid even the appearance of ambition."[3]

He assured her he would be often in Dublin, and indeed he was, commuting across the Irish Channel with great regularity, and writing to his mother that "all goes merrily here" at the Viceregal Lodge; he had student meetings to attend in Wales and more ahead in Scotland, so "it is hard lines crossing the channel so often" but "letters I think had better be sent here as this will be headquarters. I have great political talks..."[4]

Mail flew across the Channel when he was obliged to be on the English side. Ishbel was engrossed in projects to find work for the unemployed and relieve famine in Dublin, for her original mistrust of Ireland had swiftly vanished. She visited every dark nook in the city. All was described to Henry, for his commendation and advice. Should she, in view of the dreadful poverty, set a good example by not attending the Punchestown Races, canceling the Punchestown Ball at the Viceregal Lodge, and donating the money to hospitals instead? He thought she should, though Aberdeen might go. She told him of visiting the Hospital for Incurables and he replied:

It must have been very trying, for that awful place (I know it) needs all one's nerve. Do you not think the word 'Incurable' should be buried out of sight, and something substituted with at least one glimmer of hope in it? The Edinburgh one has the awful word carved in great letters across the front. I never pass it without shuddering. There is a great indelicacy and want of fine feeling still about much of our philanthropy.[5]

Costume Embroidered by Irish Girls for the Countess of Aberdeen.

Promoting Irish Industries and Fashion drawing of a gown embroidered by Irish girls for the Countess of Aberdeen in 1888.

The Aberdeens in 1886 tried to efface, in Gladstone's name, the hatred felt in Ireland for the successive English aristocrats who had held court at Dublin Castle, and succeeded in winning many hearts, if not of the Irish Tory Peers, certainly of the general public. Then the British parliament turned down Gladstone's Home Rule Bill, which would have given Ireland a quasi-independence under the Crown, close to the relationship successfully concluded with Canada nineteen years before. In the election that followed, English voters threw Gladstone out of office. Aberdeen was recalled.

On the traumatic day when they left Dublin, 3 August 1886, Henry Drummond at Ishbel's urgent request was by her side. Ishbel was dressed that day in an Irish-made dress of the kind she had worn repeatedly to boost Irish industry, of blue poplin trimmed with Limerick lace in a pattern of rose, shamrock and thistle. In their baggage was a painting of young Dudley and Archie as "Two Little Home Rulers" perched on a barrow of potatoes, by Madame Starr Cansiani.

Ishbel recounted in their memoirs the awesome emotion of the Dubliners who thronged the streets to bid them farewell.

> ...and as we turned down the sharp bend into Cork Hill, a sight and sound met us, never to be effaced from memory. As far as the eye could reach, one dense mass of human beings; no barricades — only a thin line of soldiers, who would have been powerless to keep the people back even if they had wished to do so; and the moment we came in sight there was a sudden mighty roar of voices which one could never, never describe... We found it best to stand, so that the people at the back could see, as this partly prevented their crushing forward; ... the emotion was largely that of sorrow; for it all seemed to speak of a 'might have been'...[6]

It was a matter of the heart, and to Ishbel it was largely due. An unnamed Irish journalist later compared their impact during that brief 1886 régime with former incumbents at Dublin Castle:

> Lord and Lady Aberdeen came to us in the full flush of generous youth in 1886, when Mr. Gladstone was making his first great attempt to reconcile the Irish. They were with us only six months, and during that time they endeared themselves so greatly to the mere Irish that their going away was a scene of national sorrow...

Souvenir of first Irish Vice-Regal term.

It would be hardly commensurate to say that Lady Aberdeen seconded Lord Aberdeen in the attempt to win the Irish people. It could not be said with truth of so great a personality as that gracious lady's that she seconded anyone... She has spent herself in the cause of Ireland and the Irish poor. Nothing has turned her back; nothing has stayed her. She has swept on in her irresistible course, and has fired others with something of her superb energy and courage... She would have swept the Tory ladies into her business of well-doing. But the Tory ladies preferred their own way. The way would be that of the Lady Bountiful. I am far from saying that some of Lady Aberdeen's ways did not scandalize them. The common people came too near her. She has that divine pity for childhood that she could gather her arms full of Dublin slum children at a Vice-Regal picnic for the poor of Dublin and romp with them like a merry girl. 'Such things are most unbecoming the wife of the Viceroy', said a Tory lady to me.[7]

Drummond was sobered and deeply impressed by the farewell. Formerly apolitical, he now surprised his friends by expounding on Home Rule, taking Gladstone's side in the

Liberal schism. He held this position against the raging of his father who, like Lord Tweedmouth and many others, gave full vent to feelings against the Irish. Home Rule was now thoroughly out of fashion. Drummond blithely parried Ishbel's attempt to have him run in the summer election, and respectfully declined the invitation from Gladstone that came at her instigation. He did appear on platforms in support of young Captain John Sinclair, Aberdeen's aide-de-camp, who had yielded to Ishbel's urging and joined the political fray.

The vengeful vituperation heard in England after Gladstone's defeat went very hard with Ishbel. She was only 29. The ascent to power had given her a sense of fulfilment and confidence never experienced before. Now she must endure her father's wrath and a sense of unjust betrayal.

Gladstone had closed the debate on the Home Rule bill with a Herculean speech:

> Go into the length and breadth of the world, ransack the literature of all countries, find if you can a single voice, a single book, in which the conduct of England towards Ireland is anywhere treated except with profound and bitter condemnation. Are these the traditions by which we are exhorted to stand?[8]

Ishbel wrote in her journal: "The truly grand old man made a magnificent closing speech and a passionate appeal. But they hardened their hearts to him and lost this golden opportunity."[9] And in a letter to Henry as the election results became clear,

> We scarcely know how to live through the day... Do you know J.R. Lowell's poem:
>
> "Once to every man and nation comes the moment to decide
> In the strife of Truth with Falsehood, —
> For the good or evil side."[10]

So the reaction to the Irish experience was predictable. Ishbel's gloom and suppressed anger brought on violent headaches. Finally, at the end of 1886, Aberdeen was persuaded to take her on a world tour, in the hope of lifting her spirits. Rosebery strongly advised it, saying they owed it to themselves to visit the outposts of the Empire. Drummond wrote:

In his letter A. announced you had some 'Plans', and as I have some small experience of the magnitude of your conceptions I was thrown into violent excitement for three days. I turned over all the possibilities, and finally concluded that the Powers of Europe had elected you to the Throne of Bulgaria and that I was to go at once to witness the Ascension..."[11]

The Aberdeens booked passage in December, first to India, then Australia, and across the Pacific to the United States. Henry was urged to accompany them at least part way, but his university duties would not permit it. Instead, as far as Australia, their companion was John Sinclair who had so valiantly fought for Ishbel's sake in the summer election. He had been defeated, of course, and had suffered another fall as well when a polo pony tipped him off the saddle and set a foot on his face — he had presented a brave but badly mangled visage to the electorate in that campaign, and wore a heavy drooping moustache thereafter to disguise his scarred lips. Sinclair, son of Lord Pentland, had become a great favourite with Henry Drummond, who loved his ebullient spirit and dubbed him "The Boy." He was a good traveling companion and Ishbel was sorry to part with him on the far side of the world.

Ishbel was not a good traveller. She had accepted the respite in the hope that quiet weeks on board ship would allow them "to make a plan for some definite purpose..." When she got as far as the Taj Mahal she wrote in her journal that "it seemed to hold out an unattainable perfect pattern, and therefore to bring a sense of one's own dismal failure."[12] On the next lap, to Australia, weather was bad and Ishbel described "plunging through the tail of a storm, when it needed an argument on some favourite subject like Women's Suffrage to enable me to brave it out at meals."[13]

In vain did Henry's letters urge her to succumb to "Travel Fever":

But is it not good? And really wholesome, and tonic, and expansive all round? And what new proportion it gives to things...Do you know your last letter was the lightest and brightest you have written me for a year? You see you have been carrying half the universe on your shoulders... Well, my birthday wish is that you won't be so serious, please.[14]

He, meanwhile, was putting in a quiet winter of lectures and study, and beginning his next book, *The Ascent of Man,* all of which he vivaciously described to her in a faithful flow of letters. *The Ascent of Man,* which would have nothing like the popular success of *Natural Law in the Spiritual World,* had moved in the direction of man's social and political obligations, a direct result of the Aberdeen influence. He wrote to complain that the season was dull, even new books were dull, and a recent poem by Browning "quite unintelligible."

In May as university classes ended he received a persuasive invitation from Dwight L. Moody to lecture to Moody's student's at Northfield, Massachusetts. The idea was appealing. Henry could surprise the Aberdeens somewhere in their journeying, for they would be in the United States to see Ishbel's two younger brothers, now set up as ranchers in the American West. On the point of making his travel plans he had a telegram from Ishbel. He wrote to his mother:

> A funny piece of clairvoyance. Last Tuesday, just as I was thinking of taking my berth a Telegram from Australia, from the Aberdeens, came in. 'Do meet us in America. Telegraph Auckland.' I wired back: 'Coming'...[15]

A telegram was a supreme event for those lucky enough to live in so great a scientific age. The single word sang through the wires, bouncing under seas and across continents. "What a marvellous thing it is to receive a Telegram!" Henry had written.

Ishbel received hers on arrival in San Francisco in June, along with a "whole stack" of letters, stopping at the Post Office even before being driven to their hotel. It was a fine way to be welcomed to North America — along with the four-foot-high floral harp they found waiting for them in their hotel suite. Resident Irish plied these Home Rule luminaries with attentions. As they crossed the United States emigrant Irish and Scots vied for audiences. Ishbel heard of Irish-American violence around the occasion of the Queen's Golden Jubilee, but recorded the opinion of a sincere young churchman, Mr. Norman MacLeod of Milwaukee, that "the Dynamiters are numerically few."

The Aberdeens arranged to meet Drummond at Niagara Falls once Drummond's Northfield lectures were over. Drummond, for his part, thoroughly enjoyed the U.S., where he had more invitations to speak than he could handle, and said he could make his fortune there very quickly if that were his goal; he established a rule, however, to charge for "science" lectures but not for "religion". He wrote to his mother from a train speeding to Northfield:

> This is a good day for traveling, and if one gets thirsty, Appolinaris, Ginger Beer and sandwiches are to be had on the train. Many of the trains have a dining car and the newest thing is a bath and a Barber's shop. They guarantee a shave at 60 miles an hour without a scratch.[16]

Lord Aberdeen also delighted in the marvels of railroad travel (and the wonders of the typewriter operated by a young woman who typed some letters for him at one of their stops). But the swaying speed made Ishbel ill, while the rough adventures in buckboards, through broiling heat, across stretches of Texas and Dakota to visit her emigrant brothers were only to be endured and not enjoyed. Her contributions to the joint travel journal mocked and criticized the crude ways of Americans.

Then, overnight, a transformation. On 12 July Lord Aberdeen wrote in their journal:

> Cataract Hotel, July 12. Found telegram from H. Drummond, would be here at 8. Much impressed by falls, and water angry and sea-like, great roaring of water constantly heard but not annoying — gives sensation of strength. Our first view of falls was in a train from the Canadian side. H.D. arrived all safe to-night. Niagara is very noisy.
>
> July 13. [in Ishbel's hand] Niagara still very noisy but everything else *rüjig*... After luncheon drove to Whirlpool Rapids, crossed to Canada and had afternoon tea at the Canadian Falls. *Wunder, wunderbar....*[17]

A few days later Drummond was sending a sad letter after their departing ship;

> "How quickly it becomes dreamland again; and one picks up the threads of real life once more just where they were dropped. I cannot believe I really saw you and A. here. It was

so short and sudden, and you passed away like a weaver's shuttle. I spent the Sunday in Newport and often looked over the Atlantic..."[18]

Drummond remained in North America that fall for a round of evangelical meetings, in which he was joined by Sinclair. Henry conceded that Princeton and Yale men were quite equal to English undergraduates on average, and found a challenge in lecturing at Harvard where the professors seemed to be all Unitarians and skeptics. Meanwhile he and Ishbel, by mail, conspired to promote public concern for Indian students educated in England and unable to find employment and, in a second cause, petitioned the queen on behalf of the girl-widows of India. Wrote Drummond:

"I never really realized before what a politician you are and hope you will not be angry at me for saying so."[19]

Ishbel was not in the least offended. The label was proudly worn. She had been speaking on public platforms ever since the return from Ireland. A first major event was the annual Liberal party gathering in Birmingham Town Hall, 7 November 1888 before an audience of thousands, when the Manchester *Chronicle*'s patronizing comment was that her speech "had no suggestion of the bluestocking or of hysterical rhetoric, and was delivered in a clear sweet voice which thoroughly fascinated the audience and was heard perfectly everywhere." She had been actively engaged in building a Women's Liberal Federation in England and a second one in Scotland: she became president of both. She set out her true vocation boldly:

We Women have often said we are politicians because it has been shown to us that we cannot do our duty either to our own homes or to our country without being so... [Some critics thought politics 'degrading' but they] must be faced out. The criticism comes from (1) a very partial view of what a woman's life should be and (2) a low estimate of politics...[20]

But it was becoming difficult to handle her political frustrations. From Ireland came disturbing news of repression under the Tory administration's Coercion Bill, while Arthur Balfour, Aberdeen's old friend and best man at their wedding, was now the Conservative Secretary for Ireland and was known there as "Bloody Balfour". In England the Liberal party was badly torn. The trade unions talked of sending members of their own to parliament instead of supporting Liberals. There were moments when one could believe class violence was imminent.

> ... the revolution which has been gathering so long. The people will feel their power: what then? The upper classes are defiantly determined to keep all they can; the conventionality of society binds its slaves down. Many of the best people withhold from what they feel is the contamination of politics.[21]

When women were given the vote in municipal elections Ishbel was asked to test the waters as a candidate. Because she owned no property in her own name she could not satisfy this fleeting ambition. In the event two women were elected to the London County Council, but their eligibility was challenged and the court disqualified them.

Enforced absence from Henry was added to political frustration. On return to Britain late in 1887 both of them were met with serious family problems. Ishbel was kept at Guisachan for weeks by her mother's serious illness. She felt chained to the patient's bedside. At the same time Drummond's father was terminally ill, and Drummond spent what days he could spare from his work at his parents' Sterling home. A rendezvous in Edinburgh in November, and at Haddo House in late December that year, took careful planning and were accomplished only with a sense of guilt and truancy from filial duty.

A letter from Henry in December expressed his concern for her unhappiness:

> My dear Eisdrubail. I had a letter half written to you a few moments ago but I threw it in the fire, for the post has just brought me your letter of yesterday. Words altogether fail me and I do not know how I dare intrude upon such woe as yours. These are terrible terrible pages you send me...[22]

The anguish Ishbel was experiencing during these months is attributed by her daughter to a hard questioning of religious faith, a re-examination of values. The journals Marjorie Pentland apparently destroyed would have thrown more light. Pentland writes:

After she had come through the battle she wrote in her locked journal of the tempests of doubt which had swept over her in those two years: 'It was terrible to go on day by day as if all were the same. I thank God that that blackness, with all its horrors, has passed. Henceforth I accept nothing but the truth, no standing still, always fresh truth. How that scorches a past life, honest enough but superficial, trivial...'[23]

Ishbel sent Henry a copy of her new "Confession of Faith" which she said now replaced the church doctrine she had grown up with. Henry's reply was far from reproachful: "How infinitely simpler, grander, more human, and more practical than the one one has had to give up! What more could one wish to work from, or work to?"[24]

Complicated feelings surrounding her mother's illness were part of the same conflict. Marjorie Pentland writes that Ishbel confessed to wishing her mother would die. Ishbel had in her "locked journal" justified such thoughts out of sympathy for the suffering her mother had endured.

And now as the fever rose and the doctors warned me there could be no hope, how I thanked God that the misery was over for her. The others thought me strange and cold, but how could I feel otherwise who had seen more than they of her life-long trouble, of her hourly self-sacrifice — I too who as she came slowly, painfully back to life, saw the look in her eyes as she asked me, 'Will he [her husband Dudley] be different?'[25]

But was this the real, and only cause of the death wish? It was also her mother who had put her into corsets at the first sign of pubescence, imposed the rigidity of proper behaviour, taught submission to the dictates of society and the church. And she had for so long championed her mother in the contest with her overbearing father! Cause enough for migraines.

Ishbel even turned on Henry, in accusations not identified. He replied:

What a dreadful letter you have sent me. Please don't, and remember I'm not made of vulcanite. You know you never gave me even a hint that you wished me to come to Haddo House for the Thursday and Sunday until I was inextricably fixed here with a heavy programme to get through... You who work like a tiger, or like a hundred tigers, must have

patience with a poor wretch who can only work like a snail...
so please don't say such dreadful things. If you had written
me a week before you did I could have arranged to come... But
I must draw breath after this wail and take a walk in the
rain.[26]

Late in 1889 Ishbel collapsed briefly under the strain and
was ordered off to bed.

I doctored myself for a day or two, but got furiously headachy
and feverish; A. sent for Dr. Maclagan from London and I
was pronounced to have nervous fever, followed by jaun-
dice.[27]

Dr. Maclagan sentenced her to a full year of recuperation,
doing nothing. Private correspondence, a few magazine articles and an attempted novel (in which Henry took a lively
vicarious delight) were now her only outlets. She heard from
Liberal party leaders as from a far-off battlefield. Richard
Haldane, who later became Secretary for War under Campbell-
Bannerman, wrote of the Women's Suffrage Bill he and
Edward Grey introduced (futilely) from the Opposition side
and, having heard she was hoping to resume some activity,
warned:

I hope you will not undertake the business of at least two
Cabinet ministers as before. The worst of being about the
only woman trying to keep abreast of all new departures is
that you cannot avoid having a great deal to do. The only way
is to delegate all detail.[28]

Henry sent her various things to read, and the gentlest of
admonitions and comfort:

Holiness is an infinite compassion for others; Greatness is to
take the common things of life and walk truly among them;
Happiness is a great love and much serving.[29]

It was the last of these precepts Ishbel would cherish.
During her confinement to her room Lady Tweedmouth
descended on Haddo House, and though Henry was at first
pleased that Ishbel had her mother with her, particularly
when Lord Aberdeen took a break and went off to spend some
time at his London clubs, which struck Henry as very odd

behaviour, he soon learned that friction was mounting between the two women, and wrote that he hoped she had managed to restrain herself and "*not* have it out with Lady Tweedmouth," though he "well knew the torture of suppression."[30] He visited her when it seemed prudent, writing afterwards of how hard it was to see "the shame in your eyes at being ill." When Aberdeen returned home Drummond mocked:

> Give my sympathies to the 'Man about Town' on his return to captivity. Why not pave the various drives at Haddo, put on a hansom or two, with a Club at the Lodge Gates and a Smoke and Fog producer at the Gas Works?[31]

Despite her doctor's orders, Ishbel resumed work, increasingly, with the Women's Liberal Federations, and responded to invitations to speak. A newspaper report on the opening of a Home Industries Exhibition in Dundee indicates how well she got on with the public:

> Lady Aberdeen is not only good to listen to but to look at, tall, generously proportioned, with a frank mobile face which lights up with a capital sense of humour, vivacious dark eyes, wavy brown hair. Her bonnet was of dark blue velvet and yellow honeysuckle, its strings clasped with a fly brooch of diamonds, pearls and sapphires. Among other home industries she advocated poultry farming...[32]

Her headaches recurred and her physician again urged rest and a change of scene. They tried a spring trip to Italy, which merely reinforced her opinion that classical art was "sterile". A longer restorative journey was proposed. Lord Aberdeen would take his wife to Canada in August, returning in November. Ishbel agreed — only because she would be separated from Henry in any case. He was off to Australia and the New Hebrides, rounding the world to land in America. She intended to travel across the North American continent and meet him on the Pacific coast.

PART III
CANADA

Chapter 7
1890: the Tourist

I shbel's doctors and well-wishers had consigned her to a year of rest, quiet and inertia. It was an impossible prescription. As long as she remained in Britain she was caught up in the flow of political events, which brought little tranquillity. The Liberal party had split on the Irish question. At the election late in 1886, 78 "Liberal Unionists" deserted. They would soon attach themselves to the Tories.

Lord Aberdeen must surely have been affected by the action of these Liberals of his own class, the Liberal peers and gentlemen Whigs. But Aberdeen stayed with Gladstone. He insisted that, once converted, he never felt afterwards "even an inclination to deviate from the central path of Liberalism."[1] He had a Christian conscience, and he had come to see the Gladstonian tradition as "Christianity in politics."

Ishbel felt more keenly the political frustrations of Britain, as the eighties became the nineties. What was happening to Liberalism? The working classes were threatening to go their own way, the Whigs had left. With other anxious Liberals Ishbel looked for renewed hope and glory overseas, in "Greater Britain". A provocative treatise had come from the pen of Sir Charles Dilke, who had been called "the fastest rising star in the Liberal heavens"[2] until a scandalous divorce case ruined his career.

In April 1890 as Henry Drummond sailed for Australia, Ishbel provided him with Dilke's latest book; *Problems of Greater Britain*. On reaching Melbourne Henry reported that he had "read Dilke according to instructions, and feel very wise and Imperial Federationally". He vowed to carry Dilke's ideas here and there about Australia as he toured. "We *must* take this jolly child a little nearer its grey old mother," he vowed.[3] His next letter was less resolute, for he had dined with a young couple, the husband an Australian lawyer who had roughly discouraged his English wife from talk of England, or any wistful hope of returning there. "From which I gathered," Henry wrote, "that he represents the faction of young Australians who hate us and all our ways."[4]

It was a salutary experience for the proponents of a more closely knit Empire. Ishbel would learn the same lesson in Canada. The concept of Imperialism was being challenged. Gladstone was adamantly opposed to the "waste" of military defence abroad, and equally concerned with the principle of liberal self-government for all peoples. He not only sponsored Home Rule for Ireland but endorsed Southern secession in the American Civil War. A 20th century historian, George Malcolm Young, has described the confusion of the period, "...all the emotions, from an almost religious fervour to an almost religious horror, with which the name and idea of Imperialism affected Late Victorian minds, according as it was regarded as the Mission of an Elect People, or Exploitation by Superior Power."[5]

Then there was Ishbel's good friend William Stead, the short, red-faced, red-bearded "human torrent of good causes",[6] who had just begun publishing his *Review of Reviews;* he espoused a union of the English-speaking world which he called "Sane Imperialism".

The winds of change were circling the globe. It was a good time to stir abroad.

Ishbel wrote voluminous letters, later collected in the form of a journal but addressed originally to John Sinclair, "The Boy", her friend and Drummond's. To Sinclair she could say:

> Spirits greatly revived by a telegram from Yokohama saying that H.D. starts next Thursday for 'Frisco... Sorry he is not coming straight to Vancouver as it would have been nice to welcome him off his ship... Beginning to chafe at not hearing from him...[7]

The Aberdeens paused first at Quebec City where the Citadel, the viceregal residence on the heights above the St. Lawrence, was made available to them. In the fine weather of those August days Ishbel "ventured out on a wooden terrace on the battlements leading out of the beautiful ballroom put up in Princess Louise's time here, to sketch".[8] Imperial displeasure was invoked when she looked cityward, to view: "a deserted square tenanted only by a poor bear chained to a high pole, and a few Dominion soldiers loafing about. One cannot help regretting the withdrawal of British troops from a place like this, if only for the sake of sentiment and picturesqueness."[9]

How could she describe the people of Quebec? "Everything certainly looks strangely un-English and yet it is not Continental and in spite of their French origin, we thought the people scarcely looked cheerful — and there is a look of settle-downedness... which seems unlike the typical colonial. The crops we saw were wretched — almost too wretched to be taken seriously. The houses have a curious look of being built for contingencies of either extreme of climate — verandas and green doors with netting against insect torments, green sun shutters, and then sloping roofs with a curve apparently arranged for snow."[10] They had gone on a picnic drive to Montmorency Falls in a borrowed viceregal carriage. If the population looked neither English nor properly French, clearly it was not American either, and that was all in its favour. Of the beautiful falls and its steep rock stairway she wrote, "If this were in America, doubtless there would be advertisements on the rocks and all sorts of tourist arrangements. We are much struck by the universal civility and gentle courtesy of the people — no pushing."[11]

She was less attracted by Quebec's Premier, Honoré Mercier, who as they proceeded to Montreal "joined the train after a bit and came in and had a long chat with us. He is very French in all ways, and does not inspire one with confidence".[12] Mercier had swept the Rouges to power in Quebec in 1887 on the strength of his fiery wrath at the hanging of Louis Riel. It was Mercier who now introduced her to the convulsive problems of trade relations with the United States, where the McKinley Bill to increase tariffs was before Congress ("five cents per dozen on eggs for instance," Ishbel wrote). Spurred by this impending blow and dismayed by a persistent agricultural depression in Canada, Liberals in this country were working up a case for "Commercial Union" with the U.S. It was a devastating idea, in Ishbel's view. What hope for Greater Britain?

Things were calmer in Montreal, where they stopped at the Windsor Hotel and were invited to dine with "kind hospitable Sir Donald Smith" of the Hudson's Bay Company and the Canadian Pacific Railway. At his home her education in things Canadian was resumed; she learned for example, that the Indians of the West, unfortunately dying out due to tuberculosis, "loved" the Hudson's Bay Company. She also met enchanting Père Lacombe from Edmonton, always a welcome guest in that house, who talked of his "sauvages". Lacombe, she was told, was "high in favour with the magnates of the CPR because while it was in the process of being laid down he was always able to pacify any of the wild Bloods or Blackfeet tribes who threatened to wreck the enterprise".[13] When she saw that Lacombe was not comfortable in English Ishbel switched to French, and was amused at his surprise. She wrote Sinclair: "Both he and Sir Donald say that the English residents here scarcely ever know French. This seems strange, does it not, where the majority is so French?"[14]

By the first of September they had arrived at Hamilton, where they would spend their family holiday. They would stay at Highfield, secured for them by the Governor-General, Lord Stanley's son Eddie, later Lord Derby, after a fretful protest that there were no rich people and consequently, no suitable houses in Canada. Highfield was a pretty villa described as "domestic Picturesque Gothic",[15] built in 1860. Here they were fussed over by Senator William E. Sanford of the city, who had located the place for them. Ishbel found it adequate, though the grounds were "really pretty small" — a

"Highfield" formerly 362 Bay St. S.   Arthur W. Wallace

"Highfield", Hamilton, Ontario.

mere thirteen acres. (Later the acres were subdivided and the residence became a boy's school, at 362 Bay Street South in the growing city. It was demolished by fire in 1918.) As Ishbel saw it in 1890, Hamilton was a quiet, clean little place, where terrible feuding went on between the minority Roman Catholics and the Orangemen. She found it easy to follow her doctor's instructions and decline most social invitations. "Truth to say," she told Sinclair, "our public appearances in Hamilton such as going to church are rather painful and decidedly comical. We are so evidently regarded as belonging to a Museum of Curiosities."[16]

Here the four children joined them. They would stay together in Hamilton until Haddo had to return to school. Their eldest son was now eleven, his health a source of constant worry. From sickly babyhood he had passed into delicate boyhood, and was now subject to epilepsy, a disease never named in Victorian times, nor in Ishbel's journal. Haddo had gone to Cargilfield with a doctor in attendance, and though Henry sometimes visited him when the Aberdeens were absent, and invariably sent cheering news of rosy cheeks and lively boyish interests, little real improvement was discernible. Haddo did not much like his Hamilton holiday and told his mother he was glad when they went to church for the last time, because the children made fun of his top hat. An enterprising downtown hatter had featured it as the "Lord Haddo hat" in a window display, "the newest shape for youths".

The other children were more content, busy with such things as capturing moths and butterflies with a mixture of honey and molasses smeared on telegraph poles near some electric lights every night. Marjorie was now ten, growing tall and spindly. Dudley, a self-contained lad, passably good at studies, passably good at sports, keen on all things mechanical, was seven, and Archie, the darling of the group, nearly six. Ishbel, busy as she was, found time for her children, and surrounded them with care and affection. When Marjorie wrote her biography in 1952 she recalled no grumbling or rebellion in the nursery — everyone fell in with Mother's plans in good spirit. In 1890 Marjorie had written an "effusion" titled "Mother's Qualities", preserved by her father. It said:

Mother is beautiful, kind, loving,
ingenious, busy, bright,
friend-like, sympathizing,
strict in some ways, indulgent in others,
merry, playful, attentive,
has a silver bell for her voice
and is altogether very GOOD.[17]

One congenial neighbour in Hamilton was Colonel John A. Gibson, Provincial Secretary in Oliver Mowat's Liberal Ontario government. Gibson hoped to see Macdonald defeated in the next federal election. Mowat had scored for the Liberals against Ottawa by extending his provincial boundaries far to the north-west through a direct application to the Privy Council in London: this was contrary to Macdonald's policy of retaining small provinces, with others created as settlement expanded. The Liberals were appearing everywhere as the champions of local or provincial rights.

The political weather was rough. Macdonald had hanged Riel. There was conflict in the North West over use of the French language. The President of the Ontario Conservative Union, Dalton McCarthy, had set up an "Equal Rights Association", meaning the subjugation of the French: "This is a British country, and the sooner we take in hand our French Canadians and make them British in sentiment and teach them the English language, the less trouble we shall have to prevent", said McCarthy. Adding to the general discontent was the depression in agriculture and trade. CPR shares had dropped sharply.

Ishbel wrote: "[Gibson] in common with others of his party are for making commercial union with the States, the avowed policy of the Liberals. He won't have it that this would lead to political union. Nevertheless it is difficult to see how it could be avoided."

When she went with Lord Aberdeen to open an Industrial exhibition in Toronto, they continued the discussion with Premier Mowat. "These eternal questions of duties and customs and tariffs rather confuse me, and seem to land people in all sorts of difficulties if they are to act consistently," Ishbel observed. Still, "really we feel that Canadian politics are the only politics worth knowing about at present".[18] The convalescent Countess had found a draught of her favourite brew.

The Aberdeens' travel plans were geared to letters from far-off Pacific places as Henry kept them up-to-date on his schedule. At the end of September they left the three children in Hamilton to travel further, their destination Vancouver. They stopped in Toronto where they found themselves at the dinner table of Colonel George Denison, one of a prominent family of United Empire Loyalists, Conservative to the core. Denison was head of the Toronto branch of Imperial Federationists. Ishbel was dismayed to find how thoroughly the Canadian Tories had taken up this cause. Edward Blake, "the *practical* leader of the Liberal party" (he had turned over the nominal title to Laurier) seemed reluctant to identify himself with Imperial Federation. Ishbel said Blake had first declared himself in favour of the idea, then withdrawn. She added that Blake had "never personally canvassed his constituency" on the issue, as though she suspected a good many Imperial Federationist Liberals lurked in the underbrush.

She was probably right. English-speaking Canada cherished a fairly general view that Britain was the seat of their loyalty and the home of greatness. It is aptly expressed by Lorne Murchinson, the rising young Ontario lawyer in Sara Duncan's *The Imperialist,* who exclaims to his sweetheart as he leaves for England:

> I'll see England, Dora; I'll feel England, eat and drink and live in England, for a little while. Isn't the very name great? I'll be a better man for going, till I die. We're all right out here but... I've been reading up on the history of our political relations with England. It's astonishing what we've stuck to her through, but you can't help seeing why — it's for the moral advantage. Way down at the bottom, that's what it is...[19]

Ishbel's political assessment was correct, for the "economic union" policy cost the Liberals the next election and their last chance to beat the doughty Sir John A. Macdonald.

Meanwhile Ishbel enjoyed the novelty of their surroundings. She tried to explain to Sinclair how different Toronto was from "the old country idea of the size of a town of about 150,000 inhabitants," having so much more open space. It was "beautifully laid out in wide streets, and all the newer houses have lawns and gardens of their own."

Ottawa, where they traveled next, had a population of 40,000. Since Confederation a cluster of fine stone buildings had gone up near the parliament buildings on Sussex Street. When the Aberdeens looked out from the Russell House hotel they saw a handsome city hall south along Elgin Street, and a colonnaded post office just to the north. The popular Russell House, four-storey, with 250 beds, stood at a spot that has now disappeared from the Ottawa scene, the south-east corner of Elgin and Sparks, for at that period Sparks extended across what is now Confederation Square. Politicians stayed there on temporary business in the capital, and the capacious lobby was a congenial meeting place for dealers of all kinds.

Ishbel admired the parliament buildings on their fine site and went back a second time to sketch. Her comment on meeting the durable Prime Minister, Sir John A. Macdonald, who received them at Earnscliffe, was a sly "He certainly is like Dizzy in appearance," for rumour persisted that he was Disraeli's offspring. Macdonald spoke confidently of winning the next election, dismissing Liberal boasts.

Sightseeing took them to the new Geological Museum on Sussex Street — "how H.D. would enjoy it!" — and also a saw mill, turning huge trees into planks". One day they drove out to Government House, locked up in the Stanleys' absence so that they saw only the gardens, the toboggan slide, and the covered curling rink. Another day's trip took them three miles south to the experimental Farm, where new strains of hardy wheat for the North-West were being developed. At dinner in Ottawa they met leading Conservatives, including Macdonald's youngest minister,Charles Hibbert Tupper. He made a favourable impression, unlike his bombastic parent whom they knew in his capacity as High Commissioner in London.

Before they left Ottawa, Ishbel checked out the booksellers. Sure enough, she was able to report to Sinclair that two editions of Henry's *The Greatest Thing in the World* were on sale — "one horrid and cheap for 20¢, and the other slightly better at 35¢... but everywhere it is the same cry, they cannot keep a copy in the shop."[20]

Drummond, almost in spite of himself, was growing rich from this popular booklet. He wrote to his mother on his return to Glasgow that autumn:

Another event of the week has been the purchase [at auction] of a silver tea set — rather a good old thing of William IV date. I have long been wanting the genuine article... [also] a hundred pieces of old Wedgewood [sic] Dinner Service... for £5. Wedgewood China when real is, it seems, the most valuable of all... These extravagant purchases... come from The Greatest Thing's pennies.[21]

For the long trip West Lord and Lady Aberdeen traveled in style in a railway car with white mahogany fittings, with a separate dining car and attentive porter, provided for them by Sir Donald Smith and the officials of the CPR. Their next stop was Winnipeg.

Now they were approaching the Canada of their imagination, wide, green, empty — accepting the outcrowded poorer classes of the United Kingdom. Lord Aberdeen had paid £2,000 into the Secretary for Scotland's fund to settle fifty Highlanders at Killarney, Manitoba. The Aberdeens would see for themselves how those immigrants were faring.

On this trip and again in 1891, Ishbel was also concerned to follow up and report on the servant girls whom she had helped to send out from the other side. In 1883 she had become first president of the Ladies Union of Aberdeen, concerned with the welfare of young girls crowding into the city from family and domestic service, taking jobs in factories if they could, but always perilously close to crime and prostitution. The Union's "Lily Band" tried to keep them moral (that is to preserve their virginity). An Emigration Committee selected those who "though poor, were of superior intelligence and moral character"[22] for assisted passage to the colonies. Most preferred to go to Canada. So a brisk business had been developed in that direction by the Ladies Union.

Canada is the best place for girls. It is our own land still, if one may say so, it is the nearest colony, and the people are so glad to get the young women that they are as a rule exceedingly kind to them.[23]

The adventurous young emigrants were being despatched under strict supervision. They complained they were treated like prisoners en route. They arrived, chaste and sound, to an overwhelming demand for their services. Unfortunately what the girls had in mind were positions as parlour maids or housekeepers in upper class households, and instead the majority of the jobs were as "hired girls" in the North West, where they would be expected to milk cows and feed chickens and hoe gardens as well as cook and clean. "Of course our girls are generally useless for such work", the Aberdeen ladies admitted.[24] They tried to exercise care, but other organizations were less scrupulous, and Lady Aberdeen was upset at the fate of many ill-suited job applicants. On the train approaching Winnipeg she sought out several women riding herd on London orphans and hopeful servant girls in the colonist coaches of their train.

In Winnipeg they were surprised when their own family immigrant, Ishbel's younger brother "Couttsy", turned up from Dakota. "He has had a bad time of it," Ishbel confided in Sinclair, "between droughts and losses of stock generally... His neighbours are not nice people to associate with, and everything is mortgaged... We are going to get a report on the profitability of selling the place and then try to get Coutts over into Canada into some civilized part, probably British Columbia."[25]

Lieutenant-Governor and Mrs. Schultz and the people of Winnipeg welcomed the Aberdeens warmly. Ishbel wrote: "they seemed a particularly nice lot of people — in fact we are more taken with the appearance of the inhabitants than of the town which is not much yet... The houses are sort of scattered pell mell as if you had thrown them down in a handful, a big one and then a little old log hut by the side of it, and then a store and so on and of course weeds everywhere."[26]

Winnipeg might shock them, but they could scarcely believe their first view of the prairies on a bright early October day. They traveled south to Morden and Manitou and on to Killarney, over scarcely perceptible prairie trails "in what they call a Democrat — a sort of long four wheeled cart with two seats one behind the other." Ishbel marveled at the soft elasticity of the soil which carried their wheels with minimal jolting, she had praise for the beautiful sky, fleecy clouds and indescribably brisk bracing air." But there admiration ended. Here was settlement in the raw. She wrote: "May Heaven preserve us from ever being fated to banishment to the far-famed wheatlands of Manitoba! Oh the inexpressible dreariness of these everlasting prairies!.. Wooden shanties, most of the size we would put up for a keeper's shelter at home, but here inhabited by farmers owning some hundreds of acres and some half-dozen children... Nowhere yet on the prairie have we seen even a geranium pot, or a young tree planted..." It was a miracle that people in such surroundings were capable of "fostering higher tendencies". Yet little schools were being built, wherever there were fifteen local children to attend them, and when they stopped to visit one at Northcote a little student "answered some questions on English history quite intelligently."[27]

Their own Scottish settlers had made out poorly. Each family had been set up with £175 for passage, and on arrival a pair of oxen and a cow. To survive until harvest they had goods on credit from Mr. Lalor, the storekeeper — they were "in his hand". Some 17 of the original 50 immigrants had given up their homesteads and taken to working for wages around the country. There was little evidence of the pride and independence they had hoped these people would find in owning their own land. But, Ishbel pointed out, "The experiment could scarcely have been made with more risky people unless it be London paupers", for many had been unemployed for years, hanging about the coastal towns of Scotland hoping for jobs as fishermen or boatmen, and had never known a grim land like this one, which exacted such heavy toil merely to survive.

Pondering their credit problems with Mr. Lalor, Ishbel wrote, "It is curious that Co-operation should never have struck root in this country. One would have thought it would have done so well."[28] Her perception was only slightly premature. Farmers had barely ploughed their first furrows. In only a few decades the Co-op store would become a feature of every village. In 33 year's time a new Farmers' Union at the town of Ituna would let loose a messianic leader with all the independence of spirit that could be desired, to create, like a new religion, a farmer's Wheat Pool for the co-operative sale of their grain. That messiah was however, not a transported labourer from the north of Scotland but a Jewish lawyer named Aaron Shapiro from the U.S. west.

As they left Winnipeg, half the train they were traveling in left the track with "a great jolt" a few miles out. Their private car at the back of the train stayed upright. Ishbel tried a sketch of the upturned engine, like an unfortunate iron beast on its back in the ditch. No one was killed. They were on their way again the next day.

Increasingly impatient to meet Henry, Ishbel canceled their proposed stop in Calgary. They rattled through the Rockies in a state of dizzy wonderment, surfeited with beautiful scenery", dashing from window to window and trying vainly to sketch or photograph — for Ishbel had brought on this trip her newest acquisition, a box-like Kodak camera with a dangling cord and shutter release. On 10 October there was a first mention to Sinclair that her husband had developed a desire for a "shanty", as he put it, in Canada. British Columbia was clearly the place. Then at last she was able to report:

> At Donald our hearts were much comforted by receiving the following telegram, "San Francisco Oct 11. Just arrived leave tonight reach Vancouver Tuesday morning horribly slow. H.D." So at last we are on the same continent and shall get nearer one another hour by hour.[29]

The Aberdeens managed to meet Henry in Victoria on time, but only by swallowing their Presbyterian scruples and traveling on Sunday across from Vancouver. The happy reunion was accomplished.

The next two weeks would be frantic, with some engagements canceled to keep in step with Henry and take passage with him out of New York on 26 October. They had only one day in Victoria, "ridiculously like an October evening in the south of England, the same damp sort of smell and sense of greenness all about." They had one day, also, in Vancouver. On that day they acquired, sight unseen, an inland tract of land that would satisfy the wish to set up Coutts on British colonial soil and also answer Aberdeen's whim to possess "a shanty" in this country. They had blundered into a chapter of pioneer adventure that would drain their purses, while with a golden spade they left a clear imprint on developing Canada.

They paused at Banff. There, with Henry for company, Ishbel's adjectives whirled in giddy pleasure, without a trace of the critical irony that sometimes peppered her letters. "...just glorious and if I began to describe all the perfections and delights of the place and the weather and the views and everything it would be endless... Henry and I had a good walk and a sketch and a drink at the sulphur springs and a sight of the open hot sparkling green swimming-bath and cave...

We walked down to the station — Henry and I — on Friday night to have a last whiff of Banff air and were taken up within a few minutes of the place by A. driving furiously in his democrat."[30]

In Winnipeg Aberdeen was scheduled to speak to a formal luncheon, Drummond was to address a crowd of students, and Ishbel to meet with a group of women at Knox Church.

> We were annexed at the station by various dignitaries of Church and State... I went in solitary glory guarded by Mrs.Taylor, the Chief Justice's wife, Mrs. Scarth, the Dominion M.P.'s wife, and Mrs. Duval, the wife of the pastor in whose schoolroom the meeting was to be. It turned out however that after the evening service nearly all the ladies had stayed and as the schoolroom was already full, those in the latter place had to be conducted into the church and I had the rather formidable task of addressing 1400 ladies from an elevated platform beneath the pulpit. They were very nice however and very responsive... H. Had a good meeting too...[31]

Ishbel did not deliver the expected platitudes. The stark prairie homes she had seen had stirred her deeply. In her daughter's biography a section of her talk that day is given:

> Who are to be brought up in the homes scattered over the prairies, in the log huts standing so pluckily in their clearings? How can you make them a strength, not a weakness? What is the practical thing to do? Could you not get the names of newcomers from the immigration agents and forward to them from time to time such papers, magazines, books as you could get together. There must be many such in Winnipeg. A reminder of this sort from home — a picture to brighten the walls, the competitions in the magazines, would often be a real interest in the little bare homestead so far out in the world. And if you could add a packet of flower seeds you would foster the love of beauty which can lift up lives engrossed in material needs.[32]

Within weeks the "Aberdeen Association for Distribution of Good Literature to Settlers in the West" was born; by Christmas it had mailed 82 parcels. Ishbel got the CPR to carry parcels from eastern Canada free; she got Stead to put a request for parcels from Britain in the *Review of Reviews,* she got £100 from Andrew Carnegie for paper, string and postage. Year after year monthly parcels were sent to many hundreds of farm homes. Ishbel herself gave full credit to the women of Winnipeg:

The women who had arranged the meeting I was addressing happened to be gifted in a peculiar degree with powers of organization and imagination.[33]

It was a first demonstration of what, time after time, would be the fruitful outcome as Ishbel's silver-voiced appeal connected with the inexorable competence of Canadian women. A deluge of mail confirmed the need. One mother wrote to tell Ishbel how her children danced for joy and wouldn't go to bed when the parcel came. In a 1911-12 report when the Association had eleven branches from Halifax to Victoria a Lloydminster farmer was quoted:

The parcels you have been sending me are read by people 14 miles east of me, and 12 miles north, so you see they reach quite a number. The parcels never stay at my place, but are circulated far and wide. I do not know when they have done traveling, as I never get them back. It is pretty hard for anyone here to buy magazines this year, as everyone is frozen out and all the wheat is practically good only for cattle food.[34]

The 1911-12 report noted that:

Dr. Sutherland, traveling secretary for Methodist Home Missions in the West, always gives the highest praise to Aberdeen work: to his personal knowledge it is an estimable boon to hundreds of lonely settlers, many of whom have stated that the books and letters have saved their minds from getting unhinged.

Following the report a delegate to the Association meeting affirmed: Friendship, letters and books make for Empire building."[35]

After Winnipeg the party separated. Lord Aberdeen went on alone to fill speaking engagements in Ottawa. He rejoined Ishbel and Drummond in Hamilton where they picked up the three children and all took sail from New York.

"We were very glad we came by the Umbria," Ishbel concluded in her letters to Sinclair. "The last night or two had nice sits on deck in the moonlight until the deck-washers came and turned us off... Canada will soon look like a dream."[30]

Ishbel and her husband visited Canada again the following year. Her keen observation, her concern for the immigrant population, the roots they struck in the Okanagan, and her mounting political interest, brought to Canada in due time a Governor-General's lady very unlike her predecessors.

Chapter 8

1891: The Anglo-American Design

The Aberdeens and Henry Drummond were back in Britain, and visits and letters between Glasgow and Aberdeenshire were once more in full flow.

Of course all will be ready for you at the end of this month or the end of any other month, week, day or hour.[1]

They chuckled over memories of their Canadian trip on "the great, the immortal, the unballasted CPR", of all the world's railways the one most suggestive of sudden annihilation."[2] Henry scolded Ishbel for immediately taking up again all her many interests. He sought to lighten her mood with the latest society tales — as when the gallant Lord Rathbone of Liverpool reversed the common recipe for removing wine stains by applying salt. Rathbone, to set at ease the lady next to him at dinner who had just overturned the salt-cellar, said not to mind, and emptied his glass of claret over the salt. "Please don't say you're too tired to laugh," wrote Henry, "though I am getting frivolous and you are a highly serious person."[3]

Ishbel had now undertaken to publish a monthly women's home magazine, initially for the members of the Onward and Upward Association across the Scottish countryside, though with wider aspirations: "We want to make it the very best magazine for women."[4] Drummond was a staunch supporter, and as delighted as she when the lively magazine found a ready audience, reaching an eventual circulation of 15,000. In October of its first year he was writing:

O & U is going to have a real future. We smiled when you started editing *but* — well, as usual!⁵

A red-covered children's magazine, *Wee Willie Winkie,* nominaly edited by the Honourable Marjorie Gordon, became a supplement. Henry, though deep in a revision of "that old fossil, 'Natural Law' ", willingly undertook to act as interim editor in September when the Aberdeens made their next trip to North America.

This time their chief aim was to lift money from the pockets of rich Irish-Americans. Ishbel had kept up a persistent initiative on behalf of Irish improvement. Among other enterprises she had persuaded her husband to buy a house in Belgrave with a ground floor leased to the Irish Industries Association (of which she was president) for the selling of lace, red Connemara cloaks and unbleached linen by the yard. With the coming of the World's Fair in Chicago she pressed for an eye-catching exhibit there. As Marjorie Pentland describes it:

> Her committee, prepared to consider sending a show-case, were startled by her proposal of a full-sized model bride with wedding presents, alongside a full-sized Irish cabin with live workers making the goods.⁶

The cabin would expand to an Irish Village, a village square where dancers performed Irish jigs, and a replica Blarney Castle. The long-term goal was to bring on such a thirst for Irish goods that a store could be profitably run in Chicago — even with duties of 60 per cent against lace.

Alongside the major goal of raising funds for this enterprise was a more modest one — a holiday on the side — to see the ranch in the Okanagan purchased the previous year, where Coutts was now installed.

This time Ishbel's long letters were addressed first to Henry and second to John Sinclair. They would form a second three-and-a-half month Journal. She had feared her letters to Sinclair the year before were "dry as bones" but was persuaded of the delight and interest they had inspired in several readers.

So Drummond and Sinclair heard of her first in New York, at "a very delightful comparatively new hotel just opposite the Central Park; just opposite, another huge building is rearing itself, called after the Savoy." With the Aberdeens was their daughter Marjorie who was during the journey to have lessons for two hours a day under her mother's tutelage. They spent one afternoon in Central Park snapping pictures of "the quaint little grown-up overdressed New York children." In New York the Aberdeens were hounded by reporters, but at least the curiosity of the press could be deflected to the Irish exhibit at Chicago — "about which they can really be of some use."[7] Press manipulation came readily to the Countess.

They were quickly out of New York and on to Northfield; they had accepted an invitation from Dwight Moody, so long revered by Drummond, to visit his evangelical college. The young students paid a minimal fee and did the work of the place themselves, and though Ishbel was a bit wary of the fundamentalist religion inspiring the establishment she praised it for Henry's sake, while her affable husband "was enchanted with the student waitresses."[8] Ishbel questioned Henry about Moody's proposal to visit Scotland, for it was her conviction that religion had advanced there to an extent that left Moody far to the rear. She also reported rumours that Moody's more fundamentalist followers were disturbed by the "broad" ideas of Henry Drummond. As for Ishbel herself, the closed mind of earlier religious adherence had become open and receptive since her tortured self-examination five years earlier, when she had resolved that henceforth she would seek "nothing but truth." Every Sunday there was church attendance, but always in a questing and questioning mood.

Leaving Northfield the Aberdeens made the leap, as they did so frequently, from plain Christian endeavour to the pleasure-seeking palaces of the wealthy. They traveled as far as Montreal in an elegant railway car got up with every comfort and lent for their convenience by President Webb of the Wagner Palace Car Company. Ishbel's conscience was pricked by the "difference that a private car does make when one is journeying like this",[9] but could not help enjoying herself, especially when Webb's brother asked them to stop off at his Vermont estate of 4,000 rolling acres on the shore of Lake Champlain. Dr. W.S. Seward Webb had married a Vanderbilt and given up his surgical practice to devote himself to luxurious living — Shelbourne House had 110 rooms and a butler imported from Blenheim Castle; the impressive facade curved in a great arc above terraced Italian gardens.[10] Pheasants and a deer forest, a stud-farm that included horses from the stables of Ishbel's godmother Lady Burdett-Coutts — the "conspicuous consumption" was American but the model was "the English style".[11] The United States of America blazed and shone. Ishbel observed:

> I think it is the continual bright sun and glare that one feels more tiring than anything during the first weeks in America.[12]

She entered Canada again in a mood more critical than on her former visit. At the home of Sir Donald Smith she was not sympathetic to the boasting of potentates of the CPR and Hudson's Bay, in their talk of large land holdings acquired in government deals. "...and what in return? The people go to the States, and the CPR charges such high freights that they become prohibitive."[13]

The town of Ottawa seemed charming to her, as it had a year earlier. At the Russell House the good justice minister, Sir John Thompson, "came in this morning at breakfast to greet us, looking very much the tower of strength that he is to the Government."[14] But the political atmosphere in the wake of Sir John A. Macdonald's death in June was turgid and uncertain. The Conservatives had won the election under his leadership. But his death had thrown the ruling party into a state of violent agitation. Thompson had turned down the chance to succeed as prime minister, in favour of Senator John Abbott. There had been a third contender in the wings, Sir Charles Tupper, a great blustering warrior from Nova Scotia, and only when this "old tramp", as Thompson called him, had made it clear he did not intend to leave his post in Britain as Canadian High Commissioner did Thompson feel he could safely abandon the field to Abbott.[15] Thompson's reasons were personal but shrewd — having recently changed his church affiliation from Protestant to Roman Catholic, he wished to give the public a little time to digest his censurable behaviour. Abbott headed a caretaker government which would last only until November of the following year.

Thompson would then without much fuss take over the position of Prime Minister. The smooth transfer would be effected by a fairly unanimous cabinet decision, followed by the formal summons from a largely indifferent Governor-

General. It would seem on that occasion that Canada had reached a constitutional independence. And yet the respective powers in the land were not yet clear, and the attitude of the Queen's high court at Rideau Hall toward the government of the day depended greatly on the temperament of the incumbent.

In September 1891 Parliament was in session when the Aberdeens dropped in, and they spent several hours in the House of Commons, where the atmosphere was not uplifting. The "Liberals" (and Ishbel put the word in quotation marks in her letter, as though she was not sure they deserved the name) were "intensely sore and bitter" as they attacked the government over the latest scandal, involving the Minister of Public Works, Sir Hector Langevin. But these Canadian "Liberals" were "indefinite" in her estimation, especially over the uneasy triangle with the United States and Great Britain. "From their manner of talk they almost give colour to the idea they are hankering after union with the United States, though they say it is not so," she wrote as she reported conversations at a small party Prime Minister Abbott had for them at the close of the evening's debate. And the Liberals had their own scandals, such as the involvement of Honoré Mercier with Langevin.

As they left Ottawa's unsavory atmosphere, Ishbel's letters to Henry were full of "do you remember"? His to her were as wistful:

> It does seem strange to think of you and A. on the old CPR once more... I wish I had a round of Banff with you or even Medicine Hat...[16]

Regina was dismal. She was glad to get back on the train. "All day long we traveled through those dreary alkaline prairie lands," she was writing on the last day of September. Even getting as far as Calgary was a relief, for at last the line of snowy peaks could be seen on the horizon, and there was also a sense of larger enterprise. It was range country. In the hall and dining-room of their hotel, the Alberta, one constantly saw "stalwart gentlemanly looking young Englishmen striding in, showing their nationality unmistakably"; all the talk was of ranches and horses and herds. The Alberta Hotel (which still stands on the corner of 8th Avenue and First Street South West) surprised Ishbel by its size, "quite out of proportion to the size of the place, [but] doing well." All in all, said Ishbel, "a thriving little place and has all the air of a coming town",[17] though it had been on the map for barely seven years.

They stopped again at Banff. For Ishbel, the place lost its enchantment without Henry's company. Now she could see with disapproval that the population was not worthy of the scenery, being made up largely of "loafers who came to live on the tourists."[18]

At Banff they met Lady Macdonald, Sir John A.'s widow. Agnes Macdonald was restlessly trying to pick up what was left of life for her after her husband's death. She had been born fifty-five years earlier to a plantation family in Jamaica, moving to Canada with her brother Hewitt who became Macdonald's secretary. A quick courtship in 1867 led to her marriage to Sir John: she was 31 at the time, described as "tawny... rather 'raw-boned' and angular..."[19] Yet in her fifties she had a towering majesty, reflecting the status she had achieved as the Prime Minister's wife when she had become a force to be reckoned with in Ottawa. Lady Macdonald was as partisan as Ishbel. She was fiercely loyal to her husband and his memory. She despised Sir John Thompson — Ishbel admired him. She would have chosen Sir Charles Tupper as the next prime minister — Ishbel despised *him*. It would make for an interesting confrontation in the shadowed green dining room at Banff Springs Hotel, at that time a wooden mansion of impressive size, built in 1888 by the CPR.

Ishbel entered the field of combat to find Lady Macdonald already ensconced, her table a centre for a cluster of good Conservatives paying homage. The Aberdeens were ushered to a table, their rank and identity immediately known to most of the people in the room.

When Ishbel learned that the stern but handsome lady in black was the Earnscliffe hostess they had missed seeing when they called on Sir John A., she was ready at once to extend condolences. Before she could move, their waiter appeared with a note from Lady Macdonald's table. It was addressed to "Dear Ishbel" — a surprise. Then she saw that the sender was one of Lady Macdonald's guests, Mrs. Herbert, wife of the general commanding Canada's militia. Ishbel recognized a London friend of her girlhood. Now this was convenient — a note could be returned renewing acquaintance with Mrs. Herbert and easing the way to an introduc-

Lady Agnes Macdonald.

tion to the tight-lipped widow. There was an interval. Another note came from Mrs. Herbert. Lady Macdonald, she wrote, had been so recently bereaved that she was not quite ready to receive new acquaintances. The Aberdeens had to concede, for the moment. Mrs. Herbert after lunch left her party to join Ishbel for some London reminiscing.

This state of affairs continued for a day or two. When there had been quite enough time given, Ishbel looked to Mrs. Herbert for an explanation. Lady Macdonald, she noticed, had no difficulty in meeting a number of lunchtime guests. Mrs. Herbert was on the spot, and admitted weakly that the widow was "strange", and "took fancies against certain people", nor would she ever change her mind. And, Ishbel enquired, was there any particular reason why Lady Macdonald had taken a fancy against *them*?

Mrs. Herbert confessed under Ishbel's level gaze. The Aberdeens were Liberals and friends of Mr. Gladstone. Lady Macdonald told Mrs. Herbert, "she did not want to have anything to do with people whose whole object would be to pull down all that Sir John had done *if they could.*"

Ridiculous! said Ishbel, describing it all in her letter to Henry. Rank and position could not countenance such a bold-faced snub. At the next opportunity Ishbel sent a more direct request to the Lady Macdonald table. And even as the waiter turned to make his way in that direction, Lady Ishbel rose to her own statuesque height, and in full view of the attentive audience, proceeded across the room in his wake. Lady Macdonald read the note, glanced up "poising herself to send back a negative answer" and found Lady Ishbel smiling at her side. It was unfair. Ishbel outranked her in poise, in youth and grace, and had a husband in tow. Lady Macdonald acknowledged their presence with a bow.

"She melted, and ended by practically accepting an invitation to Haddo House next year," said Ishbel, and went on, "One cannot help being sorry for her, poor lady, in her unconcealed grief over her loss of power. She appears not to try to hide how much she feels the difference in her position."[20] That power had been wielded in mischievous and deceitful ways, Ishbel continued, and it was a relief to know she and A. would have little more to do with the deposed first lady of Ottawa. Ishbel's final thrust was only a little wicked. She thought it would be a good thing if Lady Macdonald resumed writing for magazines, since "some little things that we have seen of hers are very brightly done."[21]

There followed a visit of nine days in the Okanagan valley to see their new holdings, which turned out to be not quite what they had expected. But Lord Aberdeen was caught up in the adventure and in Vancouver that fall arranged a further purchase of 13,000 acres next to the town of Vernon. Ishbel, with only a few misgivings, plotted and planned with him.

By mid-November they were in Chicago, engaged in their special mission to raise funds for the promotion of Irish trade and especially for the great world fair exhibit. "The game has been worth the candle... Machinery has been got into motion,"[22] Ishbel wrote to Henry on 12 November. With pledges from Mr. Carnegie, and from the proprietor of the Chicago

Herald and other successful Irish-Americans, thousands of pounds were committed. She made the rounds of leading dry goods stores where the goods might be retailed, enjoying a practical discussion of the matter with "Mr. [H. Gordon] Selfridge, Mr. [Marshall] Field's partner," of which she liked to remind him when Selfridge later opened his impressive London store. She extracted an offer from him to buy the lace wedding dress that would be the centre-piece of the exhibit, and a kind donation of glass show-cases and wax figures; from the Archbishop of Chicago came a promise to instruct his clergy to use Irish poplin, embroidery and lace in ecclesiastical vestments — "another splendid outlet."

Much business had to be done at "interminable state dinners" arranged in the Aberdeens' honour. The social leader in Chicago was Mrs. Berthe Honoré Palmer, wife of the rich and powerful owner of the Palmer House hotel, which had 225 silver dollars imbedded in the floor of its barbershop. Mrs. Palmer was chairman of the board of Lady Managers of the 1893 World's Columbian Exposition.

The Palmers' private residence was a castle on the shore of Lake Michigan and had cost $700,000. Its uncertain architectural style had been described as "eclectic Gothic". There was a red velvet ballroom. There was a 60-foot conservatory. There was a very large gallery to house Mrs. Palmer's bathroom with swan-shaped sunken tub. As Ishbel said, a "gorgeous habitation". In her usual blunt style she deplored the luncheons:

> It is an extraordinary thing that these hurrying scurrying Americans should sit two hours over their luncheon... It is a veritable mystery to us how these people, especially the women, survive, with their heated rooms into which not a breath of fresh air is allowed to wander, their spun-out unwholesome meals and their want of exercise. In these four days we have done as Rome does, for the sake of attaining an end, and I feel as if another two days will absolutely suffocate one and soften any brains that one has left. It is beautiful bright bracing weather outside and I pant for some air. They never seem to walk or use anything but a closed carriage.[23]

When they crossed over the border briefly to Toronto Ishbel wrote: "It is real nice to be in Canada again. There is an indefinable difference which does make all the difference."[24]

When they proceeded to Boston they met, it seems for the first time, the Canadian leader of the Liberals, Wilfrid Laurier, who was pressing the cause of better trade relations along with a scrupulous political separation. His orations were receiving attention. Laurier had "a most interesting talk with A. about Canada's future."[25]

They lingered in Boston, New York, and Washington, and on these visits met not only wealthy expatriated Irishmen but a rich variety of other Americans. They were welcomed at Wellesley College where Ishbel felt her daughter respond to the idea of higher education. They discussed Temperance with Mrs. Frances Willard, women's suffrage with Mrs. Julia Ward-Howe and social work with Miss Jane Addams. In New York Ishbel made an important contact for Irish industry in "Mr. Baumgarten, 321 Fifth Avenue, the very very swell head-decorator man here in the States who has decorated the Vanderbilt houses etc and who will give us orders if we send him designs." They "dined with the Carnegies another night and went to hear an Oratorio at the very charming Music Hall he has put up..."[26]

They visited Oliver Wendell Holmes, "small, alert, beaming with geniality... the poet and the autocrat..." in his study with deep bay windows overlooking the Charles River and Boston Harbour... He gave us all three a book apiece and had quite a little flirtation with Marjorie, ending up with an embrace."[27] A souvenir of that visit was preserved by Holmes and discovered by a later admirer, Toronto educator James L. Hughes:

[Holmes] directed my attention especially to a model of Grandfather Harrison's white hat, made from redeemed Treasury notes. 'That,' said he, 'was given to me by the little daughter of Lord Aberdeen... '[28]

While Marjorie was sitting quietly making a paper hat of old Treasury bills, Lord Aberdeen asked the patriarch to comment on a current news item about the "antipathy naturally existing between Englishmen and Americans". Holmes, used an abstract metaphor to indicate there was no likelihood of better relations in future.

Ishbel and her husband were unhappy with such opinions, and believed them untypical. They had been so well received, there was such power and spirit in America —

Ishbel's whole instinct was to bring this nation into renewed relationship with Britain. She had listened to expressions of impatience with Canada, as an impediment to amicable relations between the two "great powers", London and Washington. Canadian interests were brushed aside like those of a clamouring child. The British ambassador to Washington, Sir Julian Pauncefote, was certainly of this view. He had been obliged to negotiate with the Americans over sealing on the north-west coast, which the United States had pre-empted. It would have been settled so peacefully except for Canadian protests! Ishbel pondered this information. "Canada is a bit of a difficulty between [sic] a complete understanding", she wrote.[31] She, personally had found a larger perspective — while sympathetic to Canada which with its strong prevailing British sentiment was a better place to settle such unsettled people as her brother Coutts.

In her letters to Drummond and Sinclair, as her journey drew to an end, she reported her earnest efforts to promote a vision of a vast British-American alliance. The United States would become an important partner, perhaps almost equal to Britain in time, in an immense world-wide development for peace and progress. She talked to the bright girl students at Wellesley and she wrote:

> I wish these girls could be inspired to make that great English-speaking Alliance, about which we dream, a reality. But indeed it seems to us less and less an impossible dream to see fulfilled even in our time. The idea is not far below the surface in some form or other in many minds. We never neglect an opportunity of speaking of it and very often, much more often than not, there is a very cordial response...[29]

The ideas of Wilke and Imperial Federation she had brought with her on her travels were not discarded, but evolving. First, there was the Canadian Liberal purpose to achieve a greater independence, as a self-governing nation which still recognized allegiance to the Queen. Apparently Australia had the same aspirations. Imperial Federation must "of necessity be modified". She poured out her thoughts:

> Now why should not the Imperial Federation League recognize this attitude and in drawing up the scheme now under consideration provide, firstly, for the full representation of

Colonies who wish to remain in the same position as at present together perhaps with power to elect their own Governor and at the same time recognizing that some may wish as time goes on, further or full independence, and *then* suggest the plan of entering into an Alliance, under the same flag, with representatives from England, ports open, and still an arrangement by which young colonial men might obtain a certain number of Commissions of the British Army... Might not something of the sort be devised which to all intents and purposes, would leave the Colonies as much as ever bound to us or more so, yet with the pride and ambition of an independent people and forming part of an Alliance into which the States might not be unwilling to enter, later on.[30]

Glorious prospect! She could let the matter of Empire rest there for the moment. They were sailing home to Britain, North America behind them, anticipating another election, Gladstone's return to power, and the resumption of their place in Ireland.

They sailed on the *City of Paris.* Their most interesting fellow passenger was Annie Besant, an English feminist and activist who had been tried and convicted of purveying obscene literature — a pamphlet on birth control — in 1877. Mrs. Besant gave a shipboard talk on Theosophy, dream consciousness, and the astral plane. Ishbel reflected:

Her address was a powerful sermon... She said the saddest thing about Christianity is that it is the religion which has departed most from the spirit and teaching of its founder. Is this true? ...Will the papers get hold of A. presiding [at the meeting] and will there be a row?[31]

Back at home, they had native Indian artifacts to hang in the corridors of Haddo House, and Ishbel would publish a series of travel sketches first in *Onward and Upward* and then in a well-illustrated book, *Through Canada with a Kodak.*[32] When they decided to build an important addition at Haddo House, a large hall for community entertainment, they added a whimsical line of fluted roof, after the fashion of rural Quebec. Souvenirs of a country with which they expected to have only a limited future association, as landowners in the far West.

Chapter 9
The Okanagan Ranches

L ake Okanagan in mid-British Columbia lies like a pretty scarf let fall across the landscape. It is 69 miles long and about two miles wide, and deep enough in the middle to accommodate its own sea monster, Ogopogo. Sea monsters seem to live a very long time, and this one was first sighted by the Indian tribes long before white settlement. In any case, the Okanagan Valley is a distinctive feature of British Columbia, as favoured in its way as the beautiful Pacific Coast, and a bountiful provider of apples, grapes, and other fruits through extensive irrigation. It is cut off by mountain ranges east and west. It is marked at the southern tip by the town of Penticton and at the northern end by the small city of Vernon. Almost at the half-way point, in a flat valley with a backdrop of hills, lies another town, Kelowna, grown from the spot where Lord and Lady Aberdeen in 1890 made their first investment in Canadian real estate. Lord Aberdeen was not yet governor-general. But he was a Scottish earl, and his coming to the valley roused the speculative interest of others, opened settlement, provided a romantic past for today's local historical societies, and added to *We Twa* further idyllic reminiscence and a record of good work done.

But magnanimity had its price. A story comes to light in a Scottish lawyer's anguished letters, Ishbel's dashed hopes, and the mutterings of grandchildren who believe today that far too much of their ancestral inheritance was lost in the wash of Ogopogo.

"Poor old Coutts," Ishbel's brother, was to be set on the road to fortune, established on a baronial acreage and subsidized over a few initial years until wealth poured in from his Canadian estate.

That was the dream in 1890 when the Aberdeens, on a day's stop in Vancouver, met their fellow expatriate George Grant Mackay, who had once carried out road-building projects for Ishbel's father. He filled their ears with tales of the fabulously rich unclaimed interior. They entrusted him with $10,000 to buy up 480 acres near an Oblate missionary outpost run by Father Pandosy. It was on a landing where a hotel and a few other buildings were going up — present day Kelowna. Mackay was confident that a railway would come through from Vernon; investments were bound to increase tenfold.

Mackay was, throughout their dealings, using the Earl's name to his own advantage. He bought up land next to their purchase and laid out a townsite which he called Benvoulin.

Coutts arrived with a footloose companion, his foreman, named Eustace Smith. The pair led an indolent life with plenty of shooting, late nights at the local tavern, and the construction of an extravagant ranch house with gold Japanese wall paper, seven chimneys, and no insulation.

In 1892 Lord Aberdeen's Edinburgh lawyer, George Jamieson, tried to curb the disastrous flow of spending. He traveled personally to British Columbia and reported at length. The whole undertaking was a disaster and:

> I am afraid Mr. Smith has rather encouraged than checked the not unnatural feeling that an English earl is fair game. The house is a pretty one and contrasts of course very favourably with those in the community but... it is badly finished...[1]

A costly and drafty house was the least of their disappointments. The Aberdeens visited the estate in 1891 and refused to be daunted, though they found no access to the lake or any other source of water, the old farm buildings were dilapidated and flea-ridden, and Ishbel's brother was totally indifferent to the realities of agriculture. Ishbel fell in love with the country which with its pretty surrounding hills made her think of Guisachan in the Highlands, so she named Coutts' new place after her childhood home. She busily plotted new farm ventures, and on the train heading east after their 1891 visit wrote to Drummond and Sinclair of her husband's resolve to build a jam factory:

> Now please rack your brains for good names and advertisements wherewith to compete with 'Crosse and Blackwell' and their likes... [we are] thinking of 'Premier preserves'... It would be nice to see poor old Coutts a rich man after all.[2]

By then, however, the shrewd Mackay had given up on the place. The railway wasn't coming through after all. Mackay persuaded the Aberdeens to shift their interest north to Vernon, purchasing a vast ranch acreage called Coldstream from pioneer Forbes George Vernon. Mackay had in fact got himself thoroughly enmeshed in the affairs of Vernon, Aberdeen, and an outfit called the Okanagan Land Development Company. Aberdeen in 1891 laid out £50,000 for the 13,000-acre Coldstream Ranch.

Mackay persuaded Aberdeen that the jam factory should be in Vernon. From Haddo House Aberdeen pressed forward with this enterprise, advertising in Britain for a jam factory manager. In fact, the overall crop of the district was scarcely able to support such a venture at that stage, and Aberdeen's own holdings were many years away from producing any fruit at all. It was his misfortune to have his advertisement answered by a self-styled "confectioner and fruit preserver", G.W.F. Krauss, who was hired at once and given a free hand to buy all the necessary pots and ladles for the proposed factory. Krauss and his wife had their way paid to Vernon where they put up at a hotel, and their systematic swindling was climaxed in an attempt to compromise the bachelor Coutts Marjoribanks in an unsolicited visit by Mrs. Krauss to his ranch home. The lawyer Jamieson fumed; eventually the Krausses were sent packing.

Courtesy Mr. Cameron.

"Guisachan", (Kelowna, B.C.) originally built by The Honourable Coutts Marjoribanks. A paper chase party in 1905.

Ranch House, Coldstream, Vernon, B.C. from a snapshot taken by Ishbel.

Through Mackay's influence parts of Coldstream Ranch nearest Vernon were subdivided into small fruit farm holdings, to be leased or sold to settlers "of a very good class... a good nucleus for the future: — we ought to get in time a really high-class little community here."[3] Naturally, Aberdeen chose to be extremely generous, with deferred payments and guarantied sources of irrigation.

When the 2,000-head of cattle at Coldstream mysteriously dwindled under Coutts' management, Jamieson tried manfully to recover some of the unreasonably high original price of £50,000, and outsmart the seller Forbes Vernon, accusing him of setting an inflated price and not submitting an accurate inventory. But law suits were threatened, Vernon held Aberdeen to his contract, and rather than risk embarrassment to the [by then] new Governor-General mortgages were arranged in Scotland to pay off the debt. In 1894 Ishbel was despondent:

> The fruit at Guisachan was a failure, owing to alkali... it has been a big loss to plant all those trees down there... [at Coldstream] our 800 cattle are only a loss and after entailing

wages and food all winter sell for less than the hay itself would have fetched... This year there will be a big deficit.[4]

Eustace Smith left after a year and a half, to be replaced by a new foreman, Edward Kelly, who complained to Mr. Jamieson:

There is no Cash Book or Journal... I shall have to get any information I require from you as Marjoribanks knows nothing of anything connected with the estate... Mr. Smith must have a cheque book in his pocket as cheques have come in that have been taken from some book I cannot find...[5]

A few months later Kelly, grown bolder, told the lawyer that when he took the job he was unaware that "the place was the laughing stock of the country." But Kelly for all his zeal failed to turn the fortunes of the place around.

The jam factory was built in the spring of 1893, but no jar of "Premier preserves" was ever produced. In 1896 during an extended holiday in the area the Aberdeens held a grand ball in the factory, sending the *Vernon News* into raptures: "The most brilliant assembly" in the history of the city " had enjoyed music and dancing until three in the morning, and refreshments not only on the main floor but at a 'recherché supper' in an upstairs hall". Alas, sighed Ishbel to her journal: "We wish the building could have been put to its proper use."[6] It was bought much later by the Bulman Cannery Company, and destroyed in a fire in the 1930's.

The difficulty in securing markets had been an important obstacle. Ishbel made overtures to the great men of the CPR who had dined them in Montreal, to supply their hotels and trains with fruit and vegetables. To that end, a party of these important gentlemen, led by Sir William Van Horne, paid a visit to Coldstream in 1895.

They arrived unexpectedly. Marjorie and Archie had been left in charge. Lord and Lady Aberdeen had gone down the lake to Guisachan and were returning with various produce and dairy supplies. A farm cart was sent to Vernon landing to meet the Aberdeens' boat, but the trail home was rough and muddy and to everyone's consternation an axle stuck and wheels refused to turn. The Aberdeens got out to lighten the load; they pushed and shoved, only Lord Aberdeen's ingenuity saved the day. They had butter among their provisions —

Hon. Coutts Marjoribanks and his foreman, Mr. Kelly, Horse Shoe Ranch, North Dakota.

it could be put to no better use than greasing the stubborn axle. His Lordship and the driver went to work, successfully. So, very late, they pulled up to the ranch-house door, finding two children rigid with self-conscious politeness and the small parlour bulging with "the great Panjandrum of the CPR" and his party.

How to serve an adequate lunch was the immediate crisis, but one way or another it was done. "The supplies at the ranch nearly gave way, though Marjorie and I were alone conscious of the horrors of the situation and happily H.E. did not notice."[7]

After lunch a surprisingly agile Van Horne kept up with other guests in a tour of the place, and the affair ended happily with promises secured for sales of Coldstream and Guisachan produce. Afterwards Van Horne wrote: "Mr Angus and Mr. Clouster came away from Coldstream Ranch with quite a new idea of the possibilities of British Columbia, and we are all most gratified to Your Excellency for one of the most enjoyable afternoons we have ever spent."[8]

As a holiday retreat the Okanagan ranches provided Lord Aberdeen and his family with much pleasure. Ishbel wrote in her journal that her migraine headaches were completely forgotten at Guisachan and Coldstream.

In October 1894 the Aberdeen family left heavy duties at Ottawa for a welcome respite of ten days in the house Coutts had refurbished at Coldstream. Ishbel felt the delicious sensation of being alone in their own small house.

> There is a wonderful charm in feeling that one is once more on one's own domain and that one need not ask permission from the Government before moving a plant or ordering a plate or a duster.[9]

Even their staff had dispersed, most occupying the hired men's quarters. As Ishbel, Johnnie, young Marjorie and Archie, looked into each other's face over a plain dinner table they felt "as if we had regained our individuality." It was a considerable change for the lady who at Rideau Hall had introduced an unusual degree of majesty at state occasions, wearing a diamond tiara to parliamentary openings, her silk train carried by pages dressed in velvet. Now her chief worry was the skunks in the chicken house. As for Lord Aberdeen, he even more than Ishbel dreamed and planned. The desire

Back at Haddo House, with Sinclair (L) and Drummond (R).

to hide away in relative obscurity seems to have been a predominant trait among the Aberdeen heirs. Like his brother, like his neurotic father, he was not temperamentally suited to play the heavy-handed landlord at Haddo House. Here he would have liked to establish a benevolent presence in a bountiful young land, encouraging and assisting freehold farmers, not tenantry.

Coutts withdrew completely from the enterprise when their father, Lord Tweedmouth, died in 1894, and Coutts received his inheritance. He went back to England for a while, married Agnes Nicholls and returned to build a charming house, Invercraig, on Lake Kalemalka. Their daughter was named Ishbel, in appreciation of the sister who had stood by Coutts so loyally during the period of paternal disapproval. Young Ishbel married Allan Surtees: two later generations of the Surtees family are resident in the Okanagan.

The Aberdeen name was preserved for many years on the prow of the first CPR stern-wheeler, which plied the Okanagan on regular runs after 1892. But their property passed after a few years into other hands. Coldstream now lies within the B.C. Agriculture and Land Preserves and thus may escape urban development for some time to come; it is owned by Macdonald-Buchanan in Britain and operated through Canadian directors. In 1967, when local historians across

Canada celebrated the Centennial of Confederation by publishing pioneer records, Vernon's archivist wrote: "The Earl of Aberdeen, in purchasing the Coldstream Ranch from Forbes George Vernon in 1891, initiated the commercial fruit-growing industry in the Okanagan."[10]

Well-deserved tributes were paid. Privately, though, the Aberdeens admitted their personal loss: "Neither the purchase money nor all that was spent on development ever came back," Ishbel wrote in their memoirs, "and the results of our investment in B.C. have been very sad."[11]

Chapter 10
Rideau Hall

There is a river, the streams where of shall make glad the city of God.

T he psalmist of old had become Henry Drummond, the place was the city of Quebec, on the rainy Sunday evening when the Earl and Countess of Aberdeen took up their new post in Canada. They were gathered for family worship at the Citadel, a high fortress on a rugged cliff, the dark St. Lawrence moving far below. Henry saw this setting as very like the inspiration for King David's song. His discourse was that the mightiest fortress, to withstand assault, depended on more than impregnable rock. With that particular power he sometimes possessed, he mesmerized his listeners. He was speaking to reassure a woman taking up what she regarded as a huge, almost impossible task. With sure instinct he chose the one line of the 46th Psalm that uttered joy. The river of life, bringing gladness, the sweet grace of God, flowed beneath and beside, and would sustain them. Ishbel would recall his words throughout her life.

The Aberdeens had come ashore on the rainy morning of September 17, 1893, met by a sodden, huddled official party. Met also by Henry, "True to his promise".[1] He had stayed on after meetings in the United States, to meet the Aberdeens and steady their first uneasy steps as the Queen's surrogates in Canada. Ishbel was afraid, even terrified. Afraid she would not do enough. Afraid she might fail. Henry was there, and gave support.

They had been in Chicago in May, overseeing the Irish Village exhibit at the opening of the World Fair, when they were informed that Lord Stanley was resigning following the death of his father and his succession to the Derby title and estate. Aberdeen would be appointed to Ottawa forthwith. The trying year-long hiatus since the 1892 election was ended. They returned first to Britain, and came to Canada in September.

They left behind a Britain perturbed by bombings in France, anarchist terrorism in Spain, and the ravings of her own revolutionaries. The Liberal government with its uncertain majority was seeking to reconcile this epidemic madness with liberal freedom of thought. The 1892 election had brought into parliament four Labour M.P'.s, cutting into what Liberals had always felt was their constituency, the "common man", and overtures were being made to absorb these M.P.'s into their caucus. For Ireland, in an attempt to downplay Home Rule, the new government had appointed as Viceroy, Lord Houghton, a stiff and inarticulate widower of 35, who was to mollify the Irish peers by keeping as low a profile as possible without disappearing from public view. The Aberdeens' Irish friends regarded his appointment as calamitous. The government quickly brought forward the promised Home Rule bill. It was under debate in parliament as the Aberdeens left. When they reached Rimouski, the *S.S. Sardinia* paused to pick up mail and a *Montreal Star* reporter, and before he could interview them they demanded news of the vote at Westminster. The bill had been defeated. After that Ishbel agreed to answer questions, since it was understood that the Governor-General did not. "It was necessary to explain to this gentleman that I had not given a Home Rule address on board and that the Irish girls at the Village have not all left and gone into saloons...," she wrote.[2]

Ishbel resumed her now confirmed habit of keeping a journal. The letters were sent to Henry Drummond and John Sinclair (who had won a seat in parliament in the 1892 election) and to family members, but circulated also to Gladstone and to Rosebery, both of whom commented on its usefulness.[3] In November Gladstone wrote: "Many thanks... It is sympathetic (which might otherwise be expressed by saying it is *yours*), it is business-like, it is satisfactory; it is all it should be..."[4] In 1896 he responded to information on the contentious Manitoba school question when he commented: "Canadian politics are not always interesting on this side..." the Journal filled a gap.[5] There was similar appreciation from Rosebery " It cleared up many misconceptions."[6]

The swearing-in ceremony for Lord Aberdeen took place at the Legislative Assembly in Quebec City. For a week the

The Earl of Aberdeen, Governor-General of Canada 1893-1898, and Lady Aberdeen.

party remained in residence there. Photographs were taken, they attended a lacrosse game, and privately they enjoyed "romping in the ballroom"[7] with Drummond leading the frolic. Ishbel was 36 years old. She loved to dance with an agreeable partner. There was dancing almost every evening after dinner during that first week, attended by an instructor in Canadian dance. Ishbel described the new steps:

Dancing in Canada has its own peculiarities. The waltz is particularly difficult to pick up. It is a mixture of *deux temps* and *trois temps*, danced v. slowly and they always reverse here. Then there is the 'rush polka' and the 'bon ton', a pretty old Virginia dance something like a *pas de quatre,* and then the Saratoga quadrilles are v. popular and are much more lively than our quadrilles, all the couples dancing at once, the top and bottom dancing with the sides instead of with each other. We had a real good bit of exercise before getting to bed.[8]

The livelier the dance the more Ishbel enjoyed it. Some days later she reported on their first ball. She had decided to conclude it with a reel. None of the guests could be persuaded to take the floor and the reel was performed by Ishbel herself, with two of their stalwart aides-de-camp and Miss Wetterman, the children's governess to complete the square. Those in later years who have seen Lady Aberdeen as a strait-laced Presbyterian might have looked on in surprise.

Ishbel spent much time about town with Henry, a fact not unremarked by the press, during their initial week in Quebec city. He accompanied them on September 25 when they went by private car to Ottawa for a day. Aberdeen had agreed to open a Central Fair there and appear at a lacrosse game. It was 11:30 in the evening when they reached Ottawa, and Aberdeen and the rest of the party elected to sleep on the train. But Ishbel and Henry took a cab to Government House and explored the place before retiring to bed, then breakfasted together ("a bright morning") and "ransacked all over the premises and grounds"[9] before they rejoined her husband at noon.

Her first reaction to the viceregal residence was that the Board of Works must at once provide an addition. When the family and staff were accommodated there would scarcely be any space for guests — three or four at the most. Also, the family dining-room was gloomy and *smelled of kitchen,* though the ballroom added in Lord Dufferin's time pleased her. She would find, alas, that the Board of Works was not very free with additions, and like all of their predecessors would bemoan the inadequacies of the house, its awkward distance from the city — two miles through woods in those days — and its undistinguished site, close by but not on the Ottawa River.

While she and Henry were exploring, Aberdeen opened the lacrosse game with a fatherly speech about keeping the game clean, and avoiding the rough-house that had sent more than half the Ottawa team (the "Capitals") to hospital the previous Saturday in an encounter in Montreal.

Ishbel looked at Ottawa critically on that quick visit, noting especially the condition of the streets, "so full of pitfalls and ups and downs that it seems wonderful that any springs can stand them."[10] They were soon in Montreal, which was sophistication itself by contrast. When they entered the city thousands of people turned out to get a glimpse of them as they drove from the station to the Windsor Hotel. A formal reception at City Hall saw Ishbel in pink and white brocade, and with the first of the very large bouquets that would everywhere encumber her. She thought this first one lovely, made of pink roses and white heather, but she noted next day that she would like to have a word with the florist, for the bouquets were "v. heavy and v. wet — so wet that yesterday one entirely ruined my dress." She had on these initial appearances to assume her proper role as smiling consort, entering the Windsor banquet room *after dinner* to be seated behind her husband, and silently taking note of Mr. Laurier, the Opposition leader, and the enthusiasm of the cheers that welcomed him. She judged him a brilliant speaker. When Lieutenant-Governor Chapleau also made a charming speech, appearing a popular as well as an urbane figure, her perception of Canadian politicians took its first upward turn. "H.E." pleased the crowd with "little stories" — Aberdeen's speeches alternated between fatherly advice and funny "cracks", in which the frugality of the Scottish race figured prominently. Later he would publish two little illustrated volumes of his humour.[11]

Drummond had stayed with them as they came to Montreal, but at that point had to be off to speak on Evolution at the University of Chicago. They would not meet again until both visited the World Fair in October. For some weeks she clung to the hope that he would be offered and would accept a post as principal of McGill University. For whatever reasons, this did not materialize.

Still, there were their handsome aides-de-camp in constant attendance. Chief ADC was Captain Beauchamps Urquhart who cut a fine figure in the full dress kilt of the Cameron Highlanders. Others were Captain Kindersley of the Coldstream Guards, and Robert Munro-Ferguson ("Bob") and David Erskine, both resplendent in the dark green and gold of the Scottish Archers. All were tall young men, whose first formal appearance at the swearing-in ceremony in Quebec had evoked the approving comment that no previous governor-general had brought with him so splendid an escort.

It was mid-November before the Aberdeens finally moved in at Government house. There followed the tiresome task of installing servants (with the right "tone" morally). "Domestic adjustments seem interminable."[12] Mama, back home, rounded up and sent out laundry maids who could be trusted not to shrink the woollens. Instead of contracting for dairy products with Mr. Clarke, who ran the barns and pasture on the Rideau House grounds, Ishbel brought in "our own splendid dairy maid Johanna Doherty" to see to the butter and cream. She dismissed the Government House chef, Fanconnier, who had served the Stanleys and the Lansdownes, declaring him "very extravagant — and not a good tone in the kitchen", and brought over their London chef, Gouffé, with his head kitchen maid. Gouffé, threatened to leave two weeks later, unable to bear the limitations of colonial victualing, and pleading that he could lose his reputation. He was "smoothed down". Then a storm rose between old and new servants. Accusations of flirting were made against Ishbel's personal maid, Jessie Gunn, and stoutly denied; the housekeeper, second maid and groom of the chambers were dismissed. They had been, in any case, "awful Conservatives".

Despite these tempests, the democratic process of a new Household Club was set in motion at Rideau Hall as it had been at Haddo House. There were meetings, educational and social evenings, shared by master and mistress. Scurrilous reports soon appeared of a governor-general worsted at chess by the butler, of guests aghast at the disrespect of footmen. The Mintos, who succeeded the Aberdeens, picked up and circulated these stories. The sly slander was felt keenly by Ishbel who, in household management, could be quite as autocratic as any lady of high degree. When it came time to write her memoirs of the Canadian experience she opened with pages of painfully amused denial. She did *not*, as a writer for a Boston Sunday paper claimed, startle housemaids by ordering them to remove their caps, "that badge of servitude"; she did *not* "play hide-and-seek and such games with the housemaids and footmen at all sorts of odd hours". Her purpose in entering into the personal and social lives of her servants was solely to uplift, and put something in their heads besides their obsessive interest in lacrosse and hockey.

The Aberdeens built a chapel, which after their tenure was dismantled and shipped West to serve a church mission. They turned the finest state bedroom, the oval room from the house's original structure, in present times reserved for royal guests, into a charming schoolroom for their children. Rideau Hall was not run on its usual lines between 1893 and 1898.

Lady Stanley had passed on to Ishbel peevish counsel about the inadequacies of local shops:

> There is no good dressmaker in Ottawa... [there is] a very good man for tailor-made dresses in Montreal, called Milloy; he is expensive and troublesome but can make very well ... I made an arrangement with a dressmaker or rather with Rupell and Allen [London] and they sent me out dresses, tea gowns, bonnets, etc., etc., everything I needed. I was advised to do this and it answered very well and saved a great deal of trouble. You can get nothing good in Canada in the way of gloves, ribbons and stockings, boots or shoes. We had to have everything from England.[13]

At Rideau Hall, (Government House), Ottawa, Lord and Lady Aberdeen and their four children.

Ishbel, on the other hand, reported her husband's elegance in a new long beaver coat, the fur on the outside instead of serving as lining, bought from the popular Ottawa furrier, H.H. Devlin; she dressed her children in bright blanket coats with contrasting trim and remarked, after the first tobogganing party:

> Scarcely any blanket coats were worn today excepting by our own party. It seems a pity that the fashion for this national costume should pass away when it is so light and warm and when it gives opportunity for so many bright colours on the winter scenes.[14]

Skating and tobogganing parties were now an established feature of Government House entertainment. Through Miss Wetterman the Aberdeen children were also introduced to skis, an innovation in Ottawa. Ishbel first shunned the toboggan slide, afraid she "hadn't the head" for its dizzy speed, but she succumbed, and even persuaded a Cabinet minister, Mackenzie Bowell, to take the plunge with her one day. Canadians were obsessed with sports. Prime Minister Thompson rose in Ishbel's estimation because he ignored them, an attitude reflected by Edward Blake when he visited in January:

> It is somewhat refreshing in the midst of an entourage entirely possessed of a mania for winter sports all day and all night to find Sir John [Thompson] admitting that he has never seen a game of curling and Mr. Blake saying he had never seen hockey...[15]

Ishbel thought hockey alarmingly dangerous. After watching a game between Ottawa and Montreal early in 1894, when one player's nose was broken, another badly cut in the mouth and a third knocked unconscious, she wrote:

> There can be no doubt about its roughness, and if the players get over keen and lose their tempers as they are too apt to do, the possession of the stick and the close proximity to one another gives the occasion for many a nasty hit. [Another time she said that she was sure *she* would murder her opponents at such close quarters, with a stick in her hand.] Yet there are many men and boys here in Ottawa who practically live for hockey. It must be said that it is beautiful

to see the perfection of the game — the men simply run on the ice as if they were on the ground.[16]

A week later at the Quebec Winter Carnival she could only describe in rapture the vision of skaters in masquerade costumes performing with "utmost grace... a sight to remember". Still, one Carnival seemed to be enough; she declined in succeeding years, pleading more urgent business.

Lord Aberdeen, on the other hand, not only took a lively interest but demonstrated considerable skill in winter sports:

> I am not sure that some of the people half approve of receiving a G.G. who ventures to have some acquaintance with skating and curling and sleighing & does not need being instructed in these arts.[17]

She had probably read the Toronto *World* (6 January 1894). His Excellency had skipped a rink in a curling game and "pranced and gyrated on the ice like any plebeian", when his side scored.

Ishbel was sensitive to public opinion, which had been decidedly mixed on their arrival. As she anticipated, the country was run by Conservatives. The Aberdeens' partisan support of the Liberal party in Britain — more particularly *her* partisanship — had prompted cautionary words from the Colonial Secretary, Lord Ripon, as they assumed their duties. He had pointed to the wide difference between viceroyalty in Ireland, essentially an arm of government, and the non-partisan, non-political posture expected of Canada's governor-general:

> Party politics of any kind are entirely outside his sphere. With contested questions whether political or social he can have nothing to do... Your Government will be Conservative; you are a Liberal; they will be Protectionist; you are a Free Trader. So that all along the line you will be shut out from following publicly the natural bent of your inclinations... Such restrictions are irksome and you, and I fear Lady Aberdeen also, will find them so...[18]

Aberdeen committed himself to this requirement: "I venture to predict that you will hear no whisper of complaint..."[19] Yet from Canada even before they sailed the whispers rose. Sir Donald Smith, stout supporter of Sir John A. and the Conservatives, was writing:

The fact of Lord Aberdeen's being a great favourite with Mr. Gladstone will not predispose many in his favour; but I believe he is earnest, and industrious, and a Scotsman of rank and lineage, which in itself signifies a great deal. Then, as I need hardly remind you, there is her ladyship![20]

Tories in Canada fastened on the Aberdeens' known sympathy with Home Rule and their exertions in the U.S. on behalf of the Irish. The Toronto *Telegram* editorialized:

All the Governor-General needs to do is remember that Gladstone is no idol here, and that Canada has more reason to dislike than he has to like his Fenian friends in Chicago.[21]

But then the Liberals had been fully as vindictive against the Stanleys, appointed in their time by British Conservatives. J. W. Longley, Attorney General of Nova Scotia, had written to Edward Blake: "There can be no doubt that Lord Stanley is a complacent partisan who would not disturb them [the Macdonald government] if they should rob the treasury of millions and debauch every department of the public service."[22]

For Ishbel, the deepest hurt was the personal sniping that appeared in the press to a degree unknown in Britain. She wrote, apparently in one of the diaries or letters since destroyed:

No stone was left unturned to have unpleasant things said about us; the dislike of myself which I stumble upon occasionally is a disagreeable shock, I confess.[23]

The Montreal *Daily Witness* said:

Lady Aberdeen has much more prominence than the average wife of a Governor-General, and in fact, much more is written about her and her work than about His Lordship...

In build, Lord Aberdeen is slight, of medium height, with sloping shoulders. He is a rather delicate-looking man, with soft black moustache and beard, very smooth dark hair, sympathetic violet eyes, and has a nervous manner very different from the average cold, placid Britisher...

Her Excellency, as we must from this on call her, seems to have a heart big enough to sympathize with the poor of all the countries on the earth...[24]

There was sarcasm in the latter comment, for who in his proper mind wanted an unbridled philantropist at Rideau Hall? The Ottawa *Journal* put in a quiet dig about her political bent:

> [She is] a handsome woman, above medium height, possessed of a cultivated mind, kind heart and great strength of character... She is somewhat of a politician also...[25]

The Winnipeg *Free Press* was content to say, "The Earl of Aberdeen will make a pattern Governor-General and the only doubt about Lady Aberdeen is that she may try to make us too good."[26]

Barbed comments, along with distorted tales of democratic antics with her servants, put Ishbel under great strain. She found relief in walking and riding, and wrote home:

> ...Just the prosaic practice of riding makes me feel saner; I am quite ashamed to find how much better a place the world can look during and after, a ride. Then Monarch [her Skye terrier] makes me try to run frivolous races with him. To-day he and I sallied forth in a biting wind and had our reward in coming on a bevy of pine grosbeaks all twittering away together...[27]

She was very homesick. She wrote to John Sinclair:

> We banished settlers often think of you reveling in the luxuries of the Palace of Westminster. Five or six years away look horribly long. All that we preach about the grand destiny of this country is true, and I hope that we shall be able to be of some use here. But now and again you must let me tell you how weary I am of stifling artificiality; I cannot write with the perpetual smirk I have to wear... There's a little burst! Anyhow it has been a great consolation to me to put up a picture of Mr. G. in every room.[28]

When formality was required, Ishbel seemed bound to outdo the Tories at their most splendid. She wore velvets, silks, brocades and laces, diamonds and tiaras, with a sash of Gordon tartan to the St. Andrews ball in Montreal, and at their first state dinner at Government House a gown of "blue satin with pansies... beryls and star tiara" and a train, carried by her two youngest sons garbed as Elizabethan pages. To be

Ishbel on "Blarney", Ottawa.

attended by lads dressed in blue velvet with lace ruffles, their white satin capes trimmed with beaver and gold lace, was somewhat sensational even for the ostentatious Nineties.

Dinners and levées were held to receive the élite of Montreal, Quebec City and Toronto as well as Ottawa. In Quebec Ishbel arranged simpler affairs as well as formal ones, urging guests to bring their children, and providing "games of tug-of-war etc." for them, while she "introduced hot chocolate with whipped cream for the French ladies, which is greatly appreciated."

Lady Aberdeen, as wife of the Governor-General of Canada.

In Toronto, the first grand reception was held in the provincial legislative buildings on 25 October 1893. She said, "A great turn-out of officers made us look very smart."[29] The Aberdeens shared the dais with Lieutenant-Governor and Lady Kirkpatrick, the Premier Oliver Mowat, and Provincial Secretary Colonel Gibson. A very long procession of Torontonians passed before them. Most contented themselves with a handshake while "some tried a bit of a curtsey, though not many," and the frank appraisal of the curious left Ishbel "pretty tired". Still she appreciated Toronto's good manners, so lacking in the capital.

In Ottawa during the winter season she set herself to entertain all the Members and Senators and their wives in a succession of state dinners, six or seven dinners with 60 or 70 people at each. Inviting the wives was an innovation, but Ishbel thought it would cut down on the drunkenness that had reputedly marked the men-only dinners hosted by Stanley. Since many wives never came to Ottawa this resulted in a preponderance of males, and occasionally, a dinner at which Her Excellency was the only female present. Their Tory successor in office, Lord Minto, deplored the whole idea, and reverted to the men-only functions.

Ishbel wrote:

> We have had a horse-shoe table made for these dinners and His Excellency and I sit together in the middle of it... then comes the tussle after dinner to get around and speak to each and to remember to show that one remembers each by saying something appropriate.[30]

It was a great way for her to feel in touch with the politics of the country, and she was pleased to find "so many nice people among the Senators and the M.P.'s", which she attributed to the predominance of Scots and Irishmen compared to those from England, who had found their way into public life.

The Governor-General's Levée on New Year's Day was by long tradition a male-only occasion and Ishbel could only report that John Grant, the butler, thought it had passed in reasonably good order, despite the tendency of the guests to have four or five glasses of champagne apiece. They were soon, as at Edinburgh, overspending their expense funds to an alarming degree.

The first parliamentary Opening, an occasion for the ultimate in formality, was shadowed in March 1894 by the death of Ishbel's father. Government House went into mourning, the servants in black liveries, for a six-week period. Ishbel could not be present at her husband's first Throne Speech, though she was relieved when she was told it had gone off well. "Whatever else he may or may not do," said Ishbel of her husband, "he can always be trusted to do full credit to such ceremonials."[31]

It was permissible to attend their first court Drawing Room on April 28, held in the Senate Chamber. Their Excellencies stood on the dais above the parade of Ottawa's finest, acknowledging bows and curtsies for an hour and a quarter. "It seemed to me a worse ordeal than at home," she wrote. "First there is the Entree, to which very few have right, then Senators and their wives — then M.P.'s — and then everyone else."[32] Ishbel's black gown had a train — " it makes the whole affair more finished," but afterwards she concluded that, since others were copying this affectation and "it would be a needless expense when most ladies are not well off," it had best be discouraged. It was a season also for sheer trailing veils and tall plumes tucked into coiffures. These seemed "more in keeping" for Ottawa ladies of modest wealth, and were encouraged.

Then there were the At Homes at Rideau Hall. Her plan was to hold these every fortnight for "what are considered Society people... trusting them not to all come together". Ishbel paid a visit to the Electric Car Company to sound them out on running tracks up back roads to Government House. To travel there by streetcar "would be a great convenience to people on party nights for the hacks charge as much as $5 for these expeditions and this is a considerable sum to the Civil Servants of which Ottawa Society is so largely composed."[33] A delegation of cab drivers, lamenting that their business would be ruined, stalled that proposal.

Despite the cost, 350 "elite" people turned up for the first of the Rideau Hall entertainments. They listened to a Ladies' Quartet from Toronto, a tenor from Chicago, a violinist from Montreal, and a harpist named Sullivan brought to Canada as a member of their own staff. Ishbel hoped this imported talent made a favourable impression, though the women guests seemed, after supper, to be in a great hurry to leave:

The ladies behaved somewhat boisterously in the cloak room and quite upset our calculations by vaulting over tables arranged for giving out cloaks and insisting on going for their bundles themselves and no reasonings or entreaties would make them abstain from this. Of course there was dire confusion... We think of sending out a little printed note explaining cloak room arrangements next time with the invitations.[34]

A year's acquaintance with the capital culminated in a "long talk about Ottawa society and its ways and its wishes" with her good friend Lady Annie Thompson, the prime minister's wife. "Lady Thompson sums up its chief demand in saying, 'Feed them, feed them, feed them — nothing else will satisfy them.'"[35] In 1895 after a reception in Montreal Ishbel was writing: "There is no pushing and struggling and they ask for things civilly..."[36] and Ottawa again suffered by comparison.

A Ball at Rideau Club to celebrate opening of new rooms. Were forcefully impressed by the boorishness of Ottawa manners as compared to all other parts of Canada.[37]

Raising Ottawa's cultural level impressed itself as a priority from the first experience with a "dreary performance at the Canadian College of Music. Mr. Smyth the principal is the organist also at St. Andrew's and greatly spoils the services by his bad training of the choir."[38]

Patronage of the arts was among her duties:

Mr. [Archibald] Lampman read one of his own about the surroundings of Ottawa and one of Bliss Carman's; Mr. Duncan Campbell Scott read a charming production very badly. Miss Pauline Johnson recited some of her poems in her Indian dress and with much dramatic power.[39]

She had not been long in Ottawa before she made a brave but futile effort to launch an Ottawa public library. It was opposed by the Roman Catholic Archbishop because the church would have no voice in the selection of books; a library had to wait for the philanthropy of Carnegie.

Occasionally Ishbel herself participated on the cultural circuit. Her journal on 31 May 1895 told of an evening in the

Massey Music Hall of Toronto where, before 2,500 people, she "lectured on the present Irish literary scene."

> I wore the new cerise dress which Fanny chose for me covered in the deep flounce of black Limerick [lace] which Mama gave me, which was made for her by Papa's order after a new design of roses, shamrocks and thistles intertwined with ivy. It was much admired and enabled reference to Irish Industries to be brought in... I confess I enjoyed the evening. The audience was very responsive.[40]

But always it was back to Ottawa, and a renewed effort to improve its manners and culture. The backwoods capital could also exhibit a parochial intolerance. One of Ishbel's first acts of clemency was to lift the social ban against Mrs. Addie Foster, wife of Thompson's finance minister. Mrs. Foster had been divorced before remarrying. She was introduced to Ishbel one morning at St. Andrew's Church, one of the few places she seemed able to attend.

> She had never yet been received at Government House and it seems to us that this has been v. unfair. She divorced her husband — an American — in America for cruelty and desertion for six years, and married Mr. Foster some time after.[41]

Ishbel opened the doors by inviting Mrs. Foster to their first concert, and was rewarded with a private assurance that the Fosters were most grateful. She was even more convinced she was right when she was told that Mrs. Foster's exclusion had been due to "a fad of Lady Macdonald's, who ruled society in Ottawa with a rod of iron."

Days at Rideau Hall were brightened by entertaining guests from across the Atlantic. Novelist Paul Bourget came on a letter of introduction from Lord Dufferin. He gained a warm welcome when he admired the writings of Henry Drummond. Bourget was in the process of gathering material for yet another book on the United States as seen through European eyes. It would, on publication as *Impressions of America* (1895) earn the wicked riposte of Mark Twain. But Ishbel felt she had helped the traveller toward truth:

... he does not appear to be enamoured by what he has seen so far. He is especially horrified by the type of rich, fashionable and luxurious women at Newport, who appear to him to be the worst type of irresponsible wealthy women that he has seen. I hope I have been able to give him some letters which will at least let him see there is another side to womens' life in the U.S.[42]

William Stead, who arrived soon after, leaned the other way. He was inclined towards the Americans (he was wooing promoters of an American edition of *Review of Reviews)*; it was his view of Canada that seemed uncharitably harsh. At Government House Ishbel nursed him through a bad cold, and listened with serious interest to his revelations about "Julie" and his other supernatural associates. She felt she had set him also on the right path by describing for him Canadian virtues and potential.

He has come to believe in Canada and her future v. heartily, which is a great result to have attained; and he is very anxious to make his American edition serve our ends; with this in view he wants us to write his American editor, Dr. Shaw, who is a real thorough-going American and wants to clutch B.C.[43]

At the end of May 1894, Ishbel returned home briefly. She had kept close contact with the Irish exhibit at Chicago's World's Fair, and had helped wind up its affairs and set up an Irish dry goods shop in the city, and she had sent the Irish maidens safely home from their spinning and dairying in the make-believe village. Now she decided to report back to her Irish Industries Association in Dublin, earning a respite from Ottawa burdens. She would leave her husband to his own devices and take all of June and July at home.

She wrote her husband of the wonderfully grateful reception in Ireland. She spoke to a large crowd in Cork, where her efforts at the Fair were extoled. She was given the Freedom of the City of Limerick, the first woman to be so honoured. At Tralee the crowd held up banners of welcome, though one, "Bring back Our Home Rule Viceroy!" she tactfully urged her hosts to have removed. She inspected mills, shops and hospitals, proposed progressive new projects, and was praised in the press for her "practical benevolence."

And Henry Drummond came to share the last days of her visit in Ireland, going on with her for a week at Haddo House. She wrote sparingly to her husband of their time together, yet reported:

June 16. H. D. and I were in a car together most of the day. It is delightful going about in a car [the Irish two-wheeled jaunting-car drawn by one horse] — it is so cheery and cosy and seems to lend hilarity to the whole proceedings. We had first-rate horses and drivers & had lots of fun. People working in the fields... At one place I tried to spin but the wheel was broken & I promised the old lady a new one... I fear for our reputation in this hotel — we were up about 12 p.m. with hunt the slipper and hunt the whistle.[44]

Many things in Britain had changed. Gladstone, afflicted with failing eyesight, had resigned in March, and Ishbel's visit to him was in the nature of a holy pilgrimage — "a sacred peaceful sort of halo of restful farewell over it all..." Rosebery had succeeded him in office, not with much conviction or joy. Rosebery had never recovered from his wife's death, and projected a debilitated air of sardonic fatalism. He would write Ishbel six months later from Downing Street:

From here there is nothing bright to report. Poor Randolf's [Churchill's] artificially preserved decay — for it is nothing else — is intensely depressing. Then the government obviously does not prosper. That would not matter if it would end. Let it end or flourish. The fear is of a process like Randolph's — a long-drawn decay. And yet the government has not deserved ill of the people.[45]

In the summer of 1894 in a brief letter to Aberdeen, Rosebery said he had "caught a flying glimpse of Lady Aberdeen; but she prefers Ireland to England and Scotland, which is depressing to the inhabitants of the two subordinate countries."[46] Rosebery had seen Ishbel on her brief visit to London. There she had stayed with Teddy and Fanny, was taken off by Fanny to buy new gowns, and there she also caught up on political gossip with John Morley, the Campbell-Bannermans and other stout-hearted Liberals.

Haddo House "looks but too painfully homelike and attractive," she wrote from there, "rhododendron, hawthorn, birds singing like anything..." Reminders of Canada were an intrusion. She poured out her vehement displeasure at the impertinent visit of Senator Sanford's son from Hamilton, an offensive young man "dressed very much like an American and wearing patent leather boots."

> [I] told him that as he was a young man I would venture to give him a little advice and that the next time he wished to visit a lady he did not know, he had better write a note and find out if it would be convenient to receive him... ' in this case, you would have saved much trouble, as I could have written and explained that it was *not* convenient.' I effectually subdued the scamp. But Mr. Muirhead began to look so terrified that I had to desist.
>
> Did you ever hear of such a piece of impudence? Except indeed when the people came and sat in my room that evening in Ottawa and turned over my books and magazines... Ah! You good people who have stayed over there, you may be glad not to have to feel for a little the contrast of home, then go off. Everything is so perfect here — the civilization, the gentlemanliness, the nice plates, the taste of everything.[47]

How hard it was to give an appropriate little talk on Canada that evening to the working party of her Onward and Upward ladies: "I have to bite my lips not to make disagreeable remarks about Canada and to extol the country and its future."[48]

Its future. One could always look resolutely in that direction, and set oneself the task of the empire builder. Ishbel, in late July traveled back to Canada. The country might be full of people with no manners, the press rude, the Tories in control — but her duty lay there and she would find the means of transmuting both ennui and wrath into something useful to others and satisfying to herself.

Chapter 11
A Women's Parliament

"G ood works" spell tedium to those involved in a rich
and satisfying social life. Ishbel's response to the
rival attractions of society and charity was the
opposite. She found social demands stressful and tedious, her
regal manner disguised an odd streak of shyness, of self-
disparagement left over from an awkward childhood. It was
particularly difficult to maintain her countenance amid the
"smart set". In Halifax, 20 August 1894, after a reception
given for the Aberdeens by General Montgomery and his wife,
she wrote: "It is a terrible thing to process through a smart
crowd like that, to most of whom one has been introduced, and
so one ought to shake hands and say the right thing at the
right moment... there are moments when one wishes the
earth would swallow one up."

Her natural element was the vigorous, adrenalin-rousing
battle of reform, when she stood armed with conviction and
faith in a just cause. She looked into the dark unhealthy
corners that most Canadians preferred not to acknowledge.
In late October 1893 she visited a new YMCA building in
Toronto and asked plain questions. When she was told that in
this young city 800 cases of destitution had applied to the "Y"
for aid the previous year, she said: "So much for the common
saying that there are no poor here."[1]

The wretched poor in Quebec City, at an Ursuline Convent Home, shocked her, "Rows of poor wee babies and poor
old people. We send the scraps from our kitchen here."[2] In
Halifax there was a poor-house to visit, with 300 occupants,
where the viceregal party handed out a quarter-pound packet
of tea to each woman and a fig of tobacco to each man. These
were Lady Bountiful gestures. Ishbel needed constructive
work to do.

As soon as she touched the Canadian shore she was off to
discover what plans were made to receive the poor immi-

grants from the same ship. She visited the reception centre in Quebec City, inspecting the stores of food and bedding provided for sale for the long trip West.

She discussed immigration with the politicians and authorities. It was her impression that the Irish and Scottish were better material than the English. At the Caledonian Games in Georgetown, Prince Edward Island, she had a sense of mystic transportation to the grounds of Haddo House, "so persistent was the Scottish type of face... It was touching to see the weather-beaten old Scottish faces under their Highland bonnets gazing up at H.E. as he spoke in answer to their addresses."[3] In addition to those from the British Isles she noted new arrivals from Germany and Scandinavia, which she considered acceptable. She was dubious about a more exotic mix. Before long she encountered the Chinese on the western coast, and did her best to surmount a considerable culture gap:

> Somehow it is difficult to feel towards a Chinaman as a real human being, but today we were brought for the first time into contact with some of the superior men, some of them quite good looking and all dressed in green or blue silk with coats of black satin or silk with ornamental buttons, their pig-tails well brushed and dressed... Here at least they still have the control of the Japanese, for the latter work for them at less wages than the Chinese will work. Our first visit [the Chinese Benevolent Society as hosts] was to an opium refinery. We were shown all the processes from the time it is brought in. Up to a year ago a great deal of opium was refined here for the purpose of smuggling it into the United States. But since the duty on raw opium has been taken off there, the trade has been diminished and there are now only three refineries in this city instead of 17.[4]

On they pressed to visit a Joss-House — "where these strange folk carry on their worship," and accepted with as much grace as they could a very potent cup of Chinese tea: "the leaves had to be scooped aside for drinking, [members of the party were] making wry faces and trying to invent epithets to express politely their appreciation.." A visit the next day took her to a Methodist Chinese Girls' Home "where girls who had been brought from China for the wrong purposes were being brought up. They seemed a cheery lot and sang God Save the Queen with great heartiness."

In her viceregal role she had taken on a deeper concern extending to all inhabitants of the country. She no longer saw the dispossessed Indians through a tourist's eyes as "pictur esque". Traveling west with her husband in the fall of 1894 she noted in Regina: "The Indians suffer terribly from scrofula and consumption."[5] In Calgary, the Indians who had gathered to present an impromptu sports program "presented a sad appearance and gave rise to many sad thoughts — for there is little hope for them."[6]

She took up the cause of immigrant domestic workers. "Truly there are horrible tales related... It is utterly wrong and cruel to encourage [unsuitable] girls to come out. It must result in utter failure both for themselves and for their employers. Good strong general servants, ready to fall in with the ways of the country, and who have *not* been told that they are sure to marry comfortably in Canada, are what is wanted... Tonight in the Home [a Girls' Friendly Society Home in the little town of Indian Head, Saskatchewan] there were five girls just arrived, three of these were 14 to 15, delicate half-grown sort of girls from Essex or thereabouts, and quite unfit for the rough and tumble they will assuredly meet."[7] She wrote articles for the magazines back home, she talked to members of parliament, she urged an organization of "friendly visitors" on this side to assist girls in adapting to a new way of life.

Canadian Children's Aid Societies were just being organized. She and her husband visited inaugural meetings in Toronto and Ottawa, and she was impatient with the long-winded self-importance of the speakers and the cold apathy of audiences. In May 1894 she was furthering a petition to the Ottawa Police Commissioner urging that trials for children be held separate and apart from those for adults.

The great shame of illegitimacy shrouded and smothered charitable feelings toward foundlings. In Montreal, in late November 1893, she visited two institutions in Montreal, a Maternity Hospital and a Foundlings Hospital, both established as very progressive efforts to rescue these unfortunates. Ishbel found the hospitals well managed, and described the prevalent customs that had led to their inception:

> There is no registration of birth necessary in this province at
> all. The influence of the priests keeps up a v. strong feeling
> about illegitimate children & the consequence is that it is

accepted as a belief that the kindest thing is to baptize these children and then facilitate their exit from this world as much as possible. The practice both amongst R.C's and Protestants has been to take such children to the Grey Nuns & to hand them over with a sum of $10 to be provided for as best they might. The babies are farmed out with the result according to their own showing that the percentage of deaths amongst such children some years has been as high as 90 p.c. & one year, actually 99 p.c.[8]

In the maternity hospital there were separate wards for married women, to shield them from the contamination of the unwed. Both institutions she visited had to endure a grudging charity at best, while there continued to be "popular feeling against them."

The same attitude was apparent in Ottawa when Ishbel pressed for a maternity hospital there. She presided at a City Hall meeting for the purpose, but attendance was small and she met "a curious prejudice against the plan." On 1 March 1894, she visited a private establishment in Ottawa, run by Miss Wright, who feared a Maternity Hospital would put her out of business. "She takes poor girls in here to be confined, *if* they will stay for twelve months, take care of their children, and do laundry work — she also takes discharged prisoners and imbeciles. She is a real good earnest girl but narrow, and does not like to be interfered with. An air of squalor and closeness pervaded the establishment — about 26 women and 20 infants."[9] A group of more broad-minded doctors and concerned women nevertheless set out to raise funds for a new maternity hospital in Ottawa which opened a year later despite "much prejudice against it." Ishbel was elated, describing her part in the achievement as "unlocking the door, which unfortunately would not open at first when unlocked."[10]

Ishbel found in Toronto that this new country treated its working girls exactly as they were treated in England. She described it for her Journal readers:

It is disturbing to think that sweating and all its attendant evils should have already so firm a hold here. Just the same old set of circumstances as at home — homework and married women's work underselling the work of women wholly dependent on their earnings... The sort of prices which prevail are 14 cents for a boy's coat with three pockets, button-holes etc, taking a day and a half to make — 35 cents for a grown-up coat — 50 cents a dozen for overalls, etc — thread of course having to be supplied by the workers. Then in factories girls by the score earning only two dollars a week and afraid of giving up their work because there are hundreds of others ready to step in their places — fines, unsanitary conditions and no woman inspectors.[11]

A Woman's Protective Association had been organized in Toronto but the factory girls were afraid to join. Some of their number had been dismissed for attending meetings. Ishbel became a Patron of the Toronto Protective Association, lending it respectability. She brought its president to Ottawa in late 1893 to address a small gathering of working girls at a private home on Cumberland Street. She became Patron of their small union also, encouraging them to pay 10 cents monthly into a fund to provide sick benefits for themselves when they fell ill. She spoke boldly to the press against an act by Ottawa authorities to repeal an early closing law in the city shops. Shop girls who had been able to go home after twelve hours' work no longer had that protection.

Where was Ishbel to find the machinery to undertake reform? In Canada there were no benevolent peers, no powerful Wilberforce, Owen or Shaftsbury to call on. Ishbel put her faith in the efforts of enlightened women. The response she aroused among Canadian women was evidenced by Emily Willoughby Cummings, a Toronto journalist who became an active supporter. She wrote reflectively to Lord Aberdeen when the time came for their departure to tell him what she had felt unable to express to Ishbel herself. She said that *she* had a reputation as strong-willed, but Lady Aberdeen "has a wonderful influence over me, an influence so strong that I doubt if I could resist it even if I tried. When I am with her I am perfectly conscious that I am a better woman with higher ideals and purposes ... When I said this to Her Excellency she said laughingly, 'that is quite opposite to the idea most people have of me'..."[12]

In Canada when Ishbel came, women had just begun to organize nationally in other than church groups. There were two main issues: Temperance and The Vote. Ishbel's view of the Temperance women, the WCTU, was not sympathetic:

A deputation of some 50 ladies from the Quebec Branch of the WCTU came with an address today to me. Received them in the ballroom — afraid I can scarcely have pleased them, as I told them we were not abstainers and could not be in accord with some of their methods, although — etc.[13]

The Enfranchisement group was small but feisty, so was the scattered band seeking the right to higher education. Ishbel could work with such women. But she had broader plans.

In the United States in the 1880's an international group, led by American suffragists Elizabeth Cady Stanton and Susan B. Anthony, had devised a base for reform action beyond the winning of the franchise. Frances Willard and May Wright Sewell, strong advocates of access to universities for women students, joined in. A first convention of a new International Council of Women met in Washington in 1888. Member Councils in western Europe were nursed into being. A second grand convention was held in 1893 to coincide with the World's Fair in Chicago, where the ICW was formally established 19 May. It looked to Great Britain for a new president; it chose Lady Aberdeen. She was informed by cable that she had just been chosen president of an international organization she had never heard of.

She accepted with alacrity.

So in Canada that autumn she had the instrument "ready to her hand". Canada had sent delegates to the big Women's Congress in Chicago and two Toronto women, Mrs. Willoughby Cummings and Mrs. Mary Macdonell, had returned as provisional president and secretary of a Council for Canada. They resolved to ask Lady Aberdeen, now in Canada, to assume the presidency, and an inaugural meeting was scheduled for October.

Beginning with that October meeting Ishbel used the many official viceregal appearances across the country to organize local Councils. It may be suspected that the need to set up the Councils sometimes determined the timing of official visits, with Lord Aberdeen an agreeable partner. (He had directed his own philanthropic work to furthering the "Boys' Brigade", an earlier version of the Boy Scouts.) In October 1893 they took their special train to London, Hamilton and Toronto. In Hamilton Ishbel made a point of meeting Mrs. Adelaide Hoodless, a countrywoman already embarked on the task of organizing Women's Institutes in rural areas and promoting courses in "domestic science" in public schools.

(Her own child had died of typhoid, acquired through drinking unpasteurized milk, and clean milk was a strong element in her crusade.) Ishbel had "a talk" with her, and Mrs. Hoodless came to the big Council meeting in Toronto and agreed to serve as national treasurer. The wives of lieutenant-governors agreed to be vice-presidents.

Among these women, Ishbel especially admired Emily Cummings. "One of the main movers in this scheme," she wrote, "is a very nice little woman, Mrs. Cummings, a widow and a lady of good connection in Toronto. She was left very badly off by her husband who died about a year ago and at present she is writing the weekly Woman's Page for 'The Globe'. She has been appointed secretary..."[14] Ishbel addressed the large afternoon meeting in Toronto's Horticultural Pavilion (Allan Gardens in later years) in a speech, described next day in the *Empire*, that was warm, inspiring and thoroughly practical:

> We are beginning to realize that all the divisions we have put up between ourselves, the narrow grooves along which we accustom ourselves to run, our want of knowledge of one another's interests, one another's sympathies, one another's work, is keeping us back from fulfilling our life's mission for God and humanity...[15]

Together, the barriers overcome, Canadian women could meet new needs, especially among working girls who lacked decent lodgings and cheap midday meals, and in fostering an organization dedicated to preventing cruelty to children. She moved the resolution to set up the National Council of Women (seconded by Mrs. Tilly of London) and wrote that night in her Journal: "It is wonderful to feel and see the intense desire and readiness of the women for some such movement as this."

The Aberdeens stayed over in Toronto two more days. The new NCW executive met: "Mrs. Cummings, Mrs. Hoodless, Mrs. Macdonell and two ladies who were not appointed so ought not to have come." Then she toured Loretto Roman Catholic girl's school with Archbishop Walsh, "a dear old man evidently v. Liberal" who had read the news report of the NCW meeting with hearty approval and would encourage "his ladies" (of the Catholic faith) to join. The next day there was a "long talk with Mrs. Cummings."

During the year that followed three groups, the Women's Art Association, the Girls' Friendly Society (sponsors of immigrants) and the Dominion Women's Enfranchisement Association affiliated at the national level. But the priority was to carry the organizing spirit to local towns and cities, where literally dozens of Councils sprang into being. Ishbel restricted her work abroad for the International Council of Women to an attempt in May to bring a British group into the fold. The challenge lay closer at hand, to build the Canadian body into a tower of strength as an example for other countries to follow.

Questions of faith were the first vexation. Ishbel met with and organized a "v. cordial" group in Montreal in November, but choosing a vice-president, preferably French-speaking and Catholic was delayed until Archbishop Fabre could be brought round — "The ladies themselves want to join." The women of Quebec City were separated even more sharply by language as well as religion: "Fancy the wives of both Presbyterian ministers neither understanding nor speaking French *in Quebec!*" wrote Ishbel.

The preliminary meeting in Quebec was discouraging: the Catholics were strict and the Protestants narrow, and both groups fiercely divided among themselves. "None of the ladies present ventured to speak. Some gentlemen came to the rescue." She would encounter the same traumatic dumbness in Edmonton in October 1894, when "the ladies were allowed to bring their male belongings as escorts," and were in consequence "intensely silent." When she visited Edmonton the following year the men had been left at home and the ladies read their reports "nicely but shyly".

Ishbel was not unprepared for religious rivalries. They were part and parcel of the times. She had noted the alarming burst of activity of the Protestant Protective Association in southern Ontario, with its strident campaign against Thompson, Laurier and all other Catholics in politics, and its efforts to dissuade voters from casting ballots for Catholic candidates at any level of government. She bent her diplomatic skills to achieve a balanced representation in those holding office in the local Councils of Women: in Montreal a Protestant president and Catholic vice-president, in Quebec City the opposite arrangement. Ottawa ladies thwarted her efforts by nominating additional vice-presidents and upsetting the balance, then choosing as Treasurer Mrs. Henrietta Muir Edwards (later one of the famous five Canadian women who, in the 1929 "Persons" case, signed the petition which changed the British North America Act and gave women eligibility to the Senate). Ishbel saw her in 1894 as "rather aggressively Evangelical, in a post which will bring her in contact with the R.C.'s." She sighed: "The election of officers at these public meetings without nomination previously is a mistake."[16]

Her greatest triumph was in persuading the Councils to open their meetings with a moment of silent prayer. A prayer of *some* sort was considered essential — but what prayer and by whom? She ran into the dilemma first in south-western Ontario. A crowd of 2000 thronged her inaugural meeting at the London Opera House, but this auspicious welcome was diluted:

> There was a great desire here to begin the meetings with Bible and prayer — this could not be if we had any intention of keeping the R.C.'s and others... A very aggressive little person, Mrs. Thornby, president of that *very American* W.C.T.U., asked the question publicly if we were to include societies not acknowledging God and Christ. I pointed out that we were to include all societies and institutions. Most seemed quite satisfied... but she will doubtless give trouble and would not mind excluding R.C.'s, Jews, Unitarians and Quakers... Mrs. [Elizabeth] Tilly [representing the King's Daughters] was nervous and afraid of the W.C.T.U...[17]

Jewish women had joined the Councils in Montreal and Toronto and "helped us heartily"; despite opposition from the Archbishop of Montreal the Catholic ladies were also joining — was this to be upset by the London W.C.T.U.'s motion to introduce an avowal of Christian faith in the constitution? Ishbel wrote in her Journal, as the first annual meeting opened in Ottawa in April 1894:

> Women here who have generally only as yet had to do with organizations on a religious or church basis cannot under-stand... I was beginning to fear a real outbreak of contro-versy and hard words. But once more I am rebuked for want of faith; for now just at the moment some of the best and most earnest women in London, after many volumes of agonized correspondence began to see the light and I had a telegram

last night to say... they accepted the original constitution without alteration and that they also join in the nomination of Lady Thompson and Mme Laurier [both Catholic] as joint V-P's... I have great, great hopes of this Council making a meeting place for all.

It was strange to note the unaccustomed sensation which came over the assembly as we all knelt for a few minutes in silent prayer for the opening of the meeting. The mere fact of being able to do this, with the full sanction of the ecclesiastical authorities seems good and hopeful...[18]

She was not yet out of the woods in this issue. As the new executive met at Rideau Hall at the end of the convention a deputation of London ladies insisted on an audience and "gave it us hot about 'unworthy compromise', 'shirking', 'praying with base motives', etc... I tried to answer as courteously as possible, but felt boiling..." The question had to be put to a vote at each local Council, to appease the London diehards.

By then locals had been formed in half a dozen cities and towns in Ontario and Quebec, and during the remaining months of 1894 Ishbel would personally establish them in the Maritimes and in the prairies as she and her husband journeyed east and west.

Aug. 14. St. John. A real busy day... at lunch sat next R.C. Bishop Sweeny and got him to consent to his ladies joining a Council... Meeting at the Mechanics' Institute at 3: 1,300 seated, many standing... Lady Tilley, pres.; Mrs. Turnbull, V-P; Mrs. Dr. Travers, V-P, an R.C. lady, sister of the Bishop, a great triumph and surprised everybody... So far, so good...
Aug. 24. Halifax. Meeting of the Local Council. Mrs. Montgomery Moore [wife of the British commander of the Fleet stationed at Halifax] and Mrs. Daly [wife of the Lieutenant-Governor] on my left and right... The W.C.T.U. very cordial here...
Aug. 28. Yarmouth. Forming their Council. This is a very go-ahead little town of 8,000 inhabitants with an exceedingly good ocean service to Boston...These provinces never cared for Confederation... and they still need to be made much of and made to feel that they are as directly linked with Great Britain as ever they were... The Women's Councils appear to have great possibilities... It all means so much more fresh

responsibility, but after all that is what we are here for.

Sept. 25. Port Arthur. H.E. visited Fort William, three miles away. A good deal of jealousy between the two towns... At 4, meeting at Town Hall for formation of Local Council, Mrs. Gibbs of King's Daughters taking initiative... Council to be for the District of Thunder Bay.

Oct. 12. Maple Creek. A raw little town represented by a rough little crowd of rude children at the station... A talk to some ladies, with the result that probably another Local Council will be formed here...

Nov. 7. Victoria. Our 17th wedding day. A wonderful meeting held in the Theatre for the formation of a local Women's Council. Place packed to the roof, and Lieut-Gov. and Mrs. Dewdney who were supposed to be opposed to it asked to come and were very cordial. The Bishop also has given us much more personal help than any other Anglican Bishop in Canada... A strike of Post Office clerks. They get only $29 a month, an allowance [for higher West Coast living costs] promised but not paid, owing to the mismanagement of the Dominion authorities... the sympathy of the public is very much on the side of the men... We like Victoria *very* much...

Nov. 16. Donald, B.C. Looked in at a local dance which brings everyone together every Friday night. The arrangements were all quite primitive and no attempt at evening dress. The floor master not only announces dances but *calls:* 'Salute your partner... Grand chain *Sway* to the right,' etc... They seemed to appreciate our coming. Mrs. Spragge wants to form an East Kootenay Local Council for many small places nearby...

Aug. 2, 1895. Qu'Appelle. To see the Indian mission schools. We have done our duty to the Show [Agricultural Exhibition, Regina]; H.E. has gone round the stock and through many tents of exhibits; we have sat in the grand-stand for hours and watched races of many kinds, broncho busting, musical rides, polo, horse and cattle parades, and the inevitable jugglers and clowns and other monstrosities of a Fair of this kind... I also had a little preliminary meeting about the Women's Council in our tent on the grounds, the ladies of the W.C.T.U. being the main people... One of the young ladies valiantly attacked H.E. [because] beer was served on the grounds. H.E. rose to the occasion and defended the beer & they parted friends, though doubtless the young lady was not convinced. It is a pity that the Temperance women should adopt this rabid tone... They train their younger women to be so self-asserting... They are essentially *American*...

Twenty local Councils were flourishing by the end of 1895. They were developing briefs, petitioning governments and forcing public debate on: supervision of immigrant children and immigrant servant girls; providing visiting nurses to care for the sick in their own homes; starting manual training and domestic science courses in schools; setting up employment bureaus and relief for the unemployed; appointing female officers to all charitable institutions receiving government grants; appointing female physicians in insane asylums; legislating equal pay for men and women teachers; arranging care of the aged poor in special homes instead of the common jail; endorsing international arbitration for the peaceable settlement of national disputes; promoting patriotic feelings in Canadian schools.

Ishbel said, after the first [1894] annual meeting:

I have never presided over any assembly of women where such attention has been paid to points of order and business-like proceedings and the whole tone has been very high throughout. In fact, the high level has been a revelation to the women themselves — they could not repress their astonishment at being themselves.

Her part

had been a bit of tough work to get this through... to get the really nice and influential women to take it up... For ourselves, our connection with the Council will prove of infinite value, as it will bring us into contact with all sorts and conditions of women who work for the good of the community. Through them we get our hand on the pulse of the country in a way in which we would never hope to do in the usual course of traveling about, holding formal ceremonies and receptions.[19]

The National Council of Women of Canada would continue to grow and flourish under her skilled guidance — while she sent her private secretary, Miss Teresa Wilson, to Europe to keep up contacts for the ICW.

But meanwhile, suddenly, late in 1894 after scarcely more than a year in Canada, the Countess Ishbel of Aberdeen found herself heart and centre of a political intrigue that called into play the native guile and shrewd political instinct that were as much a part of her as human sympathy and the call to

Front Entrance Rideau Hall, Ottawa, in the 1890's.

service.

The Tory government was faced with another leadership crisis. For the second time in three short years since the death of John A. Macdonald, a new prime minister must be chosen for office. Honest, upright, sagacious Sir John Thompson, with whom the Aberdeens had formed a most amiable relationship, died unexpectedly in London on 12 December 1894. There was no obvious successor in the cabinet. Events of the days and weeks that followed have been passed over lightly by most historians. Yet the part played by an uncertain Governor-General and by his wife who was very certain indeed, were such as might have eclipsed in significance the 1926 "scandal" of Lord Byng, who used his viceregal power to call Meighen to office against the advice of embattled Prime Minister Mackenzie King. The constitutionality of Byng's action has been laboured for over sixty years. But what of the Aberdeens? Have historians been unable to accept the boldness of the true politician at Rideau Hall who was a woman?

Chapter 12
December 1894

S he had thought the Liberals a poor lot, scarcely worth the name, when she saw them in Opposition in late 1891. She kept her eye, somewhat anxiously, on Wilfrid Laurier, looking for signs of greatness. Hesitation and uncertainty, as well as poor health, had marked the extended transfer of leadership to Laurier from Edward Blake. There had been vacillation in finding a convincing policy to put up against John A. Macdonald in the 1891 election, and a dismally unsuccessful flirtation with the notion of "reciprocal trade" between Canada and the United States. When in 1892 Thompson succeeded as Prime Minister, Laurier appeared to resign himself to this fresh evidence of Tory resilience. Canada might well be Conservative for evermore.

Still, eagerly and hopefully, Ishbel recorded after her first significant meeting with Laurier:

> May 19 [1894]. Mr. and Mrs. Laurier and Dr. and Mrs. Bourinot dined tonight. M. Laurier as leader of the Opposition has not been able to dine before. *He is a brilliant man* and very agreeable socially — talks English v. well — is an immense admirer of the Scotch.

In his rise to prominence in the party Laurier had shown great promise. He had severed the party's ties with the discredited *Rouges*. At the same time he had managed to affirm that church and state must keep respectfully separate, and this had gone over well in Quebec as well as the rest of Canada. His youthfully zealous declaration in 1885 that he would have "shouldered a musket" at the side of Louis Riel endeared him forever to the French. His eloquent admiration for British institutions had been equally effective in Ontario. As an orator no one could match him.

Lord Aberdeen, about 1894.

All fall, in 1894, there had been talk of an early election. After all, this parliament had been running for more than three years, under three Tory prime ministers. Thompson had never looked better. Cabinet members like young Sir Charles Hibbert Tupper were keen to win re-election before Laurier found his feet as Opposition leader. Charles Hibbert had voiced his fears to the prime minister after Laurier "made a triumphant march to the Pacific Coast, received every-where with open arms."[1] No one doubted there would be an election soon, probably when the prime minister returned from London.

On 26 November 1894, the Aberdeens had moved to Montreal to take up residence for the winter. They had taken the Sir John Abbott house, "roomy, comfortable and decorated in good taste." Ishbel had gone shopping, on very icy streets with the horses slipping and stumbling, and had purchased some "bits of furniture". Marjorie and Archie were enrolled in a YWCA cookery class and in Miss Barnjum's physical drill class where they would use Indian clubs and dumb-bells. Marjorie celebrated her fourteenth birthday, bewailing the loss of her youth. On 10 December the Aberdeens held a Drawing Room, the smart Montreal ladies decked in veils and plumes.

Then, on Wednesday, 12 December, Ishbel wrote:

> A black day indeed for Canada, for Sir John Thompson died suddenly at Windsor Castle shortly after being sworn in as Privy Councillor by the Queen... The news could not be believed here... As for ourselves, his friendship has been one of the brightest features of our stay in Canada.[2]

Thompson had just been seated at luncheon at Windsor Castle when he suffered severe chest pains. He retired from the room, but returned shortly, insisting all was well. A few minutes later he collapsed from a massive coronary attack It was learned that his physician in Ottawa had that fall pronounced him reasonably fit but with a potentially troublesome valvular disease of the heart. The Prime Minister was only 50.

The British newspapers were full of shock, eulogy and speculation. The Queen expressed grief. The Colonial Secretary, the Marquis of Ripon, was so strongly moved that he arranged the outfitting of a ship of war, the *Blenheim*, to convey Thompson's body home to Halifax. The Times by the next morning had its despatch from Ottawa: "Business is practically at a standstill here, and the people are gathered in groups at the street corners discussing the political outlook... A great blow to the country..." Reuters in Montreal had already cabled London that: "It is expected that the Governor-General, who is now in Montreal, will send for Hon. Mackenzie Bowell, the Minister of Trade and Commerce, to form a new Ministry," a guess based on the fact that the old senator was Acting Prime Minister in Thompson's absence by virtue of seniority. Actually, Bowell had been around for many years as a sop to Anti-Catholics; his association with the Orange Lodge was well known. Of late he had proved an encumbrance in cabinet and Thompson had been waiting for the appropriate moment to retire him. He had delayed too long.[3] Reuters modified the premature assumption a day later, saying "cabinet conferences were proceeding" on the question of succession.

British papers declared the successor would be Sir Charles Tupper, Canadian High Commissioner in London, to whom "probability points" as "the only possible choice". The Glasgow *Herald* (13 Dec.) went so far as to testify that "Sir Charles Tupper, now in England, can alone unite and lead the Conservative party, which has been in power in Canada for 22 of the 28 years which have elapsed since Confederation." A *Leader* reporter approached Tupper, but was scolded for impertinence: the query was "quite improper" and the assumption "totally unauthorized". The doughty stentorian statesman from Nova Scotia was a man who radiated power, with a leonine head, bristling sideburns and square, clean-shaven jaw; he had bullied his province into Confederation and had been highly valued by Sir John A. Macdonald. But if he had any private intention of succeeding Thompson he did not make it known during those first agitated days in London. Indeed, he succumbed to a severe bout of influenza and, according to the *Standard* (22 Dec.) was advised not to go back to Canada on the *Blenheim* with the body.

On that first black Wednesday, half a world from London, every flag in the small city of Vancouver was flying at half-mast by noon. The papers came out with deep black borders; all outgoing trains were heavily draped in black crape. Charles Hibbert Tupper, Sir Charles' son, Minister of Marines and Fisheries, was traveling that day from Victoria to New Westminster. He remarked on the flags lowered on their staffs, and was dumbfounded when he ran into reporters on the station platform who told him the grim news. For once, young Tupper guarded his tongue. He told the *Empire* he couldn't imagine who the new leader would be, and broke away to cancel engagements and find a train to Ottawa.

Traveling in Ontario, where church bells were sadly tolling by noon in every city and hamlet, two other cabinet ministers were engaged in a pleasantly successful political tour. They were J.C. Haggart, Minister of Railways and Canals, and J.C. Patterson, Minister of Militia. Haggart was a self-made, blunt-spoken Perth miller with a Mark Twain moustache and an uncanny political instinct: they liked him in the rural ridings and small towns where most Canadians lived in the 1890's.

He and Patterson arrived in Listowel at noon and were handed an Ottawa telegram. It said: "Thompson died at Windsor" but so incredulous were the pair that both thought it must surely mean Thompson had "dined" there. The message confirmed, they also canceled meetings and caught an Ottawa-bound train. Did Haggart know that he had been Thompson's choice to succeed him, as Lady Thompson was telling Lady Aberdeen by noon the next day?

On Parliament Hill another leading cabinet minister, tall, poker-straight George Eulas Foster, Finance Minister, was first in Ottawa to learn of the London despatch. Foster was a former classics professor from the Maritimes, believed to be very intelligent and incorruptible. He also would be seen as a possible leader.

With a colleague, Foster hurried through corridors to the Senate offices to inform Bowell. Bowell insisted it was only a newspaper rumour. Sandford Fleming, who happened to be on hand, offered to wire the CPR cable office for confirmation. When it came Bowell burst into tears, and said he couldn't possibly be the one to go and inform Lady Thompson. ("It is your duty, Mr. Bowell," Foster told him sternly.)

In Montreal, the governor-general and his wife had received the news. Ishbel's first thought was for Lady Annie Thompson, who had become her dear friend. She knew there was surprisingly little money in the family, and several Thompson children to educate; she knew how dearly Sir John and Lady Annie Thompson had loved and supported each other. She wired the house on Ottawa's Somerset Street and asked if Annie wished her to come; the answer was yes. Ishbel organized everything for a quick departure to Ottawa at 9:30 next morning, 13 December.

Her journal adds, almost as an afterthought, that "H.E." decided to go also, to "be on the spot to consider for whom to send to form a ministry... It is a delicate situation."[4]

In fact so delicate and difficult did it seem that Aberdeen had cabled London, asking the Colonial Secretary for advice. Strictly speaking, whether or not Aberdeen appreciated all the niceties of the situation, instructions could not properly be given by Britain to a self-governing ex-colony, but Aberdeen had obviously felt the need for guidance. Ripon carefully distanced himself from the decision in his reply received in Ottawa next day.

Aberdeen's cable, decoded, reads:

> Secret. Wednesday night. I would like L. [his Lordship?] advise regarding present situation. Bowell acting Premier is elderly and has not commanding influence although an estimable man, but an orangeman.
>
> Minister of Finance Foster for an alternative is undoubtedly ablest. He is a Protestant but not bigoted. Sir John had high opinion of him.
>
> Doubtful which has most following or which would be preferred as leader by party in coming elections.
>
> On public grounds I would deprecate either Sir C. Tupper's. I go to Ottawa tomorrow morning.
>
> Please telegraph instructions.[5]

His reason for "deprecating" the Tuppers, father and son, were best known to himself, but seems to have been as much a matter of personal prejudice as anything else. The older Tupper, bluff, arrogant, bombastic, usually victorious, was not Aberdeen's sort of fellow. Possibly some of Tupper's dealings in London on steamship lines to Canada had seemed nefarious. The son, equally strong-willed and more volatile, had the advantage only of a shorter list of political misdemeanours.

At 1:30 on Thursday Lord and Lady Aberdeen accompanied by their secretary Arthur Gordon and Aide-de-Camp David Erskine, pulled into the Ottawa station, to be met by Thompson's distraught secretary Douglas Stewart. It is likely that the Aberdeens had as they traveled had a chance to read some of the previous day's Canadian papers, where detailed accounts of the tragedy mingled with speculation. The Hamilton *Spectator* "demanded" that Sir Charles Tupper be called. The Hamilton *Times* thought this development probable. The Hamilton *Herald* concurred: "Sir Charles Tupper may possibly be asked to take the leadership, and in some quarters the Honourable John Haggart is looked upon as a possibility." The Toronto *World* picked Haggart — if he would not accept, then George Foster. Between them, Foster and Haggart could come to an understanding and assume command, the *World* maintained. The Montreal *Star* considered the two Tuppers, though one, Sir Charles, was "too old", the other "too young". The Montreal *Witness* said: "Everything points to the succession of Sir Charles Tupper." The London *Advertiser* said: "It is to the veteran statesman who fills the great position of High Commissioner of Canada in England that the eyes of the Liberal-Conservative ranks may turn instinctively for leadership." The Toronto *Globe* had the same view: there was a general feeling at City Hall that "Sir John's death would not strengthen the party in Ontario, unless Sir Charles Tupper could be induced to come back from England and lead the party." There were other kind opinions about both Foster and Haggart.

For the acting Prime Minister, Senator Bowell, no paper had a word of commendation. One put it bluntly: "Mr. Bowell is narrow-minded, limited in his views, and an Orangeman, and certainly not acceptable to a large section of the party."

Ishbel set down her own summation. She assessed the contenders:

> Mr. Mackenzie Bowell was only appointed premier in Sir John's absence... Mr. Foster the Minister of Finance is an able man, a good speaker and a good man, but [there is] that clique against him and his wife, because they married in the United States after she divorced her husband... And Mr. Haggart who is the strongest man is admittedly a Bohemian. Mr. Mackenzie Bowel himself is 75 [in fact 70], rather fussy and decidedly commonplace, also an Orangeman — but he is a good & straight man & he has great ideas about the drawing together of the colonies and the Empire, as was evidenced by all the trouble he took about getting up that Conference.[6]

On arrival, the Aberdeens were driven first to the Thompson home where Ishbel spent an hour or two with the stricken woman whose husband, the centre and whole concern of her life had suddenly left her. But Lady Annie Thompson was a strong woman, and while she poured out her acute grief, her concern for her sons and daughters, her fear of the future, she also turned to Ishbel to make certain that everyone knew at once where the political succession ought to lie. She, like the Aberdeens, detested Sir Charles Tupper, and for more valid personal reasons, for she had ample evidence in letters from her husband of Tupper's brazen manner of taking credit for achievements (when both were consultants with the British delegation in negotiations at Washington) that rightfully were Thompson's. In response to Annie's concerns, Lady Aberdeen "was able to reassure her as to H.E.'s intentions about this. Never if he could help it should Sir Charles be again in Canadian politics."[7]

Lady Thompson insisted that: "Mr. Haggart was the man that would be best able to keep the party together", which she said had been her husband's view.[8] She was anxious to see Lord Aberdeen, for the decision would not wait.

Ishbel recorded, of that long conversation, "She is unfortunately a bit cynical, and looks upon politics as a game of chess, but she has a clear head and good judgment and has been of infinite use to Sir John."[9] But Ishbel, in the first of a number of highly dubious actions that day, did not accept Annie's judgment nor give Aberdeen a chance to hear it. Her own solution to the crisis was rapidly forming in her mind.

As soon as she could leave her friend, Ishbel went up to her husband's office in the Parliament Buildings where Aberdeen was waiting for her arrival. He had just received Ripon's cable in reply to his own:

> This is not an occasion on which instructions can be given by Her Majesty's government. But my advice as a friend is to ask the acting Premier after consultation with his colleagues to come and advise you as to whom you should send for to form an administration. This is preferable to your making any independent selection.[10]

It was a most significant cable, one which unfortunately has missed the eye of those recounting these events. It appears never to have been read by Canadian historians, perhaps because it was unavailable in the Public Archives in Ottawa, although on record in London. It was not an endorsement of Bowell. It said plainly that Aberdeen ought to get advice from the cabinet, through Bowell, and Aberdeen ought *not* to make his own decision.

Aberdeen in his memoirs, tells a different story:

> ...I decided to consult, in a non-official manner, the Colonial Secretary, not merely because of his position as such, but because he was a reliable personal friend. I therefore cabled in cipher to the Marquis of Ripon, explaining the situation; and I received a very considerate reply in which Lord Ripon

Historical Ball, Senate Chamber, Ottawa, Lord and Lady Aberdeen front centre, 1896.

said that, although he could not advise in an official capacity, he could, as a friend, express the opinion that, on the whole, the circumstances which I mentioned regarding Sir Mackenzie Bowell seemed to indicate a balance in his favour.[11]

Ripon had said no such thing. The mists of time, and the self-serving caution of old age, apparently altered Aberdeen's recollection. His story has, however, been used in several places as the reason for his subsequent choice.

So there was Aberdeen, on his own in Ottawa. If he followed Ripon's advice he would insist on collective advice from the cabinet as to which new leader would be preferred by the Conservative party, with its commanding majority in the House of Commons. If the ministers, jostling among themselves, did not provide him with a name, he might at least have consulted prominent Tories, of whom there were plenty in the capital and in Montreal. Instead, with one slight exception, he conferred with no one but Bowell himself — and his wife Ishbel.

Her *Journal* records that for the rest of that day she was with her husband almost continually. She read the cable from

Ripon. A short time later a note was sent to Bowell. It requested a "preliminary" chat; it also suggested that Bowell take prior counsel with his colleagues. Ishbel waited until Bowell's reply came back.

What it said was that as to consulting his colleagues, it seemed unlikely that any of them would agree. But *he* would be happy to come for a talk, "leaving H.E. quite free to send for someone else afterwards," as Ishbel records it.

Bowell was plainly putting himself forward for the job, without any backing from his cabinet. He was interpreting Aberdeen's summons as an invitation.

Ishbel left her husband at that point, and he had his first talk with Bowell. A mutually amiable conversation took place, discussing the funeral arrangements among other things. In the minds of both men, whatever the exact words used, it was also a move in the direction of a formal summons to become prime minister. It is known that they also talked of dissolving parliament, and Bowell was given to understand that, as prime minister, he could make this move without the necessity of consulting his cabinet. Aberdeen appeared to anticipate an immediate election.[12]

After Bowell left Aberdeen called in one more visitor, a somewhat thick-witted senator, Sir Frank Smith, minister without portfolio. As a Catholic it was assumed he could clear up the one hesitation in Aberdeen's mind: Bowell had been Grand Master of the Orange Order of Ontario — would it be seen as an affront to the Catholic population if Bowell was called? Smith told Aberdeen, according to Ishbel's journal, that Bowell had been careful never to offend an R.C. That seemed to suffice. Aberdeen saw no one else; he left his office for Rideau Hall, to join Ishbel.

Ishbel records rather tersely what happened next. "After a bit we drove back to the [railway] car for dinner." Their dinner ran late. After it, "H.E. returned to the Office and sent for Mr. Mackenzie Bowell and commissioned him to form a government." It was now 10 o'clock in the evening of 13 December. "And I returned to Lady Thompson to tell her personally of H.E.'s decision."[13]

One ludicrous development added to the political clamour that followed. In Montreal the *Witness,* a Liberal paper, seized on the curious summons to His Excellency's office of Sir Frank Smith, a nonentity. To everyone's astonishment, Smith confessed with some pride that Aberdeen had called on him to form a government, but he had modestly refused: "Yes, it is quite true that His Excellency did me the honour... but I told him... it would not suit me..."

This fantastic notion was only marginally worse than the actual selection of Mackenzie Bowell, the dull and rather petulant little printer-publisher from Belleville. The general lamentation of the press when the call to Bowell was made known is perhaps most eloquently stated in the grieving of the Halifax *Chronicle* that "so ordinary a politician" would become prime minister.

Leading members of the Conservative party were shocked and distressed. They wrote to each other about Bowell's weakness, age, remoteness as a senator from the voting public, and total inability to assume command. They wished they could find "honourable ways" of resigning. Even Sir Charles Hibbert Tupper, whose life blood was politics, talked longingly of retiring though he supposed one must soldier on.[14]

It had been a most peremptory proceeding. It is not even possible that the Aberdeens were unaware of Bowell's limitations. They had been in the country over a year; Bowell had dined at their table. Ishbel had been frank enough about his failings in her journal. Yet they foisted Bowell on his party and on the country. The question remains: why?

Ishbel, amid all the tributes to Thompson and sympathy for the family that filled page after page of her journal on 14 December, included one fact that had leaped to her mind even as she contemplated the choices. *There would be an election and the Liberals could win it,* "taking all things into consideration and Laurier's attractive personality and eloquence contrasted to the want of any strong man or even any outstanding figure amongst the crowd of commonplaces in the Cabinet."[15]

An opportunity was open to Aberdeen. He could use the unique prerogative of his office to call in a man unable to prevent a Liberal victory. It would all be over soon. An election would be held, and in the two-month campaign the silver tongued Laurier would be facing absurdly incompetent Bowell. This delightful "scenario" (to use a modern term) would in the event be frustrated by the vanity and vacillation of the man they had put in power.

Bowell undertook to make a few necessary changes in the cabinet before the new swearing-in, and he was given a few

Sir Mackenzie Bowell, Canada's Prime Minister December 1894 to May 1896.

days to do so. The Aberdeens took the train again late on the 14th for Montreal. But Ishbel could not resist going a step further. She was impatient to contact Laurier, who was at home in Arthabaska, attending to his law practice. Was Laurier alert to his great opportunity? She had to find out. Of course she couldn't travel to see him in person. But the journal says:

> Dec. 16. Mr. Erskine came back in the small hours this morning and brought good news of *his mission*.

There was an ostensible mission. It had to do with getting all-party agreement in the House of Commons to provide Lady Thompson with an annuity.

Mr. Laurier had already written to Mr. Ives suggesting the grant from Parliament.

There was the actual mission.

> They are also fully alive to the great desirability of getting such men as Mr. Fielding [William Fielding, Premier of Nova Scotia] & M. Joly [Henri Gustave de Lotbinière, former Quebec Premier] to join the Government if the Liberals come in. The difficulty will be to get them to leave the provinces, but surely they may be stirred to do this even at some personal sacrifice when they see the greatness of the opportunity. For it is very evident that with them now lies our hope as far as calibre is concerned, now that Sir John and his strong hand have gone. If only Laurier proves to be big enough.[16]

She finished the day's entry with a jab at the remnant cabinet which was apparently unable to agree on the wording for the funeral wreath: "A fair example of what we have to expect for the present."

Mr. Erskine's trip to Arthabaska, despite all precautions, was discovered by the diligent *La Presse* of Montreal, though it mistook the name, and credited Captain "Kinderly" (Captain Charles Kindersley, A.D.C. and Master of the Horse) with making the secret journey. *La Presse* headlined the story: "Was Mr. Laurier Consulted by the Governor-General?" Laurier issued a blunt statement dismissing the story as "devoid of truth" and "absurd".

Ishbel had tried to be a little too clever with that manoeuvre. It was relayed promptly to Bowell's ministers in

Ottawa, where much foot-dragging and wrangling impeded the formation of the government. The story had the effect of speeding up the process. The hold-outs decided to get in line. Some months later Ishbel heard of this from young Sir Charles Tupper whom she had, through various friendly overtures, gained as a confidante. On 18 July 1895 she recorded a long conversation with him:

> It seems that many of the present Administration were kicking at serving under Bowell, and were in fact refusing to do so. Several of them had decided to ask for an audience from H.E., to put the question to him personally... They were talking over this plan one evening some days after Sir Mackenzie had been commissioned to form a Government when it was heard that a paragraph in the paper, or rather a telegram to one of the ministers, stated that an A.D.C. of H.E. had been seen with Mr. Laurier. 'We all turned in like sheep to the fold, at the very rumour.'[17]

Bowell's administration was sworn in 21 December. There were few changes, though young Tupper had been won over with the Justice portfolio. Foster continued in Finance, Haggart in Railways and Canals. The government's main weakness, apart from Bowell himself, was the lack of good Quebec representation. Joseph Auguste Chapleau, one of the best and most moderate, had resigned in anger in 1892 over the failure of the government to over-rule the Manitoba legislature's decision to eliminate the sparsely attended Catholic schools in that province. Thompson had made the mistake of moving Chapleau out of politics to a lieutenant-governorship. There were few others of note. Dogmatic, unpopular Auguste Réal Angers continued as Agriculture minister. An even more dubious link with Quebec lay in Adolphe Caron, the Postmaster General — he would soon be the object of serious charges of scandal. Bowell, fearing to call an election, would be propelled into the Manitoba crisis with a party seriously undermined.

Sir John Thompson was buried in Halifax, 3 January 1895. Lady Aberdeen had undertaken to provide the pall to cover his coffin for the lying-in-state in the legislative building and the Cathedral funeral service. She had chosen white poplin, to be edged with a gold fringe and embroidered with a large gold cross. The finishing and embroidery were entrusted to the sisters of the Convent of the Good Shepherd in Montreal. But Ishbel herself did the careful sewing attaching the fringe, in an eerie late-night solitary vigil on New Year's Eve 1894. As she stitched, was she planning the burial of Thompson's party along with the corpse?

At least the pall looked splendid and appropriate when finished, its white and gold shining dramatically against the sombre black in which the Cathedral was draped for the occasion. Ishbel, looking down, felt also a burst of affection for her husband:

> H.E. looked very young and dear in his high seal with all the elderly men by his side, and right in front of him between him and the bishops was the coffin covered with our white and gold pall on which only the queen's wreath and our own lay, others being placed all round... The gold and white of the pall glistened out beautifully in the light of the many candles and electric light and seemed to focus one's thoughts on the glorious side of his life and death and to take the sting out of the nation's loss...
>
> The funeral car was the only blot in my mind for it looked heavy and out of proportion like a great four-post bed on wheels, quite apart from the horrid black plumes above and the six draped horses... It is still hard to believe that it is really Sir John we have been burying.[18]

One disquieting incident arose that day when Joseph Ouimet, the new minister of Public Works, "hinted" that he and the other cabinet members had learned "the fact of Mr. Bowell refusing to consult his colleagues about whom they wished to be Premier when H.E. invited him to." This "fact" would be "brought up", Ouimet intimated. They were not yet out of the woods. "But why did Mr. Bowell let this be known is the question," Ishbel demanded of her journal.

Two days later Bowell was knighted by her Majesty's good grace and appeared "very pleased" with himself. The cabinet apparently decided not to make an issue of Bowell's too-eager grasp at power. At least for the moment, the government held.

Meanwhile Ishbel set about establishing friendly communication with the leader of the Opposition. In one exchange of notes, when Laurier apologized to Ishbel for the roughness of political life, she reassured him: she had been "brought up from childhood in the atmosphere of politics."[19] She wrote delightedly in her journal of a subsequent "pleasant little talk" with Laurier in which the Opposition leader said "he would be very glad if I would write to him or let him know of anything he could do on any future occasion... I v. readily entered into a compact so to do."[20]

Bowell in office proved himself inadequate enough to satisfy all doomsayers. Subsequent testimony supports the opinion that he was a disaster for his party and the country. One of the strongest condemnations comes from Sir Joseph Pope, assistant clerk of the Privy Council, and former secretary to Sir John A. Macdonald, who in his memoirs wrote: "There followed days of weak and incompetent administration by a Cabinet presided over by a man whose sudden and unlooked-for elevation had visibly turned his head, a ministry without unity or cohesion of any kind, a prey to internal dissensions until they became a spectacle to the world, to angels and to men." Pope said sharply that Bowell was "as little qualified to be Prime Minister as Lord Aberdeen was to be Governor-General."[21]

In their series of sketches of Canadian prime ministers, Christopher Ondaatje and Donald Swainson describe Bowell's appointment as "ludicrous", and state that: "His short regime was an unmitigated disaster."[22]

Bruce Hutchison sounds bewildered as he writes: "How it [the Conservative party] came to choose Mackenzie Bowell is not clear even today... In choosing the fifth Prime Minister, *presumably after he had sounded out the cabinet*, Aberdeen was scraping the bottom of the barrel... A tiny, stupid man..."[23]

Joseph Schull says that in the cabinet of December 1894: "No one could agree on anything but the incapacity of Bowell."[24]

It cannot be pleaded that Aberdeen had a lack of better candidates. Of the men at hand, John Haggart was not only anxious for the job but seemed the most credible choice. He was liked personally by Sir John Thompson, whose own sterling qualities have only recently been fully presented in the biography by P. B. Waite, Haggart might have a "Bohemian" reputation, but it was no obstacle in Thompson's mind even though he himself was a devoted family man, and on occasion critical of the peccadillos of others, including Sir Charles Tupper. Thompson saw Haggart as the victim of an unfortunate early marriage, to a hometown girl, Caroline Douglas, described by Thompson as a "wild virago". Haggart was a politician's politician, tough, business-like and practical, with the sagacity to stay clear of political scandal in his constant dealings between railways and government—though in Perth he is remembered in a 300-yard gratuitous extension of the Tay Canal to serve his own mill, a stretch of waterway still called "Haggart's Ditch". He continued in politics for forty years, the longest record for any Canadian M.P.

Or George Foster might have served with a rather arid distinction.

But if Aberdeen had conscientiously looked for the ablest man to lead the Conservative government in December 1894, he would surely have called Sir Charles Tupper. Tupper had the contacts and influence to repair Conservative strength in Quebec, a vital consideration. It was believed he could have persuaded Chapleau to forsake the soft life of Spencer Wood to enter the cabinet again. After all, Tupper was firmly in favour of restoring the Catholic schools in Manitoba, which had been the cause of Chapleau's resignation.

Tupper was judged "bold, contemptuous, audacious... with roots of greatness. In constructive genius he has had no equal among the public men of Canada," by the contemporary correspondent and one-time editor of the *Globe*.[25] Sir Joseph Pope described him as a man "whose courage and amazing vitality evoked the strongest admiration alike from friend and foe."[26] Two modern Conservative analysts laud him in similar terms. "Tupper towered above his Conservative colleagues in political astuteness, and in the vigour and breadth of his conceptions," writes Lowell C. Clark.[27] And Heath Macquarrie argues: "He had been Macdonald's most able lieutenant for years. Tupper not only had a renowned reputation for his share in achieving Confederation and launching the National Policy, but his personal contacts abroad, in the Colonial office and the financial world, would ensure all possible assistance in obtaining new markets for Canadian products and improved oceanic transportation..."[28]

It is worth recalling that Queen Victoria, who personally disliked Gladstone as fiercely as the Aberdeens disliked Tupper, tried hard after Disraeli's defeat in 1880 to avoid calling on Gladstone to take office. She sought an alternative, she stalled, proposing Lord Hartington or Lord Granville instead. But Queen Victoria backed down and yielded to the advice of the majority party, swearing in Mr. Gladstone.

In 1894 Canada had had little experience in these procedures. Each succession had been indicated by a fairly obvious choice, which the governor-general put into effect after deliberation and consultation. The course followed by Lord Aberdeen is without precedent. It has been assumed that he simply followed Ripon's advice. There is another explanation, that the choice was a deliberate one to put in office a prime minister whom Wilfrid Laurier would have no difficulty in defeating at the polls. If this is the case, it was a flagrant abuse of the office of governor-general. The impropriety of his action mocks the tradition which allows the governor-general his one significant prerogative — to call on a new prime minister to replace the old. The rational expectation is that he will choose one who is likely to succeed.

The question remaining is the extent of Ishbel's part in the appointment. Of the two, Ishbel was the politician. Aberdeen alone could have made a foolish choice, but he had a high sense of propriety, of doing the right thing. And Ishbel's dominating role during Aberdeen's term is well known. Sir Charles Tupper once raged that Aberdeen was "a weak and incapable governor under controll [sic] of an ambitious and meddlesome woman."[29] Sir Joseph Pope was aghast at her interference, as he saw it, in affairs of state, relating a tale of Lady Aberdeen examining Treasury Minutes and consulting a deputy minister about them, to the D.M.'s horror.[30] Lowell Clark writes of her consuming interest in her husband's business: it was intolerable that she even knew what was going on or was "permitted to discuss" such matters.[31] These were Ishbel's political enemies. But John T. Saywell, in his extensive biographical introduction to her published *Journal,* wrote: "Almost at once she seized the initiative and retained it for the five years they remained in Canada. Aberdeen often followed where she bravely led... Aberdeen was not tough-minded, and even in his official duties as Governor-General often leaned on his wife for support and direction."[32]

These men knew, yet did not fully credit how boldly Ishbel guided her compliant husband in pursuit of the high goal of Liberal victory. The subsequent year and a half spin out the intrigue at Rideau Hall to give Canada to Wilfrid Laurier.

Chapter 13
1895

B owell, in line with his private agreement with Aberdeen, appeared ready to resign as soon as the air cleared on the Manitoba School question. A political hiatus occurred, while the Judicial Committee of the Privy Council pondered that matter. The Aberdeens resumed their sojourn in Montreal. Marjorie and Archie had remained there, joined by Haddo and Dudley on holiday from their schools in Britain, while their parents arranged the succession of the country's government. The Swedish governess, Miss Ebba Wettermen, brought them skis, something new in the Aberdeens' experience. "Enormously long wooden snowshoes, " Ishbel explained, "six and eight feet long. The children are managing them nicely."[1]

With maternal pride she reported a "delightful picture" of Marjorie painted by Wyatt Eaton, whose portraits of the great men of the CPR, George Stephen, Sir Donald Smith and William Van Horne, had brought him acclaim. Eaton had taken one look at Archie and decided he must also paint the charming small boy. "The opportunity of my life."[2] The result, showing a pink-cheeked wide-eyed angel in ruffles and blue velvet — the page costume — was completed more than a year later. It was probably the last of Eaton's portraits, for he was already in poor health. Ishbel was enchanted by the painting. "It is absolutely charming, very like, & beautifully painted. It will be quite a family possession... We hope to send this picture to the Academy for Mr. Eaton next year." Notman took family photographs.[3]

That year Ishbel, approaching her 38th birthday, was concerned about putting on weight. There was little opportunity for exercise during Canadian winters unless one went in for "violent games". She resorted in March to "one of those saddles for taking mechanical exercise" which she installed in her boudoir.[4]

The Aberdeens while in Montreal arranged an elaborate historical pageant designed to edify as well as entertain. Fourteen-year-old Marjorie starred first as Madeleine de Verchères and again as Evangeline in a series of tableaux. "Over two hundred people took part belonging to all the leading families of Montreal [French and English] and this in itself has produced a nice feeling," Ishbel wrote.[5] The program ended with the singing of "God Bless Our Fair Dominion", a tentative national anthem that failed to retain its popularity. Ishbel's youngest brother Archie turned up for the event. He, like Coutts, had failed as a rancher in the American West and he was in poor health. He was taken temporarily on staff as an extra aide-de-camp, Aberdeen bearing the cost. Archie Marjoribanks was now engaged to a southern belle, Myssie Brown, *not* in Ishbel's eyes a wise choice.

In February Lord and Lady Aberdeen returned briefly to Ottawa. The Privy Council decision for which they had all been waiting had been reached. It pronounced that the federal government had indeed the right to disallow the Manitoba Act. But since this was merely permissive, the government must now decide how to cope with the raging passions on both sides of the argument. The cabinet gave the impression on the whole of favouring "Remedial Legislation" but certain ministers disagreed. Those who feared the political cost of such an arbitrary move against a province wanted an election first. Those fiercely in favour of preserving Catholic schools wanted a bill then and there, before an election.

Bowell appeared to be swayed by the larger group. Rather dolefully, for there is no question he was enjoying his sudden elevation to the prime minister's office, he sent word to Lord Aberdeen that the government would dissolve for a May election. The next day he appeared in person to confirm this decision. The Governor-General asked him to set forth in writing the reasons for dissolution and, well satisfied, went back to Montreal.

He returned five days later. Bowell had reversed himself. He had been persuaded to stall a little longer. The government would allow an "appeal" against the decision of the Privy Council, with a hearing at which the Manitoba government could present its case again.

Ishbel was furious at Bowell's "characteristic indecision".[6] Her private hope for an upset in an election was heightened

Dressed for a court occasion, Lady Aberdeen with Marjorie, Dudley and Archie.

by a visit from the Oblate missionary priest from the West, Father Lacombe, who had much to say about the peril to the country of leaving the Manitoba situation unresolved. "He is very clear that the Government will be hopelessly defeated if they do not settle the question before going to the country," Ishbel wrote with rising anticipation.[7]

Whether the Conservatives had more to gain than to lose by calling an election at once was producing a stalemate in the cabinet. Bowell wavered from one side to the other. On 18 March when the appeal hearing was exhausted the cabinet held another all-day meeting, "but have again sent a message to say they have been unable to come to a decision — that news is getting a little stale."[8] It had gone on throughout the winter; the Aberdeens saw their neat scheme to set up Bowell for an immediate election foundering.

Again Lady Aberdeen filled up the time with a busy social program. She went without her husband to Washington, Baltimore and New York, taking with her handsome Bob Ferguson. She visited President Cleveland and his "pretty and attractive" wife. She took the occasion to visit congress:

...The scene presented would appear an impossible one. In the vast hall as one enters, one is conscious of a sort of subdued hubbub in a close and stifling atmosphere. As one's eye becomes accustomed to the scene, one perceives one member smoking a cigar, another a pipe, another sitting with his feet on his desk enjoying a joke with his neighbours, some writing letters, some walking about, some whistling or clapping their hands to arrest the attention of the pages... The speaking is only done by grievance mongers for their constituents.[9]

When she had time, she expanded on her observations:

The ultra-fashionable set at Washington, led by a few to whom expense is no object, raises one's whole inner antagonism... my antipathy to the essential spirit of the American people, their customs, their everything, grows every time I come in contact with them, and my thankfulness that there is still such an essential difference between them and the Canadians — how any Canadian with a grain of common-sense or self-respect can even consider the possibility of his country throwing in its lot with the United States is as much a mystery to me as the craze young Englishmen seem to have for marrying American girls...[10]

This remark was prompted not only by brother Archie's attachment to Myssie Brown but by the engagement in Washington of Lord George Curzon, whose meteoric career as under secretary for India had brought him great public attention, to Mary Victoria Leiter, daughter of a Chicago millionaire: "She looked lovely in a gorgeous gown but oh! he is taking a big risk if all accounts be true."[11]

Ishbel had gone to Washington in her capacity as president of the International Council of Women to attend the Triennial meeting of the U.S. National Council, and she spoke, not without feeling "very quaky", at a dinner where Rudyard Kipling and his wife were among the special guests. She thought Mrs. Lowe-Dickinson [sic] the incoming U.S. NCW president, hardly up to the calibre of her predecessor, Mrs. Wright Sewell, a leading suffragette, but she adored the aging Susan B. Anthony. Despite her reaction to their "tone and talk and ways" she formed a positive opinion of the group, whose conduct of meetings was an example Congress might well have followed. Ishbel had her own political world to run. She came away determined that British women now organized in a National Union of Women Workers must become an affiliate of the ICW. They could then take responsibility for the next international gathering, to be held in London, and give a better direction to the ICW.

On her way to rejoin "H. E." in Toronto, Ishbel attended a somewhat dismal Women's Council affair in Hamilton, where a luncheon had been scheduled for 1:30, was delayed by a blizzard, and turned into a full-course dinner "at 4:30 of all terrible hours". Her train arrived late and the food had turned chilly, but they all worked their way gravely through numerous courses, "the ladies somewhat self-conscious that something out of the way was going on." Toasts were called for, but no wine appeared on the table through the strong intervention of the WCTU faction. "I innocently imagined we were intended to drink them in water but telegraphic looks went around when I lifted my glass and then I discovered the Temperance people had decided that it would be inconsistent for women to raise their glasses at all." On this memorable occasion, "toasts" were responded to mutely, while the ladies kept their hands in their laps. "The Jewish women of the Council" had dissociated themselves from the others with a subversive gesture: they had sent up some claret and moselle to the house of the President, Mrs. Lyle, where I went to take off my things." But Ishbel had left the bottles to the pleasure of Mr. Lyle and Bob Ferguson, who dined alone while the ladies were "disporting themselves" at the Royal Hotel at their comfortless great meal.[12]

She attended a more congenial Council meeting in Toronto. Her husband had come to the city to take part in a curling bonspiel and "came home the proud possessor of a grand silver mounted broom... He enjoys being able to play with the stones here instead of the irons at Ottawa." Ishbel found time to attend the provincial legislature where she was escorted by the Sergeant-at-Arms to a chair on the floor of the chamber on the right of the Speaker, as she was accustomed to sit in Ottawa, and there she reveled in the dignified atmosphere and the striking contrast to the United States Congress. "Let the friends of annexation visit the two, and say which would be the better for being annexed."[13] After these diversions the Aberdeens re-entered the long argument in Ottawa, more impatient than ever to accept Bowell's resignation and let the country proceed to an election. Bowell, however, confessed that "still the government cannot make up its mind as to its intentions."[14]

One member of the cabinet had certainly made up his mind. It was the younger Sir Charles (Hibbert) Tupper, Minister of Justice. Paradoxically Ishbel was drawn to the bumptious Tupper — ignoring his unconcealed loyalty to his terrible father. The younger Tupper wanted an election at once — so did Ishbel. *He* argued that such a show of resolution would bring the Conservatives back into power before it was too late; *she* was sure they were already doomed.

Young Tupper hoped to hasten the process by presenting a "Remedial Order" to Manitoba, instead of bringing legislation before the house. The Order was approved by cabinet 19 March, signed by His Excellency 21 March, and issued to Manitoba forthwith. Ishbel rejoiced. "It is something to be thankful for that they have at least come to this decision... Their own supporters are getting utterly disgusted by the long continued shilly-shallying attitude."

But now Senator Auguste Angers, the leading French Canadian in the government, dug in his heels. There must be a Remedial Bill, he insisted. If there was not, he would resign and perhaps take other Quebec members with him.

Bowell swung over to his side. Parliament had not been sitting during the entire cabinet wrangle. Bowell now called

Sir Charles Hibbert Tupper.

it into session for April, for the purpose of introducing a Remedial Bill. Its progress through parliament would of course mean another long delay.

Tupper, infuriated, now threatened *his* resignation. He wrote to Bowell that he was indeed committed to remedial legislation if Manitoba failed to respond to the Order, but an election was necessary: "we can do nothing effectively or properly without a direct mandate from the people." Moreover, "fear of defeat" in an election was unworthy: "I cannot be a party to a course dictated by dread of the people." Their policy must be "fearless". What Bowell was proposing was "indecent".[15] He accused the Prime Minister of giving in to those ministers who wanted to stall a while longer.

Bowell's reply is interesting in that it refers back to his "call" by the Governor-General, and an assurance given by Aberdeen that as Prime Minister Bowell wouldn't need to consult anyone about calling an election. Aberdeen expected him to do so immediately. So now this vain little man, sure of his authority, chose *not* to call an election. He told Tupper that perhaps the country would cool down a bit if an election was deferred.[16]

In another exchange of letters, Tupper raged: "The ship could have been saved by pluck." The rest of the cabinet had tamely followed Bowell: "Not a man stood by me... when I protested an old man's folly and tyranny."[17]

Hot-headed Charles Tupper had talked himself into a position he would have difficulty reversing. Should he resign in solitary protest? At this point a letter came to him from Lady Aberdeen, saying she wished to see him, and could he come for lunch?

The invitation became a dinner engagement the following evening, 27 March, with Sir Charles Tupper and Lady Tupper the guests of the Aberdeens at Government House. "We both talked to him, and to her."[18] It was a most friendly conversation. Every effort was made to persuade Tupper not to resign. Ishbel stressed his fine prospects if he could practice a little patience. To clinch the matter they wired the strong man of the Conservative party, Senator Drummond, to come up from Montreal and talk to Tupper. As a result, Tupper met with Bowell, reached an accommodation, and stayed on. He was quite overwhelmed by the Aberdeens' show of friendly concern, and wrote:

> Lady Tupper and I feel under deep obligation to her Excellency and yourself for your exceedingly kind consideration of the most difficult problem of my life. We have earnestly dwelt upon all you were both good enough to say to us.[19]

What were Ishbel's motives here? The most bluntly political interpretation is that she saw that Tupper stood alone and his single resignation would not endanger the government. As long as he stayed in Bowell's cabinet, however, he would be a constant irritant, demanding an election — playing their game.

Tupper's motives probably coincided with hers. The press speculated that Tupper had an eye only to his own future, wanting an end to the embarrassing spectacle of the Bowell regime, foreseeing a Liberal victory and a term in opposition, and himself as leader of a resurgent Conservative party when the tide turned. In May, when rumours of his resignation were again current, the Montreal *Star* said that Tupper's colleagues were "down on him" because "they resent his aspirations for future leadership *at the price of a present Liberal victory*."[20] Was it Ishbel who planted the seed of this ambition?

Or was she merely showing a warm-hearted concern for a bright young man imperiling his career? "Sir Charles is the strongest man no doubt in the Government and one with a future if he can but curb his temper and be less overbearing. We have made great friends with the Tuppers over this and they have really been v. nice."[21]

What is beyond doubt is that she made an ally, in truth a political accomplice, of the younger Tupper, who would shortly be bringing her tales of caucus and party, and their difficulties.

In July Ishbel wrote a comprehensive summary of the Manitoba school crisis for her friends and colleagues back home. She fully appreciated the angry divisions within Canada:

> A pretty pickle is it not? I think it is often not recognized what a great difficulty had to be contended with in the government of this country through the necessity of every Administration having to be practically a coalition Ministry having a French speaking section and an English speaking section, and not only having to represent different races &

creeds strongly antagonistic to each other, but also different Provinces each with different interests & with different provincial laws. But woe be to the Premier who forgets these different elements & thinks merely of a broad Liberal or Conservative policy.[22]

Her remedy for the current debacle was a Liberal federal government. Since Manitoba's government was Liberal, "it is rumoured that they would be found more tractable if their own Party with Mr. Laurier at its head were to be returned to power in the Dominion Government." Laurier appeared "very confident of being able to deal with the question satisfactorily" though he was equally determined not to be drawn into announcing their policy whilst in Opposition." Laurier was in fact infuriating the cabinet with his posture of smiling silence, while the Conservatives tore themselves apart.

Parliament had opened in April, as Bowell had promised. The Speech from the Throne was designed to satisfy the hardliners: it promised legislation to disallow the Manitoba Act. The formal Opening was enhanced for Ishbel by the presence of her elegant sister-in-law Fanny (Churchill) Marjoribanks, who was as clever about politics as Ishbel herself and an invaluable factor in brother Teddy's steady rise in the. British Liberal party. She created a favourable stir in Ottawa's social circles and "it is like a dream to have her here."

> On Friday Fanny and I went down to the House to hear the beginning of the debate on the address. Laurier spoke v. well & Fanny agrees with me [sic] us that he is the outstanding figure here. Mr. and Mme Laurier came here to supper on Sunday to meet Fanny.[23]

It was an exhaustingly warm, humid spring, of the kind that Ottawa Valley frequently conjures up to set its inhabitants awash in perspiration and befuddle the brains of parliamentarians. All the trees were in leaf by 10 May. His excellency was reported hammering up mosquito netting on the ballroom windows to save the ladies' bare shoulders from extreme torture. "The carpenters were to have put up screens several days ago, but Board of Works men are proverbially slow." She went to Toronto for the NCW annual meeting and complained that to "rush around & make civil speeches etc with the thermometer at 98° & one's face streaming, one's hair sopping, one's garments clinging to one & all the dye coming off is o'ermuch of a good thing." She must see about having "dresses and underclothing made as if for India."[24]

Nevertheless they had a highly successful Council gathering. The press remarked on Lady Aberdeen's "spirited and graceful" opening speech, and the high quality of the proceedings.

> the keynote of this harmony of feeling was set by the admirable judgment and tact with which its distinguished President conducted the business from beginning to close. Firmness, punctuality and courteous consideration for all characterized the rulings of the chair...

Ishbel had intended another visit home that year, but had apparently been distracted by Ottawa's politics. For the first time in many months her journal mentioned Henry Drummond. He had written them after a long silence on 24 May from Biarritz, striving to make light of his calamitous illness. He did not describe it as cancer of the bone, but as "an exceedingly rare 'rheumatic' affection involving the whole trunk... very hard to cure. Greenfield expects it will begin to yield presently... I hear Her Excellency is likely to be over in the summer but I fear my tether will not let me go within reach of Britain for a long time yet."[25]

Ishbel accepted his determined optimism, saying, "It is *horrid* but happily they seem confident of ultimate cure." She stayed on in Canada, postponing a visit until Henry might be well again.

On 19 June Manitoba made its response to Ottawa's Remedial Order. The province was adamant, declaring financial inability to fund two school systems where only one would do. Events were again pushed towards crisis.

Yet Bowell did not bring in a bill. Instead, pressured strongly from both sides, he sought another delay. On 8 July he had a statement read by Foster as House Leader in the Commons, seeming to find some hint of conciliation in the Manitoba reply. It proposed to prorogue the session and allow the summer and fall for further consideration, calling parliament back to a new session in January. Then a Remedial bill would be introduced, if no settlement had taken place in the interval. Since the maximum term for that long parliament — which had begun with Macdonald and racked up three prime ministerial changes thus far — would end in April 1896, he was prolonging the agony and uncertainty to the extreme limit.

Of course there was revolt. Again it was Auguste Angers who first threatened resignation if they rose for the summer. Bowell appeared to believe this was bluff, and sent his secretary Payne to ask the Governor-General — the Aberdeens were in Quebec City — for permission to prorogue and hold a January session. Aberdeen thought it spelled trouble, but was given to understand that all had agreed. On 9 July Bowell wired frantically for His Excellency's return — he was in deep trouble again. Not only Angers but the two French Canadians next in line in the Cabinet, Adolphe Caron and Joseph Ouimet, were determined to quit.

This promised to be too exciting to miss. Ishbel returned with her husband to Ottawa where they put up at the Russell Hotel. Here Bowell called, "very despondently", with the three resignations in his hand, and the news that the most Orange of his Ontario members were rebelling from the opposite position — because a bill had been promised in January! The Whip expected a government defeat on the motion to prorogue.

"This seemed definite enough ", wrote Ishbel. An election was surely at hand. Aberdeen agreed to the resignations, but just as he was about to cable Her Majesty and the Colonial Office of the upset in government, his secretary brought him word that it had all blown over. Caron and Ouimet, though not Angers, had been persuaded to stay on. "Senator Drummond in his role of peace-maker and purse-bearer contributed largely to this conclusion", Ishbel said.

She was seated in the Commons almost continually that week, to watch events. Her presence aroused comment in the press. The Ottawa *Free Press* reported that when Mr. Foster appeared to have a little throat trouble she passed him some lozenges, which fixed him up nicely and let him get on with his speech. The *Evening Journal* said His Excellency's secretary accompanied her and appeared to be taking notes. "The Princess Louise used to sit on the floor of the House occasionally but no other vice-regal lady ever took the amount of interest in politics that Lady Aberdeen does."[26]

She was there as the debate wound down.

Mr. Laurier's speech was masterly—very bright and playful and never bitter nor showing any disappointment which after all would have been natural considering how near he came to being Premier that day. Sir Charles Hibbert Tupper spoke the best of the Govt. in an aggressive style of course and taunting Laurier for not declaring his policy. Laurier sat and smiled...[27]

Though Ishbel found it impossible to stay away from the Commons her conscience troubled her.

I sometimes feel that sitting on the floor of the House as I do, between the Speaker and the Treasury Bench as I do, that I hear too many of the secrets of the Ministry, and their various small confabs. I believe on the whole however that this going to the House may be a real help in the future both to H.E. and myself. He cannot come in any fashion, and it makes a wonderful difference in the knowing and understanding of the men to see them as they are in the House.[28]

Laurier again met all her expectations in a "worthy" and statesmanlike speech devoted to conciliation. It was a speech in which he put his heart beside the hearts of all Catholics: "I wish that the minority in Manitoba may be allowed the privilege of teaching in their schools, to their children, their duties to God and man as they understand those duties and as their duties were taught to them by their church." But "imperious dictation" was the wrong approach. "The hand must be firm and the touch must be soft; hitherto the touch has been rude and the hand has been weak," he told the House.[29]

While the Canadian parliamentary session dragged to a close, doleful news was reaching the Aberdeens from Britain, where the Liberals, fighting their first election without Gladstone, were losing at the polls. Of personal concern was the defeat of John Sinclair, still called "B" for "Boy", in Dumbartonshire.

Defeat had been apparent during the lack-lustre period of Lord Archibald Rosebery's leadership. Now Lord Salisbury led a new Conservative administration, and placed in the office of Colonial Secretary Mr. Joseph Chamberlain, a man intensely disliked by the Aberdeens. They feared the dislike was mutual, and their performance would be closely watched. Gladstone from his retirement wrote to reassure them:

And then you have Chamberlain on your back; but I think the permanent staff of the Office may be relied on to do all in their power to prevent injustice.[30]

The Canadian parliament rose, the newspapers deploring it all in large type:

After the Crisis — A Rattled and Demoralized Party. Mr. Bowell Admits Defeat. Ontario Offended, Quebec Not Reconciled.[31]

Aberdeen appeared formally on Parliament Hill to give royal assent to a bundle of bills, and in the Senate Chamber "there was but a sprinkling of ladies. The ladies appear in morning gowns and I sported my pretty new white silk spotted with rose buds and trimmed with silk — it was immensely admired."[32]

They were to take the train for the West for a prolonged vacation. Before leaving, Ishbel took a step even more inappropriate to her position than usual. She sent word to the younger Tupper that she would much appreciate an informal, confidential chat. It took place 15 July. Ishbel admitted, "What I said to him has its dangers." What she asked was that he act privately as their informant during their absence in case things went badly askew in Cabinet. "I asked him therefore to write to me as a friend, so that there might be no impropriety about seeming to pass by the Premier... Sir Charles entirely entered into the proposition and its delicacy & readily assented to my proposition..." The two had a frank exchange of confidence about Bowell's shortcomings. Ishbel made no pretence of defending their appointee — let Tupper try his hardest to undermine him! She decried Bowell's "weakness and consequent shiftiness. He is altogether in the seventh heaven at being Premier and fancies that he can emulate Sir John Macdonald's genius in managing his party, and succeeds only in creating universal mistrust..." Tupper in turn related various frustrating experiences with Bowell and told her how difficult it had been in December to get the ministers to serve under him.

Tupper was easily persuaded of Ishbel's kind intent. The voice was sweet, moderate and firm, the smile pleasant, the bearing of the viceregal lady always most gracious. So immature a young man as Charles Tupper was soon persuaded to act an unofficial spy on the lady's behalf. She had her first "confidential note" from him the following day "in consequence of our compact."[33] On the Sunday following she "drove to Sir Charles Tupper's little cottage on the Hog's Back after church" to follow up that matter. She felt they were now on a nicely intimate footing, and she and her husband could be off to the North West with some assurance that they would know instantly if the government got into further trouble.

All the way West at the end of July there was talk of little but the Manitoba school question. In Winnipeg Premier Greenway called on Aberdeen and declared "the whole province" to be against any concession. At Regina, where they opened a large Agricultural Exhibition, the Aberdeens talked to Mr. and Mrs. Scarth (from Winnipeg) and heard dire talk of annexation to the United States rather than submission to a Remedial Bill imposed by Ottawa. Ishbel was alarmed. It occurred to her that Confederation might be preserved through a tactful intervention by "our leading men at home", if someone was prepared to come out an deal with the matter.[34] She fired off letters to both Rosebery and Gladstone. Neither gentleman favoured the idea. Gladstone wrote that "the dilemma that has arisen is one strictly belonging to the Dominion and not to the Imperial authorities."[35] Rosebery turned down her direct invitation to him: "I have in the first place a great horror of external people interfering in colonial affairs... I am gloriously happy at recovering a measure of freedom..."[36] Glad to be out of office, he was in no mood to set out for Canada on a dubious mission.

On the West Coast people seemed less stirred by the turmoil in Ottawa. The Aberdeens arranged a ball to be held in Victoria's Military Drill Hall. Ishbel said it "won over the smart set". One young woman who received an invitation wrote an effervescent description to her father in Ontario:

> Oh! What a week this has been! It nearly kills us all when the Governor-General pays us a visit... I was presented and curtseyed. It was such a chance to show off the new mauve silk, 400 people to gaze at it as I curtseyed. I didn't hurry over it either. It was beautiful... Supper was too small to be of much nourishment... Lord Aberdeen made a speech at the Convent and made complimentary remarks about my lectures. I had quite a long talk with him. He told me funny Scotch stories of course...[37]

In Vancouver the Aberdeens took time to attend an evening's entertainment given by Mark Twain. "We took all the children, thinking he was a character they should see. I am not sure if I like him... He ended with an essentially stupid ghost story. We saw him for a few minutes afterwards. He has the strangest slopingest sort of head at the back with long fair hair about his neck."[38]

Ishbel also described but did not visit the lepers' colony on an island off the coast. Chinese immigrants showing symptoms were kept there, visited every three months by a doctor who brought them medicine and supplies. One Englishman had been removed to the island, and had quickly succumbed. "This does not seem a sufficient provision, and surely the Govt. who imposes restrictions and banishes the poor wretches should care or them properly to the end. The Englishman who died endured great misery."[39]

They spent a long vacation at the Coldstream and Guisachan ranches. Occasional word reached them of Ottawa affairs, but they were far removed from the disarray described by the Privy Council clerk, Joseph Pope, who suffered through that Ottawa summer:

> I remember it was almost impossible to get public business transacted. Weeks passed without a Treasury Board being held. When at last a necessary quorum was obtained, the Governor General had gone out to his country place in the mountains of British Columbia and the papers had to be sent after him... with the consequence that public business during that unhappy summer was well-nigh paralyzed.[40]

What Ishbel did not know was that several leading members of the Cabinet had become desperate, and determined to force the Prime Minister from office. What they planned was the worst possible move from her point of view. They would bring back old Sir Charles Tupper from London to take over as leader — their one remaining hope. Rumours may indeed have reached Ishbel. She wrote Sir Charles Hibbert in August to ask innocently if his father would join his mother in Nova Scotia to celebrate their approaching Golden Wedding anniversary. Then in October she sent a direct query on the strength of their "compact":

Shall I be very rude if I say that your silence has been very comforting to me? And at the same time we have felt sure that if there were any real reason for His Excellency to return to Ottawa, you would have let us know...[41]

Tupper responded with the information that things in Ottawa were in a sad state. He added: "Efforts are being made to reorganize the Government and it is not improbable that Mr. Chapleau, and Chief Justice Meredith may be with us. This of course is very confidential."[42]

The threat of "reorganization" was the warning signal. The Aberdeens would fulfil social commitments in Victoria and return at once.

Strong letters were being exchanged among top-ranking Conservatives. William B. Ives, Minister of Trade and Commerce, had a letter from fellow Tory R. H. Pope in Quebec. An election must take place within six months and:

> There is no man but knows the truth so far as the ability of our Premier goes. It is utterly impossible for that man to lead our party to victory in the coming struggle... Now then, we have to have a man as Premier of this country who will be able almost instantaneously, considering the short time we have at our disposal, to place the deliberations of the Government upon a higher level, and also by his very presence there to make the public realize that a change has taken place. I know of no man who can do it better — and of course I do not know if he can do it — than Sir Charles Tupper the High Commissioner... The presence of this man would give courage and hope & I fancy might be the means of inducing other and better men to enter Parliament & possibly bring Chapleau in...[43]

A copy of this went to the younger Tupper, strengthening his appeal to his father that went out 4 November, the same day he wrote to Ishbel of "reorganization": "It seems a downright shame to follow tamely an old man to the slaughter when if we were up and doing with a real leader we could march on to victory... I verily believe if you could visit Canada on some excuse the party would run up and form under you..."[44]

Others also implored the older Tupper to return and take leadership. Sir Charles cautiously agreed. A stratagem was

Sir Charles Tupper, Prime Minister May to July, 1896.

devised. Bowell was persuaded to ask him to come home — to talk over arrangements for a new trans-Atlantic steamship line.

Sir Charles arrived in Ottawa on 15 December. It was almost a year since Bowell had been placed in the Prime Minister's seat — a lost year for the Conservatives.

Ishbel, her husband and family, arrived back in Ottawa at about the same time. Faced with this mighty challenge to Liberal hopes, Ishbel had no thought of yielding the field to legitimate politicians. Instead, she sent an entreaty to her young friend and protegé, Captain John Sinclair, to join them in Canada as Aberdeen's "special secretary". She knew she needed at her side someone of greater political acumen than the soft-hearted Aberdeen. Sinclair accepted. His British Liberal colleagues were not happy with his decision. In fact his old campaign manager would follow him all the way to Canada to try to persuade him to come home. Rosebery wrote spitefully to Ishbel that she was jeopardizing Sinclair's position in the party: "The Liberal party is in a grievous plight, and it will be remembered hereafter, whether or no men helped in these days of darkness." What could possibly justify such a sacrifice? What was so important *in Canada?* "He will make a charming sympathetic Secretary I grant!"[45]

To be so misjudged by an old friend may have grieved Ishbel but it did not deter her. She must be ready for whatever form the "reorganization" of Cabinet would take. The emergence of old Sir Charles Tupper over the eastern horizon had to be met and countered.

They had put in office an incompetent, expecting an early election, an easy Liberal win. Bowell had clung to office, and the country had been put through a year of unparalleled paralysis and frustration. Instead of a modest deference, at last, to the will of the ruling party, the Aberdeens were now ready to try by every means possible to forestall this new threat to Liberal hopes.

Chapter 14
1896: Traitors & Curious Conversations

O n 2 January 1896, the last tumultuous session of that long seventh parliament of Canada began. There was little snow. His Excellency and his wife arrived on the Hill by carriage instead of sleigh, the postillions wearing livery instead of furs. "I wore my blue velvet, made to look very pretty combined with my white & gold and were much admired. H.E. got through both English and French versions of his Speech v. well..." A state dinner for 80 to 90 people was held at Rideau Hall that evening: "successful... I dining as the only lady."[1] The Speech promised Remedial legislation. After the Opening there was a week's adjournment of the House.

January 4th, "the storm burst over the political horizon." It was the occasion of the famous "nest of traitors" revolt. The Conservatives had capped their year-long troubles by losing two by-elections in Quebec; this news precipitated events, according to Ishbel, "together with the planned presence of Sir Charles Tupper Sr. in the country."[2] A harried Bowell had hinted to Aberdeen of "some caballing against him". Foster and Haggart had come to see the Governor-General and inform him of their intention: seven of the Cabinet members had summoned up the courage to resign, to force Bowell out. They had agreed on the elder Tupper as their leader: they would wish Aberdeen to call on him to form a new, last-ditch administration. The seven ministers were Haggart and Foster, the younger Sir Charles (who would stay out, so as not to overburden the Cabinet with Tuppers), Walter Montague (no portfolio), William Ives (Trade and Commerce), John Wood (Inland Revenue) and Arthur Dickey (Secretary of State). The seven might have been nine, but cautious T. Mayne Daly (Interior) and Donald Ferguson (another Minister without portfolio) dropped out at the last minute.[3] A flustered Aberdeen sent them away, telling them fastidiously that he could receive such information only through the Prime Minister.

On Sunday the 5th Bowell came to luncheon. The unusual importance of Aberdeen's wife in these affairs was recognized by Bowell, who specifically asked her to stay as he talked it all over, "and H.E. was glad, under the circumstances, to have a witness."

Bowell told them that Foster and Montague had been to see him, followed also by old Sir Charles. He had been handed the resignations of the seven men. Sir Charles had then offered him various incentives to resign, indeed almost anything if he would vacate the prime minister's seat. The effect on Bowell was to make him cagey. He had insisted on a night to think it over. "He feels rather pleased with himself at not having fallen into the trap of resigning at once." Instead, he hastened to his old benefactors the Aberdeens, for advice and support.

He returned to them in the evening for another worrisome discussion. The Aberdeens backed him up; they urged him not to give in.

They sought first to justify their support — ignoring the legitimate concerns of the seven — by condemning the revolt as an act of "treachery", expressing horror at this sudden mutiny on the heels of a Throne Speech setting forth policies the entire Cabinet must have concurred in. Such was Lady Aberdeen's immediate response. By evening the Aberdeens had developed a position to sustain the beleaguered Prime Minister. One of the rebels' complaints was that Bowell had not replaced Angers after his resignation in the spring; the by-elections had shown how weak they were in Quebec. Bowell had made some effort to recruit another French Senator, Masson, who had declined; the matter was urgent. So, said the Aberdeens: remedy that situation, make "every effort" to get new French Canadians in the Cabinet. Further, said they, it was imperative that Bowell "keep to his pledge of bringing in remedial legislation and putting it to the test [of an election] & not to throw the country into the hands of one who would doubtless deal with it only in such a way as would suit himself."[4] This was putting tenacity on a nobler plane: Bowell must go on for the good of the country and to save it from base Sir Charles.

Much strengthened, Bowell went home from Rideau Hall for a night's sleep. Next morning he attempted to stall the rebels who, finding he was not prepared to give way easily, decided to increase the pressure by letting the world know their intentions, and their reasons. They wanted to issue a statement to the press. Since the extent of the Governor-General's authority was still so vague, they felt it appropriate to check out this move with Aberdeen, and at 2 o'clock they sent round a copy of their press release with a request from Foster for permission to give it to the papers. Aberdeen said the proper place for such a statement was in the House of Commons, and refused his permission. It was Ishbel who then checked out the constitutionality of that refusal with the Chief Clerk of the Commons, Dr. John George Bourinot. Bourinot apparently confirmed that they had taken "the right course", since to issue such a statement was "indecent".[5]

The rebels, waxing desperate, next sent the younger Sir Charles with George Foster to see Bowell and try to "soften him down".[6] And the dejected old man weakened. He sent a message to Aberdeen, asking to see him that day. His note said:

> I see no change in the aspect of the situation and fear that there is no solution of the present problem than for me to resign. I shall however defer final action until Wednesday next.[7]

Both Aberdeens went that evening to his office. They bolstered his failing resolution with sympathy for the cruel way he was being treated and sought to reassure him. "But he *is* weak and there is no mistake about it", Ishbel wrote.[8]

Why did the Governor-General, who had been ready half a dozen times in 1895 to accept Bowell's resignation, so stoutly reject it now? It's been said that Aberdeen thought Bowell ought to carry out the Throne Speech promise of a remedial bill.[9] But there had been a Throne Speech to the same purpose, and a Remedial Order in 1895. Only one thing had changed: Sir Charles Tupper had appeared on the scene. Resignation now did not mean an immediate election and a Liberal victory. It meant switching leaders to give old Tupper a chance to finish out the session, rally Conservative forces, and lead a revived party into an election contest. Ishbel revealed their only real concern: Bowell must not be allowed to "throw the country into [Tupper's] hands."

The seven ministers carried out their threat to resign.

> January 7th. The sitting of the House this afternoon was very short... The statement was read by Foster... was rec'd in dead silence. The Conservative party seemed paralysed and dumbfounded... After the debate [Bowell] who had been sitting behind me by the Speaker's Chair went over to the Opposition leaders and shook hands with them all, saying audibly, 'It is such a comfort to shake hands with honest men, after being in company with traitors for months.'[10]

Others thought they heard "nest of traitors".

On 7 January Ishbel found more telling reasons for keeping Bowell on instead of Tupper. She wrote of new information received: "we know that the retiring Ministers and Sir Charles mean to drop the remedial policy although they are individually pledged to it & have renewed their allegiance to it so lately as last week in the Speech from the Throne."[11] Where had this intelligence come from? Saywell surmises: "Bowell was undoubtedly her informant."[12] But the *Journal* which recorded over several pages the various meetings with Bowell failed to mention this as an argument put forward by the Prime Minister. Bowell's complaints had been of how badly he had been treated personally by the "traitors".

The more likely source was Wilfrid Laurier, with whom Ishbel was in touch several times on 7 January. On the morning of the 7th Ishbel had dropped in at the Russell Hotel to see her National Council secretary, Emily Cummings, who was lodged there in her capacity as a correspondent ("Sama") for the Toronto *Globe*. Laurier was also staying at the Russell. It was Ishbel's idea to use Mrs. Cummings as a go-between. "As she is always in communication with me about the Council, her comings & goings will not be considered unnatural and it is well at this juncture to have some means of communication with the leader of the Opposition."[13] Laurier had agreed, and Emily Cummings as his messenger had called on Ishbel at noon and again later in the day. That evening Ishbel's journal ascribed to Sir Charles and his friends a *hidden agenda* to drop the Remedial bill. Terrible consequences to Canada would ensue. The policy attributed to Tupper later proved quite false. Tupper would in due course fight furiously to pass the bill. Laurier was feeding Her Excellency some highly questionable rumours.

Laurier through Emily Cummings also presented a new solution to the situation. If Bowell resigned, it lay within Aberdeen's power to call to office the leader of the Opposition, without recourse to an election. "If Sir Mackenzie fails in reconstruction, in spite of the fact of the Conservative majority in the House & he puts forward his reasons & also precedents for such action on the part of H. E."[14] This was a new and tempting alternative, a shortcut to Liberal power.

Ishbel went with John Sinclair to the Senate that evening to hear Bowell respond to the resignations. "Not well done... showed his mortification... very plainly." She spent some time working her way among the Senators, pressing them to urge Bowell to add the needed strength to his Cabinet, and stay on.

The following day the drama heightened. Laurier pressed his case.

> Mrs. Cummings came again with missives from the same quarter this morning. There is one reason for sending for Laurier which is doubtless very cogent. At present he and his party want to deal fairly with the minority — the R.C.'s in Manitoba. But if a government under Sir Charles Tupper or any other against or lukewarm about remedial legislation came in, they would gather round them all the P.P.A. (Protestant Protective Association) & all the anti-Catholic feeling in Ontario and then the two provinces of Quebec and Ontario would be face to face for a deadly combat. Already the fact that the seven Ministers who have resigned are Protestant, that five of those who have stayed with the Prime Minister are R.C., is beginning to give rise to reflections...
>
> The Liberals are confident of sweeping the country if they come into power now — but if Sir Charles comes into power and dissolves, he will not hesitate to use means fair and foul to bribe the country into returning him. This is not mere supposition — his past record is clear enough on this subject.[15]

While Ishbel pondered Laurier's fresh arguments she went again to the House of Commons to watch proceedings, and Bowell turned up again in Aberdeen's office and again tendered his resignation. Aberdeen stoutly refused to accept it, urging Bowell to take "all time necessary to reconstruct his Government & carry through the policy [in the Throne Speech] before resigning. The old gentleman quite plucked up courage again..."[16]

While Aberdeen thus pursued their strategy of keeping Bowell in and Tupper out, his lady had gone off on the new tack. Perhaps it would indeed be possible at this juncture to call in, not Sir Charles, but Wilfrid Laurier. She would have liked to enquire further into the possibility, but the next day "much to my disgust, Miss Wilson reminded me at breakfast that I had promised to go to the Ladies' Morning Musicale this morning. So we trotted off, leaving H. E. to cope with Dr. Montague who came to discuss the matter of the anonymous letters against Caron... I came back just in time for a little talk with A. before he drove into town to the office to see Sir Mackenzie..."[17] The Prime Minister, like a buffeted beach ball, again tendered his resignation which was again refused. It would appear that the Aberdeens had decided to give Bowell one last chance. If he was unable to make good, and returned one more time to submit his resignation, it would be accepted and Aberdeen would move at once to call Laurier.

It was obviously Lady Aberdeen, not her husband, receiving the pressure from Laurier. A number of people sensed that she was the real power at Government House. Other ambitious M.P.'s with their own ideas about the leadership approached her; the Ontario Conservative McNeill, who was violently anti-Catholic, came to tell her that he and some others were not keen to have Tupper as leader and would prefer Chief Justice Meredith or Professor Weldon, both strongly anti-Catholic. Ishbel responded by introducing him to Captain Sinclair, who would take care of him. Her real interest now was the scheme to call Laurier. Sinclair was sent to Bourinot "so that every step may be taken on safe ground." She conferred privately with the Presbyterian minister of St. Andrews church, Mr. Herridge, "wishing to find out what might be termed the outside independent thinking citizen's opinion on the position." Herridge appeared a judicious choice. While he saw the strength of her argument, he made some enquiries on his own and told her after church the next Sunday that: "In the House, the majority of the Conservative M.P.'s are in favour of Tupper's leadership... The pressure of feeling he is the only man is of course very great."[18] Ishbel was unmoved. If Sir Charles was widely popular that only made him more dangerous.

The younger Sir Charles now presumed on his privileged friendship with her to ask if he might call. His purpose was to insist that the Conservatives were still strong and he was "very confident that his party will win at the General Election if properly led."[19] More to the point, young Sir Charles denied the rumours that his father secretly opposed Remedial legislation.

Laurier was challenged on that point the following day at a Government House skating party. The Liberal leader said he still felt that "the source of division is the school question". But Ishbel prudently dropped the accusation against Tupper. She felt she had grounds enough for refusing Tupper a chance to govern Canada, though the Aberdeens were both reticent about their reasons for dislike.

She was elated by the growing intimacy with Laurier. That day she introduced Captain Sinclair to him "and hinted that he was a confidential friend. So the two went off for a walk and talked the whole matter over and what would be the course to take if he did come in. Dissolution of course at once. And he says he could form his Cabinet in three days and he is very confident of the country if he is in power at dissolution — but if Sir Charles were in power, this might be different... I had a little talk with him when he took me to tea."[20]

On the same evening Ishbel, resplendent in purple, trailing a train edged with ermine, and attended by her pageboy sons, presided over a Drawing Room in the Senate Chamber. All moments of private conversation hinged on Cabinet making. Bowell had got Senator Desjardins to join and was hopeful. He had also asked the older Tupper to serve under him but they were at odds on the admission of the seven rebels. "Bowell says he would never again sit with Foster, Haggart or Montague. So that's over for the present."[21]

Ishbel imagined her dealings with Laurier were unobserved. But gossip was rife, especially in Liberal quarters. James Edgar, the fussy little Liberal M.P. from Ontario West, who wrote puffed-up letters to his wife Matilda from that centre of conspiracy, the Russell Hotel, said on 6 January that "the situation looks promising. I hear a great deal, and think that neither Bowell nor Tupper can succeed in forming a new ministry. Chances are at present that after an adjournment Laurier will be called on."[22] Four days later he told his wife that it was impossible to answer her questions about "The true inwardness of the situation"; everything was still speculation. Still, "I lunched with Laurier at the Club today on his treat, and everybody kowtows to him... I must go and put my name down at the Rideau [Club]."[23]

T. Mayne Daly tried on 12 January to press Bowell to settle with Sir Charles, warning him, "I feel as satisfied as possible that if you cannot succeed in arranging matters by Tuesday His Excellency will call on Laurier, beyond a doubt."[24]

Yet Ishbel was surprised when on Sunday afternoon Senator Frank Smith dropped in. "He evidently thought that the alternative was Laurier, but I took care to utter no syllable which would lend colour to such a supposition." She was sure she had been entirely discreet, and no one knew of the long discussions in which she, her husband and Sinclair went over the situation" in all its bearings up hill and down dale night after night."[25]

Round came the note the next afternoon from the younger Sir Charles to "vex" her further. He had it, he said, "on good authority from Government House that in no event wd. Sir Charles be called for. I sent back a most unequivocal denial."[26] Her reply to "My Dear Sir Charles" was that, "No one can *possibly* have the authority for making any statement regarding His Excellency's intentions. So I thank you for contradicting the assertion to which you refer, which has not a shadow of foundation."

But denial could not save her. Her improper complicity was too obvious. Her *Journal* at this period is full of political dealing, irritation at distractions such as demands of the NCW, and even annoyance when her husband went to some trouble on behalf of the legitimate government: "The whole day from 11 to 6 has been employed by H.E. in patching up the quarrel between Caron and Montague... Here is another service to the Conservative party!"[27] Her attitude and actions fanned the rumours.

The Conservatives settled for a compromise that would keep them in power. On 13 January Bowell arrived after dinner; the Aberdeens were waiting in anticipation of a resignation they would not this time refuse. Instead, Bowell had come to terms with the "traitors" and with Sir Charles Tupper. "He consents to take the whole of the deserters back again. And this after all the protestations!"[28]

The older Sir Charles joined the Cabinet as Justice Minister while his son dropped out. Bowell was still Prime Minister — the Aberdeens had won that essential point. He would remain as leader until the end of the session. But a deal had been struck with the "bolters". Bowell had promised to switch places with Tupper as soon as the House dissolved. Tupper would lead the party into the election.

"And so the crisis ends — for the present."[29] The Aberdeens had in fact won the battle. Bowell's year and a half in office had been terminal for the Conservative party. Tupper's brave fight would begin much too late.

The younger Tupper was bitterly frustrated — though still confident of Lady Aberdeen's friendship towards himself and his wife. He denounced those ministers who had not joined the revolt and strengthened it. "Ferguson, Costigan and Daly (not to mention Caron and Ouimet) or any one of them are responsible for Bowell's lunacy and the great injury done our party during the 'crisis'. Had it not been for them Bowell would gracefully have gone and Sir C.T. would have been Prime Minister and our victory would have been certain... We have now a government not much better than the last, and if Bowell is not out of the way at the G.E. we are doomed beyond peradventure..."[30]

The press, Ishbel reported, considered the whole situation so bizarre it had run out of expletives.

The senior Sir Charles had now to get himself elected, which he did very handily in a Cape Breton by-election, "giving rise to very violent things being said. One reads some of Sir Charles' statements with amazement. But he has been very plucky & has gone through a tremendous strain for a man of 75",[31] Ishbel acknowledged. She could afford to be magnanimous.

The by-election coincided with the birth of a grandchild, the younger Tupper's son; they named him "Victor". And the younger Sir Charles wrote to Ishbel, asking her to be the infant's godmother:

> You placed me under a heavy debt of gratitude for your advice and friendship last spring... Remembering all this we were bold enough to contemplate asking permission from Your Excellency should the little stranger be of your sex to call her after you. Our girl however turns out to be a boy! Would it be permitted to call him Victor *Gordon*?[32]

Ishbel sent her consent, saying that being godmother in this case would mean much, since she and the father had been brought together "in so peculiar a way during these last weeks."[33]

Chapter 15

1896:The Sun Rises for Laurier

During the winter of 1896 other matters besides politics sometimes occupied the viceregal family. The children recklessly enjoyed the famous toboggan slide. "Archie goes from the top of the steep slide on Norwegian skis, a performance none of the gentlemen can do, and they none of them mind anything — they go down standing or sitting or kneeling or anyway."

Haddo had his seventeenth birthday. He was in such precarious health, his epileptic seizures worsening, that he was kept with his parents for a time. Special doctors were in attendance, including Dr. Tait Mackenzie. (As a noted sculptor, whose works are still exhibited, Mackenzie drew his inspiration from Greek statues of the male form.) Ishbel admitted Haddo's incapacity obliquely. It looked, she wrote, "pretty different to what might have been expected if one looks back to Jan. 20 1879" when the bells rang out at Haddo House as at the birth of a prince. Asked what he would like for his birthday, Haddo said he'd like to watch his mother go down the slide. She accordingly "forced myself on exhibition to my family & was taken down three times... All one's insides go from one and one's brains too."[1]

Ishbel also took time out from politics to arrange an Historical Ball of grand proportions, to be held in the Senate Chamber 17 February. She described her plans:

> At the outset, the project had a great deal of cold water dashed at it — there was not time — people would not dress — people had not the money and so on. Then we arranged with Montreal costumiers to provide dresses for gentlemen from $5 to $10, wigs and shoes extra, and give designs for costumes for ladies, leaving them to have them made up, then came the political crisis. The costumiers came & took rooms at Ottawa and sat there and waited, but no one came — everybody was at the House of Commons.

Public Archives Canada.

(Left to right) Archie, George (Lord Haddo), Marjorie, Dudley.

Dr. Bourinot, the clerk of the House of Commons & a great authority on constitutional history was our mainstay. He suggested all the personages we might represent and their characteristics and entered into the whole affair with enthusiasm... The last fortnight has made a great difference. Now you hear everyone anxious to trace out the lineage & deeds of General This and Admiral That...[2]

She was succeeding in her object of stimulating the interest of young people in Canada's past, and away from "the everlasting discussion of hockey varied with Ottawa scandal."

A thousand people attended. "A scene of equal brilliance never seen in Canada. Lord Dufferin's fancy dress ball, of which people still talk, could not compare with it", gushed the Ottawa papers. Eight ladies had been assigned to organize costumed dances for eight historical periods, and Ottawa people learned the gavotte, the pavane, the bourée and other delightful steps. The sets were performed in turn before the viceregal party of 59, brilliantly dressed in contemporary elegance.

Bourinot, chronicler of the event, declared passionately: "The Past in mimic guise met for the nonce the Present..."[3] At the conclusion the viceregal party performed the intricate State Lancers: "We felt it was rather formidable to get through & some of our Cabinet Ministers got very far astray."[4]

Lady Aberdeen wore violet brocade trimmed with Honiton lace and purple violets, amethysts, pearls and diamonds. Among the Aberdeens' guests were Mrs. Potter Palmer of Chicago, who was gratifyingly impressed, and the Canadian soprano Mme Emma Albani who had made a debut at the New York Metropolitan Opera five years earlier.

The Historical Ball was of course complete with supper: "They eat very largely here & we put lots of sandwiches and jellies in the tea room as well as the supper room to keep them quiet." Dancing continued until four in the morning. Ishbel wrote to Lady Thompson in Toronto: "It certainly did go well — and for the time being Ottawa is pleased with us and with itself. But how long will it last?"[5]

Politically, "we continue to live in a volcano and there are constant rumours of new resignations from the Ministry... Mr. Laurier came and had a long talk with me last week... A more statesmanlike view of things than the others — he does not grasp at power."[6] A remarkable comment, given Laurier's efforts to win her support and fuel her prejudice against Tupper!

Laurier thought it well to outline for her his carefully conceived position on the Manitoba school issue. The controversial Remedial bill would be presented 11 February. Laurier would have to break his protective silence. His closest,

Lady Aberdeen, about 1894.

shrewdest adviser was Israel Tarte, and Tarte's advice was surprising. Everyone supposed Laurier would, like most French Catholics, support the bill. Tarte reminded him that French Catholic votes could be taken for granted; what Laurier had to do was please the temper of the English Protestants. He must vote against the bill offering to *mediate* with Manitoba.

Laurier did not underestimate Ishbel's power. And he remembered, if she quickly forgot, that he had prophesied disaster to the country under Tupper if the bill was not passed. It must have taken all his eloquence to explain to her the new situation. What, asked Laurier thoughtfully, would be the effect on the country if Quebec M.P.'s were seen to have forced this unwanted law on the western province? Immediately after he called on her, Ishbel wrote in her journal: "If this Bill is passed by the vote of the French Members from Quebec of both parties, the cry against French ascendancy will become a yell and then what hope will they have for their schools in the other English provinces?"[7] Later she added that if the Bill was "carried through and imposed on Manitoba against its will, [it] will produce such a lamentable civil war."[8] Laurier had been persuasive, Ishbel predisposed to believe him.

In such shifting political sands, the remainder of the 1896 session would be hazardous. "It is well for us that Captain Sinclair has been persuaded to stay for at least a few months & succeed Arthur [Gordon, Aberdeen's secretary]. His knowledge of political life and his tact and discretion will be invaluable... Our object is to get at least all the French R.C. M.P.'s dined before Lent..."

On 3 March Laurier took his stand in parliament. He accused Sir Charles of forcing Nova Scotia into Confederation instead of leading the province by persuasion, and of wishing now to force Manitoba to change its school system instead of patiently exhausting "all means of conciliation." Laurier had received a threat, through Lacombe, that the Church would exert opposition against him in the election if he did not support the bill. He turned that threat to advantage by reaffirming his belief that no political leader should be bound in public affairs by the dictate of the Church — in this, he said, "I am a Liberal of the English school". He said, "I am here the acknowledged leader of a great party, composed of Roman Catholics and Protestants as well, as Protestants must be in

the majority in every party in Canada. I will take my stand...
on grounds which can appeal to the conscience of all men,
irrespective of their particular faith, upon grounds which can
be occupied by all men who love justice, freedom and tolera-
tion." It was stirringly spoken and it ended in a motion to
reject the bill with a "six-months hoist". Said Ishbel, "His
French followers cheered."[9] The vote on his motion was
defeated by the government, second reading was resumed.

It was a chaotic House as Sir Charles did his utmost to
force the bill through before time ran out on 23 April. All other
business was suspended. Writes O.D. Skelton:

> It was in vain that for a hundred hours the House was held
> in [continuous] session; Dr. Sproule read the Nova Scotia
> school law; John Charlton read the Bible passages pre-
> scribed in Ontario schools, Colonel Tyrwhitt went through
> Mark Twain and Bibaud's History of Canada, always prom-
> ising to come to the point, and barely a clause went through.
> [10]

The usual courtesy disappeared. When Sir Charles raged
against obstruction, Laurier retorted, "Whose fault was it
that we did not meet until January second, that we found the
Cabinet divided into two factions, calling each other imbeciles
and traitors, and that six weeks of this dying session elapsed
before the bill was brought down?"

James Edgar, who had a nose for scandal, wrote to his
wife: "It is aggravating to find members getting bought up by
office to vote for the bill... Government are having an awful
time of it. The debate is really greatly against them."[11] By 19
March, "At this moment a very decent fellow, Moncrieff is
speaking but I am sorry to say he is obviously drunk and
getting drunker — drinking gin and water. He has knocked
his tumbler over once and sent for more. Six o'clock will soon
come and shut him up."

Ishbel was told scandalous tales by Mr. Taylor, the Conservative Whip: the previous night "they had what they called
a Symposium and finally Mr. Davin, M.P. for Assiniboia was
called on to give a Blackfoot Dance in the Smoking Room.
They had a long table with refreshments put up & Mr. Davin
wound up his dance by springing on this & jigging down the
centre, kicking over bottles and tumblers & plates at every
step."[12]

On 21 April Edgar was writing his wife again: "There are some serious troubles yet in the Cabinet — evidently all is not yet smoothed out for Tupper to succeed Bowell." And: "That old villain Tupper is at his old tricks offering to buy up the whole country with their own money. His proposal to build seven branch railways in P.E. Island is a hard blow for poor Davies and his five Island seats... I hope it won't make CPR hostile for I would dislike to fight Van Horne..."[13] The raucous mood of parliament would carry into the looming election.

So impossible was the situation, past hope of bringing the Remedial bill to a vote, that Sinclair and Aberdeen conspired to put the seventh parliament out of its misery. While traveling to Toronto they "concocted communications to Sir Mackenzie and to the Privy Council."[14] Supplementary estimates must be passed and money voted for rifles for the militia — the Remedial bill debate must be brought to a halt. These views were pressed on the government; with one week to go the House switched to Estimates and then dissolved.

Before the formal dissolution Ishbel managed to steal the headlines from the embattled House with a near tragedy. It was late April but outdoor exercise, walking or even riding, was still impossible through the deep mud and puddles of Ottawa. Ferry service had resumed across the Ottawa River to the pretty north shore, and on a fine spring day Ishbel with John Sinclair and the groom, John Keddie, took a light carriage across with her beautiful chestnut ponies, Cowslip and Buttercup. Rivers in spring flood, horses dancing in release from winter confinement, a lady in a mood as gay as theirs, conspired in danger. Ishbel took the reins on a shore circling Pointe Gatineau. The fast-moving water had flooded the road at intervals but local drivers with their carts were ignoring the splash; Ishbel urged Cowslip and Buttercup through. Cowslip shied, a carriage wheel hit a submerged hole, the carriage spilled, they were all of them thrown out into the icy Gatineau River rushing at peak level to empty its waters in the Ottawa.

> Before we knew where we were, the ponies had disappeared into the river and the carriage, half overturned, followed and the waters closed over them. I found myself on my back in the water, — Boy was looking over me for a moment & smiled & said, 'It's all right'. I tried to smile back again & then remem-

bering that I had been told one ought to float in such emergencies I stretched out my feet...[15]

Keddie couldn't swim but got on top of the carriage and kept himself from going under. Sinclair, supporting Ishbel with one arm, used the other to try for shore. Her thick winter clothes soon dragged her down and "my head got under water which was not at all pleasant (and he says he thought things looked very nasty then)..." Sinclair made it to shallow water and both were on their feet with Keddie, when a row-boat of rescuers reached them. The ponies were carried downstream.

We walked home, first going to the curé to ask him to prevent any sensational message being sent off from the telephone office. We came across to Rockcliffe by a small boat... and then walked home to tell our news and to get into hot baths... Poor A. He *was* in a state... We had a little dinner with Laurier tonight and were at home afterwards for any Senators or M.P.s who wished to say Good-bye before the end of Parliament tomorrow, & all had heard of it & were full of it.[16]

Aberdeen cabled reassurances far and wide, but the papers, and their daily mail, made much of her "miraculous escape". Rosebery wrote: "If Sinclair is really the rescuer I forgive him for remaining!"[17] As she entered the Senate chamber in full velvet and lace regalia next day, the assembly rose as usual at their entry, and began clapping, which was unusual, and was interpreted as congratulations on her survival. "Her Excellency was agreeably astonished at the ovation..."[18]

A bell was presented to the Pointe Gatineau Church of St. Françoise de Sales, on May 9, 1897, and installed in a service of thanksgiving for her deliverance from a premature death. In 1972 the bell with its inscription: "Gratias Domino, Ishbel Aberdeen, John Sinclair" was rescued from obscure neglect, restored, and housed in an arched enclosure next the church. Gertrude Holt, the moving spirit in this latter-day project was, fittingly, the President of a unique Ottawa institution, the May Court Club, founded by Lady Aberdeen in 1898.

For a time Ishbel lost her nerve in approaching horses. She was grateful to John Sinclair for acting as riding master and insisting that she ride again:

Frozen in Time. Ice Sculpture of dramatic upset of Lady Aberdeen and carriage in the Gatineau River, 1896, won first prize in Ottawa's Winter Carnival 1987.

> B. had rather a time with me... I abused him well at first but he took no notice... He was determined that I should get back my confidence.[19]

Three days after parliament ended, with an election set for 23 June, Bowell went through with his contract to resign and let Sir Charles Tupper assume the leadership. There had been one more amiable family affair, the christening of small Victor Gordon Tupper, when Ishbel and old Sir Charles were both present, oddly, as the baby's godparents. Next day she recorded her chagrin at having to swallow the bitter pill at last, and watch her husband summon Sir Charles to take over the government. There "did not seem to be much choice. But still... a distasteful job. It seems so untrue to the country to have to put it in the power of such a man..." She described the "wonderful" way in which the "old Cumberland warhorse" found no hesitation in accepting.

Tupper threw his remarkable energy into remolding the cabinet to lead the party into the election, but with no great success. Chapleau turned him down. The best he could manage in Quebec, the crucial province, were men like Angers iden-

Dedication of a Bell, church at Pointe Gatineau, Quebec, 9 May, 1897, in Thanksgiving for escape from drowning.

tified with the ultramontanes. Tupper's attempt to pass the Remedial bill weighed in his favour with the bishops, who issued a statement aimed at support for Tupper to be read in Quebec churches 17 May. The Church's authority in civil matters was now balanced against Quebec's desire to elect a French prime minister.

At the other end of the spectrum was the traditional Tory vote, the die-hard Orange Order, deeply offended on the same issue. A skilfully organized Conservative party of the kind Macdonald had led could have handled both ends. The party was in no shape, in spring 1896, to accomplish that feat.

Laurier achieved support among middle-stream Canadians — the happy position his party held thereafter as decade followed decade. Among his successful recruits were Fielding, ex-Premier of Nova Scotia, and Mowat, ex-Premier of Ontario. But Tupper fought hard:

> ...fighting like a lion, as I have explained, against tremendous odds. Through no fault of his, he had no chance. Had he been called upon when Thompson died, the outcome might

have been, and probably would have been, different, but the late Government had made such a mess of everything they had touched that nothing could save their successors.[20]

Ishbel's emotional involvement had been at a fever pitch throughout the session. It had burst out in foolishly reckless driving; it had revealed itself in her impatience with those duties where patience was required. After a meeting of the Home Missionary Society of St. Andrew's Church she had written:

> Mr. Herridge was there and spoke and so did I, and he agrees with me that this species of meeting of about 30-odd ladies forming three sides of a square & looking very good & very impenetrable is the most alarming audience possible and that one's natural impulse is to leap over the table or dance a jig or do something dreadful so as to create a diversion somehow.[21]

Now Ottawa was closed down; legitimate politicians took to the hustings, and clandestine politicians had little more to do to influence affairs. Ishbel had a new typist, the very efficient Georgina Dallas, who was "good at not grumbling over long hours", and her own hours were lightened. The family went off to Quebec City where she and Haddo enjoyed themselves by walking early to St. John market and returning through the town, their baskets heaped with chickens, vegetables and flowers. "I am sure one could have a lot of fun here."[22]

In Quebec they followed with close attention the campaign of Sir Henri Joly Lotbinière, a Liberal and a Protestant. "In this province the two candidates still have joint meetings... The country people look forward to election meetings as their great dissipation & both men and women turn out... Their great complaint is when they are too short..."[23]

From their vantage point at the Citadel they looked down on Dufferin Terrace on election night, and the huge screen erected there by the *Electeur* newspaper, with a "magic lantern" positioned to project the voting results as they came in over the wire. Great crowds gathered. "But even before it was dark, the returns which were read out indicated that the unexpected had happened and that the Province of Quebec, which was supposed to have been handed over to the Conservative Party at the bidding of the Bishops, had gone overwhelmingly for the Liberals." The three outstanding Quebec Conservatives, Angers, Desjardins and Taillon, lost. Results across the country gave Laurier a majority of 28, with five Independents. Sir Henri Joly was elected. From Caribou in the North West came a win for Mr. Bostick, their own special M.P. (representing an area that took in the Okanagan) a young Liberal who was editor of an enterprising "really capital weekly newspaper".

It was a smashing triumph, the first of such magnitude and promise for the party that had always been second in Canada. The extent to which the Conservatives were regarded as the nation's government is reflected in the 1897 edition of the *Canadian Parliamentary Companion,* a semi-official compendium of government data, which even at that date referred to the Tories as "the dominating political party," which after the election was "obliged to give way to a Ministry from the Liberal party."

The next bitter wrangle, one rather thoroughly discussed by historians and those concerned with constitutional matters, began to take shape 24 June, the day after the election. Laurier called on Captain Sinclair to urge that "it would be a great injustice to the Liberal party" if Tupper's defeated government should attempt before formally resigning, to fill up vacancies in the Senate and on the bench with Conservative henchmen.[24] Laurier had promised a Senate seat to Mowat, and had other good Liberals to be similarly rewarded.

But Tupper was still Prime Minister, and would remain so until he resigned or met parliament and was defeated in a vote. He chose to remain at least until all the recounts were in. And he chose not to present himself humbly at the Quebec Citadel to acknowledge his defeat to Aberdeen. Instead, he sent word to the Governor-General that his presence in Ottawa on public business was desired. Aberdeen replied haughtily that he had Dominion Day duties to take care of in Quebec City. The main duty was attendance at a bicycle race.

So July 2nd they took a train to Ottawa and at three o'clock met Tupper for the first time after the election. Ishbel could not repress a scornful admiration.

> The plucky old thing came down blooming in a white waist-coat and seemingly as pleased with himself as ever. — He did not at all appear as the defeated Premier come to render an account of his defeat and its cause to the representative of

the sovereign. Not he! Down he sat, and for an hour and a half he harangued H.E. on the enormity of sending Minutes to Council...

H.E. said but little at the time & gave his visitor tea at the end; but after a great talk he and B. went to work...[25]

They drafted a lengthy and carefully worded Memorandum which dealt with the dispute over Minutes and also, at length, with Tupper's main point, which was his intention while he was still Prime Minister to fill up the Senate and judicial vacancies with men of his choice. In Tupper's view, a governor-general had no alternative but to accept the advice of his prime minister in such matters.

Sinclair, warned ahead of time by Laurier, worked mightily to prove otherwise. Tupper as Prime Minister had never met parliament; he had just been soundly defeated by the voters. It was unfair and improper that *he* should seize the political spoils of the election.

Tupper was wrathful; the war was on. Canadians might not understand all public issues, but they did understand patronage. The lines were drawn, the papers bellowed, the constitutional authorities were called in. Aberdeen had Sinclair strengthen the arguments of the Memorandum and go over it with Bourinot. This was not in Ishbel's province: she "went into town to find a present for H.E. to give B. today, as it is his birthday & I chose a jolly little Kodak." The revised and improved Memorandum was despatched again to Sir Charles Tupper.

One of those pleasant little sidelights to history provided the setting for the next move in this drama. The three conspirators in a mood of elation headed down Sussex Street in their carriage, carrying a tea-basket and planning a little outing on the Rideau Canal on an "electric launch". As their carriage made the turn onto Rideau Street they were hailed from a cab going the other way — it was the Prime Minister's secretary, Mr. Payne, and he was frantically waving a large blue envelope. Everyone pulled to a halt; the envelope was handed in. Payne drove on. Aberdeen ripped open the envelope: inside was a notice of resignation by Sir Charles on constitutional grounds. Aberdeen's attempt to deny the nation's Prime Minister his right to make appointments would be broadcast as far and as bitterly as the old warrior could do it — and Tupper was well known in London, where Aberdeen's friends were in Opposition.

Ishbel described with relish their bravado:

> We thought that we could not do better than go on the launch
> & consider the famous reply in peace in mid-canal. Which we
> did, A. making himself responsible for working the boat. But
> presently a big steamer hove in sight & A. drew to the right
> to let her pass. And so we got among a lot of weeds which
> wound themselves round the screw and precluded further
> motion. Here was a nice predicament — the G.G. stuck in the
> Canal without anyone to help him & the Premier waiting to
> give in his resignation at Government House. However it did
> not come to that. A. and B. got the boat to the side & there
> we got temporarily stranded.[26]

Were they abashed? Not in the least.

> Then we had tea and discussed the memo & were relieved to
> find that it was not formidable though very crusty.

The tea things were tucked back in the basket; His Excellency and Captain Sinclair worked under and around the boat, untangled the reeds and pushed off to the centre of the channel. A boat crowded with interested boys pulled up and offered help. The three, still undaunted (it seems a pity the jolly little Kodak was not focused on their good spirits), got safely home and "had a long evening of discussion — or rather night — and finally the line for the next day's interview having been decided Captain S. drew up all the chief points for H.E. to keep on his table."[27]

Sir Charles Tupper did in fact resign on this constitutional issue, and he got all the publicity he hoped for. Aberdeen's autocratic behaviour caused a raging debate in the press. The *Mail and Empire* wrote editorially: "This is the first time since we have enjoyed the right to govern ourselves that the representative of the Crown has declined to be guided by his Ministers."[28] The *Daily Spectator* said it had always been assumed that Canada's governors-general should be appointed from Britain to ensure their impartiality. "But the recent action of Lord Aberdeen has dissipated the Canadian idea, and has shown the people of this country that a Governor General appointed by the imperial government can be a partisan and a very small one at that: that he can prostitute his office to allow small pickings to his political friends..."[29]

Whig papers said Canada was lucky to have a high-principled governor like Aberdeen who was not afraid to prevent the "vultures" from seizing the spoils even after the people had turned them out of office.

If Tupper hoped the British Colonial Office might reprimand Aberdeen or perhaps even recall him he was soon disappointed. Chamberlain was disgruntled because Tupper had presumed too much on their common party allegiance and had even claimed that Chamberlain had given him support in the election. That was going too far. Chamberlain had no time for Canadian local affairs. "He won't even answer what he is asked about — the Allan Line for instance –which affected Imperial interests", Ishbel scoffed.[30] In answer to Aberdeen's lengthy report on the whole affair Chamberlain had expressed routine approval, while cautioning "discretion".

Laurier was sworn into office 11 July and opened a new parliament in mid-August. There Tupper Senior denounced Aberdeen and his "secret advisers", and was taunted by the Liberals. Tupper ostentatiously returned the golden gifts that Aberdeen had sent for his wedding anniversary. He maintained a fierce vendetta to the end of his days. Young Tupper joined in, made rudely aware of the fragility of viceregal friendship. He declared his inability to attend further social functions at Government House, "without compromising my self-respect".[31] Lady Aberdeen asked futilely for courtesy towards the Queen's representative but young Tupper abandoned courtesy:

> From my point of view, as I have already ventured to say, Lord Aberdeen appears as a Chief of a political party; and in his capacity as our Executive Head resembles more the President of the U.S. Republic than Her Majesty.[32]

The younger Tupper was author of an article sent to the *Northern Review* in Britain, repeating his accusation that Aberdeen had placed himself at the head of the Liberal Party in Canada. Sinclair took on the job of framing Aberdeen's reply, one of the last of the valuable services he performed for them. At the end of the year he departed to contest — and win — a by-election in Forfarshire. Ishbel was desolate.

There is a terrible blank in the house and no crutch to lean upon. Only those in the house know what a difference B's living in it has made to everybody. He seems to have won all hearts by his sunniness and tact and constant thought for others. But only the innermost circle know what he has been and how much, how very much we owe him both from a public and a private point of view.[33]

So Laurier took power, wearing the lucky charm Ishbel had sent her maid, Miss Gunn, to give him, as in an old romantic Highland custom of farewell to a hero who goes forth to battle. It was a sprig of white heather. With it he was given an enameled white heather pin as a more lasting souvenir.

Things settled down comfortably in the relationship between Governor-General and Prime Minister. "He [Laurier] was a loyal friend as well as a faithful counsellor, and with such a combination the course of transactions could not fail to run smoothly", Aberdeen recalled.[34] Young Archie called his most tuneful canary "Sir Wilfrid". Ishbel could be observed to doze, after a busy day, as she sat in her husband's study while Aberdeen and Laurier went over public matters.

Laurier "settled" the Manitoba school question without bloodshed or annexation of the West by the U.S. agreement was reached in November. Religious instruction by clergymen was permitted in the public schools after hours if parents or school board requested it; some Catholic teachers were to be hired; French instruction could be provided where population numbers warranted it. The Manitoba government was clearly the winner, and Catholics remained angry, but other Canadians were ready to wash their hands of the interminable debate.

Sir Charles Hibbert Tupper retired to Vancouver where he practiced law. Sir Mackenzie Bowell stumbled periodically into the Senate chamber where he was leader of the Opposition until 1906. He went home to Belleville at last and died in 1917.

The Liberal Party of Canada flourished like the well-known green bay-tree. Laurier had 15 years as Prime Minister. The party marched on after his death; it has been the governing party in Canada for the greater part of the present century. It has long survived the party of Gladstone and Asquith that handed on its name and a largely inappropriate set of political principles. And Ishbel went quietly — and sometimes not quietly — about more seemly pursuits.

Chapter 16
In the Queen's Honour

I tinerary for His Excellency and Lady Aberdeen, Sept. 8. Oct. 2: Toronto, St. Thomas, Windsor, Chatham, Sarnia, London, Peterborough, Stratford, Goderich, Brantford, Woodstock, Port Hope, Lindsay, Brockville, Picton, Amherstburg etc., Markham. Object: to visit agricultural fairs.

Ishbel's Journal:

> Sept. 8 [1896]. It is a weary grind, this process of being received at the station by the Mayor and Aldermen & perhaps a guard of honour, then a solemn drive around the town...
>
> Sept. 26. ...another week of 'progress' as it is called, through Ontario — that is, being bucketed from one place to another by night & going through the round of being received at the station, addresses presented, a procession round the town, reception at the Fair grounds, and attempt to go round the exhibits in the midst of a huge crowd, a long luncheon with nothing possible to eat, & visits to various schools, hospitals, convents & other institutions. We live our days to the tune of *God Save the Queen,* from the moment the train stops till it departs, & one sometimes wonders inwardly whether the moment will not arrive when instead of keeping up an inane smile, one will not seize someone and turn them around or shake them... I fear this is all horridly ungrateful... I think there has been a general desire to show that the feeling of the country was not with Sir Charles in his attack on H.E. At Peterborough the platform was fairly stormed and it collapsed — it was not high and no one was hurt... Next day another platform began to crack, & at the evening reception at Goderich the crowd became utterly unmanageable and fought with the militia brought in by Capt. Wilberforce's request to help keep the passage way. The mayor sent for the police & threatened to arrest any man who gave trouble, but there was a great discomfort and the poor wretches who

struggled through to the so-called 'reception' and to present addresses looked decidedly disheveled & irritable...

The electric light went out, & we finished our entertainment by the light of a single oil lamp...

The antidote, the recipe for survival, was good works. Ishbel had visited hundreds of communities, many very small, many almost without amenities. When she talked to women it was the lack of any help to call on in emergencies they minded most — when a child was dying, when a husband's arm was caught in machinery and severed. One died, or one lived, maimed and crippled.

There was an obvious solution. It was to provide a local nurse to go out among the people, or two nurses in a tiny hospital, a doctor too if one were very lucky. The National Council of Women had heard papers presented at their annual meetings on the care of the "sick poor". For some this suggested an urban slum. To the settlers of the North West it meant also an accessible refuge in the nearest town or village. For Ishbel, it turned promptly and practically into organized action, to accomplish at once a grand nation-wide plan for visiting "district" nurses, patterned after the British Institute of Queen's Nurses that had been established ten years earlier to honour the Queen on the Golden anniversary of her reign. Fortuitously, the Queen's reign was now in its *Diamond* anniversary year.

In 1896 Ishbel had quietly proposed to two Vancouver women that their Local Council send off a letter to the Executive for the National Council annual meeting that year. Another strategic suggestion brought a resolution from Halifax on the same theme. The resolution to take action to provide nursing and health care to the needy — to press the government for assistance — passed that 1896 annual meeting. Now, early in 1897, she was ready to go to work on the project. She undertook personally to secure government financial support through a grant — perhaps a million dollars — speaking privately to Prime Minister Laurier and his Minister of the Interior, Clifford Sifton. She had private discussions also with some of Montreal's leading doctors and believed they approved. An inaugural meeting to announce the national plan was set for 10 February, and Laurier promised to be there and give his support.

Unfortunately the Press got hold of the scheme and the *Herald* put it in print and is booming it finely...[1]

This was doubly unfortunate because it not only took the edge off the formal announcement on the 10th, it also left insufficient time to check out the original concept of "home helpers" with those whose co-operation was most urgently required, Canadian doctors and nurses. Ishbel, as she sketched out the plan, envisioned a sturdy, cheerful, practical nurse who would not be above preparing a nourishing meal for a family in case of sickness, and who would certainly charge nothing like the two dollars a day for home care agreed on by the fledgling profession of trained nurses. That "helper" would also, like her counterpart in Britain, act as midwife. Ishbel thus, with one stroke, managed to offend both the graduate nurses, fearful of the undercutting of their hard-won professional fee, and the doctors, who were doing their best to keep all nurses in a handmaiden role, and would not tolerate any threat to their own monopoly in obstetrics. In those days many doctors were indeed struggling to make a living; there were not enough wealthy patients. The plan was announced as promised 10 February, Laurier moving the resolution.

But Ishbel had barely got that initial meeting out of the way when there were interruptions. She had to be off to Tennessee to her brother Archie's wedding. Archie Marjoribanks was a near-invalid, but he and his Myssie Brown were about to be wed. Ishbel barely disguised her skeptical view of the union. She spoke of "Brother Jonathon", an allusion to the Biblical "I am distressed for thee, my brother Jonathon", and when she got to Nashville she said the bridegroom was "looking rather peaky".[2]

Nothing could be further from Ishbel's taste than the life style of Nashville's important families. The Southern belles were pretty, she had to concede, but fatuous in conversation. And very shrill: "We certainly did not come across the soft Southern voices of which we had heard so much. The parrot house at the zoo is the only thing one can compare one of these receptions to..."

Smugly she compared her Marjorie, brought up in wholesome English schoolgirl style, to these pampered damsels. Marjorie told her in horror that the girls she had spoken to knew nothing of bicycling, shooting, fishing, cooking or games.

"They just seem to go to parties every night and then stay in bed till twelve o'clock every morning!"

The tall, athletic daughter abominated feminine clothes, and it was a struggle to get her into her bridesmaid's attire. Ishbel wrote: "She considerably resented having her hair put up and putting on long petticoats and skirts and a low bodice and she was like a young colt throughout the performance."

Myssie, on the other hand, was beautifully gowned and radiantly happy, and the church was mobbed by the curious, with thirty extra police assigned to restrain them, at some expense to Archie. After a honeymoon in California the pair would move to England, to live at Bath near Lady Tweedmouth. Culture shock and a difficult mother-in-law awaited poor Myssie.

The wedding was mid-February. There follows a gap of almost three months in the Journal. Then it was May, and Ishbel was able to look back and set down with some composure the shock of Henry Drummond's death on 11 March, just before her fortieth birthday:

"...the dying out of a great light..," she wrote.[3]

Few had known, she said,

> so full and so perfect a friendship with one whose character and nature ever seemed to reveal new richness and new perfection the closer one came to him. None can know what it has all meant to us except himself and B. and ourselves. It has all been so perfect and there has never been a shade over our relationship since that first evening when he came into the drawing-room at Holyrood in May 1884 and when we seemed to know one another right away...

Ishbel had postponed a visit home the previous summer because of Henry's illness. She had been confident that he was improving in recent weeks and he held out that hope. He had written only of "the stupidity of being ill". She had been living in the expectation of seeing him in July, "and he himself thought that by that time he would be so much better. He had lost all pain and was beginning gradually to regain power of movement..." Only Sinclair ("B.") had not been deceived. Sinclair had gone immediately to Tunbridge Wells when he arrived in England for his election campaign. Just before returning to Canada to tidy up official business he had gone again to visit Henry, and had concealed his alarm, in the face of Henry's insistence that health was returning. Henry died before Sinclair reached New York.

"I received the day after his death some Tunbridge Wells violets sent to me through B.", Ishbel wrote.

The illness had so physically demolished Drummond that she could scarcely bear to recall her last sight of him in 1894 at Haddo House, when he had still appeared so alive and full of grace. What helped in this, and in overcoming the inevitable sense of guilt that "it was not given to us to be able to have had him to care for, as we might have had if we had been at home", was something Drummond himself had once said: "Our last real good-bye to a friend is the last day we see him in health."[4] The words would form a litany in her mind along with the other gentle phrases she cherished.

"His mother wrote me a beautiful letter and sent me a bit of his hair which had become almost white..."

The ghostly lock of hair is concealed in the back of the framed miniature of Drummond at Haddo House. On the frame itself is engraved a phrase from the 46th Psalm: "There is a river", which had been Drummond's blessing on their work in Canada.

Ishbel did in fact make a short visit to Britain as she had planned. Her letter to Drummond's mother was written from Haddo House:

Many thanks indeed for your kind letter, for the pin and book, I can only assure you that these dear tokens of our dear brother receive a fresh value by being entrusted to us in so loving and trustful a way by his mother. You have indeed been most generous to us... But most of all do I cherish your gift of his dear hair.[5]

The letter continues with the sad comment that every place she goes has so strong an association with Henry that her grief increases, and finally she thanks Mrs. Drummond for a gift she had sent for little Archie.

Lord Aberdeen helped arrange a memorial service at the private chapel they erected at Rideau Hall. Sinclair, the trusted friend and link with Henry, reached Ottawa just in time for that noon service, designed to take place at nearly the same hour as Henry's burial at Sterling.

"I can write no more about this, although memories are crowding about me."

Large gaps appear over the subsequent two years of her *Journal*. Henry had so lately been the recipient whose opinion she most dwelt on as she wrote; the Journal, circulating among a select few, had Henry always as a principal target. He had never failed to express his delight in her descriptions, even in his last letter from Biarritz.

The days at Rideau Hall fell into a flat, stale pattern. Sinclair returned to England in early April, "and he took away our little Archie with him to begin his school life — and thus the house is left with a most dreary silence and quietness brooding over it."[6]

She had a hard task to perform in this early period of mourning. The University of Chicago took pride in its female graduates and the women on its teaching staff. But its solemn Convocation rites had never been addressed by a woman. Largely through introductions to President Harper and others by Henry Drummond, who had lectured there in 1893 when Ishbel was caught up in the World's Fair extravaganza, an invitation had been extended to Ishbel to break that tradition and appear as honoured Orator on the Convocation platform. She had hesitated, then she had agreed.

"I consented for April, thinking it would please Henry and I wrote to him all about it, and when the time came, he was gone, and the motive for my going was gone."

Bravely she launched her discourse with a bit of fun: was this an April Fool's joke, this appearance on a previously male platform of a woman, and a woman innocent of college education? The crowd filled a vast auditorium "with great round galleries mounting up into the roof", all very hushed and still, according to local tradition, which admitted no jolly student outbursts or applause. "If I had not been warned, I should have thought I was getting into an absolute mess", she wrote.[7] In fact she was an unqualified success, as even the Toronto *Saturday Night,* which liked to regard vice-royalty with cool amusement, had to admit. The magazine's correspondent noted that she appeared on the platform "gowned in salmon silk, draped with black lace. She wore a single flower and a flashing jewel in her hair. Perfectly at home, she spoke with a clear enunciation... sober, thoughtful, interspersed with some very delicate shades of humour... [she] has won golden opinions..."[8]

The message she chose would have appealed to Drummond. She spoke of reconciling divisions among men and women, class and class, of seeking harmonious society. Ishbel told the collected lady and gentlemen scholars of Chicago that instead of moving proudly into a university elite they must repay a social debt. Every home that received a university graduate must be quickened and enlivened by that impact. It was as much the concern of male graduates as of educated wives to give a broader understanding back to the homes they would found as parents. Viewed otherwise, the university experience "becomes like a separate compartment into which none but the initiated may enter, and it loses thereby half its vitality and half its meaning ", she told them.

She spoke too of the "Woman's Age" in which they found themselves in the 1890's. They were going through a transition into true equality of the sexes, she said, and hot tempers would in due course give way to a fine and healthy comradeship.

> There are many of us who, whilst rejoicing in the new opportunities... yet have always felt that the banding of ourselves apart from men for various objects must be regarded in most cases as a temporary expedient... and it must not be allowed to crystallize into a permanent element in social life. Man was not meant to live alone, — but still less was woman.

She was proud that her voice carried in that large hall without strain. It could have been a terrible ordeal, "but I did want to say what I did say, so that was fulfilling Henry's rule."

Almost immediately after the Chicago visit Ishbel acquired honours nearer home. She was awarded an honorary degree at Queen's University, this time breaking precedent in Canada. "There was a proposition at first to create a special degree for women but ultimately it was thought best to give me the ordinary LL.D. and a good deal of interest was taken in the new departure."[9] Sir Sandford Fleming was Chancellor.

Queen's had no tradition of decorum at convocations. Here the undergraduates kept up a merry row, each recipient of a degree fair game for song and comment from the galleries. "I simply quaked... However they were very good to me and were quite silent all the time I was speaking... They sang 'For she's a jolly good fellow' and shouted 'What's the matter with Lady Aberdeen? She's all right, you bet!' Everybody was most kind..."

At the end of June she left for Britain, taking Marjorie with her. There were things to arrange, launching Haddo at Oxford and Dudley at Winchester. What would have been the greatest delight of the visit became a sad pilgrimage to Stirling, and a quiet talk with Henry's mother. Ishbel had passed the hours on shipboard reading Henry's letters "with a view to arranging them", and as she drew near Ireland she wrote in her Journal: "It is difficult to believe he will not be there to meet me. He was with me in Derry last time."

There was a round of family visits: to her mother at Bath, to Teddy (Lord Tweedmouth) and Fanny at Brook House, and to Aberdeen's mother. With Teddy and Fanny she was drawn briefly into prominent British Liberal circles again, attended a court ball, talked with Sir Henry Campbell-Bannerman who was taking over the leadership and with John Morley. The Jubilee celebrations were at their height. Wilfrid Laurier had, in part through their proposal, received a knighthood. He shone in London as the senior Prime Minister of the dominions and was much courted and dined. Ishbel met him with Mme Laurier at the Cecil hotel and wrote, "He is looking very well and not a bit spoilt."

Much of her time, with a weekend given to a final call on the Gladstones at Hawarden, went in passing on the reins of the Irish Industrial Association, while remaining Past President, and setting in motion the wheels of her next enterprise, the meeting of the International Council of Women scheduled for the following year in London. She must talk the English "Union of Women" into changing their name to a "National Council", and the discussions with their members and with various Jubilee guests to Britain were trying. "The German ladies disagreed with everything", while the leading spirit among British women, Mrs. Mandell Creighton whose husband was Bishop of London, was determined that her group, if they consented to host the affair, would retain a right of veto over the subjects for discussion. Mrs. Creighton was uneasy about outlandish resolutions that might come from lady reformers in various countries of Europe and America. She was asked, "What sort of subjects would you think it necessary to ban?" And Mrs. Creighton answered, "Marriage, divorce and all the New Woman ideas." Ishbel decided it was going to take more than a year to bring these opposites into one convention hall, and the Quinquennial Meeting was postponed to 1899, when she expected to be back in Britain.

This done, she and Marjorie sailed back to Canada, accompanied by the two younger boys, on holiday.

In these months, when Ishbel tried to adjust her life to Drummond's loss, her thoughts centred much on her quartet of children. Their lessons, their proper development, their sports and hobbies and games, had always received her careful supervision and whenever possible there was a daily period of personal instruction and reading aloud. At Stanley House, a very rustic holiday fishing lodge purchased by the previous governor-general in the Gaspé, on the Baie de Chaleur, she encouraged Marjorie, Dudley and Archie to build huts, to put on little plays for household entertainment, to write journals.

A degree of formality between parent and child seemed only good manners to her. Her children when they wrote letters addressed her curiously in the third person. But she was pleased at independent spirit and playful humour, determined not to follow the stifling and fear-ridden regimen of her own childhood. That summer at Stanley House she spent more time than usual watching her younger offspring, observing their prowess at swimming and boating, joining them when they rode, dreading the swift approach of fall and the boys' return to school. Dudley had daily lessons to make up for poor marks in Latin, French and English, but this second son was active, of an engineering turn of mind like his father and supremely happy telling his mother "his greatest idea of bliss is never to change from what he is, never to grow older, and spend all his time between this and Harrow." As for Archie, he shone in scholarship and in much else, the light of his mother's eyes.

During the quiet weeks on the Gaspé Ishbel also took time to wonder whether her husband's term in Canada had been the great period of service to the country she believed it would be that late autumn day in 1893 when they had listened to the pure eloquence of Henry's voice. *"There is a river, the streams whereof shall make glad the city of God."* The river of beneficence that must flow from their persons to the farthest reaches of Canada. And these musings brought her back to her project of visiting nurses, the work at hand.

Enmity to the scheme had developed by June, even before her visit home. The first protests had come from the nurses. Their struggle was still in progress, to establish their work not only as a profession but even as a decent vocation: not long past was the pre-Nightingale era of the nurse as despised and gin-drinking drudge. Many doctors looked on their efforts with the greatest suspicion; the nurses responded by creating boundaries which they were careful not to overstep, and by accepting work only as assigned by a supervising full-fledged medical man. To fit into this emerging pattern of things it was essential to revise the original concept; the "Victorian Order of Nurses" would employ only graduates from accredited nurses' training schools now developing within Canada's hospital system. To this diploma might be added special training by the Order itself in the techniques of home care. With this revision, the nurses could fall in enthusiastically with the scheme, and did so. The "Home Helper" idea would re-surface at intervals during the VON's long, excellent history of service, as a secondary stratum of assistants or, in to-day's parlance, "Homemakers". As for midwifery, it dropped out of sight as a function of the VON. Though VON nurses devoted much-needed care to mothers and infants they did not deliver babies except in dire circumstances with a doctor at least notified and "on call".

Ishbel had accepted the nurses' conditions in time to prevent much damage from that quarter. At a public meeting in April in Toronto where she spoke with some difficulty, apologizing for her severe cold — it was all too soon after Henry's death — she was already calling explicitly for "this order of thoroughly trained nurses".[10] The meeting did secure some lasting support in Toronto, notably from Roman Catholic Archbishop Walsh who wrote to her husband: "I am delighted to learn that the meeting at the Pavilion was a great success and that it promises excellent results. Lady Aberdeen's programme for her great undertaking is, in my opinion, marked with great good sense and practical wisdom, and, if successfully carried out, will be fraught with untold blessings for the Dominion."[11]

The change in regard to the nurses had its price. It would all cost a great deal more, for the trained nurse would expect a salary of about $300 a year while the Order could charge the patient only twenty-five cents an hour or some fraction thereof — often nothing at all. Community committees as fund raisers thus became eminently important to the plan, especially after Sir Wilfrid Laurier reluctantly told Ishbel he could not provide the hoped-for one million dollars from federal coffers. An all-party vote in parliament would be needed, and would be impossible to secure. Rejection by the Tory side of the House could be traced directly to the virulent charges against the Order now emanating from doctors' associations. Coincidentally Sir (Dr.) Charles Tupper, Opposition leader, had been a practicing physician and the first president of the Canadian Medical Association.

Ishbel had appealed widely to the general public. She had even sent an appeal to every public school in Canada:

> If the Queen herself should appear in your classrooms and ask you to do something for her, what a rush and competition there would be to do it! Well, Her Majesty has asked us all to do something. She has said, — 'Make This a Year of Jubilee to the Sick and Suffering of my Dominion!'[12]

The Queen had not exactly said this, but a trickle of nickels and dimes — no million dollars — arrived at Rideau Hall. Meanwhile in many places the all-important fund-raising committees were suspending action in the face of the doctors' assault.

In snobbish Toronto the doctors had opposed her from the start. Toronto's favoured weekly, *Saturday Night,* in a not-unsympathetic column, "Between You and Me" written by "Lady Gay" (Grace Denison) confided:

> A physician was airing his thoughts for my benefit to-day about the proposed Victorian Order of Home Helpers, which the Countess of Aberdeen is thinking of setting up. 'There are more trained nurses, and good ones too, than can find even a reasonable amount of work', he said decidedly. 'Look at the scores turned out yearly from the hospitals, unable to get engagements at even five dollars a week — I know some who would go for three!' Whereat I was much enlightened... I have often wondered how a fund would prosper to pay these trained nurses to attend and care for and advise our many sufferers among the patient poor.[13]

There was in Toronto an irritated feeling that Ishbel was far too condescending in her vice-regal role. This found accurate expression in a subsequent *Saturday Night* front page piece that delved into her personal motives:

> Rightly or wrongly, Her Excellency the Countess of Aberdeen is very widely suspected of a desire to use Canada as a footstool. Her scheme for founding an Order of Nurses would

have been taken up with enthusiasm only that people have a disagreeable feeling that anything that might be accomplished would only be taken as evidence of how much an Intellectual Lady can do even with a raw people in a wild country. There can be no doubt that Her Excellency is guided in this matter by motives that are beneficent and resolves that are highly generous. If she succeeds, — and I trust that success will crown her efforts, — a good institution will have been founded, and the credit, almost entirely, will have to belong to her head and heart. Yet success has been made very difficult by the fact that the Countess has shown that she must always be promoting something or emancipating somebody. Since coming to Canada, Lady Aberdeen has shown undoubted intellectual ability and a marvellous energy, yet she has ever created the impression in the Canadian public mind that she is conscious of the fact that in whatever she says or does, she is in the presence of an observant and gifted autobiographer who will ultimately do her justice in the eyes of the world and posterity, whatever the rabble of the hour and the place may say or think... Canadians are regarded by Her Excellency as wax figures to be moved here and there, and grouped thus and so in a series of pictures which will later on illustrate the great volume containing the story of her career...[14]

Which may have been shrewd psychology but was hardly charitable. What politician has not seen his exploits in large print, even as he performed them?

The Ontario Medical Association on June 3 dealt her a savage blow. It passed a resolution asserting that "it would be neglecting a serious duty if it failed to express its most unqualified disapproval of the scheme, on account of the dangers which must necessarily follow to the public should such an Order be established."

A similar resolution was passed by the Medical Society of Winnipeg: "with our more perfect knowledge of the Country in attending the sick, we feel that the scheme, at any rate as far as Manitoba and the North West is concerned, will prove an entire failure."

Now the Toronto *Globe* advised its readers: "An Order established against the advice of the medical societies and organizations of the Provinces would find its influence impaired. That is a result which all must be anxious to avoid."[15]

On Ishbel's first visit to Toronto after the trip to Britain, "the most absurd ideas of our plans were propounded to me."[16] She found staunch supporters here and there — in Ottawa

Professor James Robertson, Dominion Agricultural Secretary, familiar with the needs of the North West, who was acting as secretary of the VON Provisional Committee Ishbel had set up, and in Toronto a few prominent figures like Archbishop Walsh and Senator George A. Cox, President of the Bank of Commerce, who had joined the Provisional Committee. Cox arranged discreet meetings for her, and "most of them were successful." She thought it "very curious", though, "how business men will condemn a scheme without even asking what it means."[17] She talked to nursing superintendents. Then she discovered that meeting in Toronto was the British Science Association holding its annual meeting for the first time in the largest Dominion. ("Our last experience of the British Association was when it met in Aberdeen & we took a house in town for the week & Henry Drummond stayed with us and knew exactly which sections & which wise men to take us to hear.")[18] The 1897 President was Dr. Thomas G. Roddick, Montreal surgeon, who, as Deputy Surgeon General to the military unit despatched to the North West in 1885, had command of the first small group of Canadian army nurses. Roddick was head of Ishbel's Advisory Committee of doctors — most of them in Montreal.

Thus it happened that the prestigious Association received and passed a resolution "that in the opinion of this meeting the organization by a system of district nurses throughout the Provinces of the Dominion would afford invaluable help in the treatment of disease and be a great benefit to the sick poor of this colony."[19] Many British guests must have looked puzzled at this appearance on their agenda of a very parochial matter. Dr. Barnes of Carlisle, seconding the motion, said severely that he was surprised at the lack of any system of district nursing in Canada, a remark not calculated to please Canadian men who rallied to voice antagonistic views. Roddick dodged: details had still to be worked out, he told the gathering.

With her husband Ishbel was now taking another of their exhaustive tours, this time into the Maritime provinces. In Nova Scotia she was much aware that they had entered "Tupper country", yet she held a score of meetings intent on setting up VON committees.

They ventured into Cape Breton, "where no Governor General had penetrated", and at his Baddeck summer home met Alexander Graham Bell who, having given the world the telephone, was occupying his thoughts with an experimental flying machine. His wife Mabel, a Bostonian, "a deaf and dumb lady who was taught to speak and who undertakes all the duties of life in a wonderful way", had invited Lady Aberdeen to address her "Young Ladies' Club of Baddeck" . Mabel Bell's keen eyes more than made up for lack of hearing. In a graphic letter to her daughter in the United States she described her carefully planned luncheon for thirty guests, and the fidgeting of the Governor-General who, placed beside her, seemed totally unable to deal with her disability.[20] Aberdeen in fact became so agitated that signals were passed across the table: "Mrs. Kennan saw his wife elevate her eyebrows to him in a peculiar way so he quieted down until the ducks were served." But,with three dessert courses were still to come, Aberdeen's tolerance was exhausted and he stood abruptly, requiring hostess and guests to follow suit, and the party moved on to the afternoon gathering of Baddeck young ladies.

Ishbel, fortunately,was a great hit at the meeting, praising warmly the garlands and arches carefully prepared by townspeople, especially the schoolchildren. A correspondence developed between the two women, Mabel Bell seeking advice in setting up needlework classes for Baddeck girls to develop home industry, and receiving good advice and assistance from Ishbel.

At St. John, New Brunswick, Ishbel and her husband met with "a gathering of medical men convened to cross-examine me about the Victorian Order. As they were by way of all being antagonistic this was rather formidable... Dr. Travers made it clear that in his opinion the nurses would interfere with the province of the doctors, and another got up and asked, 'Is there really any district in Canada which needs nurses?' However the outcome was distinctly good..."[21] The St. John *Globe* noted that she had come to the city "particularly to advance a philanthropic scheme in which she is the principle mover in Canada, and the furtherance of which she has displayed zeal, earnestness and great business ability."[22]

Another meeting, another committee formed at Woodstock: "I feel that I have quite become a traveling lecturer with my bundles of pamphlets too which I distribute everywhere but it is the only way to make it go. And it *is* moving along now."[23]

What turned the tide decisively in the VON campaign was the inspired introduction of a "world authority" to the debate. This coup followed a visit to Princeton University where Aberdeen received an honorary degree. Princeton's President, Dr. Patton, occupied his position with great dignity, Ishbel conceded, "But as he sat in his President's chair to-day under his marble canopy one could not help thinking how Henry Drummond would have looked there. He was approached regarding the Presidency of this University but declined..." They met Dr. Woodrow Wilson, the future American President.

Of great significance to Ishbel was the meeting that followed, in Boston. She was the speaker at the Tremont Temple where a capacity crowd, including many expatriate Canadians, had met to hear her describe the plan for a VON, and to put $330 in a collection plate to support it. No one there knew that she had received that morning a letter from Professor Robertson, on behalf of the hard-pressed Provisional Committee. In view of the storm of adverse publicity, he advised her to give up the VON idea. Ishbel chose to ignore his timidity.

At the reception following the meeting she "met Miss [Charlotte] MacLeod, the Lady Supt. of the Waltham Training Home for District Nurses founded by Dr. [Alfred] Worcester of whom I have heard so much".[24] Miss MacLeod, a native of St. John, New Brunswick, was a "sweet, gentle feminine little person but with great reserve of powerful character behind." Ishbel learned that Waltham was only ten miles out of Boston and rearranged travel plans to visit the school the next day.

There she prevailed on Dr. Worcester to come to Canada and sell the VON. She was so confident of success that she also begged for and got the services of Miss MacLeod for a three-month initial period once the VON was in operation.

Dr. Worcester has recounted with some merriment his response to Ishbel's invitation.[25]

"I went to Ottawa little expecting what a perfect mess I should find."

He met with the Provisional Committee and worked with them through an all-day session involving a Montreal delegation. He was appalled that only a handful of Ottawa doctors deigned to put in an appearance. He therefore contrived with

Ishbel to set up a drinking-and-smoking free-and-easy late-evening occasion at Rideau Hall, Ishbel going off to bed. Twenty-five doctors came, "to have it out with him". He reported to Ishbel that for the first hour they were bitter and totally unreasonable, but when time and sympathy and liquor had done their work, "bye-and-bye they came round and ultimately became quite enthusiastic."

Next day they trooped back to Government House to meet with Ishbel. And she wrote: "A miracle has occurred! The Ottawa medical profession, as a body, has owned itself converted to the scheme for establishing the Victorian Order of Nurses."[26] She had Dr. Worcester work his magic at a meeting of the Ottawa Council of Women, and again at the Nurses' Institute. Ottawa was on side.

Next, with key members of the Provisional Committee, she followed the Montreal delegates back to that city to straighten out points in dispute. To her surprise good temper reigned. "It all ended in congratulations and pretty speeches and general jubilation. So again the walls of Jerico have fallen for Dr. Worcester... when he passed through on Monday and saw all and thought them almost hopeless."[27]

Unconquered still was the last bastion, Toronto. The leading Toronto opponent of the VON was Dr. Charles O'Reilly, house surgeon of the Toronto General Hospital and medical superintendent of its nurses in training. He was a close friend of former Lieutenant-Governor Kirkpatrick, of strong Conservative persuasion, who with his wife fostered much hostility towards the Aberdeens. Another urgent telegram brought Dr. Worcester a second time to Canada, to perform his final miracle. In Dr. Worcester's account:

> The change of heart on the part of the Ottawa doctors had had small effect, if any, upon their more numerous brethren in Toronto, where there existed a wider-spread and more bitter hostility to the Aberdeens than in Ottawa, where they had become better known. As the telegram warned me, if I should again enter the fray, I need expect no mercy from the enemy.
>
> Only too plainly I needed every possible reinforcement, for retreat was now of course out of the question. Remembering Dr. Osler's many previous kindnesses, I begged him to introduce me to his former Toronto colleagues. He promptly wired, urging me not to go into such a hostile camp and to

have nothing more to do with 'those Aberdeens', but adding that, as he had no idea I should be wise enough to heed his warning, he had already written to some of his friends there not to scalp me at first sight. These letters of his proved to be my salvation. And I cannot resist mentioning here with what glee, years after, when he had been closely associated with Lady Aberdeen in her anti-tuberculosis work in Ireland, I reminded him of his former very different opinion of the Earl and his Countess.[28]

Establishing contact with Dr. Osler's friends, all of whom advised him to get out from under the Aberdeens' roof, check in at a decent club and forget the VON, Worcester learned that Dr. O'Reilly was their main pillar of strength and he proceeded, on his first day in Toronto, to the General Hospital to meet the man and a few of his colleagues.

Ishbel explained: "Dr. Worcester had a terrible ordeal to go through the first day, for he decided to go right into the den of lions... and they gave it to him hot in a manner which pained him sorely, for they made no secret of their want of respect for nurses generally."[29]

St. George's Hall was rented the following day, and personal invitations from Her Excellency ensured that nearly two hundred medical men gathered to "scalp" him, while they partook of sandwiches and strong spirits. Says Dr. Worcester: "I spoke for an hour, but none listened." Then he invited questions, and got very rude ones. How much were the Aberdeens paying him? Did he think it was *decent* to come to Toronto to "instruct" them? Did he think they were going to be bamboozled because the name of the Queen was tacked to the title of the Order?

To all this Dr. Worcester applied an agile good humour. Shrewdly guessing that Victoria in fact rated very high with these gentlemen, he picked up that final question. He expressed astonishment that the great Queen, whom all the world admired, including a mere New Englander, should not receive respect from her Toronto subjects, and that her royal wish for a nursing order in her Dominion should be treated with contempt. This sobered them (since none of them knew that the Queen had precious little to do with the undertaking thus far). The doctors even ventured to apologize, and finally they cheered him. Dr. Worcester recalls:

Although it was past midnight, none of my excuses prevailed, and I had to go with some of the leading physicians and surgeons to their club. There they plied me with questions about the whole scheme of district visiting nurses, and promised their support at the great public meeting the next evening. For my bursting headache they insisted on whiskey and soda as the sovereign remedy, promising most faithfully to see me safely back to Government House...

There though he would have preferred to creep off to bed, he found the Aberdeens waiting up for him and:

I had to tell them all that had happened, while Lord Aberdeen brewed tea for me over their grate fire. For the lemon, that he insisted I must have in it, the good man himself went down to rummage in the pantries...

The public meeting that climaxed his Toronto visit could not fail to be a *tour de force*. Ishbel recorded: "Dr. Worcester's address at the public meeting was splendid and moved many to tears and there was no doubt after that that Toronto would be all right."

Charlotte MacLeod as first Lady Superintendent of the Victorian Order of Nurses arrived in November 1897, and the first twelve nurses were formally accepted into the Order that month. Eight communities from Baddeck to Vernon, British Columbia, had soon applied for nurses, guaranteeing their salaries and uniforms for at least a year, local Councils of Women helping in almost every case. And as the nurses went into operation, sometimes working out of small community hospitals, their assistance became much valued by the doctors, and testimonials flooded the annual reports of the VON.

Late 1897 saw the opening of the Klondike in a frenzied rush for gold. In this sensation of the moment Ishbel saw unparalleled opportunity for the VON. The tent cities of the Yukon gold fields were desperate for medical care.

Early in 1898 a letter from Lady Aberdeen filled several columns of the Toronto *Globe*:

I think it will interest your readers to know that the four district nurses who are to form the first contingent sent into the Yukon district by the Victorian Order of Nurses have now been appointed, namely, Miss Powell... Miss Payson... Miss Hannah... and Miss Scott. All these ladies are fully trained nurses and have splendid testimonials from leading physicians. They are fully aware of the hardships which they will have to face. The Government has decided to send our nurses forward under care of the detachment of troops which is to start about the end of April, and the present plan is that they accompany them all the way to Fort Selkirk, the probable capital of the district... May I hope that your readers, and especially friends of Klondikers, will subscribe to our Klondike nurses' expedition...

The rugged journey inland from the Pacific coast, the hardships endured in Fort Selkirk and Dawson City, were duly reported by Miss Powell and her letters were widely publicized by Lady Aberdeen. The *Globe* also sent along in the company of the nurses a female reporter, Faith Fenton. No other VON exploit was ever quite so adventurous. The enterprise, springing from Ishbel's fertile imagination, brought the name of the Order wide recognition.

By 19 May 1898 the Royal Charter, signed by Victoria, was finally secured, and with it royal permission to use and adapt the Queen's Nurses' badge and uniform. Even more cherished was a hand-written letter to Ishbel from the aged and ailing Florence Nightingale:

There is little fear but that any dissentient medical men will quickly learn from actual experience to appreciate the value to them of the District Nurse as an intelligent handmaid and not an interfering interloper. Heartily do we wish success to the Victorian Nurses and to all Canadian workers in this good cause. Again and again I give you joy of your beneficent work, and I am overflowingly your servant, Florence Nightingale.[30]

Ishbel would on their departure turn over to her successor the growing VON portfolio, so that the governors-general and their wives could maintain the royal link that gave a special importance to the association, soon many thousand strong. Some of her final hours in Canada were spent drafting by-laws for the VON, so that she could say at last:

Now we flatter ourselves that our Bye-laws [sic] and regulations are not only eminently wise and adaptable to the varying needs of different districts of Canada but also that in some aspects they are a distinct improvement on the Queen's Jubilee Institute rules.[31]

No gift to Canada has proved more valuable a commemoration of Lady Aberdeen's "reign" at Rideau Hall.

Chapter 17
A Difficult Farewell

The Aberdeens were not allowed even to leave Canada without debate: did they leave by choice or were they pressed to resign? In the first place, there was no "normal" term of office: previous governors-general had varied their stay from four to six years in the Ottawa post. Aberdeen, however, seemed to believe the departure premature, and sought to explain it in their memoirs. He carefully set forth his letter to Laurier in May 1898, which spoke of "private and family claims and interests" preventing him from filling "the full term of six years". In a footnote he said the correspondence must be made public to correct the "strange error which occurs in a biography of Sir Wilfrid Laurier, by Mr. O.D. Skelton."[1]

That "error" describes increasing friction between the Aberdeens and Joseph Chamberlain, Colonial Secretary. Chamberlain's appetite for imperial glory was leading towards the Boer War. According to Skelton, Chamberlain "neglected no opportunity of preparing the ground. In the summer of 1898 a new governor-general and a new commander of the Canadian militia were appointed..."[2]

In Canada rumours of Aberdeen's "recall" were afloat for months. They appeared to originate with Sir Charles Tupper, a strong figure in the campaign to rouse public sentiment in support of Britain's position in South Africa. Certainly the next Governor-General, Minto, would come to Canada very much Chamberlain's man. John W. Dafoe described Laurier's "continuous struggle with Lord Minto, a combination of country squire and a heavy dragoon, who was sent to Canada as Governor-General in 1898 to forward by every means in his power the Chamberlain policies."[3] In Canada there was some disappointment in the choice, made known in mid-July, since the country had come to expect someone who ranked rather high, "a Prince, or a Duke, or at least a commander-in-chief"[4] and Minto was known only as the military officer under Middleton in the North West Rebellion, who had afterwards organized an adventurous Canadian contingent of voyageurs to proceed up the Nile to the relief of Kartoum.

Preceding Minto in mid-1898 came the new Commander-in-Chief of the Canadian Militia, General Edward Hutton. His appointment was also from London. He was one of those officers who found ambivalence and conflict in the role, preferring to consider himself responsible to the War Office in London, with little regard for the Canadian Minister of Militia. His predecessor, General Gascoigne, had managed this dual accountability quite aimiably. Hutton would exceed his authority, since he believed his primary duty was to muster Canadian troops for Britain. He would be recalled after two years, when even Minto found it impossible to get along with him.

Though raising troops for Britain was a contentious issue, there was plenty of imperialist sentiment around. A Canadian stamp issued in 1898 showed a map with British possessions in red and the legend, "We hold a vaster Empire than has been." Goldwin Smith could write: "Toronto is the centre of jingoism and almost its circumference",[5] but in fact the excitement could be found well beyond Yonge Street. Loyalty to Britain shone forth everywhere in the English-speaking parts of the country. Meanwhile Britain had become very jingoistic indeed. Chamberlain led, and fed, the patriotic outbursts. Even in 1896, soon after his appointment, he had put thoughts on paper to his leader, Salisbury, saying:

> I think what is called an 'Act of Vigour' is required to soothe the wounded vanity of the nation [after the ill-fated Jameson Raid]. It does not much matter which of our numerous foes we defy but we ought to defy someone. I suggest... the immediate preparation of a force of troops for Capetown sufficient to make us masters of the situation in S. Africa.[6]

Chamberlain was determined that the colonies contribute their full share of those troops. On this issue, if on no other, he must have regarded Aberdeen as an impossible, representative of the Crown in Canada. The Aberdeens were clearly of that Liberal school opposed to British imperial expansion and in particular the quarrel with the Boers which carried with it: "an uneasy sense of ignoble motive, a glitter of the gold mines of the Rand, an aura of predatory capitalism, commercialism and profit.'"[7] Gladstone died 19 May of that year, after a few short years of retirement during which he had viewed affairs with increasing pessimism.'"I am contented with my half century', he said more than once, 'I do not envy my successors'" —so wrote his biographer.[8] Rosebery spoke sadly of "this bloody war", while John Morley thought England had lost all sense of moral direction, and even the old Whig Harcourt said, "In these days of lust of Empire we are a little in danger of losing some of the instincts of a governing race."[9] Such remarks brought epithets of "pro-Boer" and "Little Englander".

Some Liberals denounced the war all the more righteously because they were still in the process of discarding grandiose ideas of their own, of the high moral benefits Britain ought to bestow on various lands around the globe. No individual exhibited this dichotomy more richly than William T. Stead, an old friend of the Aberdeens, more particularly of Ishbel. Stead pursued fierce journalistic campaigns, first on the side of Cecil Rhodes and Sir Alfred Milner as heroic protagonists of "liberal imperialism" and then, as both demonstrated their bellicose intent, in remorseful breast-thumping at his error in judgment and his share of responsibility for a cruel war. Over several years he poured out letters to Ishbel, a favourite correspondent: "My responsibility in South Africa is very great, and no one knows it more than myself..."[10] Ishbel responded, "We cannot shirk the consequences of our own actions... be they what they may."[11]

The Aberdeens were no sooner back in Britain than they justified Chamberlain's darkest suspicions. Lord Aberdeen joined Stead and other Liberals in 1899 in what they called the International Crusade for Peace. Stead was at that time publishing, along with his *Review of Reviews*, a second journal called *War against War*. (Stead, incidentally, had little time left to pursue burning idealism. He was one of the ill-fated passengers on the Titanic in 1912.)[12]

If Aberdeen kept from their memoirs any hint other than "cordial" relations with Chamberlain over retirement in 1898, he must have been still less inclined to air a nastier innuendo that Tupper raised in the House of Commons and some newspapers saw as a further reason for Aberdeen's departure. This had to do with the Laurier government refusing approval of a steamship line contract Tupper had negotiated with the Allan Company of Glasgow, and putting in its place an agreement with Peterson-Tate, whose president was Ishbel's brother Teddy, Lord Tweedmouth. In the more rabid Tory papers Tweedmouth was portrayed as a millionaire who had "spent most of his time for ten years in handing out big checks" to the Liberal Party of England: "All that he received in return was a beggarly peerage" but now he stood to benefit substantially. "Dastardly and cowardly" said the Liberal press of these accusations.[13]

The press kept the issue of forced retirement alive. The Hamilton *Spectator* said in June that while the Tories were generally glad to "sing goodbye" at the formal farewells, Tupper could afford to say little because of his knowledge of the fact that Aberdeen has been recalled before his time was up."[14]

There were, on the other hand, personal reasons enough for leaving in 1898. Aberdeen put first his wish to see more of his elderly mother in London; he had always had a close attachment to her and had been unable to make the long trans-Atlantic journey during his term of office. Second was cost. They were very much in debt as a result of overspending on what they saw as the requirements of their office. Chamberlain wrote to their successor:

> I think I ought to say that Lord A. informs me that the expenditures of the office during his tenure of it has exceeded his salary by about £5000 a year. [The salary was £10,000.] I am under the impression that this is more than is necessary...[15]

A pressing reason also was their distance from the boys' schools. Poor Haddo was having a difficult time of it. In a weak and ill-formed hand he wrote frequently to "My Dearest Mother", signing himself "Mother's own St. George" in what appears to have been a pathetic attempt to live up to the name she used to inspire valour. He apologized to her for the epileptic recurrences which he called "warnings": "... when lunch was half through, I had a very bad warning, having to make a tour round the room, with Prof. H. following me..." "Another attack... I called out but was not heard: luckily I had my clothes clips on, which prevented me from falling out of bed... Mother will well understand that these attacks do the contrary to helping me with my work. I can't rouse my head to work when it is so full of nerves going on like they do..." As for golf: "I so seldom get good strokes." And in May, on reading in the papers of their end of term, "the joyful resignation is officially announced... I hope it is true..."[16]

So whether or not the Aberdeens were pressed to resign remains in doubt. The indications are there; the proof is not.

It could not in these circumstances be a wholly graceful exit. Bad-tempered opinions of the Aberdeens persisted almost until their boat left the dock. One city, Hamilton, even refused to host a farewell reception that summer. Yet Ishbel had, through the final months of their term, devoted herself to mending differences and recovering goodwill.

In August 1897 she and her husband had been entertained at a garden party at the Toronto home of Goldwin Smith. Smith among his various vehemently expressed opinions left no doubt that in his view their office in Canada was anachronistic and redundant. "The viceregal court at Ottawa struck him as a childish parody of British monarchy which wasted money and encouraged the worst type of social snobbery", according to his biographer.[17] For the August 1897 occasion Smith kept a firm check on such feelings, turning their visit into something approaching a state reception of dignitaries from some foreign land. Ishbel wrote:

> Yes, the Goldwin Smiths! Who would have thought that the day would have come when H.E. and Goldwin Smith would have been seen hobnobbing together & H.E. drinking his host's health in a silver goblet belonging to the first Governor of Ontario. [How "curious" that Smith] should be the man to receive us in the most absolute royal manner, every point of etiquette being most formally observed — red cloth — the Goldwin Smiths themselves on the doorsteps and he hat in hand all the time ready to fetch anyone we wanted to speak to. It was all very funny. They have a lovely place [The Grange, now embodied in the Art Gallery of Ontario in Toronto] — quite one of the oldest houses in Toronto with beautiful grounds.[18]

Toronto, said Ishbel, "considers itself the centre of the Dominion, although in truth it is very provincial." She had preferred Montreal, and it dawned on her, perhaps in consequence of the Goldwin Smith reception, that Toronto was jealous, felt snubbed, and that therefore, "We have to dispel this idea before we go."[19]

As might be expected, her assault on Toronto was magnifi-
cently done. She engaged the provincial Government House
for six weeks in November and December 1897, during the
interval between the occupancies of Lieutenant-Governor
Kirkpatrick and Laurier's appointee, Sir Oliver Mowat. She
wrote down the reasons for that visit:

> A. & I were perfectly aware that in the "Queen City" we had
> but few friends. Society was dead against us, led by Lady
> Kirkpatrick, who for some reason best known to herself
> appears to have conceived a violent antipathy to us from the
> outset, [and] who began by circulating all the silly stories
> about our domestic arrangements — servants not wearing
> caps, cook playing cards with H.E.... The Conservatives, of
> which party Toronto is the centre, were against us — not
> only because of the Tupper affair of 1896 but also because of
> our original sin in being Home Rulers & followers of Mr.
> Gladstone. The Orangemen were against us — for we had too
> many Roman Catholic friends and were too partial to Mon-
> treal & Quebec. The good people whose capital is also
> Toronto, were also against us, for had we not championed the
> compromise of silent prayer being used for the opening of the
> National Council instead of the audible. The great army of
> the Temperance people were against us — for we had
> expressed ourselves clearly averse to prohibition. And the
> last battalion to be ranged against us was that of the doctors,
> organised in virulent bitterness & complete ignorance by Dr.
> Charles O'Reilly against the Victorian Order & all its friends.
>   And the only thing to be done was to go straight ahead as
> if totally unconscious of the opposing hosts.[20]

Dr. Worcester's miraculous diplomacy defeated the "last
battalion". For the rest, there was a six-week campaign that
took the Ontario capital by storm. There were visits to every
institution and association of any consequence and an assiduous courting of Toronto's leading citizens. Her Excellency was
At Home on three successive Sunday afternoons at Government House, and the curious came and came again, each
afternoon a greater success than the previous one. There were
two dinners a week until almost everyone with the proper
clothes to wear had appeared at their table. There were four
Tuesday "Cinderella" dances for the younger set.
  The fine old Government House, which stood until 1912 in
a park-like setting on the present site of Roy Thompson Hall,

was partly the reason for the success of these affairs. It "lends itself so splendidly to entertaining", Ishbel wrote. "All the reception rooms communicate with each other by big doors and there is complete circulation all round the big central Hall from which a very wide staircase communicates with another vestibule above where people can sit out. The ballroom too opens by five doors into a big conservatory... and good cloakrooms too. Government House at Ottawa cannot hold a candle to it."[21]

Dazzled and impressed by viceregal splendour, the people of Toronto were also given multiple occasions to catch a glimpse of the warmer human side of the Aberdeens. Ishbel's six-week diary notes visits to Upper Canada College, St. Margaret's College and a flower show; suppers for notables; a Massey Hall concert; appearances at the Canadian Yacht Club, a Hunt Club meet and breakfast (where it was reported that "Her Excellency looked exceedingly well in her neat habit, a red wing lending a jaunty air to the black round hat."), a Salvation Army meeting; visits to Knox College, Grace Hospital, the Infants' Home, the Armouries, a Pure Food Show, the Orphans' Home and the Girls' Home; a St. Andrew's Dinner at the Queen's Hotel, a Hospital Bazaar, an Art Club gathering; visits to the Women's Medical College and the Sick Children's Hospital; an Osgoode Hall luncheon; visits to St. John's Hospital, a Women's Art Exhibition, the House of Providence for old people, St. Michael's Hospital, St. Joseph's Academy for Girls, Havergal College, Bishop Strachan School for Girls, the Fred Victor Mission, the Home for Incurables, the Central prison, the WCTU, the Ladies' Presbyterian College, the Loretto Abbey Convent, the Children's Aid, the Conservatory of Music, the Veterinary College, the Victoria Curling Rink, the Mercer Reformatory, the Victoria Skating Rink, the Haven and Prison Gate Mission, the House of Industry, the Old Folks' Home, the College of Music, the Western Hospital, the Globe printing office — and a few more, with church attendance twice on Sundays in the temples of various faiths.

This frantic performance was but prelude to the noblest grand ball of all time. It was held to climax their visit, on 28 December. They engaged the Armouries, despite its forbidding size, and easily filled it. At the first stage of planning Ishbel was able to enlist a true blue-blood, Major Septimus Denison, the Colonel's younger brother, who had been ADC to

Government House, Toronto, (1868-1912).

the Duke of Connaught, as Master of Ceremonies. He would continue to serve in their retinue during their final year as ADC to Aberdeen.

Everyone of note was soon angling for an invitation to the ball, for it was to be another of those lavishly costumed affairs that had inspired the press to lyric heights in Montreal and Ottawa. The motif this time was The Victorian Era. Tableaux and dances of great versatility celebrated the advance during their sovereign's reign in extending imperial rule to a quaint variety of smiling people; the glories of art and literature were depicted; then sports (hunting, tennis, archery and golf but *not* hockey); and finally industry, some ladies being attired as codfish and Marjorie managing to impersonate forests, while men were dressed as telephones, ladies had wings on their shoulders and postcards sewn to their gowns to celebrate the postal service, and a sparkling ensemble announced the arrival in the civilized world of electricity. Four hundred people were needed to produce this stunning montage. Another 2000 looked on from tiers of seats, and many of these were also "in fancy dress, and related more or less definitely to one or other of the sets."[22] The viceregal party must of course top it all, and did so, in velvet and silk and jewels, with pages and maids-in-waiting, trumpeters and courtiers, and two lieutenant-governors (from Manitoba and Ontario), with staff, in attendance on Their Excellencies.

The Aberdeens had tried to involve the Queen herself in this display, seeking a felicitous message from Windsor Castle. Their cable and letters were unhappily ignored. Aberdeen was inspired to manufacture a message from an earlier royal acknowledgement of his Jubilee congratulations. This did just as well, bringing the Toronto host to their feet in a spontaneous rendering of "God Save the Queen". Surely Victoria ought to have forgiven them this slight impertinence, but in fact she sent a sharp note of reprimand to Joseph Chamberlain, who passed it along to Rideau Hall.

Food was not wanting at the party. Ishbel thought they had done very well with an outlay of $2,100 to caterers Henry Webb and Company, who supplied "hot soup, hot little beef things, cold quail, cut up meats and all manner of sweets... Five hundred people could sit down at once at round tables and there were 100 waiters..."[23] Dancing followed into the early hours of the morning.

At the end of December this viceregal visit ended, and the Aberdeens turned the handsome house over to Lieutenant-Governor Mowat. On the final day but one, Ishbel received a visitation that went far to justify all she had attempted, for she had broken through to the very core of Toronto's defences, the ladies of high society in the town. No less a person than silver-haired Mrs. John Strachan requested an opportunity to call. Ishbel returned that afternoon from a charitable Christmas Tree party, to find her dressing-room packed full of Toronto's finest matrons, even including Lady Kirkpatrick. Mrs. Strachan read a prettily worded address, which spoke of appreciation and gratitude for all that had been arranged for the city in the previous six weeks. It was not only gracious but so surprisingly warm-hearted that Ishbel could scarcely find words to reply.

When they took train next morning they found their car festooned with roses. When they reached Ottawa a full turn-out of Laurier and his cabinet greeted them like campaigners returned from the field of conquest.

Ishbel seems to have made a particular effort to appear magnificent on the formal occasions of their last year in

Canada. Her gowns and jewels brought superlative comments in the press. On 3 February at the Drawing Room held in the Senate Chamber after the parliamentary opening, the Governor-General wore court dress to receive the bows and curtseys of the capital's élite — white satin knee breeches, silk stockings and buckled shoes, a dark blue coat braided with gold, and across his breast the Order of St. Michael and St. George. Beside him Ishbel glittered in a diamond necklace and a gown of dark green satin with steel embroidery, her feathers and veil creating an imposing headdress when added to her best diamond tiara, with the added touch of a pink rose in her chignon. The Ottawa *Free Press* reported that she had changed to a gown of pink satin with Duchesse lace for their Rideau Hall reception — "and that magnificent tiara of hers made of immense uncut emeralds and diamonds. Her throatlet is of the same gorgeous mixture of precious jewels. A person seeing them for the first time described them to me as barbarous in their magnificence."[24] A reporter from England writing a piece on "A Colonial Drawing Room" was quoted in the *Mail*: "... like a London crush — only, I think, even finer. Colonial women dress more daringly."[25]

On St. Patrick's Day it was black satin heavy with gold embroidery, the gown that had been created and presented to Ishbel by the women of Ireland, and with it golden Celtic ornaments. Thus robed Ishbel gave the formal address to the admiring St. Patrick's Literary and Scientific Association of Ottawa, whose spokesmen described the Aberdeens' 1886 term at Dublin Castle as a "golden age" of rather short duration. Ishbel's address dwelt on the Ireland of "heroes, of saints and of scholars" and the "fairy dew of natural magic" in its poetry.

Still more gorgeous were those masquerade occasions of which she was so fond. In July another "Historical Ball" in Montreal brought her to the fore representing a lady she claimed as an ancestor, since her maternal grandmother had been a La Tour. The early Acadian heroine who manned the battlements of Fort La Tour on the St. John River in 1645 was of the valiant sort that Ishbel most admired. Ishbel wore a costume in the style of the court of Louis XIII, doing Madame Françoise-Marie full honour. Beginning with a petticoat of white satin embroidered in coloured jewels, the costume added an over-dress of brocade with a short train, panniers and wide puffed sleeves, a high Medici collar of point lace and a stomacher of jeweled satin. With this went the "celebrated emeralds and diamonds. The headdress was of rich roses and ostrich tips..."[26]

The lavish entertainment at Rideau Hall that season was described in columns of newspaper prose and in the diaries of young women fortunate enough to be invited. Among these was Maud Edgar, the clever daughter of Sir James Edgar, now Speaker in Laurier's parliament. Maud saw the Rideau Hall grounds, got up for garden parties, as "a fairy garden... the paths shimmering with satin dresses..."[27]

But always, in Ishbel's mind, the glitter and pageantry must be justified on a moral plane. Maud Edgar was among those young women of Ottawa from homes of privilege who were drawn in by Ishbel in the spring of 1898 to another of her original and, as it turned out, lasting enterprises. Ishbel and His Excellency had both been favourably impressed by the pleasant appearance of several score of young women of the capital. Ishbel's lively fancy led her to propose a May Court Club, with a ritual queen and council and the encouragement to go forth and do useful community work. All that was required of the girls was to dress in pretty white frocks and arrive at Government House on May Day Eve — though Maud and several others had come earlier to help Lady Marjorie decorate the grounds and prepare diverse garlands and staffs of intertwined flowers. On a splendid spring day everyone turned out, was received by Lady Aberdeen and seated in the ballroom to hear Her Excellency give "a charming speech". It had to do with a revival of olden time festivities, dating from Tudor days in England, and revived by John Ruskin at Whitelands College. She spoke too in singularly moving tones of a similar club called simply "the '88" made up of London society girls. They had in 1888 been inspired by Henry Drummond to associate themselves in finding some outlet for a natural need to be of use and influence. Nobody wanted to be dowdy and abjure all pleasure, Ishbel said, one only wished to add a sense of coming power to be of some account and purpose in their world. Ruskin had urged: "What the woman is to be within her gates, as the centre of order, the balm of distress, and the mirror of beauty, that she is also to be without her gates, where order is more difficult, distress more imminent, loveliness more rare."[28]

In the bright sunshine of the Rideau Hall grounds there were bands and processions and the crowning, after popular ballot, of Miss Ethel Hamilton, daughter of the Anglican bishop, as Queen, with Maud Edgar and eleven others as Councillors. This was followed by such entertaining symbols of Merrie England as a May Pole dance, then a set of Lancers led by Lord Aberdeen with Miss Hamilton as partner, and "many curious things... Two beautiful cows decorated with flowers with horns covered with gilt paper and a table near them where four pretty dairy maids gave the people junket and syllabub. There was a jack-on-the-green and a chimney sweep beside him, and there was an Aunt Sally which the children threw at to get coconuts."[29]

So began an enduring Ottawa charity branching into several other Ontario cities, and giving comfort and encouragement in various ways to female students and also, and more especially, to the ill, the convalescent and their families.

In September 1898 the Montreal *Herald* used a quote from the Chicago *Record*, another instance of Ishbel's fame reverberating from other countries. Chicago had in fact many reasons to be aware of Her Excellency's existence and good works, and frequently commented on the unusual woman who reigned in Ottawa:

> She is particularly interested in the intellectual advancement of women, and during the last five years has roused the women of Canada in all social classes to improve their conditions. The wife of no Governor-General within recollection has created so much of a stir. The working girls, the shop-clerks, the servant class, the farmers' wives, the trained nurses, the schoolteachers, and every other class have received a share of her interest... Her successor at Rideau Hall, the Countess of Minto, is more of a society leader...[30]

The Chicago *Record* did not exaggerate. Ishbel's activities and energy seemed inexhaustible, and while she took the lead in introducing the "upper classes" to good works, she did what she could also for women of less social importance. The female teachers of Ottawa had been brought together to form an Educational Union. At their inaugural meeting over one hundred attended, diffident creatures whose notes rattled in their hands as they rose to speak. Ishbel helped them to devise a constitution and encouraged them to debate their own professional problems as well as the ideals of devoted service they espoused. The Union was a forerunner of the

Women Teachers' Federation of Ontario, the Ottawa branch of which was formed in 1907.

With the young teachers propelled towards organization, and the May Court girls proceeding to follow their own agenda in a competent fashion that surprised their founder, Ishbel wondered "whether something could be done to initiate Clubs amongst the Working Girls and Girls of Business in Ottawa."[31] She anticipated a link with the May Court: "We wanted to devise a plan so much whereby the society girls could be brought naturally into contact with the working girls in Ottawa, for there has been such a want of opportunity in this direction."[32]

On 20 October the Ottawa *Free Press* reported a visit by Her Excellency to the girls at work in the bindery of the Printing Bureau on Sussex Street. Accompanying her was the May Court Queen, Ethel Hamilton, and the president of the local Council of Women. She proposed that the bindery girls start a benefit society among themselves, with the object of assisting those of their number who fell ill or met with accidents. May Court and Local Council would step in to assist, but the Society would be self-sufficient — Ishbel had drawn advance advice from "some of the Labour people" and the local Workingmen's Benefit Society. "There are no women's Benefit Societies in Canada so far as we can gather, " Ishbel said. The union men were supportive, and the girls themselves, 120 of them were unanimous. They would pay a fifty-cent initiation fee and ten cents a fortnight, and each would be entitled to draw three dollars a week up to six weeks a year in time of need. "Miss Porteous the secretary is a capital girl", said Ishbel.

Farther afield, the Aberdeen Association to provide literature to the settlers of the North West, one of her earliest projects, was prospering. There were now fifteen local branches collecting and shipping books and magazines. Bundles came in from Britain and also a few from France for the packets to French-speaking settlers. Letters of thanks accumulated. In the prairie shacks during the long winters there were no visitors, no entertainment, and "the children dance for joy and will not go to sleep the night your parcel comes", one letter said.

As for her final triumph, the Victorian Order of Nurses, Ishbel could echo Sophocles: "the gods once more, after much rocking on a stormy surge, set her on an even keel."[33] She wrote as she was homeward bound that she was putting all her trust in the inestimable Charlotte MacLeod as Chief Superintendent of the Order. "Although I would have dearly loved the chance of nursing the Order for a few more months yet I believe that it is now understood and appreciated and is on an assured basis with some very loyal and solid friends to see it through."[34]

Even more firmly set on course was the Canadian National Council of Women. The annual meeting was held in Ottawa in May, with representatives from every Council in the country, from Victoria to Charlottetown, and only Calgary women unable to attend. They heard guest speakers from over the border, including Mrs. Dunlop Hopkins of New York who unfortunately began speaking "from an anti-man sort of attitude and this is never tolerated in out Council". On the agenda was a resolution demanding action against the practice of buying young women in China and importing them to British Columbia to be sold as slaves: the NCW was determined not to pretend such problems did not exist, or were not to be talked about. Ishbel spoke of the noticeable improvement that year in the "businesslike" tone of the conference: "people just say what they know and what they want to convey without any flowery speeches."[35] As the year wore on and the Aberdeens found themselves in the thick of farewell occasions Ishbel found it increasingly hard to express her admiration and affection for those "truly splendid women", and rejoiced particularly because young women like Maud Edgar, who had just graduated from the University of Toronto, were joining as members and playing responsible roles. Maud was appointed custodian of an annual fund of about $800 a year, pledges of support having been raised chiefly by Ishbel, to rent and maintain a double-roomed office in the Bank Street Chambers. Ishbel left there "my beloved desk with revolving top at which I have done all my work these past five years."[36] Her former secretary, Teresa Wilson, who had spent some months in Europe in the service of the ICW, was to take up the secretaryship of the Canadian Council.

Ishbel's last meeting with the national executive of the NCW took place at Government House in mid-October. "...a very touching but very trying Address to me, beautifully got up. It was read by Lady Thompson as Lady Laurier was not back from Quebec..."[37] Annie Thompson managed to read with only an occasional waver"; Ishbel embraced her and had a moment's trouble finding a voice to give them her own parting message. She described the Council as "a sisterhood of love".[38] (The Ottawa *Free Press* reporter, full of praise, dubbed the organization Canada's "parliament of women.") She taxed her own composure by referring to Drummond. "He dropped me a line one day giving me just this definition of happiness which he had picked up somewhere, and the words have lingered with me ever since — 'A great love and much service.'" Her husband averted the women's tears by stepping in with his usual cheery little speech, inviting them to the conservatory to be photographed by Topley.

The militant feminist from New York, Mrs. Hopkins, decided that Ishbel must have a full-length portrait of herself to present to the NCW. Ishbel thought this "a strange idea", and the future disposition of the portrait — duly executed by New York artist W.H. Funk — was left in some doubt. Funk had, according to Ishbel's journal, painted it on condition that it stay in her hands. She compromised by having a good copy prepared, intended for the parliament buildings if Laurier's wish was to be followed, but hung instead for many years in the fine oval bedroom where royalty sleeps when it visits Rideau Hall. The present Queen Elizabeth complained to her hostess that she found the portrait interfered with rest. As a young girl she was taken to visit Lady Aberdeen, who terrified her. The portrait was removed to the hidden stores of the National Gallery. For years it was not on view until Mrs. Lily Schreyer, wife of the Governor-General in the 1980's, had it brought to light, refurbished, and hung in an anteroom at Government House on 6 March 1984. The whereabouts of the earlier copy is not known.

The National Council of Women was the chief reason for subsequent visits by Ishbel to Canada. She returned in 1899, to sever her remaining ties with both NCW and VON. Chamberlain actively sought to prevent the visit, apparently because Lord Minto didn't relish her reappearance in Ottawa:

I have had a long and most characteristic correspondence with Lord A., which has ended I am sorry, but not surprised, to say in his deciding that Lady A. will go to Canada after all. He says it will only be a short visit terminating, I understand, on Nov. 2nd and she has private affairs connected with his estate to look after. I hope it will not be productive

A Meeting of the National Council of Women at Government House.

of annoyance to you, and I have done everything to influence its abandonment. I fancy, however, that Lady A. does not easily give up any idea that she has once taken into her head.[39]

Ishbel did not stay at Rideau Hall, as might have seemed appropriate, but at her own house at 578 Somerset Street, a "sweet little abode" given to her by Senator Cox. She had furnished it with many of her own pieces, and turned it over to the use of the VON. She was "in love" with the place because "for the first time in my life I am living in a house absolutely my own."[40]

Canada would see her again on several other NCW occasions, including the Fourth Quinquennial of the ICW held at Toronto in 1909. Lady Matilda Edgar was then President of the Canadian organization, and had with Emily Cummings planned and executed the affair, including a trip to the West Coast, returning through the United States, in a special train carrying the one hundred delegates from twelve different nations. Lady Grey, wife of the Governor-General 1904-11, welcomed "the ladies from over the seas" whole-heartedly at Rideau Hall. Ishbel was inspired to prepare a commemorative booklet, *Our Lady of the Sunshine and Her International Visitors*.[41]

Communication with her other Canadian enterprises would continue as well. In July 1904, when Ishbel's daughter Marjorie was married to Captain John Sinclair (later Lord Pentland), the May Court of Ottawa sent a silver heart-shaped jewel box decorated with the club's crest. Christmas cards by the hundred flowed for many years from Haddo House to every part of Canada.

In 1898 farewell from the politicians in June was accomplished in good style, though a certain amount of tact was required in the arrangements. Sir Charles Tupper had trumpeted that he would have no part in the proceedings, so Laurier found a time when Tupper would be off on a trip to Italy. The younger Tupper angrily announced in the Commons that he would view any Conservative participation as an insult to his father. The presentation ceremony took place in the Senate Chamber. Laurier moved the adoption by both Houses of a formal Address which praised Aberdeen's "unfailing courtesy and assiduous care" and his wife's "zealous co-operation". Whereupon George Foster spoke, stiffly but bravely, not going so far as to second the motion (which was seconded by another Liberal), but asserting that his party was "not blind to the many virtues of Their Excellencies, virtues which have endeared them to the people..."[42]

Conspicuous honour was paid to Lady Aberdeen. She shattered precedent when she became the first woman to speak in the Upper House. She had just been presented with a magnificent dinner service. It consisted of more than 200, pieces of Sir Henry Doulton's best "plain china", prepared by him for the individual artwork of the members of the Women's Art Association of Canada. "Ceramic artists" were much in vogue, and the decoration of the set was carefully supervised, each piece bearing a different design and depicting Canadian landscape, fruit, flowers, sea-shells and birds. It was valued at one thousand dollars, and bought at that price as a presentation gift to Ishbel from the Senate and House of Commons. It was destined to fill a cabinet made to receive it at Haddo House.

Portrait of Ishbel, Lady Aberdeen hanging in Rideau Hall, Ottawa.

Ishbel's acknowledgement, which she described in her journal merely as "rather an ordeal"[43] won her unstinting praise in the *Globe*. "It was grand as a piece of oratory, and her voice was simply thrilling. She brought tears to the eyes of all who were around her. I never saw an audience so captivated by a woman."[44]

In the autumn, when farewell banquets and receptions followed each other in inexorable succession, the Brockville *Recorder* unbent with a sympathetic bow in her direction, taking to task certain other newspapers for their "coarse wit". The *Recorder* told its readers that "Her Excellency is one of the brainiest women that ever trod Canadian soil, and sympathy of soul and breadth of thought are the prominent features of her every public word and act..."[45]

Toronto's expressions of farewell were the biggest surprise. Were Torontonians so glad to see them go that they filled the streets to cheer His Excellency as he made the first of untold numbers of speeches in the half-built new City Hall? Ishbel saw only "spontaneous kindness and goodwill and regret... utterly bewildering and overwhelming. They are a grand people..."[46]

If she felt some regret also, and toyed with the desire to stay a little longer, it was not however because of this effusive praise but because so much unfinished business pricked her conscience in those final weeks. On their journey west that summer she had noted in Port Arthur the need for a home for the aged. There was no provision for destitute old people except the jails, a situation common throughout Ontario. "Some 60 to 70 per cent of the jail population of Ontario consists of the old, the destitute and the feeble-minded."[47] She must stir the Councils of Women to add houses of refuge to their agenda.

Then, in Ottawa, she confessed "a sneaking fondness for the place itself, in spite of its shabby old Government House put away amongst its clump of bushes and in spite of dirty old tumbledown Sussex Street, to drive over which always needed an effort." And from this fondness grew "a scheme for a grand improvement of Ottawa, which if carried out would make her one day a very queen of capitals. The idea is to get a town plan made..."[48] And this she presented to Laurier and to Israel Tarte, Minister of Public Works, taking them on a drive around the Ottawa and then the Hull side of the river and proposing bridges, "a beautiful stately drive or esplanade", a park on Nepean Point and "a new and worthy Government House overlooking that lovely view of the river". Tarte, she found, was "not only enthusiastic about it but seemed to think it possible". Sir Wilfrid was "quite taken with the idea" and eager to turn Ottawa into "the Washington of the North."[49]

Ishbel's drawing of this, titled "Suggestion for Converting Sussex Street Ottawa into a Terrace Drive from the House of Parliament to a new Government House overlooking the River, 1898" remains in Aberdeenshire. But her insistence that plans should begin at once, to prevent "eyesores of buildings" from springing up, found supporters in the Laurier cabinet. Finance Minister W. S. Fielding urged Laurier to investigate the work of the District of Columbia along similar lines, giving full credit for inspiration, according to one account, to Lady Aberdeen.[50] The following year Fielding brought in legislation to create the Ottawa Improvement Commission with an annual budget of $60,000. The Greber city plan of the 1940's and the National Capital Commission with its present vast holdings of green space, heritage buildings and waterways, are direct descendants of that Improvement Commission.

Before they left the Aberdeen family relaxed for three weeks at Stanley House with the boys joining them on holiday from Britain, young Archie bearing trophies and form prizes from his first school term. They had, also, a quiet day in Arthabaska at Sir Wilfrid Laurier's home. "We talked over everything in Canada and out of it."[51] One of the last presentations was "one of those dear little red Quebec berlots sleighs as a gift from Sir Wilfrid and Lady Laurier". Before embarking they spent some time also in Quebec City, where Aberdeen unveiled the Champlain monument on Dufferin Terrace, "beautiful, full of life and movement."[52]

They sailed on the S.S. *Labrador* out of Quebec 12 November 1898, Sir Wilfrid and Lady Laurier, Mr. and Mrs. Fielding, and Emily Cummings among the party gathered to see them off. Ishbel looked at their depleted staff, four favourite aides-de-camp had gone off to fight and die in Cuba and South Africa, and found leave-taking painful. She mourned Canadians she had known with affection, particularly Sir John Thompson and Sir Joseph Chapleau. She thought too of returning to an England without Gladstone, and without Henry Drummond. On shipboard, when the Liverpool dock was not far distant, she polished off her Canadian Journal, her reluc-

Public Archives Canada.

At the Laurier home in Arthabasca, Quebeec, 1898. Seated: Sir Wilfrid Laurier, Lady Aberdeen, Lord Aberdeen, Lady Laurier; standing: The Honourable Marjorie Gordon, (unidentified girl); foreground: (unidentified child), The Honourable Dudley, The Honourable Archie Gordon.

tance in this task apparent as she wrote: "But this is not the time or the place to dwell on such thoughts [of remembrance], although they will intrude & many others akin to them."[53]

In Ottawa until recently the Aberdeen name was honoured only in one short street leading nowhere, and a fancy bit of architecture erected in 1898 at Lansdowne Park,[54] called at first the Aberdeen Pavilion (it was opened by His Lordship) but since then, more familiarly, the Cattle Castle or Cow Palace. A great many cows traipsed in and out of it at fair time, and the building in the late century is a derelict, troubling the conscience of successive city councils. In the fall of 1987, however, on the 90th anniversary of the VON, a plaque in Ishbel's honour was unveiled at Government House by Canada's first woman Governor-General, Her Excellency Jeanne Sauvé. Representing the family at the ceremony was Ishbel's granddaughter, Lady Jessamine Harmsworth, sister of the sixth Marquis of Aberdeen.

Part IV
YEARS AFTER

Part IV
YEARS AFTER

Chapter 18
Tides of Fortune

Immediately after the Aberdeens' return to Britain, late in 1898, Ishbel was invited by the Queen to dine and sleep at Windsor. Ishbel reported to Her Majesty the successful launching of the Victorian Order of Nurses. In the company that evening was the widowed Empress Frederick of Germany, the Queen's oldest daughter, mother of Kaiser William II, who was still a "friend" of Britain. They listened to a concert after dinner. Queen Victoria spent the evening in her wheelchair, and before Ishbel retired she was summoned to the Queen's side and received a kiss on each cheek

These were the closing years of Victoria's reign. In 1901 she would be dead and the corpulent middle-aged Prince of Wales would usher in the Edwardian Era. He was not a sovereign — it was not an era — to Ishbel's taste. She was more in sympathy with the attention to duty of King George V and Queen Mary, in their turn. Nevertheless the turn of the century and the Edwardian period were significant and taxing times for her.

They had returned to an England greatly changed. In London, Oscar Wilde had been delighting his sycophants with the epigrams of artificiality. Aubrey Beardsley had been perplexing the art lovers with his strange drawings in *The Yellow Book*. Those who called themselves the literati sampled the pleasures of absinthe and opium and *The Rubaiyat of Omar Khayyam* — while the stalwart British soldier quoted Kipling — who was mocked by Max Beerbohm. "Fin de Siècle" was a description for frenzied, shifting moods and fashions.

Ishbel had never been much affected by what went on in London salons. She looked for radical excitement in the Quinquennial Meeting of the International Council of Women, scheduled for June 1899 in London. National Councils had been born over the previous five years in Finland and Holland, Australia and Tasmania, to join the earlier groups in

Germany, Sweden, Britain, the United States and Canada. Delegates from these countries were joined in London by observers from Belgium, Italy, Russia, France, Norway, India, South Africa, the Argentine, Palestine and Persia — 300 participants were there. It was an amazing tribute to Ishbel's organizing zeal, delegated in part to her loyal personal secretary Teresa Wilson, as well as a reflection of end-of-century mood of the New Woman. The assembly pronounced for:

The right to equal pay for equal work;
Access to all professions according to aptitude, not sex;
State-paid maternity maintenance;
Development of modern household machinery to relieve women from household drudgery, etc.[1]

The debates, the resolutions, the reports were presented in public halls in London, with thousands of Londoners buying tickets to pack the galleries and listen. Ishbel's skills were tested in avoiding serious schisms. The most controversial question was the female franchise. Ishbel believed it crucial to present a good and solid image to the curious public, and to this end she sacrificed the urgent demand for the vote, leaving the subject off the agenda and encouraging a second forum of debate, alongside the main assembly, under the sponsorship of the Women's Suffrage Societies of Great Britain. Lasting bitterness does not seem to have resulted from this arrangement, however imperfect. The agenda of the main body was full enough: on it were issues of legal and social suppression of women, and also the threat of war and the need to establish international arbitration as a means of settling national quarrels. The ICW sent greetings to one of the earliest European Peace Conferences, then in session at the Hague. To put a nice final flourish to the proceedings Ishbel arranged the reception of the entire body of delegates at Windsor Castle.

At the 1899 meeting she passed on the presidency to the United States, represented by May Wright Sewell. But she was urged to resume the office in 1904, and her driving spirit was thereafter inseparable from the work of the ICW until her death in 1939.

Meanwhile, on their return to Britain from Canada, she and her husband "took up the old work again", leasing a house at 58 Grosvenor Square to be in the thick of the Liberal party struggle. Ishbel became President again of both the English and Scottish Women's Liberal Federations, and spoke on platforms at party conventions and at meetings everywhere.

> It was a time when we had special reason to keep the true Liberal fires burning; the South African War was being waged; free trade was being seriously threatened; Ireland was giving ample proof that even the 'twenty years of resolute government' [promised by Arthur Balfour as Irish Secretary under Salisbury] had not reconciled her...[2]

They had arrived just as the Liberals were changing leaders for a second time since Gladstone's resignation. During Rosebery's brief Prime Ministership, Sir William Harcourt had acted as leader in the Commons, though continually at odds with Rosebery. After the 1895 election, which the Liberals lost, Harcourt succeeded Rosebery as Opposition leader until December 1898, when he gave way to a more conciliatory figure, Henry Campbell-Bannerman would succeed in holding the party together during the Boer War period of anguish, and he would eventually regain office for the Liberals.

The crisis in the Liberal ranks was the split between those who still gloried in expansion of Empire and Britain's role as a "governing nation", who had favoured an increased British presence in South Africa, — and those who denounced policies of rampant imperialism which soon led to a cruel war. Ishbel had completed her political education in Canada. She was no longer persuaded that half the world's people looked humbly and eagerly to the benevolent guidance and protection of imperial England. She knew that when Chamberlain called on "the colonies" to join in a vast imperial design, there was growing distrust in Canada. The distrust increased year by year with every territorial or trade dispute settled in favour of the United States through the acquiescence of a "Mother Country" more interested in her own trade relations than in Canada's future. One of Ishbel's most faithful Canadian correspondents was Lady Matilda Edgar who wrote her in 1903:

> It seems to me the imperial feeling has weakened here. *You who know Canada* will understand the reception given to the announcement of the Alaska award. A flame of resentment

spread like wild fire through the land. It seems to have died down now but young Canada is very touchy and the subject of treaties is a sore one. Only yesterday Judge Hodgins gave a lecture before that ultra loyal United Empire Club on Canada's loss of territory through England's diplomatic blunders.[3]

Gladstone, Ishbel remembered, had never been led into rash imperial ambition. Britain must set a noble example, and must support responsible self-government in other lands as in her own. When Campbell-Bannerman as Prime Minister worked to establish a post-war responsible government in South Africa she could be proud of those who kept the "true Liberal" faith. Campbell-Bannerman had in fact throughout the war urged his fellow Liberals to keep their heads in regard to the Boer enemy. He called for fair treatment of those who would soon be "our fellow citizens" in a territory that would become part of the British Empire.[4]

Gladstone remained for Ishbel the great prophet of Liberal philosophy. He had favoured her husband, grandson of the Prime Minister with whom he had once served. On better acquaintance the attachment shifted primarily from Lord Aberdeen to his wife. In 1894 Ishbel had visited Gladstone and shared with him hours of quiet conversation. She had described it in an eight-page memorandum. Gladstone had begun by telling her wistfully: "Say what you will, I am a survival — a survival from the time of Sir Robert Peel — think of that!" He consoled himself with the thought that this last period of his life was a necessary time of meditation. But then he quoted the actor, John Philip Kemble, who said he must retire at last to "a period between the theatre and the grave." In the course of their conversation Gladstone asked her many questions about Canada and its French — English, Protestant — Catholic tensions. Later she had been pleased to discover the deference paid to him by the villagers when he went out:

> Little knots of people gathered about to see him and salute him as he started for his drive and during its course; their attitude and his and the respectful silence that prevailed was v. touching. I did not like the black hat and cape which he had adopted. He was v. much himself and v. playful most of the time — chaffing with Mrs. G. about her pronunciation of 'squarrel' instead of 'squirrel' and other words and leading her into it.[5]

When she recalled Gladstone's powerful image decades later she wrote:

> We complain of the apathy of the public in political affairs today, but I wonder if this is not the result of the present generation never having had the chance of coming under the spell of some great Leader whose whole soul was imbued with a sense of deep personal responsibility to serve his God, his Country, and Humanity.
>
> When he came into a room, conversation would at once be raised to a higher level — under the look of that eagle eye it was practically impossible to speak lightly of wrongs and sufferings of mankind, to talk slander, or admit to unworthy aims in public life.[6]

Almost immediately on Gladstone's death he became the subject of numerous biographies and many thousands of admiring words. Lord Ponsonby, whose lot it was in 1932 to contribute a Gladstone article to a compendium called *The Great Victorians*, was moved to complain: "To write about Gladstone is like writing about Mont Blanc or Niagara..."[7]

They entered the twentieth century without Gladstone. Mourning his absence, Ishbel grieved even more for the divergent path followed by his successor, Lord Rosebery. Rosebery was her contemporary and friend. In her 1894 memorandum she quoted Gladstone: "He spoke somewhat sorrowfully about Rosebery, 'I cannot understand him — he remains a closed book to me — and on the whole I feel I understand him less than I did twelve or fifteen years ago — and yet he has a vein of deep religious conviction in him. God be with him.' Later he said, 'He never consults me.'"[8]

Archibald Primrose, Lord Rosebery, was one of the most transient, least conspicuous and most inept of Britain's prime ministers, despite those personal qualities which in the 1880's made Ishbel consider him the obvious choice to follow after Gladstone. Rosebery had also liked and admired *her*, aiding Lord Aberdeen to his first political appointment in Edinburgh largely on the strength of the wife at his side. Rosebery had, says one perceptive biographer, "a humanistic admiration for remarkable people",[9] and he found young Lady Ishbel remarkable.

In October 1884 Ishbel had asked Rosebery to act as godfather to Archie, her newborn son; Henry Drummond had been asked to fill the same office, and he had accepted, humbly, this great responsibility. Rosebery's response was typical of the man:

> I am greatly flattered and consent on condition that mine is only a nominal responsibility. I am far from sure that I ought to be godfather to anybody. I can indeed be answerable for nobody, not even for myself... You will kindly explain the Brat's first name [Ian, Gaelic version of John] at your leisure. I say first because I cannot call it Christian. It appears to be some pagan remnant of the Picts...[10]

It amused him thereafter to address her as "My dear Gossip", since she was godparent also to *his* young son Neil; he explained the word originally was God-sib, or sister in God. Teasing and friendly letters passed between them. He scolded her for the fine gifts she sent Neil. The volume of her activities appalled him and he wrote, "Did you ever read the Life of the Elder Wilberforce in five volumes? It might give you useful hints in your work."[11]

He sent an unexpected note of sympathy to her when her oldest son left home to go to school: "...the first wrench of separation. It is a much harder blow than many that seem more severe, and it gave me much cause for meditation after you left."[12]

When she wrote him a long and earnest rebuke for failing to impress himself on party members when the succession to Gladstone seemed imminent, he answered, "Why do you not consider me a candidate for the commandership of the Forces, or to the Archbishopric of Canterbury? I am not a candidate for anything; and nothing and nobody can make me one."[13]

In 1892 his wife Hannah died, and he seems never to have recovered from that loss. His letters were truculent: "I am not going to any of Gladstone's meetings myself, nor am I therefore going to take or send my boys to them, so that I am afraid I cannot be of use to you."[14] Yet two months later he had the grace to sympathize with her enormous pain at not being sent again to Dublin. He impressed on her that he had had no part in that decision, "there was no one less behind the scenes, no one in fact more [disappointed] than Yours ever, R."[15]

When Queen Victoria summoned Rosebery to become Prime Minister in 1894 he was as diffident and self-conscious as he had been to Ishbel when she urged leadership upon him.

He had, in the conservative Algernon Cecil's words, a pathetic failure to perform", much like Hamlet. Cecil describes Rosebery as a Whig, though he would have disclaimed such an élitist approach to politics. Cecil's comments on Whiggery do seem applicable, however, not only to Rosebery but, in many respects, to Ishbel also:

> The Whigs were — for they are now, alas, for practical purposes extinct — a peculiar people... Their peculiarity lay precisely in the fact that they were tenacious at once of their social privileges and their political philanthropies, that they wanted to be perennially eminent and at the same time perpetually benevolent. The difficulty here is obvious enough. The contents of every purse are eventually expended; and a long series of *beaux gestes* and electoral benefactions will exhaust the finest inheritance.[16]

Rosebery moved sharply away from John Morley and the other Gladstonian faithful on the question of Empire [he began to suggest "British Commonwealth" as a better name], and even more particularly on Ireland, a country he had always detested. His theory on Home Rule was that it should be granted only when a majority of *Englishmen* agreed, since England was "the predominant partner". For years the friendship with Ishbel existed tenuously, as between Rosebery and other Liberals who were dismayed at his political course but unable to dislike him.

As for John Morley, who *had* been "behind the scenes" in 1892, Ishbel shared his loyalty to Gladstone but not much else. Morley was "a deep thinker" but not popular with the crowd. He was an earnest moralist, declaring in 1873 in his biography of Rousseau: "Those who would treat politics and morality apart will never understand the one or the other." But even he acknowledged that he was "a born doctrinaire".[17] It was a great relief to Ishbel when in 1906 Campbell-Bannerman made him Secretary of State for India, and gave the Irish Secretary post this time to James Bryce.

The Liberal party recovered quickly once the Boer War ended. At that point Joseph Chamberlain, Colonial Secretary, handed them a prime issue: defence of free trade. Britain had enjoyed free trade for more than half a century, and prospered. To most it meant lower-priced food for the expanding urban working class. In 1903 Chamberlain switched suddenly to a plan for Imperial Preference and Protective Tariffs. One of the dropouts after that miscalculation was thirty-year-old Winston Churchill, son of Randolph, who after some months of attacking his traditional party in increasingly violent terms, formally left it in April 1904 and moved toward the Liberals. In February he was a guest at Haddo House, and he wrote a somewhat pompous comment on the matter in Ishbel's velvet-bound guest book:

> Men change, parties change, governments change — even Colonial Secretaries change. But principles do not change. Whatever was scientifically true in the economic propositions established sixty years ago... will still be true as long as man remains a trading animal upon the surface of the habitable globe.[18]

In Ishbel's personal life, the early years of the century were troubled ones. On her own forty-second birthday, 14 March 1899, Lady Mary Georgina Ridley died. Though Ishbel must often have differed sharply from her beautiful and fashionable older sister such disloyalties were never spoken aloud. Ishbel commended her as a "prominent Conservative hostess" and mourned her death. For some years she inherited the care of the two Ridley daughters. In 1904 she mourned as deeply the death from cancer of Fanny (Churchill) Tweedmouth, Teddy's wife, a vibrant, highly intelligent woman whom she had been proud to claim as sister-in-law.

In 1900 her brother Archie, long in poor health, died at Bath; it was said he committed suicide. His only son Edward would also kill himself in young manhood a few years later. When Teddy's son Dudley also died prematurely the Tweedmouth line was extinguished.

Coutts Marjoribanks, in British Columbia, had an English bride, Agnes, and in 1901 brought his wife and small daughter, Ishbel Agnes, to visit at Haddo House. Despite all Ishbel's plans Coutts had never become a rich and powerful landowner in Canada's West. The great Okanagan adventure was winding down to a sorry ending to their dreams and their large investments.

Her daughter Marjorie married in 1904 Ishbel's young friend and political protegé Captain John Sinclair, who would soon inherit his title as Lord Pentland. Sinclair was much closer to Ishbel's age than to Marjorie's, yet whatever led to this turn of events did not preclude a mother's blessing, and her assurance in their memoirs that the marriage was most successful. Sinclair became private secretary to Campbell-Bannerman and later spent some years in India as Governor of Madras. There were two much-favoured Pentland grand-children.

Haddo's affairs were another matter. The unfortunate oldest son had to leave Oxford, and drifted rather aimlessly, pursuing various faddish roads to health. At Oxford he had met a classmate, Edward Cochayne who lived with his wid-owed mother Florence, a short, plain, modest but respectable woman. Haddo spoke of them frequently and in 1905 Ishbel invited them both to Haddo House for Christmas to sound them out. Ishbel and her husband were greatly concerned that Haddo's condition might be hereditary, and were firmly opposed to Haddo producing an heir. They had given him heavy advice on the subject to which he replied in confused but rebellious letters. He seemed to hint that the joys of marriage could surely be his, while avoiding parenthood, but Ishbel apparently thought this much too risky. He was in love with a girl named Evelyn, and believed he had "many evi-dences of her affection". He recognized his "responsibility to the family"; he believed there was danger of "bringing disease into the world", but he could not accept that he must never marry. Evelyn became engaged to another man — Haddo could not promise not to "direct my thoughts to somebody else."[19]

Haddo also at this point made a try for a parliamentary seat, exhausting himself in the attempt, and lost the contest.

Now in 1905 he proposed to take a flat by himself in London. In health terms alone it was a dangerous undertak-ing for him, for he was still subject to epileptic seizures. Ishbel therefore prevailed on Florence Cochayne to take the flat next his with a communicating door. Florence devoted herself to the young lord's welfare. Her letters to Ishbel reported the young man's restlessness and uncertain pursuit of women and of new miracle-working drugs and healers.

When time had established a certain mutual dependency Ishbel proposed to Florence that she contemplate marriage. Florence, in some distress answered:

> I am thinking and thinking of what you said. I love your boy
> dearly but had never thought of him in that way, and you

know he looks on me as a second mother. I don't believe anything else would ever occur to him unless suggested. I could not do that. It would hurt me to the very soul for him ever to feel contempt or anything like that for me, and don't you think he would?[20]

Since the widow would not propose on her own behalf, other measures must be looked to. Ishbel's mother, the dowager Lady Tweedmouth known to some of her grandchildren as "Granny Tweedles" was called in and settled the matter on a visit to London. Haddo accepted his manifest destiny and in May 1906 wrote to Dearest Mother: "There will shortly be a Lady Haddo in the family... I was two years out about her age. In other words she is the same as Mother."

Dudley, the second son, had passed up Cambridge as a waste of time and learned engineering on a practical level, as an apprentice in Hall Russell's shipyards in Aberdeen. How this son would cope with the duties of Earldom, should he succeed to the title, was a perplexing question. In the event, he solved matters by scarcely outlasting his delicate older brother who lived until 1965. He never took up residence at Haddo House, and turned the whole thing over to his oldest son David (a genuinely popular modern-day Lord Aberdeen) at the earliest opportunity.

Secretly Ishbel must have sighed in 1905 at the ironies of fate and the iron laws of primogeniture. Third in line was her Ian Archibald, the soul of upper-class charm, intelligence, health and good looks. At Winchester he excelled in sports as in studies; in 1903 he entered Balliol College and acquired with ease the university distinctions that had escaped Haddo and Dudley.

In 1906 a great election victory brought the Liberals back to power. The party had a clear majority, though pressed on the left by the potential threat of a large body of Labour M.P.'s. The Labour men were cajoled and favoured and brought into a satellite relationship. Then there were the Irish Nationalists, who would feel bitterly that their cause had increasingly less priority with the Liberals. The Aberdeens would have these men to deal with, for Campbell-Bannerman fulfilled their long aspiration for a second viceregal term in Ireland.

Ishbel played a discreet political role in the other public issue that tested "true Liberal" principles in those years —

female suffrage. The Liberals of Britain had been committed to this reform since the writings of their philosopher-founder John Stuart Mill. Why they never put promise into practice is hard for later generations to understand. Who were the powerful lobbyists arrayed against the move? How was the party at risk? Sadly, the intransigence must be attributed to prevalent male attitudes, as common among Liberals as Conservatives.

Ishbel carried petitions from the two Women's Liberal Federations to Campbell-Bannerman. They accomplished nothing. While still Opposition leader in 1904 Campbell-Bannerman had refused to support a private member's suffrage bill: it would be "so big a change". If he supported it the public might actually expect him to put it on his programme if elected to form a government, and "in such an event we should have too much on our hands as it is..." It was not "possible at present", though I have indicated my growing favour of the policy."[21]

Ishbel attempted to put John Morely on the spot, to oblige him to commit himself to champion female suffrage in that election campaign. He was asked to address a meeting of the combined English and Scottish Liberal Women's Federations, and present his thoughts on the franchise. He agreed to do so with the stipulation that his speech must not be publicized. At the gathering Ishbel, in introducing him claimed that the women present represented 60,000 English and Scottish Liberals working whole-heartedly to promote the Liberal cause. "When we suggest that the time has fully come when the responsibility, the privilege of parliamentary vote should be given us, the time is always inconvenient..."[22] she declared flatly. Morley admitted that Liberal procrastination in the matter was "thankless and ungracious". He promised the audience that at election time he would *go public*, making known to his constituents that if re-elected he would favour giving the vote to women.

Immediately afterwards Ishbel sought his approval to publication of his speech in a party leaflet. Morley sternly refused permission. "When I bargained there should be no reporters, I meant it", he wrote back. *"My speech is not to be reported.* I meant all that I said, but I must choose my own time and occasion for saying it publicly."[23]

When the election campaign came less than two years later Morley did not endorse female suffrage. His reason no doubt was that public opinion had turned against the suffragists because of the aggressive attitude they had begun to display. Lydia Pankhurst, whose dedication to the cause is now engraved in stone next the very precincts of the House of Lords, had founded the Women's Social and Political Union in 1903. The clamour for the vote reached fever pitch with the suffragists venting their frustration in breaking up political meetings of all parties, usually to the point of being noisily ejected. Campbell-Bannerman was given this treatment at a huge meeting in Albert Hall. Afterwards Ishbel, as spokesman for the two women's federations, wrote a letter of regret for the "unseemly methods used by certain exponents of the women's suffrage movement... We wish emphatically to disassociate ourselves from such methods, and believe that they can only retard and hinder the movement which we have so deeply at heart."[24]

Not surprisingly, Campbell-Bannerman's reply was smugly patronizing: "I am not sure that the two or three foolish ladies at the Albert Hall did not do something to enliven the meeting! But they ought to realize that no cause can be benefited by what is nothing more than a combination of vanity and bad manners."[25]

To those who admire Lydia Pankhurst and regard the suffragists as women of rare courage, treated with abominable harshness, apology for their behaviour seems cruel. Perhaps Ishbel reveals herself here at her most Whiggish. She would continue to make urgent appeals for the women's vote through the Liberal Federations and also through the International Council of Women, but she never personally advocated or approved violent tactics. Only with the war of 1914-18 war and women's patriotic performance in it, would a government give them the vote at last.

Her willingness to temporize on female suffrage was no doubt partly due to her total commitment in another sphere. The very meeting at Albert Hall interrupted by the feminists had been one in which Campbell-Bannerman made clear his commitment to Home Rule, and part of Ishbel's annoyance was because his words could scarcely be heard. Ishbel wanted to go back with her husband to Dublin Castle and see the consummation of that pact. If it all failed to turn out as she expected she never spoke of her disappointment. During the years of that second term at the Castle she also had to cope with great stress in personal and family fortunes: it appears overall as a dark period in her life.

Lady Tweedmouth spent a good deal of time in London with Teddy after the death of his wife. There she kept a firm matriarchal grip on family affairs. Under her eye was young Archie, writing exams at Oxford and following parliamentary affairs with a close attention, though distracted by what his grandmother thought was an absurd number of dinners, balls, and other social engagements. It seemed a young lady had her eye on him, and Granny Tweedles did not approve. Violet Asquith was the lively daughter of the new Chancellor of the Exchequer, an astute lawyer whose family had owned a small woollen mill in Yorkshire. Herbert Asquith's second wife Margot, a flamboyant trend-setter on the social scene, did not rank very high in Lady Tweedmouth's estimation, and there was some correspondence on the subject of the too-obvious attraction between Violet and Archie. Violet was only sixteen. Margot Asquith wrote that her stepdaughter was "warmly attached to Archie", and Lady Tweedmouth wrote in a rage to Ishbel that it was all "deplorable if it were not too ridiculous of the attractive and much sought-after boy, giving himself even that much away to an objectionable little minx."[26] The romance continued discreetly, despite Granny Tweedles' best efforts to suppress it.

In 1908 Lady Tweedmouth fell ill. She died in March of that year. Ishbel lamented her loss and extoled her virtues, and arranged a funeral cortège that looked rather like that of a head of state. "From her son's official residence the procession proceeded through the Horse Guards, down the Mall, past Buckingham Palace, up Constitution Hill, then up Park Lane and so to Kensal Green, where she was laid beside her husband."[27]

Tweedmouth had been appointed First Lord of the Admiralty in 1906, and was soon in trouble. Lady Tweedmouth had confided to Ishbel: "I am afraid Edward is harder pressed than ever and is having a *serious* time with the cabinet (this is *most private*). How will it end? He will not give way and I'm sure *he* was in the *right*."[28]

Tweedmouth was in difficulty on several fronts. He had inherited the bulk of his father's large estate, his chief assets invested in the Mieux brewery. But in 1906 the company was in bad shape. There were comments in the *Times* about mismanagement, resulting chiefly from a trade war among the leading breweries to acquire larger empires of licensed public houses. Mieux was running on a dangerously low margin without reducing its handsome dividends. Now the government, yielding to reformist clamour, was forcing restrictions on the ubiquitous pub. Compensation to the breweries for pub closures was in dispute. Mieux had gambled too heavily on uncontrolled expansion and was suffering losses. Tweedmouth was almost bankrupt. He was compelled to sell Brook House, Guisachan, and most of his father's art collection.

Although a successful Whip for the party, Tweedmouth's term in the Admiralty was generally deplorable. He was determined on expanding the navy, much against the policy of the Liberals generally. The *Times* was running editorials about naval build-up which it believed unwarranted; the newspapers believed Britain was adequately protected by international alliances and there was no immediate danger of war.[29] Pressed to reduce his estimates, Tweedmouth "at first wrote a sulky refusal, complaining that Asquith [Chancellor of the Exchequer] did not trust him and that he ought to have resigned long before rather than allow his estimates to be cut; but he eventually accepted."[30]

Then in March 1908 a sensational letter appeared in the *Times* alleging that correspondence on naval strength had passed between His Majesty, the German Emperor, and Lord Tweedmouth. An editorial expressed "painful surprise and just indignation". It condemned both the German Emperor for "secret appeals to the head of a department on which the national safety depends", and the ready compliance of a minister who apparently could be "privately influenced" by communication from "an exalted quarter".[31] Tweedmouth defended his exchange with the Kaiser as "private and personal". Lord Rosebery loyally spoke in his defence, urging the country to remember that the Kaiser was "born of an English mother" and was not the nation's enemy. But Asquith, now successor to Campbell-Bannerman, asked for Tweedmouth's resignation. Asquith formed a new cabinet which brought in Winston Churchill as President of the Board of Trade and Lloyd George (called a "thorough-going Radical" in the *Times*) as Chancellor of the Exchequer.

In June that year the *Aberdeen Free Press* reported that Tweedmouth had suffered a nervous breakdown, though less discreet journals said he had become "deranged" and there were hints that syphilis had overtaken him, as had been the case with Randolph Churchill. Roy Jenkins' biography of Asquith states bluntly that Tweedmouth "soon became insane" after taking the Admiralty post.[32] Tweedmouth left the government (he had been made to Lord President of the Council), moving to Dublin and the care of his sister, Lady Aberdeen. A lodge was made available to him there until he died in September 1909. Ishbel got up an elaborate memorial volume to honour and vindicate him.

As if the death of her mother, her sisters and brothers — the oldest ruined and disgraced — and the loss of her childhood home and her family's wealth were not enough, Ishbel was dealt the hardest blow of all in the death of her young son Archie.

Archie had graduated from Oxford in 1906 with an honours degree in history. He had decided to learn banking — perhaps with a view to rebuilding his family's eroding capital assets, perhaps reminded of his respected great-grandfather, Edward Marjoribanks, at Coutts'. He had gone off to Berlin to attach himself for a year as a *"voluntaire"* to the Dresdner Bank, following up with a stint at the Banque de l'Union Parisienne in Paris. (In one of his blithe letters to his sister Marjorie he said he had won instant respect among French co-workers when he showed them a Canadian one-dollar bill bearing the likeness of his parents.) He entered the firm of Dunn, Fischer & Co. in London. From time to time he was in Dublin, serving his father as an ADC.

In 1909 his interest in politics was quickening. The historic debate on the powers of Commons versus Lords, brought on by Lloyd George's revolutionary budget, was riveting attention in the financial world, and it brought Archie night after night as a spectator to the galleries at Westminster. He was twenty-five years old.

Late in November 1909 he was driving his new open Daimler toward London at the respectable speed of 25 miles an hour when he was struck by a car that suddenly emerged from a side road ahead. Archie was the only casualty. Shocked friends and former tutors wrote of his young vitality and good spirits, of a crystalline quality of temperament that embodied

The Honourable Archie Gordon, A.D.C. to his Father, Lord
Aberdeen, Viceroy of Ireland, 1906-1915.

chivalry and open sincerity, of his great promise. He was buried in the private cemetery at Haddo House. Among the mourners was a stricken Miss Asquith who placed on his coffin a little wreath of violets bearing the inscription, "to my Beloved".

Chapter 19
The Crown Jewels of Ireland

The Aberdeens' second viceregal term in Ireland lasted from 1906 to 1915.

> We find ourselves in difficulty in dealing with the nine years which we lived at the Viceregal Lodge... for, curious to relate, we have few records relating to that period beyond official documents... There seemed to be always so much more to do than we could possibly accomplish.[1]

No doubt, as well, the pain of family tragedies drained Ishbel during those years of the exuberance with which she had always relished her own life and described it in full detail. How much influence did she exert in those years? Did she guide the actions of the Lord Lieutenant of Ireland or offer him only counsel and advice? Her health care projects were her own, but the part she may have played in political events is not clear.

Ishbel was now entering her fifties. She was no longer the darling of the crowd, the intensely alive young woman with her small brood of adorable children who had entered Dublin in 1886. Then she had exclaimed to Henry Drummond how the avid press reported the arrangement of every curl in her coiffure. Now there was cool distance, the embarrassment of former friends, the open enmity of the Irish aristocracy.

Dublin Castle had during the Conservative régime swung back to its traditional role. It was the symbolic fortress of the ruling British with entrée held by Irish peers, many of whom, according to scornful patriots, had received their titles in 1800 for selling out Ireland in the act of union that ended the Irish parliament. These Lords were politically loyal to the Conservative-Unionist party — and desperately and vocally loyal to the Crown. Meanwhile rebellion flared in the country-side over rents and harvests, with increasingly virulent protest groups, and in Dublin and other towns among the hard-pressed workers.

While the Conservative-Unionist government remained in power there had been no Home Rule nonsense at the Castle. Two successive Viceroys, the Marquess of London-derry and Lord Dudley, both wealthy, each supported by a gracious and benevolent wife, had restored Dublin Castle to its proper "tone". In addition, economic progress had been made under the Salisbury government with a better Land Act and an active Congestive Districts Board headed by Horace Plunkett, who kept up a correspondence with Lady Aberdeen over economic and educational reform.

Said an observer:

> Socially, the two viceroyalties had been brilliant successes. The Tory Government had everything in its favour... for ten years in succession the Dublin season was ever one of splen-dour... and yet the cry for Home Rule was not less shrill nor less determined...[2]

Dublin Castle perched in the centre of the old town surrounded by its high ancient walls like a beleaguered garrison. Provisioners of a garrison run certain hazards. Dubliners generally were desperately poor, and the largesse of patronage and trade emanating from the Castle created a violently expressed ambivalence. Thackeray had mocked the scene:

> Oh what will become of poor Dame-street?
> And who'll ait the puffs and the tarts,
> When this Court of Imparial splendour
> From Dublin's sad city departs?[3]

Thackeray died in 1863 but half a century later his satire was still appropriate. True Irishmen despised the sycophants, and men like Dublin's mayor were caught in a constant dilemma.

The election of 1906 upset the traditional feudal pattern. In the British parliament the Irish Nationalists were now united in a moderate, centrist party under John Edward Redmond. In 1906 he supported the new Liberal government under Campbell-Bannerman's leadership. His objective was to gain the long-promised Home Rule, which was to grant a large measure of independence to an Ireland under the British Crown. ("Like Canada", as John Morley had always explained.) But the resurrection of this policy under the Liberals in 1906 took the form of a long-term goal; delays multiplied. In simple political terms the Liberals had a clear majority and did not depend on Irish Nationalist votes in the Commons. In Ireland, "the Nationalist Party was inclined to be sullen, realizing their futility."[4]

Increasingly Irishmen turned to the Sinn Fein (Ourselves Alone), a boldly anti-British movement preaching an Irish republic. Repeatedly its leaders were jailed for sedition. It published two vigorous newspapers in Dublin, critical of Redmond, caustic about The Castle. A resurgent literature and drama revived the Gaelic tongue and scorned to accept Castle patronage.

Into this milieu came the Aberdeens. Their status was diminished. Lord Aberdeen had some months after his appointment found it necessary to consult Herbert Asquith, Chancellor of the Exchequer, about his proper role, referring back to the controversy that had excluded him in 1892, and subsequent modification of viceregal powers. Asquith referred the matter to Prime Minister Campbell-Bannerman with the comment: "The experience of the past twelve months has confirmed the opinion previously formed, viz. that the L.L. [Lord Lieutenant] can perform his proper functions better when not a member of the Cabinet. (This remark is intended as one of general application, even apart from actual present circumstances; though no doubt it may be specially applicable to the present L.L.)"[5]

A politically-involved Viceroy was clearly not desired. Ishbel was obviously aware of the new restrictions, and the decision of the Liberals to put Home Rule on the back burner. Her reactions are not recorded, though one can imagine how she chafed at the situation. Her daughter-biographer states that "on their first night back in The Castle she wrote, 'I feel as if the years of looking forward to this business had almost worn out one's powers of being fresh about it. Our disposition is to go very cannily and feel our way...' "[6]

Their welcome back to Ireland was sympathetic to a degree, but constrained. Those who had loudly mourned their

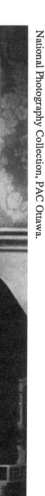

At the Vice Regal Lodge, Dublin.

departure — along with the hope of Home Rule — in 1886 turned up to greet them on their return, somewhat uneasily. They formed a deputation to present an address of welcome. The stilted occasion, according to the writer O'Mahony, "represented something as Victorian as an antimacassar." The London *Times* reported that some nationalist elements in Dublin dared to hope that the appointment had special significance, and Nationalist party leaders warned that "the disappointment of that expectation would be disastrous indeed."[7] But the nationalist *Freeman's Journal* chastised those who had taken part in the welcoming gesture. It stated firmly that the huge 1886 demonstration had not been for Aberdeen as Viceroy but for Aberdeen as "the colleague of Mr. Gladstone in his great effort to restore our ancient liberties... When those liberties are restored [we] will be prepared to address him in his official character also, but not till then."[8]

The Conservative elements began by punctiliously addressing the new Viceroy as representative of the sovereign. Their antipathy hardened, making the ceremonial office difficult.

> As time went on the Unionist landlords and their families absented themselves from the Viceregal Court, when it was perceived that the Home Rule Bill would be pressed through. Thereby they greatly diminished the brilliance of our balls and dinners, and we deeply regretted losing the company of many personal friends, but we could scarcely be held responsible for their abstention.[9]

Amid these difficulties Ishbel worked tirelessly for those causes within her province. Shortly after their arrival, late in 1906, she announced that the highlight of the next Season would be an Irish Lace Ball, with all those in attendance decked in lace. Local lacemakers had a most profitable winter. In 1909 she arranged a Pageant of Irish Industries in the style of their elaborate Ottawa and Toronto costume balls, celebrating such themes as Carpets, Curtains and Shipbuilding. Her Irish Industries Association turned over £25,000 of business a year at the Irish Lace Depot on College Green — the enterprise prospered until war broke out in 1914. R.M. Martin, its manager, recalled it as "an unique example of a great voluntary work by people of vision."[10]

Rivaling the I.I.A. for her attention was a new health league, formed chiefly to fight tuberculosis. She called it the Women's National Health Association. Ishbel launched it with a "Crusade", sending a caravan to travel the small roads into towns and villages and tell the people how to defeat the terrible killer with fresh air, rest and proper diet. The Crusade was opened in October 1907 by Sir William Osler of Montreal, then Regius Professor of Medicine at Oxford. Osler had long since revised his opinion of "those Aberdeens" who, in Canada, had so stubbornly pressed for a Victorian Order of Nurses. He gave every encouragement to the anti-T.B. project. The British parliament in 1908, after much delay, passed a Tuberculosis Act which included the compulsory reporting of all tuberculosis cases. To Ishbel's regret the Sinn Fein seized on the compulsory feature of the bill as evidence of British dictatorial attitude toward the Irish, and opposed it vehemently. But Osler wrote her:

> Of course it is without precedent, that is why it is needed. The same sort of opposition occurred in New York, but experience there is overwhelming in its favour: no single measure has been so important.[11]

The *Times* ran a long editorial praising her Crusade. It estimated that one-sixth of the population of Ireland had been reached by the lantern-slides, lectures and pamphlets of the caravan. England's death rate from tuberculosis had begun to drop through municipal efforts to preach "active hygiene measures", but the death rate in Ireland until 1907 had been twice as high as England's, and rising. In the year of the Crusade, for the first time, the rate dropped. The *Times* described Ishbel's successful efforts to get schools to give courses in home nursing of TB patients, and her pressure on town councils to augment the diet of the poor with fresh eggs, milk and meat. Her N.W.H.A. had opened an Infants' Milk Depot in Dublin, paid for, through the intercession of Lady Aberdeen, by Nathan Strauss of New York. It was an impressive story and "outsiders have no idea of the hard work, trouble, patience and whole-heartedness with which Lady Aberdeen has entered into the undertaking", said the *Times*.

Ishbel exulted: "Aren't the figures splendacious? Just fancy, the *Times* has a special article and leader about us: I can hardly credit it!"[12]

Her work was also recognized with a first prize award in 1908 from the Washington Congress on Tuberculosis, and by honorary membership, the first conferred on a woman, in the British Medical Association.

When Lloyd George brought in the Health Insurance Bill of 1911 Ishbel seized the opportunity to forward her health projects. The legislation allowed a million and a half pounds for anti-tuberculosis work. Ishbel wanted £25,000 of it, to open a sanatorium at Peamount in Dublin. She requested that the Irish Women's Health Association be designated as an "authorized agency" under the Act, to administer the necessary funds. The chief obstacle in her way was Sir Henry Robinson, head of the Irish Local Government Board. Earlier he had sent her a condescending letter: "Upon my word it is perfectly marvellous all this work about cleanliness, health and disease prevention!" But when he heard of her application for funds he advised the Treasury office against subsidizing "an association of irresponsible women."

Ishbel fought for her grant. Crossing the channel she insisted on a further meeting with Health Insurance officials, with Sir Henry Robinson present. She wrote back to her husband:

> It was war, open and declared, this morning. I was real sorry for Birrell [Augustine Birrell, then Secretary for Ireland], truly wishing to be nice to me and yet at the same time to act up to his instructions from Sir H.R. The latter made no pretence of concealing his hostility and would not give way an inch. Masterman [chairman of the National Insurance Commission] in the chair was most friendly and supporting. Mr. Birrell asked me to return at 7 p.m.; by then there had been an interview with Mr. Lloyd George, they understand that we have taken every step in conjunction with the County Councils. Mr. Birrell is writing to the Councils that we are authorized to do the work, that all speed will be made to have the buildings ready by October. He authorized the purchase of Peamount to be carried through tomorrow![13]

Peamount Sanatorium was opened on 1 October 1912, the day the Health Insurance Act became operative. Charles Masterman wrote in 1915, as the Aberdeens were leaving Ireland:

> I am proud to have helped a little bit in the work, attempting to co-ordinate the New Government Insurance work with the great voluntary agencies you have created — and despite some opposition and delay from quarters whence we should not have expected it, we did (after all), or *you* did, build the first Sanatorium under the Act, months and even years before the ordinary local authorities, in England as much as in Ireland, had even begun to think about the problem.[14]

Many touching appeals reached Ishbel from parents of children with tuberculosis, begging for treatment. The Insurance plan would not cover them — dependants were not yet eligible under the plan. Peamount's budget, even with government and local subsidies, could not carry the cost. The only salvation, as usual, seemed to lie in rich New York. Lord Aberdeen wrote Asquith proposing that he be allowed to take a brief absence from Ireland for the purpose of raising funds in America for the Peamount Sanatorium, and got a perplexed and frosty reply. Asquith said he doubted the King would approve. So Ishbel went alone. She was back in three weeks with enough dollars to make up the deficit. In another time of crisis she sold a number of her own most valuable jewels.

Ishbel did not much admire Lloyd George, the Welsh rebel springing up on the left extremity of the party. Her sympathies remained with Asquith in later years when Lloyd George took over the party and created a division — an unforgivable offence in Ishbel's view. And Lloyd George held no high regard for the Aberdeens. But he did acknowledge Ishbel's success in the anti-TB campaign. Writing to her husband in 1914 he added a gratuitous paragraph:

> I know how much we are indebted to Lady Aberdeen for all her good work in connexion with the working of the Insurance Act in Ireland and particularly in regard to the sanatorium benefit. I should be very glad if you would let her know how much the grand work she has done is being appreciated on this side of the Channel.[15]

The greatest obstacle to aid for Ireland was indifference in England. A viceregal commission set up before the Aberdeens' arrival had recommended a program of economic development for the ailing country. It would have set the British treasury back a million pounds. To Ishbel it was unbelievably short-sighted not to spend this money." Ireland was considered a nuisance", she reminisced.

The worst conditions of poverty were in Dublin itself, where over twenty per cent of the families lived in single rooms. A quarter of the male population earned less than eighteen shillings a week, while thousands had no work. "One day the whole side of a Dublin slum street fell down, killing and maiming some of the inhabitants..."[16]

Regrettably the Secretary for Ireland (and perhaps Aberdeen as well) did not press Ireland's case with sufficient zeal. James Bryce had been replaced by Augustine Birrell in 1907. Birrell was congenial enough, but not prepared to exhibit much strength or initiative in his post. He was languid in temperament and inclined to throw up his hands when the Cabinet pushed on to higher priorities. Ishbel had urged him to get House of Commons action on the Tuberculosis Prevention bill. He had duly tabled it in June 1908, but in December he was informing her from London: "I am still hopeful of saving the Bill... But a more *tiresome* crew to deal with cannot be imagined! On no account will your labours be in vain. After all to waken the country is the first and chief thing to do."[17]

So do indolent politicians silence activists. The refrain is to keep up the good work and educate the public...

Ishbel had more success in pushing through a protection bill for the handloom weavers of Ireland. It would require that "hand-woven" appear on the edge of the fabric, to distinguish it from machine-made goods now flooding the market. She met some remarkable objections. The first M.P. she hoped might propose the bill, T.W. Russel, wrote that he had questioned his wife in the matter, and had been told that neither she nor any lady she knew would dream of buying table cloths or napkins with a "hand-woven" mark on the border. Whether this indicated a delicacy in regard to advertising the quality of her linens, or possibly a preference for machine-made articles, was not explained. Another M.P. carried the bill through.

Ishbel met similar reluctance when she sought to interest government authorities in urban renewal. She was aghast at the damp, cold, crowded cellars to which her TB patients must return after treatment. If only the Cabinet would come as a body and see for themselves! She asked London for model workmen's cottages, and she got drawings and plans. George Murray of the Treasury Chambers informed her:

I will speak to the Chancellor of the Exchequer and see what can be done to meet your wishes. But I am inclined to think he may hold that we have done enough in authorizing the Local Government Board to make model *plans* for the cottages... The British Treasury is looked on by everybody in Ireland as a pigeon to be plucked![18]

A Civic Exhibition was got up, after several years of preparation. The Lord Lieutenant gave a prize to the best Report and Town Plan for the renovation of Dublin. Looking back in 1925 Ishbel sighed, "It really was a lovely Exhibition, every Section being full of life and interest... The Civics Institute of Ireland of which A. and I are still joint presidents, resumed activity after the war under great difficulties..."[19]

Ishbel's efforts were heroic, but their scope too circumscribed. She may at least be exempted from the general scorn heaped on "Dublin Castle" as inept and futile in those pre-war years. For example, a 1932 history of Ireland by the Earl of Midleton, a moderate Conservative who was a landowner in County Cork, seeks to fix the blame for the loss of Ireland by coming down very hard on "Dublin Castle" for failing to relieve the poverty of the city and thereby paving the way for the rebellion of 1916.[20] The government at London, refusing to recognize the seriousness of the situation, was the true culprit.

Even occasions for royal pomp and ceremony seemed to go wrong. In July 1907 King Edward and Queen Alexandra consented to open an International Exhibition in Dublin. When someone at the Castle was sent to bring the royal regalia to be worn for the occasion, it was reported missing.

The "Crown Jewels of Ireland" included a diamond-studded Star and Badge of some magnificence, belonging to the Order of St. Patrick and reserved exclusively for the King. Jeweled collars were put on by Irish peers in the King's presence. The regalia was kept in a special strong box of considerable size. A secure vault had been recently constructed in a building called the Office of Arms within the Castle walls, but Sir Arthur Vicars, the chief custodian, noting that the safe containing the jewels was too large to go through the vault door, had left it in the library. Someone was able to get past the sentries and through locks, remove the jewels, and leave everything neatly closed and locked again. The police could only surmise the jewels had been stolen "during the past month". They were never found.

Enquiries were launched and reputations shaken. (Sir Arthur Vicars was eventually assassinated by the Sinn Fein.) One lively rumour had it that Vicars was in the habit of giving male (homosexual) parties in the Office of Arms. A man who attended these affairs was suspected of the theft. But it was all hushed up, according to this tale, by order of the King, who was advised that the suspect could reveal matters that would compromise the Marquess of Lorne, the King's brother-in-law, who had been Governor-General of Canada from 1878 to 1883. A music hall joke had the diamonds reappearing in a necklace worn by the Queen. None of this greatly helped the status of the Irish Viceroy.

In 1911 a more successful royal visit brought George V and Queen Mary to Dublin. The festivities lasted five days, and it was the last occasion when England's Sovereigns visited southern Ireland. The Aberdeens added a new supper room to the Castle for the entertainments, at considerable cost. These days it is pointed out to tourists as "George's hall", an example of wanton viceregal extravagance while Ireland suffered.

Prime Minister Asquith visited them in Dublin in 1912, seeking the answer to the perennial Irish Question. After the latest election in 1910, Redmond and his parliamentary party had again secured a balance-of-power position and to appease them a Home Rule bill was at last introduced. But it roused violent reaction in the northern counties among Protestants. Leading the opposition was a firebrand, Sir Edward Carson, who threatened mutiny among Irish militiamen of the north if England passed the bill. Bonar Law, the new Conservative leader, was adamantly opposed to the bill.

Asquith came to the conclusion that Dublin Castle was badly run. When matters became inflamed between north and south he blamed the people in charge on the spot for not keeping events under control. He wrathfully declared, "A weaker and more incompetent lot were never in charge of a leaky ship in stormy weather, and poor old Birrell's occasional and fitful appearances at the wheel do not greatly improve matters." He talked of a "clean cut", and "the booting out of Aberdeen ...and the whole crew."[21]

Yet when that action was taken later he was soon made aware that the problem was much deeper than Aberdeen and his staff. After the 1916 Easter insurrection he realized that "resignations were not enough". It was the whole system of government, and not merely the competence of individuals, which had been found wanting. Asquith himself became quickly convinced that the Lord Lieutenant and "the Dublin Castle system must be swept away."[22]

The storms provoked by the Home Rule bill increased in velocity. The final years of Aberdeen's term saw the barometer rising. It is clear he was trying to hold back the storm, pleading with Westminster for measures he and his wife believed would strengthen the moderate centre against both the Sinn Fein and the rampant Ulstermen, but to no avail.

The Liberal government was rendered impotent by the power of northern Protestants championed by the Conservative House of Lords, and by no less a figure than George V. The King was greatly alarmed by the intelligence that his soldiers in several counties of northern Ireland felt so strongly about Home Rule, which would put the Protestants in a minority within a predominantly Catholic autonomous state, that they were mobilizing to revolt. Asquith felt compelled to repudiate his party's pledge to Redmond and his supporters, who had so faithfully stood by the Liberal party, and make a deal with the Conservatives to pass Home Rule with the proviso that it would not take effect until after the war. By then matters had gone far beyond such simple constitutional remedies.

Correspondence between Aberdeen and London records the raising of revolutionary forces, the "Ulster Volunteers", and counter-mobilization of "Citizen Volunteers" in the south. There is no doubt about Aberdeen's partisanship. On 25 April 1914 he wired Birrell that 850 Ulster Volunteers with 60 motor cars were assembled in Derry and a steamer had docked at 4.30 that morning with "about 120 motor loads of what were believed to be arms unshipped. Police and coastguards powerless."[23]

Another telegram followed on its heels, "strongly advising" the arrest of the two Conservative-Unionist members of parliament "under whose direction police and customs officers were prevented from access to Lorne Harbour."[24] He was advised to wait and do nothing until Birrell arrived.

Birrell hurried across, and in his charmingly sanguine way reported to Asquith on "the Great smuggling Coup" by the Ulstermen who "as plotters, beat us hollow... A more impudent, successful business cannot be imagined."[25] He advised against arresting anyone. He also told Asquith that he had over-ruled a written demand from Aberdeen handed to him that afternoon, that strongly put the case for arresting the ringleaders for interfering with law enforcement and preventing the constabulary from doing its duty. To let this action go unpunished would be disastrous, Aberdeen insisted. He was confident that Army regulars would back up the police if required, and put a stop to the smuggling. Birrell apparently thought the Ulster action was more formidable. He also had formed a very poor opinion of the gathering forces on the other side (strictly speaking, the government's side). He cabled to Asquith that "The National [Citizen] Volunteers are marching through Dublin today. They are not very impressive. Their complaint is 'No money for refreshments'".[26] Birrell continued to view the events as a rather amusing show.

However, in a later report to Asquith, he was frank enough about where the true guilt lay: "The landed class at the top and the Orange Lodges at the bottom are ripe for treason." He apparently believed the only sane reaction was to do nothing and hope the trouble would go away.

By July the Citizen Volunteers were successfully smuggling arms in their turn. This time, however, force was used and a riot occurred in the streets of Dublin when the military, called in by the metropolitan police, fired on citizen marchers.

As this dangerous situation escalated there was little hope for a sympathetic reception to Redmond's and Aberdeen's pleas for conciliatory measures. A few months later both were urging that Irish recruits in the great war in Europe be recognized and encouraged by allowing them to form their own regiments under their own officers and colours. An appeal by Lord and Lady Aberdeen to steer some war contracts to impoverished Irish manufacturers was turned down.

Aberdeen was told in 1915 that he was to be recalled. Just as in Canada eighteen years earlier, he was not thought sufficiently keen on raising patriotic war fervour to an effective level.

Asquith commended him, and Lady Aberdeen also, for the achievements of their nine-year term, "a term that considerably exceeds in duration that of any Viceroy since the Union", he pointed out. He proposed that as soon as the ninth year was up, "your term should come to an end."[27]

The Aberdeens protested strongly. They were convinced they were irreplaceable, and their friends among the Nationalists confirmed the opinion. They had counted on being Ireland's last viceregal couple, allowed to retire triumphantly when Home Rule ushered in a new régime headed by a merely ceremonial Governor-General. Aberdeen even appealed to the King, informing him that he was the victim of malicious enemies in Ireland who might have had His Majesty's ear. King George turned the letter over to his secretary for reply. Their son Lord Haddo wrote Asquith on their behalf, and was brusquely told: "Lord Aberdeen's resignation was formally tendered to and accepted by the King some time ago, and it would in any case be impossible to go back on it. I do not share your apprehension as to the evil consequences that may follow in Ireland..."[28]

Others did share Haddo's view. It was not out of private pride alone that the Aberdeens resisted leaving Ireland. A letter in the Haddo House Collection written after the 1916 Easter Rebellion when their successor Lord Wimborne was at Dublin Castle, reflects the opinion that their known sympathies with the Irish desire for self-rule could have moderated passions and averted trouble. Max Green, a judge in the Dublin courts and a nephew of John Redmond, wrote to them after Redmond's death:

> Mr. Redmond's death was tragic, he died of a broken heart... All his life he had the most romantic belief in the honour of English and Scots men, that their word was their bond, and it was a bitter awakening.
>
> The rebellion here filled the Cup and he never recovered from the shock. I may mention here a circumstance you are possibly not aware of, viz. that he did everything in his power to prevent Your Excellencies' departure from Ireland. He thought it a stupid blunder apart from personal considerations... He was firmly convinced that your Ex's' leaving Ireland before Home Rule was set up would give rise to the feeling here that a change of policy was contemplated...
>
> He looked upon your departure as comparable to the departure of Lord Fitzwilliam in 1795 and considered it a serious contributing cause to the Rebellion by reason of the distrust it engendered...

As was customary at the conclusion of an important service rendered to the Crown, a rise in the peerage was now in order. The Earl of Aberdeen was given a Marquessate, ranking next to a Dukedom in the aristocratic hierarchy — a Duke is directly below the sovereign. The title decided on was "Marquess of Aberdeen and Temair", the addition evoking Ireland without any attachment to an estate.

So deeply involved were the Aberdeens in the troubles of Ireland, and secretly, perhaps, so little disposed to sympathy with Lloyd George's coalition government when it came to office, that they had but slight enthusiasm for the waging of the Great War, and beyond Lady Aberdeen's service with the Red Cross expended little effort in its prosecution. They in fact spent most of the years between 1915 and 1918 in the United States, having resolved to lift £20,000 from the bottomless pockets of Irish American millionaires. They were determined to maintain Peamount Sanatorium and the children's services initiated by Ishbel, during the years of war when funds for social purposes were severely cut. It was a difficult undertaking for several reasons. Raising funds for good causes seemed to be happening on every street corner in the United States. They had talked optimistically of being gone six months, but it was two and a half years before they reached their objective, even though they practiced the strictest personal economies as they traveled.

The other problem was the turmoil of Irish relations at home and abroad. Disassociating themselves from the increasingly violent Sinn Fein was a constant anxiety, for American funds were also being assiduously sought to support the anti-British cause. So mixed were the political threads in those war years that the Aberdeens were in fact suspected of being part of this subversive action. This seems to explain the information passed to Prime Minister Lloyd George, who in mid-1917 wrote to a relative of Aberdeen's, Lord Balfour of Burleigh, by way of exerting pressure on Aberdeen to return.

> In view of the increasing difficulties created by Lord Aberdeen's continued absence in *America*, I should be glad if you would communicate with him at once in the sense of my letter of the 16th June. It is essential in the interests of the County [Aberdeenshire, where Aberdeen was Lord Lieutenant, with minimal duties] that a definite understanding should be arrived at without delay. Lord Aberdeen must return to his duties as Lord Lieutenant or I shall have no option but to advise His Majesty to accept his resignation.[29]

To this command Aberdeen sent back a rambling and somewhat plaintive reply. One is inclined to read into it a developing sense of persecution, though the circumstances are hazy at this distance:

... by what appears an insidious method, suggestions on the subject have been made not only to your office but to the King, to the President of the Council, and to the Scottish Office, together with what may be called a fifth mode of attack: anonymous paragraphs in the Scottish Press. I am quite aware that my absence gives a handle for hostile influence, but I am also aware that no practical inconvenience can be shown to have arisen in the consequence of that absence. Aberdeenshire business was very fully organized before I left, and I have been in constant communication...

Unfortunately we found the task of collecting the necessary funds... was not so simple a matter as might have been supposed... Our determination to keep the work *national* in character, acting through workers of all Churches and politics in Ireland, prevents our being able to obtain the hearty support of any one section of the Irish community here, and we have to do our work as quietly as possible to avoid controversy which might be harmful to the Irish cause and to the British government...

Unfortunately I cannot draw on my own resources, as the result of the war has been to deprive me of any income from my Scottish estates — in fact there was a deficiency after taxes have been paid, which has been only paid by the kindness of a friend during the last two years...

Our visit here has enabled us to do better service for our country than if we had been at home... Lady Aberdeen has also had much opportunity for service in connection with women's clubs both here and in Canada, and in her capacity of President of the International Council of Women can undoubtedly do more useful work for the future reconstruction period, as well as in connection with the war, here than if she were at home...

I make bold to suggest that we should look for a vindication and defence on your part, and that you will not assent to the removal of a public servant of long standing from an official position in his own County, which he has filled for thirty-seven years... As to what I have indicated regarding the real underlying character of the complaints which you have received... I cannot feel any doubt whatever. Lest you think I am too suspicious, allow me to remind you of the manner in which our removal from Ireland was effected — namely by a long continued and subtle campaign of disparagement and indeed calumny...

You will excuse the defects in the typewriting, when I explain that it has been done for me wholly (from the rough draft) by Lady Aberdeen who is only now learning the art and it has taken her the whole night.[30]

Among Lloyd George's files in the archives of the House of Lords at Westminster is a scurrilous, windy, anonymous rhyme which the Prime Minister perhaps saw as some justification for Lord Aberdeen's outrage. A Dublin enemy had written:

We've got the curse of Scotland here, in Lady Aberdeen...

Of all the Whigs and Tories who had come in days of yore,
We never had a skinflint Lord Lieutenant here before,
That hasn't got the heart to spend a cent or bawbee,
They split the ha'penny buns in two when Larkin goes to tea...[31]

James Larkin was a Dublin worker and union leader, participating with Connolly and Pearce in the 1916 uprising. It is indeed doubtful that he ever came to tea at the Viceregal Lodge.

While Aberdeen's letter makes it plain that he and his wife were more deeply concerned with the challenge of "the future reconstruction period" than with patriotic efforts to beat the Germans and hang the Kaiser, they did not escape the war unscathed. Their personal wealth was drastically depleted by wartime taxes. They knew the anguish of a son, Dudley, twice wounded in combat as an officer of the Gordon Highlanders. They suffered with friends whose sons died at the Front. In 1917 they learned of the death in Palestine of Ishbel's godchild, Captain the Rt. Hon. Neil Primrose, M.P. A letter came in December from Lord Rosebery: "My dear Gossip — though we are gossips no longer, as our Godsons are both dead..."[32] When he wrote again in 1924 he began: "My dear Gossip. I continue the old title though there are nothing but melancholy associations connected with it..."[33]

Ishbel and her husband had resumed their work in Ireland at a time when events had outrun their earnest influence. The Home Rule bill was never proclaimed. Violence mounted; there was no turning back. At Easter 1916 open rebellion marked a tragic milestone on the way to total revolt. Yet Aberdeen's successor in office, Lord Wimborne, could even then write to Prime Minister Asquith:

[It is] comic how seriously the insurgents take themselves, posting signs in the name of the republic of Ireland... Tomorrow I intend to proclaim the Irish Volunteers and the Citizen army as an illegal and dangerous association... I contemplate arrest of a considerable number of their leaders. It is our duty and our opportunity to eradicate the evil...[34]

Today's guide-book for tourist visitors to Dublin Castle, that one-time Viking stronghold that for so many centuries represented a foreign presence, maintained by force, in the capital city, contains this paragraph:

[The 1916 Easter Rebellion] proved to be the last attack the Castle had to endure. Six years later it was the scene of a handing-over ceremony performed by Lord Fitzalan, the Lord Lieutenant. A statement released to the press [*The Irish Times*] on 16 January, 1922, read: The members of Rialtas Sealadach na h-Eiram (the Provisional Government of Ireland) received the surrender of Dublin Castle at 1.45 p.m. today. It is now in the hands of the Irish Nation.[35]

Chapter 20
World and Spirit

L ord Aberdeen retired from public life in 1920 when he was 73, Lady Aberdeen 63. In that year they consolidated their affairs as best they could, selling off some properties and turning the remaining entailed estate over to George, Lord Haddo. George (who had been called "Doddy" since boyhood) and Florence took over, in a state of diminished affluence. They had difficulty meeting the agreed-on allowances to his sister Marjorie and brother Dudley, so that Dudley was obliged to fend for himself for the most part; his wife Cécile felt much aggrieved by the restricted position they occupied at Bexley in Kent, and the middle-class budget on which they brought up their five children, who would become heirs to the title. Dudley's third child, Archibald (Fifth Marquess) wrote: "The lesson I learnt from them [his parents] is that aristocracy ceased to exist as a reality at about the time I was born [1913]"[1]

Some members attribute the loss of the family's wealth to Ishbel's profligacy, though the impact of wartime taxes should be taken into account. In 1872 when John Gordon, at the age of twenty-five, inherited the estate it comprised 75,000 acres with an annual rent roll of £40,000, along with other land holdings and assets. The estate was whittled down to a residual 14,000 acres; valuable art was sold; much of Ishbel's fine jewellery had gone; liquid assets had dwindled to almost nothing.[2]

In 1920 Ishbel and Aberdeen retained for themselves a retirement villa, Cromar, which they had built for that purpose soon after their return from Canada. They chose the lovely surroundings of the Deeside, not far from the royal Family's Scottish residence, Balmoral, which had been sold to Victoria and Albert in 1852 by the Fourth Earl of Aberdeen. Cromar stood near the village of Tarland. Rosebery's architect, Sydney Mitchell, was employed to design a pretty house.

Cromar, Tarland, built for the Marquess and Marchioness of Aberdeen and Temair.

It was romantically Gothic, with turrets and a king-sized entrance, built of rose-hued granite, and its rooms were airy and sunny, opening onto terraces, fountains and a formal Italian garden. There was a private golf course, devised cunningly by Ishbel to bring the grandsons home for weekends, and there were kennels for her own champion Skye terriers. Rosebery particularly admired the place. It was full of charm, he said. "In truth I prefer it to Haddo, if I may say so." Haddo House he described as "that spacious mansion, all furnished by Bright and Mansfield, which made my blood run cold."[3]

Here the couple settled down in comfort. They wrote their memoirs, *We Twa*, resolving "not to complain of or criticize anybody who had done them harm."[4] The prose is accordingly a uniform tint of pale rose. The book was much admired in the 1920's and widely read at home and abroad.

They kept up a prodigious correspondence, much of it related to Ishbel's activities in the International Council of Women. They had, of course, a succession of visitors. Canada's most popular novelist of the time, Ralph Connor, a Presbyterian minister from Winnipeg whose real name was Charles Gordon, wrote in his *Postscript to Adventure* of the happy week he and his wife spent with the Aberdeens. He described the House of Cromar as "not a great castle... a simple, homelike mansion." describing himself as "something of a radical", and opposed to unequal distinctions in wealth and position, he nevertheless succumbed to the hospitality of this good couple, and reported that he discovered a "new world of social relationships" in "the laird's attitude toward his tenants... The spirit of this home is democracy of a very simple and also very beautiful type, a type that some Canadians apparently could not understand during the Aberdeen regime [at Ottawa]."[5] Charles Gordon apparently enjoyed Aberdeen's Scottish stories which "he told with a racy touch of pawkiness... Jolly evenings they were..."[6]

The grandchildren's memories of Ishbel date from this period. Marjorie's son, John Pentland of New York City, while he regretted the way his grandparents spent their entire life together "losing their money in good works", nevertheless was vastly impressed by Ishbel:

> She was very big; she made herself comfortable as she settled down to talk. She had personal magnetism. Her style was a one-to-one rapport in numerous small conversations. She was sympathetic toward those she talked to, but shrewd underneath...
>
> I always thought of her as someone who had discovered at an early age that she could almost do without sleep entirely. After the dinner guests left she would write letters until three or four in the morning, or even later — and the postman would arrive about six with more loads of mail.[7]

Another grandson, Archie Gordon, Dudley's son and the fifth Marquess of Aberdeen, thought he was probably her favourite, and recalled times spent with his grandmother:

> She looked the prototype of Grandmother, large, with magnificent hair; at dinner she heard the conversation at the far end of the table. Many were frightened of her, she was so imposing. She encouraged one to talk, especially about politics...
>
> A piper paraded on the terrace outside at eight o'clock to wake you all up, get you ready for an enormous breakfast, everybody in the dining-room. There were four big meals, including tea with Scotch buns and cake.[8]

This was the time when Ishbel and Johnny grew closer together and enjoyed a serene companionship. Ishbel wrote to her husband as she set off one February morning on one of numerous trips:

> Grey wintry morning; good run in to Aberdeen though roads *very* hard in the grip of an iron frost. I watched the rim of red on the horizon rising, with upward rays like the Northern lights; and I thought of my boy seeing me off from the door at 5 a.m. with the love-light in his bonny blue 'een. I do feel so ridiculously well and fresh — and I can't think why, unless it is because of your dear prayers.[9]

This felicitous life was something they could not really afford. When they came to take up their residency in 1920 it was apparent that they must operate Cromar at a yearly deficit of £2,000: the shortfall between rental income from the relatively small estate, and its upkeep. Aberdeen negotiated a deal, relying heavily on friendship, and open-ended in a way that distressed lawyers on both sides. A Tarland neighbour, wealthy Sir Alexander MacRobert, whose wife was particularly devoted to Ishbel, undertook to assume the annual deficit in exchange for title to the place on their death. Lady MacRobert died shortly after the deal was made. A second wife was much less sympathetic and insisted on extending the terms to include the entire furnishings of the house including family portraits set in the panelling of the dining-room walls.[10] "We Twa" were indeed at the end of their resources.

A few years later the MacRobert Trustees were again concerned at the size of the annual deficit. Ishbel went to them with a fresh proposition: they could have Cromar on her husband's death, probably well in advance of her own. She would move out — though Cromar had been her dream and her initiative. Johnny would be spared distress and discomfort.

They celebrated their Golden Wedding in 1927. For the occasion they were allowed by Mrs. Robert Fleming of 27 Grosvenor Square, the house they had built and occupied for a number of years in the centre of London, to hold a large reception for relatives and friends. A thousand or so responded. Gifts and letters also poured in, attesting to the high regard of friends and of any number of former servants, postmen, railwaymen and other people of all sorts and positions. Their daughter Marjorie recounts the occasion in a warm tribute to her parents' capacity to inspire affection through their never-failing interest in the lives of those around them. One of the grandest gifts was a large touring Austin presented to Ishbel by the International Council of Women. It was, says Marjorie Pentland, "destined to cover over 300,000 miles in the succeeding eleven years," for Ishbel was constantly in motion during their "retirement".

Marjorie appears in the Golden Wedding family photograph seated beside her father. She is a desolate, thin figure in heavy mourning, having recently suffered the death of John Sinclair, her husband. Her daughter Margaret ("Peggy") and son John stand near. Lord Haddo is seated on Ishbel's right while Florence, her short stature augmented by a very large hat, stands immediately at his shoulder. Dudley, a stalwart figure, stands to the right of the group, and present also are his wife Cécile and five children, David, Jessamine, Archie, Michael and Alastair.

The future of the two generations assembled with the Golden Wedding couple in 1927, all the gentlemen including two small tads, Alastair and Michael, clad in their Highland kilts, the younger women in short but not quite flapper-length dresses, would be the story of an aristocratic line coping, with varying degrees of personal success, with the scant fortune left them. Haddo (George) was childless; his brother Dudley the next heir. In 1944 George gave up the great house and estate. It passed not to Dudley, who apparently had no desire to cope with its diminishing returns, but to Dudley's oldest son David.

George, however, had a last fling at life. (He was by that time the 2nd Marquess.) He had gone to live in Sussex, and there his wife Florence died in 1937. As soon as his mother, Ishbel, was also dead he married a second time. He married a widow, Sheila Innis, and spent the nine following years in what is described by his nephews as a "disastrous" marriage which ended with Sheila's death in 1949. George lived in the south of England until his death in 1965.

Dudley then held the title until 1972, while his son David, known as "the Major" since he served with that rank in the Gordon Highlanders in the Second World War, made Haddo House a happy family residence and a community centre. A part of the ground was made over to a public park. The Major

Golden Wedding Day. Nov. 7, 1927.

became the 4th Marquess in 1972 and was the last to live on the estate. He married a charming and talented woman, Lady June Gordon, who turned Ishbel's large hall with its oddly swooping roof-line into a widely recognized centre for choral concerts and theatrical productions. David and June adopted four children to fill the nursery wing at Haddo House.

When David died in 1974 the title passed to Archibald, his brother, a bachelor who followed a career with the BBC and was the author of several books, including *A Wild Flight of Gordons*, published in 1985, the year of his death. It is an account of some of the more colourful members of his clan. This Marquess accepted the inevitable, and turned Haddo House over to the safekeeping of the National Trust of Scotland in the late 1970's. (A family wing was reserved for the use of Lady June Gordon.)

The next brother, Michael, one of the small grandsons at Ishbel's feet in the 1927 photo, was killed in 1943 in the Second World War. On Archibald's death the title therefore passed to the youngest brother Alastair, the 6th Marquess and 12th Earl. Their sister Jessamine married a man of wealth, the son of Vyvyan George Harmsworth, Viscount Rothermere, and brought up a large family.

• • •

Once Ishbel and her husband had finished their two-volume memoirs, *We Twa, the Reminiscences of Lord and Lady Aberdeen* (1925), they tried their hand at other writings. Lord Aberdeen put together a little book of his best stories called *Jokes Cracked by Lord Aberdeen* (1929) and *More Cracks with We Twa* (1929); Lady Aberdeen produced *Musings of a Scottish Granny* (1936).

Ishbel's wide range of public service was recognized in 1928 with the Freedom of the City of Edinburgh and in 1929 with an honorary degree at Aberdeen University. In 1931 King George conferred on her the honour of the Grand Cross of the British Empire (GBE), which entitled her to be known thereafter as a Grand Dame of the Empire — a not inappropriate appellation. In 1931 Ishbel also was the centre of some attention when she led a six-woman delegation, the first of their sex to appear before the august General Assembly of the Church of Scotland. She presented a petition requesting the ordination of women ministers and appointment of women as elders and deacons of the church. A curious crowd applauded her calm and measured words — but the Assembly deferred a decision on the matter.

As might be expected, Ishbel lent active support to every manifestation of the "Peace Movement" between the wars. One particular triumph was a Peace Pavilion as part of the Empire Exhibition in Glasgow in 1938 — Ishbel, at 82, was chairman of the committee to see this project through to a successful completion. A Peace Cairn remains in the Glasgow park, made up of stones brought by international visitors from around the world.

She continued her active interest in and support of the Irish National Health Association and the Peamount Sanatorium in Dublin. She also spoke on the "wireless" in 1938, in a clear, sweet voice that won her an admiring telegram from her grandson Archie at the BBC: "Clear as a bell" he said. The broadcast was directed to the International Council of Women on its 50th anniversary. Her greatest efforts were with the ICW. She held the organization together and guided its progress almost until her death, rebuilding it after the sad disunity of the First World War, when British (and Canadian) members shuddered at the idea of resuming comradeship with the hateful Germans. She tied the organization to the new League of Nations, establishing liaison with its meetings in Geneva and obtaining a clause in the Covenant opening positions on all League bodies to women.

From the time of the astonishingly successful Quinquennial meeting in London in 1899, when the ICW was a great curiosity in an era not yet crowded with international societies of all sorts, Ishbel had thrilled to an inner vision: "She had seen a glimpse of a new universe at work," her daughter wrote.[11] In one of her later writings Ishbel confessed she felt alarm as she pressed forward, as "contact with the different nations showed me the enormous difficulties in the way of bringing together these heterogeneous elements in harmonious action for the welfare and progress of the human race."[12]

Enormous difficulties had never much deterred her. The next Quinquennial was held in Berlin in 1904, the next in Toronto in 1909, the next in Rome in May 1914. At each Ishbel was re-elected president. Each was an organizational project of considerable size and complexity. Nine additional national councils, including Argentina, were added to the membership between 1899 and 1904; at that meeting profound desire was expressed for the preservation of peace, and the issue of votes for women was faced squarely and overwhelmingly passed.

A Standing Committee on the Suppression of the White Slave Traffic was set up — its message was carried to the League of Nations and became a permanent feature of the League's work between the wars. By 1909 there were 22 affiliated national councils, including for the first time Belgium, Greece and Bulgaria. A wide range of issues was explored: a new Standing Committee on Public Health was established with Ishbel as chairman; more than half that committee's members were medical doctors as more and more universities of the world graduated women in that profession.

The 1914 meeting in Rome was determinedly optimistic, yet before its report was printed the most terrible war in history had begun and the foreword added the despairing comment: "the principles for which the ICW stands appear for the time being to have passed into oblivion."[13] It would be six years before the ICW could meet again, to take up the old issues and a host of new ones in a world where the position of women was much altered. President Wilson of the United States agreed to Ishbel's request for a submission by an ICW delegation to one of the first plenary sessions of the League of Nations. Wilson called the delegates "the mothers of the world". A number of the ICW's leading members subsequently were present at meetings of the League in Geneva as delegates from their respective countries. It is difficult to form an estimate of the impact this international body made in the countries where its members, inspired by its spirited debates and far-reaching studies, returned home to propagate bold new ideas among their fellow-countrywomen.

As for Ishbel, she seems to have begun each new organizing task for the I.C.W. with a sense of profound humility and fear that success was beyond her ability. As she plunged on a sense of wonder at her own surprising success always overtook her. Her greatest challenge was to bring the members together again in 1920 in Norway, at a time when feeling against those who had been national enemies was still very strong. "As president, Ishbel called on a delegate from each council to step forward and say a word of greeting. The Austrian delegate rose in her turn, but then faltered, overcome with nervousness. Quickly Ishbel jumped up and went to stand protectingly by her side till the little speech was delivered. A wave of fellow-feeling seemed to run through the audience."[14]

> Lady Aberdeen put into her task her very best at this meeting. Of course she is always an exceedingly clever and tactful chairman, but this time she was something more, something wonderful — never tired, never impatient, her smile like a sunbeam on everyone. Her warm heart seems to give her an understanding of all the different countries' difficulties...[15]

When Ishbel was reflectively composing her thoughts toward the end of her life she wrote a short statement about her involvement with the ICW. She left it, for it was in the nature of a confession, with her Presbyterian minister in Aberdeen, the Reverend Matthew Urie Baird. She disclaimed personal credit for the leadership she had brought to the body of women. Many of the new women colleagues were professionally trained and highly intelligent, and she had disparaged herself in comparison with them. Facing recurrent obstacles she had found she had one sure resource. "As far as I could I used to make a practice of standing at a place where I could look up at the mountains", she wrote. She would repeat words from the Psalms, calls for grace and strength. And she believed herself then possessed of a power sufficient to carry through, to achieve extraordinary conciliation among opposing and diverse forces. Being of a practical mind she had thought it best not to mention this sense of an infusion of spiritual power.

As she wrote she was anticipating the tributes that would be showered on her by the ICW on her eightieth birthday. She felt, she said, "wholly unworthy" and "afraid". She decided it was time to admit, or at least commit to paper, "my sense of the enormous privilege which has been mine in being given some amazing power outside myself."[16] These experiences had also increased her effectiveness in some of her "Liberal work".

The Reverend Matthew Urie Baird had become aware of her belief in supernatural forces in other matters, and he had tried to discourage it. For many years Ishbel had been interested in manifestations of Spiritualism that were rather widely accepted: her first mentor had been William Stead with the "Julie" he drew from the shadows. Other friends — Matilda Edgar in Canada, Maggie McNeill in Ireland — shared similar beliefs. Oddly, her most open explorations of the Other World were with the rotund, prosaic and proper little Prime Minister of Canada, William Lyon Mackenzie King. She did not share his quirky obsessions with pet animals, the hands of the clock, or arrangements of numbers. But she did come to believe, as he did, in the possibility of communication with the dead, and she shared his sense of being chosen to perform the work of God.

Mackenzie King wrote to Ishbel that his first meeting with her and her husband took place in 1894 "when as an undergraduate at the University of Toronto I secured a forget-me-not from a bouquet you were carrying at the time the students unharnessed the horses and pulled the Governor General's carriage through the college grounds."[17]

That occasion was also noted in King's 1894 diary:

> I showed them into their carriage then I ran alongside it and talked to the Governor General and Lady Aberdeen all the way to Victoria College. I enjoyed the conversation with them very much.

King had visited them in Dublin in 1912, when they were attending a ceremony at Peamount. The acquaintanceship began to flourish in 1919 when Lord and Lady Aberdeen sent a letter jointly to congratulate King on being chosen leader of the Canadian Liberal Party, to succeed Laurier. Borden and a coalition had governed the country through the chaotic war years and King wrote that "the whole political situation here as in England is in a most unsettled state... His [Borden's] Government is hopelessly doomed." King wrote of "the Destiny that seems to have been shaping the events that have transpired to bring me into the leadership of the party..." He accused the Tories of buying up the Press, while on his other flank "the agrarian movements are gaining ground as a protest against the old order." His hope was "to win to our following the less extreme of those who desire progressive government"[18] — the old Liberal strategy that for this new plump little leader would pay off so handsomely.

In the 1920's King wrote with profuse pleasure of the visit Lady Pentland and "John and Peggy" made to Canada — "one of the happiest incidents of my life", which caused him acute pangs at having missed the joys of marriage and fatherhood — "life has been shorn of much that makes it tender and sweet and at its very best."[19] Peggy, he wrote, "is just too lovely for words", while he was convinced that young John was "quite exceptional" and destined to help keep "the banner of Liberalism clean as well as aloft, "taking up the political career which his father had pursued so creditably. It was Ishbel's hope that young Pentland would carry Liberalism into the next generation, and the introduction to King in Canada had been planned to promote that career choice. But King was apparently not a sufficient inspiration. Pentland soon turned to the greater enticement of the business world.

In 1933 when King was temporarily back in Opposition he wrote grimly to Ishbel of "the dangerous man at the head of affairs in Canada [R.B. Bennet]."[20] He was not consoled by her sage advice about the benefit to a political party of a degree of "insecurity". Ishbel had discovered such "benefits" in 1929 when Ramsay MacDonald was heading the first Labour government in Britain. Ishbel accepted this development with surprising equanimity, partly explained by her dislike of Lloyd George. She was friendly with MacDonald and he named his daughter Ishbel after her. His brave anti-war attitude may have appealed to her. Her attitude to Labour was not hostile — she apparently regarded it as an unfortunate and temporary misunderstanding among men who really ought to be Liberals. Of the 1929 election of MacDonald she wrote: "Lord A, and I are not at all unhappy about the results of the General Election. There are a lot of things that the present Government can do for the good of the country which they can get through easier than the Liberals..." She thought there would be an "inevitable" breaking-up of the Labour group, and this could be followed by a wholesome re-organization of the Liberals, who would then resume their "proper place..." if in the meantime the young Liberals were wise enough to remain loyal and not desert to Labour "because they cannot wait."[21] The theme would be echoed by King with his avuncular description of the CCF, now NDP, as "Liberals in a hurry."

In the 1930's King wrote to her of their mutual conviction that Liberalism was "Christianity in politics", and was humbly grateful for her interest in "my efforts to keep the banner of Liberalism flying in this part of our great Empire."[22]

Their friendship deepened after Lord Aberdeen died in 1934. King was moved to write to her: "I have come, dear Lady Aberdeen, to believe so absolutely in man's survival after death and, in one way or another, have had so many evidences, not only of the continued existence of those I love, but of their interest in and concern for me, and their guiding and guarding its every endeavour, that I cannot write of death as something which we should regret, save in that it may involve a momentary separation... I feel, too, that in mysterious ways, this assurance will be already yours." She had frequently invited him to visit them in Scotland and he now spoke of a visit soon, when they would "continue to hear his voice, and to see his smile... and as we talk, Mr. Gladstone and Mrs. Gladstone and Mr. Henry Drummond and other friends will come..."[23]

Johnny had died in March 1934 from a sudden coronary attack; he died in her arms. Ishbel in her loneliness turned to the rituals of spirit writing, seances and similar efforts to remain in touch with the dead. Her family was aware of this, and could only hope it brought her comfort.

The practical changes that came with the death of her husband certainly required fortitude. She had to give up Cromar. Parting with her household furniture and treasured portraits, including one of her mother, was difficult indeed. She accepted it calmly. She was especially grateful for Queen Mary's gesture of favour and friendship. The Queen had frequently come for tea at Cromar, when holidaying at Bal-

Queen Mary Visiting Cromar.

Gordon House, Aberdeen, where Lady Aberdeen died in 1939.

moral. In 1934 she enquired if she might buy from the MacRobert Trust a fine satinwood bookcase and desk given to Ishbel by her husband. She had it returned to Ishbel.

Cromar was vacated in September 1934. By chance this writer met in the dining-room of the Ythanview Hotel in 1978 a Scotsman who had stayed at Cromar after the 1939-45 war, when it was being used as a convalescent home for servicemen. He recalled that it was still "full of the Aberdeens' furniture", and he heard indignation expressed by loyal local people because "the old lady had been squeezed out of the place." Sometime after the war a fire destroyed it all.

In 1935 Ishbel's son the 2nd Marquess bought for her a house of grey granite at the crest of a hill, at the end of a street called Rubislaw Den in the city of Aberdeen. It was renamed "Gordon House". Though it seems sizeable enough, with grounds sufficiently capacious to include a tennis court, if not golf links, there is no doubt that Ishbel felt her lifestyle severely cramped. She could no longer entertain as hugely as she would like, and grandchildren recall being packed off to the more commodious estates of friends, where there was more going on.

There Mackenzie King visited her in 1937. He had seen her in 1936 in Geneva at the League of Nations assembly, having written to ensure they would not miss each other:

How difficult the world situation is becoming! It seems to me that at the bottom it is a conflict between the powers of light and darkness. A struggle which is not alone of this planet, but of invisible as well as visible forces which seek supremacy in the conflict between good and evil. Of this and much more we shall talk when we meet... [24]

In 1937 King was attending the coronation of King George VI and Queen Elizabeth in London, which was followed by an Imperial Conference. In February Ishbel, then nearing her 80th birthday, had invited him to visit her after the London festivities.[25] Again, she wrote to say how she regretted that King had not been able to come to Cromar while Lord Aberdeen was still alive, but she assured him: "His Excellency says he is preparing to send us a message while we are together — so you must not fail me or him."[26]

King accepted. He would go to Aberdeen immediately after the London events. He also planned to visit Dundee, the home of his famous grandfather, William Lyon Mackenzie who had led the 1837 uprising of Upper Canada, and he would be receiving the Freedom of the City of Aberdeen. He asked Ishbel to look up the home site of his King grandfather, which he believed to be Tyrie, near Fraserburgh. He told her that the more famous line, the Mackenzies, was said to have descended from a farmer known as Colin Dhu (Black Colin) who had fought for the Stuart cause.

Ishbel did her best to arrange matters for him. Various country records officers were approached; some had no information, prompting Ishbel to write in a letter marked "Private":

My dear prime minister: Would it not be possible to enlist the help of your friends on the other side to give further particulars of the whereabouts of their farms or houses in Glenshee, Dundee and Tyrie?

As I think I told you, Lord Aberdeen tells me through Mrs.D— that he is trying to find "Colin Dhu".[27]

By whatever means, a 400-year-old house was located and visited by them both that June weekend; it was said to be the house where his great-grandfather was born and wonderful things occurred like the discovery of an antique clock with its hands at the *precise time* of that birth. They accompanied by a local medium who helped these revelations along.

Prime Minister W.L. Mackenzie King, Ottawa.

Although some of his King relatives had clearly not been of the upper classes, the Canadian Prime Minister was satisfied: "There appears to have been fine character throughout."

He arrived at Gordon House in Aberdeen very late on a Friday evening, after touring Balmoral and other places of note. He had been met at the door by Ishbel. She had kept a late supper hot for him "on a little electric equipment". King, never a gourmet, described their fare as "some hashed meat or something of that sort; fruit pudding, a number of things that were easily digestible."[28]

The day following was the truly memorable one. Ishbel took him about to see Haddo House and have tea with her son the 2nd Marquess, then to see Cromar, and afterwards she held in his honour a seven-course dinner with eleven local dignitaries. (The entrée was not "hash" this time but roast spring chicken, according to Ishbel's hand-decorated menu card.) After the guests departed Ishbel and King devoted the balance of the evening to psychic matters. Lord Aberdeen indeed made a verbal contribution; so did Mr. Gladstone, though his "Love from Mr. Gladstone. Keep up the good work," seems somewhat cryptic. Archie Gordon and Henry Drummor.' sent greetings to the Canadian guest.

By now Ishbel had been told that King intended to travel to Berlin from Britain, on a divinely inspired mission to avert war. His decision to intervene personally had apparently developed when he heard Hitler described as a "mystic", probably in a pejorative context. To King this meant an otherworldly bond could be established, of great portent. He felt impelled to visit the Nazi leader.[29] He had mentioned his intention to the British Foreign Secretary Anthony Eden, saying he would seek to assure Hitler that Canada and other parts of the Empire desired nothing more than "friendly relations all round."[30]

In London, he had seen the German ambassador Von Ribbontrop and a visit to Hitler had been discussed. King saw himself as a special emissary from the British Empire, handling a commission too delicate for Britain herself to undertake. The devious Mr. King appears to have given members of the Cabinet in London the impression that he was setting out to warn Hitler of the full support which the soldiers of the Empire would throw behind England, if forced into war. To Ishbel he revealed his higher purpose.

Among the fruits of the mystical evening they shared, 19 June 1937, was a letter (either in 'spirit writing' or possibly in a memo written by Ishbel after some other kind of communication) from the dead prime minister Campbell-Bannerman. It contained scarcely more content than the brief message from Gladstone — to unbelievers these scant messages are remarkably unremarkable. King was urged to have a heart-to-heart talk with Hitler on worsening relations between England and Germany. England wanted friendship, and was prepared to recognize Germany's legitimate desires, he must say. But Germany shouldn't "frighten the life out of decent people."[31]

King was tremendously buoyed by these injunctions. He went with Ishbel to church the next morning and everything had a pattern and portent, the position of the pews, numbers in the prayer book, the words of the hymns, the name of the pet dog being carried about after the service by the Reverend Mr. Baird's daughter. "The service was quite the most impressive and most significant incident in my whole visit to the British Isles", King wrote in his diary.[32]

A month later, back at Laurier House in Ottawa, he described it fully in a long letter to Ishbel. He wrote:

> That Service spoke to me of all that our friendship has meant through the 43 years it has been enjoyed, and of all that it has come to mean in a way quite beyond the comprehension of those who are not privileged to share some of the sacred mysteries that have been revealed to us — Communion — Communion of the Spirit — alone describes it all, a communion with the Unseen, with all those we have known and loved, and with a great 'cloud of witnesses' whose experiences have been akin to our own.[33]

Ishbel's reaction was almost as passionate. She felt lonely in the days following their exciting and inspiring weekend together. "We have been living very close to those things which are eternal and invisible in a way that can never be forgotten as long as we live and which makes our friendship a marvellously sacred gift from God", she wrote.[34]

For Mackenzie King, to be psychic was to be of a higher order, and once persuaded that Adolph Hitler belonged to this elect he knew the Nazi dictator must be inherently a good person. How could it be otherwise? He went from Scotland to London where he talked to Malcolm MacDonald, Secretary of

State for the Dominions, about his proposed trip to Berlin. Remarkably disparate accounts of that talk appeared later. MacDonald told the Cabinet of King's intention to tell Hitler how valiantly Canadians would spring to England's defence if war came.[35] But King wrote in his diary that he had laid down a line of action with some force — no matter how England might be driven, she must not allow war at any cost. "I said to give this message to all, that I believe it would work out through good-will, and save the situation. I felt in talking to Malcolm a sort of feeling as though this whole country was actually looking to me to help it."[36]

So resolved, and fortified by a cable from Ishbel quoting a prophetic verse from the Bible, "For He shall give His angels charge over thee", King pressed on to Berlin. He had a talk with Nevile Henderson, the British ambassador who, though he shocked King by denouncing the League of Nations as "a horror", agreed with him that Hitler was "an idealist", and wished him well in the interview. With Goering, King exchanged pleasantries about visits to Canada where the General said he would like a chance to shoot elk or deer. King dodged Goering's questions about Canada's probable response in the event of a war between Germany and England. Canadians would consider all the circumstances at the time, he said.

Next, at noon 29 June, Mackenzie King was received at the Hindenburg Palace by Herr Hitler. They talked for an hour and fifteen minutes. King sought to impress on Hitler the symbolism of the fact that *he* had been born in a city also called Berlin (now Kitchener) in Ontario. He saw in Hitler a humble, sincere man dedicated to the welfare of his people and mankind. Hitler had "a sort of appealing and affectionate look in his eyes... a calm, passive man, deeply and thoughtfully in earnest... He is distinctly a mystic... He is particularly strong on beauty, loves flowers and will spend more of the money of the State on gardens and flowers than on most other things." King wound up his Berlin visit by attending the opera where he heard "glorious music... a triumphal end to it all", and then went back to his hotel where he slept wrapped up in his new Mackenzie tartan, like "Colin Dhu" of old.[37]

King sent Ishbel a photograph of himself which is displayed at Haddo House beside Canada's 1898 gift of beautiful hand-painted porcelain. The photo is inscribed: "Dame Ishbel. With gratitude too deep for words for the visit to Dundee, Aberdeen and Tyrie June 18, 19, 20, the crowning event of our friendship of 43 years, with abiding affection, Mackenzie King. Coronation Year 1937."

There would be other exchanges. She wrote to let him know, in May 1938, that she would be broadcasting from the BBC studio in Aberdeen a message to the annual meeting of the NCW at Vancouver. "I am given 14 minutes... It is rather an alarming job." King took care to hear the broadcast and commended her: "Your voice as clear and natural as if all were assembled in one room."[38]

There were also letters in that period in which Ishbel persuaded King and his justice minister Lapointe to release from prison an Irishman, Valentine Shortis, whose murder of several Canadians at Valleyfield, Quebec, had been a sensation during their term at Rideau Hall. Through Ishbel's influence the death penalty had been commuted by Lord Aberdeen, and Shortis sent to prison instead of being hanged. Angry Quebeckers had threatened Aberdeen's life as a result, making Ishbel rather nervous, since she knew Canadian security and protection were somewhat amateur. After 42 years in jail, Shortis was released by King's government and Ishbel received grateful thanks from the relatives in Ireland for having saved his life.

Mackenzie King, as the record makes clear, was reluctant to abandon his idea that Hitler was a fellow mystic and consequently a benevolent leader. He went to some lengths to prepare for another eleventh-hour visit to the Nazi ruler in 1939, which unfortunately was aborted by the invasion of Poland by Hitler's armies.

Though Ishbel and King were deeply sincere fellow mystics, there is no doubt which one of the two snapped back to reality more promptly when events in Europe erupted. During the Munich crisis in the fall of 1938 King praised Neville Chamberlain's policy of appeasement as "noble", and he wrote to Ishbel, "Personally, I think Chamberlain has been magnificent... I have come to have entire confidence in the course he has pursued."[39]

But Ishbel wrote heatedly "about the terrible crisis through which we have passed and the outlook for the future and our duty as Liberals." She was impressed at the overwhelming public "awakening", "the turning to God in prayer has been remarkable. And of course the sudden release from immediate danger has been wonderful too — though somewhat hysterical in London, as always apt to be..." Still, "the whole proceedings of Munich have been a deepest humiliation", she wrote. She could not believe that Britain and France acting together could not have prevented Hitler from taking his slice of Czechoslovakia, at least until the local Czechs and German nationals who wanted to escape that country had had a chance to get out. "The idea of impotency to protect these people, and the immense addition being made to Hitler's power and influence and domination of democratic power to me seem almost unbelievable", said the doughty lady of 81.[40]

She grew more furious as the events of 1939 unfolded. "How I wish I could have a talk with you about international affairs", she wrote. She described a "paralysis of fear" that had seized Britain in the face of "these unknown terrors which await us at Hitler's bidding", so that no one dared "stand up for justice and righteousness." She poured contempt on Prime Minister Chamberlain embracing Mussolini "just at a time when he was utterly going against his own undertakings in the Non-Intervention Committee and sending Italian troops to Spain and glorying in France's successes — & cheek and jowl with Hitler in spite of all his unbelievable inhumanities not only to Jews but Protestants and Catholics as well."[41]

Ishbel had had closer contact with events, through the Czech National Council of Women whose president had written to her, "We have been betrayed by our friends; our people are mad with grief."[42] On March 15, 1939, according to her daughter-biographer, Ishbel wrote in a diary: "German troops enter Prague; Czecho-Slovakia disappears. Mme Plaminkova arrested; Alice Masaryk a refugee. World opinion desperately shocked."[43]

Ishbel did not live to see her country at war again; she died just a month after that last entry in her diary, on 18 April 1939. She was eighty-two years old, and still very active, her hearing and eyesight scarcely impaired. A massive heart attack occurred after a very brief illness. She was buried in the family cemetery at Haddo House. The words on the granite stone describe her as a "handmaiden of the Lord".

In reviewing the life of Ishbel Aberdeen one impression dominates — that though she lived in the years 1857 to 1939 when women's activities were severely hampered and contained, she followed an incredibly vigorous and fruitful career. One must feel regret that she lived before women had greater freedom to act. The words of a good Liberal, Henry Campbell-Bannerman, in 1905, dismissing with amusement the foolish antics at Albert Hall of women who sought the right to vote, illustrate the almost impenetrable barriers that existed most of her lifetime. Because these attitudes prevailed she was obliged to deal in subterfuge, as a mere wife, in the exciting world of politics which would have been hers. Her achievements have been neatly divided: she is given full credit only for the philanthropies that were proper female concerns, and for leadership of the "ladies' auxiliaries" to a man's political world. She was a woman who entered fully into the spirit of her age, during disturbing and momentous times. Her acumen, generosity, zeal and loyalty would have carried her far in the first instead of the second rank of public affairs.

NOTES

CHAPTER 1

1. Henry Fawcett, *Economic Position of the British Labourer* (1865). Quoted in G.M. Young, *Victorian England, Portrait of an Age* (New York: Doubleday, 1954).
2. Algernon Cecil, *Victoria and Her Prime Ministers* (London: Eyre and Spottiswoode, 1953).
3. Ishbel Aberdeen (IA) and Lord Aberdeen, *We Twa, Reminiscences of Lord and Lady Aberdeen,* (London: W. Collins, 1925).
4. Edna Healey, *Lady Unknown, The Life of Angela Burdett-Coutts* (London: Sedgwick and Jackson, 1978).
5. Marjorie Pentland, *A Bonnie Fechter* (London: B.T. Batsford, 1952), p. 5.
6. DCM to "Annie", Milan, 23 Oct. 1842, Haddo House Collection (H.H. Coll.).
7. DCM to "Annie", 7 April 1842.
8. IA and Aberdeen, *We Twa,* vol. 1, p. 101.
9. Quintin Hogg, Lord Hailsham, *The Door Wherein I Went* (London: Collins, 1975).
10. DCM to Lady Hogg, 20 Oct. 1848, H.H. Coll.
11. Isabella Marjoribanks to DCM, 18 Oct. 1866.
12. "The Grosvenor Estate in Mayfair," *Survey of London XXXIV* (London: University of London, 1977).
13. IA and Aberdeen, *We Twa,* vol. 1, p. 103.
14. *The Times,* London, 12 April 1864.
15. IA and Aberdeen, *We Twa,* vol. 1, pp. 106-7.
16. DCM to IA, 29 Sept. 1868.
17. Ishbel Marjoribanks, "Journal", 3 Oct. 1870.

CHAPTER 2

1. Isabella M. to IA, London, 13 July 1872, HH Coll.
2. "My share and interest in a box at the Royal Italian Opera House Covent Garden with all privileges thereto" were willed to his two daughters by Edward Marjoribanks Esq., in a handwritten will, 1 Dec. 1868, Somerset House, London.
3. Ishbel M. "Journal", 3 Oct. 1870, H.H. Coll.
4. Pentland, p. 12.
5. DCM to IA, London, 13 July 1872, H.H. Coll.
6. IA., hand-written document, "Notes on the real significance of the I.C.W. to me in my inner life", 9 pp., H.H. Coll.
7. Ishbel M., "Journal", 17 July 1873.
8. Pentland, p. 12.
9. IA and Aberdeen, *We Twa,* vol. 1, p. 156.
10. "Journal", 17 April 1873.
11. "Journal", 14 March 1874.
12. "Journal", 13 April 1874.
13. Lucille Iremonger, *Lord Aberdeen, A Biography of the Fourth Earl of Aberdeen* (London: Collins, 1978).
4. IA and Aberdeen, *We Twa,* vol. 2, p. 308.
15. Earl of A. (IV) to Haddo, 20 June 1834, H.H. Coll.
16. Haddo to Lady Haddo, 1859.
17. Rev. E.B. Elliot, ed., *Memoranda of the Life of Lord Haddo,* pamphlet, (London: private printing, 1865).
18. Ibid.

CHAPTER 3

1. Ishbel Aberdeen, "Journal", 12 Sept. 1874, H.H. Coll.
2. IA "Journal", 1 Jan. 1875.
3. IA "Journal", 17 Jan. 1875.
4. IA "Journal", 20 Jan. 1875.
5. IA "Journal", 8 Feb. 1875.
6. IA "Journal", 14 Feb. 1875.
7. IA "Journal", 27 Feb. 1875.
8. IA "Journal", 14 March 1875.
9. Ibid.
10. IA "Journal", 19 March 1875.
11. IA "Journal", 27 March 1875.
12. IA "Journal", 2 May 1875.
13. IA "Journal", 27 May 1875.
14. IA "Journal", 21 Jan. 1877.
15. IA and Aberdeen, *We Twa*, vol. 1, p. 155.
16. IA "Journal", 21 Jan. 1877.
17. Dudley Coutts Marjoribanks to IA, Brook House, London, 8 Dec. 1876, H.H. Coll.
18. IA "Journal", 18 Feb. 1877.
19. IA "Journal", 16 May 1877.
20. IA "Journal", 16 July 1877.
21. Ibid.
22. Pentland, p. 21.
23. As told to the writer by Lord Aberdeen's grandson, John Sinclair, Lord Pentland, New York, 12 June 1979.
24. IA "Journal", 15 Aug. 1877.
25. "...a famous church projects its pillared portico assertively beyond the pavement on to the street: St. George's Hanover Square.... In the portico are two agreeable cast iron dogs (ascribed to Landseer) as though awaiting their their masters from matins.... Inside above all, are the weddings of the splendid." Among those exchanging wedding vows at St. George's are Shelley, Disraeli, Theodore Roosevelt, the Asquiths. Quoted in David Piper, *The Companion Guide to London* (London: Fontana-Collins, 1964).
26. IA "Journal", 7 Nov. 1877.
27. Charles Chenevix Trench, *Charley Gordon* (London: Allan Lane, 1978), p. 137.
28. IA "Journal", 31 Dec. 1877.

CHAPTER 4

1. IA and Aberdeen, *We Twa*, vol. 1, p. 175.
2. Pentland, p. 25.
3. Campbell "Lord" to Lord Aberdeen, Osiont, 14 Feb. 1880, HH Coll.
4. IA and Aberdeen, *We Twa*, vol. 1, p. 190.
5. Christopher Hussey, "Haddo House, Aberdeenshire", *Country Life*, 8 Aug. 1966.
6. "You will be glad to hear Haddo House is now firmly vested in the National Trust, with Government help, and the family providing a large endowment fund. My sister-in-law will continue to live in her wing and continue her musical activities and the contents of the Muniments Room remain the property of the Haddo House Trustees." Archibald Gordon, Fifth Marquess of Aberdeen and Temair, to the author, London, 24 Aug. 1978.
7. IA and Aberdeen, *We Twa*, vol. 2, p. 192.
8. IA "Journal", 30 Sept. 1879.

9.   IA "Journal", 1 Oct. 1879.
10. IA "Journal", 1 Dec. 1879.
11. IA and Aberdeen, *We Twa*, vol. 2, p. 11.
12. IA and Aberdeen, *We Twa,* vol. 2, p. 5.
13. IA and Aberdeen, *We Twa,* vol. 2, p. 7.
14. James Drummond of Aberdeen has recently written *Onward and Upward* (Aberdeen: Aberdeen University Press, 1983), an amusing account of these activities and their contrast with what was regarded as the proper management of servants during that time.
15. Pentland, pp. 31-2.
16. IA "Journal", 1 Aug. 1880.
17. IA and Aberdeen, *We Twa,* vol. 1, p. 199.
18. IA and Aberdeen, *We Twa,* vol. 2, p. 310.
19. IA "Journal", 22 Oct. 1879.
20. IA and Aberdeen, *We Twa,* vol. 1, p. 220.
21. IA "Journal", 2 Nov. 1878.
22. IA and Aberdeen, *We Twa,* vol. 1, p. 220.
23. IA "Journal", 10 Oct. 1879.
24. IA "Journal", 27 Nov. 1879.
25. IA "Journal", 26 Nov. 1879.
26. IA "Journal", 30 Jan. 1880.
27. Pentland, p. 42.
28. IA and Aberdeen, *We Twa,* vol. 1, p. 218 .

CHAPTER 5

1.   Henry Drummond, *The Greatest Thing in the World* (Stirling, Scotland: Stirling Tract Enterprise), 7th ed., pp. 21-2.
2.   George Adam Smith, *The Life of Henry Drummond* (London: Hodder and Stoughton, 1899).
3.   Ibid.
4.   "Grundyism", meaning propriety or prudery, derives from "What will Mrs. Grundy [a neighbour] say?" in Morton's 1798 *Speed the Plough*. Drummond's letter to Mrs. Stuart is quoted in Smith.
5.   IA to James Drummond, 15 Feb. 1924, Henry Drummond (HD) Papers, National Library of Scotland, Edinburgh.
6.   Pentland, p. 221.
7.   Pentland, p. 222.
8.   Henry Drummond to Mother, 11 Aug. 1884, HD Papers.
9.   HD to "My Dear James", 30 June 1885, HD Papers.
10. Pentland, p. 54.
11. HD to Mother, Sat. morning (1866?), HD Papers.
12. HD to IA, 20 Oct. 1885, "HD Letters", HH Coll.
13. Pentland, p. 49.
14. *World,* London, May 1885.
15. HD to IA, 15 April 1888, "HD Letters", HH Coll.
16. HD to "My Dear James", 30 June 1885, HD Papers.
17. Pentland, p. 43.
18. Rosebery, Letters, HH Coll.
19. HD to IA, 9 Aug. 1888, "HD Letters", HH Coll.
20. HD to IA, 13 Sept. 1888, "HD Letters", HH Coll.
21. HD to IA, 25 Sept. 1888, "HD Letters", HH Coll.

CHAPTER 6

1. HD to IA, 3 Feb. 1886, "HD Letters".
2. Quoted in Pentland, p. 56.
3. HD to IA, 12 Feb. 1886. "HD Letters".
4. HD to Mother, c. 1886, HD Papers.
5. HD to IA, 27 March 1886, "HD Letters".
6. IA and Aberdeen, *We Twa*, vol. 1, pp. 266-7.
7. An Irish Correspondent, *Westminster Gazette*, 14 Dec. 1914.
8. Quoted in Michael Davitt, *The Fall of Feudalism in Ireland* (London: Harper and Bros., 1904).
9. Quoted in Pentland, p. 63.
10. Ibid.
11. HD to IA, 16 Oct. 1886, "HD Letters".
12. Quoted in Pentland, p. 65.
13. Quoted in Pentland, p. 66.
14. HD to IA, 3 March 1887, "HD Letters".
15. HD to Mother, 21 May 1887, HD Papers.
16. HD to Mother, 24 June 1887, HD Papers.
17. Lord and Lady Aberdeen, 1886-87, "Journal", HH Coll.
18. HD to IA, 21 July 1887, South Framingham, Mass.
19. HD to IA, 30 Sept. 1887, Yale, New Haven.
20. IA, "Why I Am a Politician", *The Gentlewoman*, 13 Aug. 1892.
21. Pentland, p. 72.
22. HD to IA, 17 Dec. 1887, Stirling, Scotland, "HD Letters".
23. Pentland, p. 79.
24. HD to IA, 13 Dec. 1888, "HD Letters".
25. Quoted in Pentland, p. 80.
26. HD to IA, 14 Aug. 1889, "HD Letters".
27. Quoted in Pentland, p. 81.
28. Quoted in Pentland, pp. 82-3.
29. HD to IA, 12 Nov. 1889, "HD Letters".
30. HD to IA, 16 Nov. 1889, "HD Letters".
31. HD to IA, 20 Nov. 1889, "HD Letters".
32. Quoted in Pentland, p. 87.

CHAPTER 7

1. IA and Aberdeen, *We Twa*, vol. 1, p. 89.
2. R.K. Webb, *Modern England* (New York: Dodd, Mead, 1968), p. 364.
3. HD to IA, Melbourne, 21 April 1890, "HD Letters", HH Coll.
4. HD to IA, 29 April 1890, "HD Letters".
5. Young, p. 263.
6. Barbara Tuchman, *The Proud Tower* (Toronto: Macmillan, 1966), p. 286.
7-14. IA's "Letters from Canada, 1890", 26 to 18 Aug, HH Coll.
15. Marian Macrae and Anthony Adamson, *The Ancestral Roof* (Toronto: Clarke, Irwin, 1963), p. 170.
16. IA, "Letters from Canada 1890", 19 Sept. 1890.
17. Pentland, p. 86.
18. IA, "Letters from Canada 1890", 19 Sept. 1890.
19. Sara Jeanette Duncan, *The Imperialist* (New York: Copp Clark, 1904), p. 98.
20. IA, "Letters from Canada 1890", 28 Sept. 1890.
21. HD to Mother, 1890, HD Papers.
22. Annual Report, 1886, Ladies Union of Aberdeen, Central Library, Aberdeen.
23. Annual Report 1893, Ladies Union of Aberdeen.

24. Annual Report 1893, Ladies Union of Aberdeen.

25-31. Lady Aberdeen's "Letters from Canada 1890", Oct. 1890.

32. Pentland, p. 92.

33. IA and Aberdeen, *We Twa*, vol. 1. p. 294.

34. The Aberdeen Association. *Report 1911-12* (Ottawa: R.J. Taylor, Printer, 1912), p. 15.

35. Ibid, p. 23.

36. IA, "Letters from Canada 1890", 3 Nov. 1890.

CHAPTER 8

1. HD to IA, 9 Jan. 1891, "HD Letters", HH Coll.

2. Ibid., 13 Dec. 1890.

3. Ibid., 4 July 1891.

4. Quoted in Pentland, p. 84.

5. HD to IA, 8 Oct. 1891, "HD Letters".

6. Pentland, pp. 95-6.

7-9. IA, "Letters from Canada and the U.S.A. to Henry Drummond and John Sinclair", 1891, Sept. 1891, HH Coll.

10. Aline B. Saarinen, *The Proud Possessors* (New York: Random House, 1958).

11-14. Letters 1891, 10 to 17 Sept., 1891, HH Coll.

15. John T. Saywell, "The Canadian Succession Question, 1891-1896", *Canadian Historical Review,* vol. 37, no. 4, p. 311.

16. HD to IA, 6 Sept. 1891, "HD Letters".

17. "Letters", 1891, 30 Sept. 1891.

18. "Letters", 1891, 1 Oct. 1891.

19. Quoted in Louise Reynolds, *Agnes* (Toronto: Samuel Stevens, 1979), p. 28.

20-27. "Letters" *1891*, 1 Oct. to 21 Dec.

28. James L. Hughes, "An Hour with Oliver Wendell Holmes," *The Canadian Magazine,* vol. 2, no. 2, p. 137.

29-34. "Letters 1891", Nov. 12 to Dec. 15.

35. IA, *Through Canada with a Kodak* (Edinburgh: W.H. White, 1893).

CHAPTER 9

1. G. Jamieson to Lord Aberdeen, Nov. 1892, HH Coll, MSS1/40.

2. IA, "Letters", 27 Oct. 1891, HH Coll.

3. IA, "Canadian Journals", 30 Oct. 1894, PAC.

4. Ibid.

5. E. Kelly to G. Jamieson, 24 Jan. 1893, HH Coll.

6. IA, "Canadian Journals", 4 Dec. 1896.

7. IA , "Canadian Journals", 22 Oct. 1895.

8. Wm. Van Horne to Lord A., 13 Nov. 1895, Aberdeen Papers, vol. 5, PAC.

9. IA, "Canadian Journals", 30 Oct. 1894, PAC.

10. Theresa Hurst, *An Illustrated History of Vernon and District* (Vernon, B.C.: printed by Vernon News, 1967).

11. IA and Aberdeen, *We Twa*, vol. 2, p. 91.

CHAPTER 10

1. IA, "Canadian Journals", 17 Sept. 1893.

2. IA, "Canadian Journals", 16 Sept. 1893.

3. Her detailed journals for 1893-98 were deposited in the 1950s in the PAC.

4. Gladstone to IA, 10 Nov. 1893, 10 Downing St., HH Coll.
5. Gladstone to IA, 28 April 1896, HH Coll.
6. Rosebery to IA, 23 Jan. 1895, HH Coll.
7-10. "Canadian Journals", 20-26 Sept. 1893.
11. Lord Aberdeen, *Jokes Cracked by Lord Aberdeen* (Dundee, Scotland: Valentine and Sons, 1929); and *We Twa* (London: Methuen, 1929).
12. IA, "Canadian Journals", 12 Nov. 1893.
13. "Constance" (Lady Derby) to IA, 2 Sept. 1893, Aberdeen Papers, vol. 5, PAC.
14-17. IA, "Canadian Journals", 13 Dec. 1893 to 20 Jan. 1894.
18. Ripon to Aberdeen, 9 May 1893, Aberdeen Papers, PAC.
19. Aberdeen to Ripon, 30 May 1893, Aberdeen Papers, PAC.
20. Beckles Willson, *The Life of Lord Strathcona and Mount Royal,* (London: Cassell, 1915), p. 427.
21. *Telegram,* Toronto, 9 Sept. 1893.
22. Longley to Blake, 11 Aug. 1892, Blake Papers, Public Archives Ontario.
23. Pentland, p. 128.
24. *Daily Witness,* Montreal, 16 Sept. 1893.
25. *Evening Journal,* Ottawa, 18 Sept. 1893.
26. *Free Press*, Winnipeg, 18 Sept. 1893.
27. Pentland, p. 128.
28. Ibid., p. 110.
29. IA, "Canadian Journals", 25 Oct. 1893.
30. IA, "Canadian Journals", 7 May 1894.
31. IA, "Canadian Journals", 4 March 1894.
32. IA, "Canadian Journals", 28 April 1894
33. IA, "Canadian Journals", 20 Dec. 1893.
34. Ibid.
35. IA, "Canadian Journals", 24 March 1895.
36. IA, "Canadian Journals", 17 Jan. 1895.
37. IA, "Canadian Journals", 1 Feb. 1895.
38. IA, "Canadian Journals", 14 Dec. 1895.
39. IA, "Canadian Journals", 17 May 1895.
40. IA, "Canadian Journals", 31 May 1895.
41. IA, "Canadian Journals", 19 Nov. 1893.
42. IA, "Canadian Journals", 25 Nov. 1893.
43. Ibid.
44. IA, "Canadian Journals", supplementary, 16 June 1894, PAC.
45. Rosebery to IA, 23 Jan. 1895, HH Coll.
46. Rosebery to Aberdeen, 19 July 1894, HH Coll.
47. IA, "Journal", supplementary, 20 June 1894.
48. IA, "Journal", supplementary, 22 June 1894.

CHAPTER 11

1. IA, "Canadian Journals" 25 Oct. 1893.
2. IA, "Canadian Journals", 5 Oct. 1893.
3. IA, "Canadian Journals", 12 Aug. 1894.
4. IA, "Canadian Journals", 26 Aug. 1894.
5. IA, "Canadian Journals", 7 Oct. 1894.
6. IA, "Canadian Journals", 13 Oct. 1894.
7. IA, "Canadian Journals", 6 Aug. 1895.
8. IA, "Canadian Journals", 29 Nov. 1893.
9. IA, "Canadian Journals", 1 March 1894.
10. IA, "Canadian Journals", 7 June 1895,
11. IA, "Canadian Journals", 20 Feb. 1894.

12. Cummings to Aberdeen (no date), Toronto, Aberdeen Papers, PAC.
13. IA, "Canadian Journals", 30 Sept. 1893.
14. IA, "Canadian Journals", 27 Oct. 1893.
15. *Empire*, Toronto, 28 Oct. 1893.
16. IA, "Canadian Journals", 16 Jan. 1894.
17. IA, "Canadian Journals", 14 Feb. 1894.
18. IA, "Canadian Journals", 7 April 1894.
19. IA, "Canadian Journals", 14 April 1894.

CHAPTER 12

1. C.H. Tupper (CHT) to Thompson, 18 Sept. 1894, CHT Papers, PAC.
2. IA, "Journal", 11 [sic] Dec. 1894.
3. IA, "Journal", 18 July 1895.
4. IA, "Journal", 13 [sic] (actually 14) Dec. 1894.
5. Deciphered cable from Governor-General of Canada, received 13.12.1894, Public Record Office, Colonial Official. Kew Supplementary (secret) Correspondence, CO 537/113, pp. 69-71.
6. IA, "Journal", 14 Dec. 1894.
7. Ibid.
8. Ibid.
9. Ibid.
10. "Answer" R.M. 13/12/94, CO 537/113, CIF 0015, Public Record Office, Kew, Richmond, U.K.
11. IA and Aberdeen, *We Twa,* vol. 2, p. 29.
12. Bowell to CHT, 23 March 1895, Bowell Papers, vol. 14, PAC.
13. IA, "Journal", 13 [sic] (actually 14) Dec. 1894.
14. CHT to John F. McDougall, 15 Dec. 1894, CHT Papers, PAC.
15. IA, "Journal", 13 [sic] (actually 14) Dec. 1894.
16. IA, "Journal", 16 Dec. 1894.
17. IA, "Journal", 18 July 1895.
18. IA, "Journal", 3 Jan. 1895.
19. IA to Laurier, 24 June 1895, Aberdeen Papers, PAC.
20. IA, "Journal", 14 [sic] (actually 18) July 1895.
21. Sir Joseph Pope, *Public Servant, The Memoirs of Sir Joseph Pope*, ed. Maurice Pope (Toronto: Oxford University Press, 1960).
22. Christopher Ondaatje and Donald Swainson, *The Prime Ministers of Canada* (Toronto: General Publishing, 1968).
23. Bruce Hutchison, *Mr. Prime Minister 1867-1964* (Toronto: Longmans, 1964), p. 104.
24. Joseph Schull, *Laurier: The First Canadian* (Toronto: Macmillan, 1965), p. 292.
25. Sir John Williston, *Reminiscences, Political and Personal* Toronto: McClelland and Stewart, 1919).
26. Pope, 109.
27. Lowell C. Clark, "The Conservative Party in the 1890s", *Canadian Historical Association Report 1961*, p. 64.
28. Heath MacQuarrie, *The Conservative Party* (Toronto: McClelland and Stewart, 1965), pp. 55-6.
29. Sir Charles Tupper to Moberly Bell, 7 June 1897, Tupper Papers, PAC.
30. Pope.
31. Clark p. 64.
32. Saywell, Introduction, *Journal*, pp. xxv-vi.

CHAPTER 13

1. IA, "Journal", 5 Jan. 1895.
2. IA, "Journal", 9 Jan. 1895.
3. IA, "Journal", 21 April 1896.
4. IA, "Journal", 22 March 1895.
5. IA, "Journal", 15 Jan. 1895.
6. IA, "Journal", 22 Feb. 1895.
7. Ibid.
8. IA, "Journal", 18 March 1895.
9. IA, "Journal", 28 Feb. 1895.
10. IA, "Journal", 3 March 1895.
11. Ibid.
12. IA, "Journal", 5 March 1895
13. IA, "Journal", 6 March 1895.
14. IA, "Journal", 11 March 1895.
15. CHT to Mackenzie Bowell, 21 March 1895, Bowell Papers, vol. 14, PAC.
16. Bowell to CHT, 23 March 1895, Bowell Papers.
17. CHT to T. Mayne Daly, 26 March 1895, CHT Papers.
18. IA, "Journal", 29 March 1895.
19. CHT to Aberdeen, 28 March 1895, Aberdeen Papers, vol. 5, PAC.
20. Montreal *Star,* 28 May 1895.
21. IA, "Journal", 29 March 1895.
22. IA, "Journal", 13 July 1895.
23. IA, "Journal", 24 April 1895.
24. IA, "Journal", 3 June 1895.
25. H. Drummond to Lord Aberdeen, Grand Hotel, Biarritz, 24 May 1895, "Letters from Henry Drummond," HH Coll.
26. Ottawa *Evening Journal,* 20 July 1895.
27. Aberdeen, "Journal", 13 July 1895.
28. A. "Journal", 17 July 1895.
29. Oscar Douglas Skelton, *Life and Letters of Sir Wilfrid Laurier,* vol. 1 (Toronto: McClelland and Stewart,Carleton Library, 1965), p. 155.
30. Gladsone to IA, 15 Aug. 1895.
31. Toronto *Globe*, 12 July 1895.
32. IA, "Journal", 26 July 1895.
33. IA "Journal", 19 July 1895.
34. IA "Journal", 28 July 1895.
35. Gladstone to IA, 15 Aug. 1895, HH Coll.
36. Rosebery to IA, 5 Sept. 1895, HH Coll.
37. Mrs. Alfred Watt to Henry Robertson K.C., 16 Nov. 1895, Aberdeen Papers, PAC.
38. IA, "Journal", 22 Aug. 1895.
39. Ibid.
40. Pope, p. 104.
41. IA to CHT, 23 Oct. 1895, CHT Papers, PAC.
42. CHT to IA, 4 Nov. 1895, CHT Papers.
43. R.H. Pope to Hon. W.B. Ives, 4 Nov. 1895, CHT Papers.
44. CHT to Sir Charles Tupper, 4 Nov. 1895, Tupper Papers.
45. Rosebery to IA, 16 Dec. 1895, HH Coll.

CHAPTER 14

1. IA, "Journal", 2 Jan. 1896.
2. IA, "Journal", 5 Jan. 1896.

3. Sir Charles Tupper to Van Horne, 6 Jan. 1896, Tupper Papers.
4. IA, "Journal", 5 Jan. 1896.
5. IA, "Journal", 6 Jan. 1896.
6. Ibid.
7. Bowell to Aberdeen, 6 Jan. 1896, Aberdeen Papers.
8. IA, "Journal", 6 Jan. 1896.
9. Saywell, "The Canadian Succession Question," *Canadian Historical Review*, p. 326; "Introduction" to *Journal of Lady Aberdeen*, The Champlain Society of Canada, Toronto, 1960, p. lx.; and Skelton, vol. 1., p. 157.
10. IA, "Journal", 7 Jan. 1896.
11. Ibid.
12. Saywell, "Introduction", pp. lxi, lxii.
13. IA, "Journal", 7 Jan. 1896.
14-21. IA, "Journal", 7 to 12 Jan. 1896.
22. James Edgar to Matilda Edgar, 6 Jan. 1896, Sir James Edgar Papers, Archives of Ontario, MU 961.
23. Edgar to Matilda E., 10 Jan. 1896, Edgar Papers.
24. T. Mayne Daly to Bowell, 12 Jan. 1896, Bowell Papers.
25-29. IA, "Journal", 12 and 14 Jan. 1896.
30. CHT to the Rev. A. E. Burke, 3 Feb. 1896, CHT Papers.
31. IA, "Journal", 3 Feb. 1896.
32. CHT to IA, 5 Feb. 1896.
33. IA to CHT, 5 Feb. 1896, Aberdeen Papers.

CHAPTER 15

1. IA, "Journal", 20 Jan. 1896.
2. IA, "Journal", 30 Jan. 1896.
3. J.G. Bourinot, "Historical Introduction" in *Historical Fancy Dress Ball* (Ottawa: n.p., 1896)
4. IA, "Journal", 22 Feb. 1896.
5. IA, to Lady Thompson, 24 Feb. 1896.
6. IA, "Journal", 29 Jan. 1896.
7. Ibid.
8. IA, "Journal", 3 Feb. 1896.
9. IA, "Journal", 5 March 1896.
10. Skelton, vol. 1, p. 166.
11. James Edgar to Matilda Edgar, 7 March 1896, Sir James Edgar Papers, Archives of Ontario, MU 961.
12. IA, "Journal", 19 March 1896.
13. Edgar to Matilda Edgar, 21 April 1896.
14. IA, "Journal", 16 April 1896.
15. IA, "Journal", 22 April 1896.
16. Ibid.
17. Rosebery to Aberdeen, 5 May 1896, HH Coll.
18. Ottawa *Citizen*, 24 April 1896.
19. IA, "Journal", 16 June 1896.
20. Pope, p. 108.
21. IA, "Journal", 8 April 1896.
22-27. IA, "Journal", various dates, June-July 1896.
28. Toronto *Mail and Empire*, 29 Aug. 1896.
29. Hamilton Daily *Spectator*, 29 Aug. 1896.
30. IA, "Journal", 9 July 1896.
31. CHT to IA, 8 March 1897, Aberdeen Papers, PAC.
32. Ibid.

33. IA, "Journal", 31 Dec. 1896.
34. IA and Aberdeen, *We Twa,* vol. 2, p. 38.

CHAPTER 16

1. IA, "Journal", 31 Jan. 1897, PAC, Ottawa.
2. IA, "Journal", 27 Feb. 1897.
3. IA, "Journal", 9 May 1897.
4. Ibid.
5. IA, to Mrs. Drummond, 31 July 1897, HD Papers.
6. IA, "Journal", 9 May 1897.
7. Ibid.
8. *Saturday Night,* 10 April 1897.
9. "Journal", 9 May 1897.
10. Toronto *Globe* (?) April ? 1897, from an unmarked clipping in IA "Journal".
11. Archbishop Walsh to Aberdeen, 7 April 1897, Aberdeen Papers, PAC.
12. John Murray Gibbon, *The Victorian Order of Nurses for Canada: 50th Anniversary* (Montreal: Southam Press, 1947), p. 15.
13. *Saturday Night,* 20 Feb. 1897, p. 8.
14. "Around Town", *Saturday Night,* 29 May 1897.
15. Toronto *Globe,* 24 June 1897.
16. IA, "Journal", 7 Sept. 1897.
17. Ibid.
18. Ibid.
19. Montreal *Star,* 4 Sept. 1897.
20. Mabel Bell to Daisy Fairchild. Quoted in Lilias M. Toward (ed.), *Mabel Bell, Alexander's Silent Partner* (Toronto: Methuen, 1984), pp. 112-4.
21. IA, "Journal", 22 Oct. 1897.
22. St. John *Globe,* 15 Oct. 1897.
23. IA, "Journal", 22 Oct. 1897.
24. IA, "Journal", 30 Oct. 1897.
25. Alfred Worcester, *Nurses and Nursing* (Boston: Harvard University Press, n.d.).
26. IA, "Journal", 7 Nov. 1897.
27. IA, "Journal", 10 Nov. 1897.
28. Worcester.
29. IA, "Journal", 8 Dec. 1897.
30. Florence Nightingale to Lady Aberdeen, 5 May 1898, VON Papers, PAC.
31. IA, "Journal", 19 Nov. 1898.

CHAPTER 17

1. IA and Aberdeen, *We Twa,* vol. 2, p. 134.
2. Skelton, vol. 2, p. 34.
3. J.W. Dafoe, *Laurier: A Study in Canadian Politics* (Toronto: McClelland and Stewart, Carleton Library, 1963), p. 57.
4. Ottawa *Free Press,* 27 July 1898.
5. Smith to Wm. Bourke Cockran, Smith Papers, 10 Nov. 1899.
6. Chamberlain to Salisbury, 4 Jan. 1896, Joseph Chamberlain Papers, U. of Birmingham Library.
7. Tuchman, p. 68.
8. Francis Birell, *Gladstone* (New York: Collier Books, 1962), p. 122.
9. *Report of the Annual Meeting of the National Reform Union,* Manchester England, 12 March 1902.

10. Stead to IA, 3 Jan. 1900. Quoted in Joseph O. Baylen, "W.T. Stead and the Boer War: The Irony of Idealism", *Canadian Historical Review,* vol. 40, no. 4,

11. Ibid.

12. Toronto *News,* 16 May 1898.

13. Ottawa *Free Press,* 11 May 1898.

14. Hamilton *Spectator,* 9 June 1898.

15. Chamberlain to Lord Minto, 19 July 1898, Minto Papers MG 27 IIB 1, vol. 14, PAC.

16. Lord Haddo to IA, April-May 1898, HH Coll.

17. Elizabeth Wallace, *Goldwin Smith: Victorian Liberal,* (Toronto: n.p., 1957).

18. IA, "Journal", 7 Sept. 1897.

19. Ibid.

20. IA, "Journal", 24 Nov. 1897.

21. Ibid.

22. G.R. Parkin, LL.D., "Introduction", *Book of the Victorian Era Ball* (Toronto: Rowsell and Hutchinson, 1898).

23. IA, "Journal", 8 Dec. 1898.

24. Ottawa *Free Press,* 5 Feb. 1898.

25. Toronto *Mail,* 12 Feb. 1898.

26. Montreal press clipping, 30 July 1898, Aberdeen Papers, PAC.

27. Maud Edgar, "Journal", 1896-1898, Edgar Papers, Ontario Provincial Archives, MU 962.

28. IA, *Dedication* (to the first May Court Queen) (Ottawa: n.p., 1 May 1898).

29. Maud Edgar, "Journal".

30. Montreal *Herald,* 17 Sept. 1898.

31. IA, "Journal", 19 Nov. 1898.

32. Ibid.

33. Sophocles, *Antigone,* l. 180-1.

34. IA, "Journal", 19 Nov. 1898.

35. Ibid.

36. Ibid.

37. Ibid.

38. Ottawa *Free Press,* 15 Oct. 1898.

39. Chamberlain to Minto ("Private"), 7 Oct. 1899, Minto Papers, vol. 18, PAC.

40. IA, "Journal", 29 Oct. 1899.

41. IA, (ed.), *Our Lady of the Sunshine and Her International Visitors* (London: Constable, 1909).

42. Ottawa *Citizen,* 8 June 1898.

43. IA, "Journal", 13 June 1898.

44. Toronto *Globe,* ? June 1898.

45. Brockville *Recorder,* 21 Oct. 1898.

46. IA, "Journal", 19 Nov. 1898.

47. IA, "Journal", 8 July 1898.

48. IA, "Journal", 19 Nov. 1898.

49. Ibid.

50. Wilfrid Eggleston, *The Queen's Choice* (Ottawa: Queen's Printer, 1961), pp. 156-7.

51. IA, "Journal", 17 Aug. 1898.

52. IA, "Journal", 19 Nov. 1898.

53. Ibid.

54. "Mr. E. McMahon, Secretary of the Central Fair Association, writes the mayor and council saying he is instructed by the board of directors to suggest to them the propriety of inviting Lord and Lady Aberdeen to open the exhibition. Mr. McMahon further says: 'I am also instructed to say that the board would suggest in the ceremony of opening the exhibition that the new main building be named "Aberdeen Pavilion"... on Monday, 19th September.'" Ottawa *Free Press,* 29 June 1898.

CHAPTER 18

1. Board Members, International Council of Women (ICW), *Women in a Changing World* (London: Routledge and Kegan Paul, 1966), p. 23.
2. IA and Aberdeen, *We Twa*, vol. 2, pp. 162-3.
3. Maud Edgar to IA, undated, Edgar Papers, Ontario Archives, MU 962.
4. Political pamphlet, speeches given at National Reform Union banquet, Holborn Restaurant, 14 June 1901, HH Coll.
5. IA typed document, "Confidential. Concerning My Visit to Mr. and Mrs. Gladstone at Pitlochry July 3 1894," HH Coll.
6. IA typed document, "Message sent by IA for Gladstone Commemorative Dinner 16. 11. 1937", HH Coll.
7. Lord Ponsonby, *William Ewart Gladstone, The Great Victorians* (Freeport, N.Y.: Books for Libraries Press, 1932), p. 189.
8. IA typed document, "Concerning My Visit to Mr. and Mrs. Gladstone 1894", HH Coll.
9. Cecil, p. 273.
10. Rosebery to IA, 30 Oct. 1884, HH Coll.
11. Rosebery to IA, 1 Feb. 1889, HH Coll.
12. Rosebery to IA, Dalmeny Park, Edinburgh, 22 Sept. 1888, HH Coll.
13. Rosebery to IA, 13 Nov. 1888, HH Coll.
14. Rosebery to IA, 30 June 1892, HH Coll.
15. Rosebery to IA, 16 Aug. 1892, HH Coll.
16. Cecil, p. 275.
17. *Report of Annual Meeting of the National Reform Union,* March 12, 1902, HH Coll.
18. Winston Churchill in "Guest Book", Haddo House, Aberdeenshire, 1 Feb. 1904.
19. Lord Haddo to IA, 24 Aug. 1905, HH Coll.
20. F. Cochayne to IA, 27 Jan. 1906, HH Coll.
21. CB to IA, 16 March 1904, HH Coll.
22. Typed report of WLA meeting, HH Coll.
23. John Morely to IA, 25 Jan. 1904, HH Coll.
24. IA to CB, 30 Dec. 1905, HH Coll.
25. CB to IA, 6 Jan. 1906, HH Coll.
26. Lady Tweedmouth to IA, 11 July 1906, HH Coll.
27. IA and Aberdeen, *We Twa*, vol. 2, p. 192.
28. Lady Tweedmouth to IA, 11 July 1906, HH Coll.
29. "The Reduction of Armaments", London *Times*, 3 March 1908.
30. Roy Jenkins, *Asquith* (London: Collins, 1964), p. 182.
31. *The Times*, London, 6 March 1908.
32. Jenkins, p. 159.

CHAPTER 19

1. IA and Aberdeen, *We Twa*, vol. 2, pp. 175-6.
2. Charles O'Mahony, *The Viceroys of Ireland* (London: John Long, 1912), p. 323.
3. Quoted in *The Times*, 25 May 1921.
4. O'Mahony, p. 324.
5. H. Asquith, note "for the PM.'s consideration", 27 Dec. 1906, HH Coll.
6. Pentland, p. 152.
7. *The Times*, "Lord Lieutenant and Politics", 5 Feb. 1906.
8. *Freeman's Journal*, 16 March 1906.
9. IA and Aberdeen, *We Twa*, vol. 2, p. 179.
10. R.M. Martin to IA, 22 Jan. 1935, HH Coll.
11. Quoted in Pentland, p. 166.

12. Quoted in Pentland, p. 162.
13. Quoted in Pentland, pp. 169-70.
14. Charles Masterman to IA, 14 Feb. 1915, HH Coll.
15. Lloyd George to Lord A., 8 May 1914, HH Coll.
16. IA and Aberdeen, *We Twa,* vol. 2, p. 188.
17. A. Birrell to IA, 14 Dec. 1908, HH Coll.
18. George Murray to IA, 30 Oct. 1906, HH Coll.
19. IA and Aberdeen, *We Twa*, vol. 2, pp. 189, 191.
20. Midleton, *Ireland — Dupe or Heroine?* (London: Wm. Heinemann, 1932).
21. Jenkins, p. 332.
22. Ibid., p. 396.
23. Lord A. to A. Birrell, 25 April 1914, Asquith Papers, Bodelian Library, Oxford. vol. 46.
24. Ibid.
25. A. Birrell to H. Asquith, 26 April 1914, Asquith Papers.
26. Ibid.
27. H. Asquith to Lord A., 8 Oct. 1914, HH Coll.
28. H. Asquith to Lord Haddo, 9 Dec. 1914, HH Coll.
29. David Lloyd George to Rt. Hon. Lord Balfour of Burleigh, K.T., 19 July 1917, HH Coll.
30. Lord Aberdeen to "My Dear Prime Minister", New York, 20 July 1917, Lloyd George Papers, House of Lords Record Office, London.
31. Unsigned paper, Lloyd George Papers.
32. Lord Rosebery to IA, 12 Dec. 1917, HH Coll.
33. Lord Rosebery to IA, 18 Feb. 1924, HH Coll.
34. Lord Wimborne to Asquith, 25 April 1916, Asquith Papers.
35. J.B. Maguire, *Dublin Castle, Historical Background and Guide* (Dublin: Office of Public Works), p. 16.

CHAPTER 20

1. Archie Gordon, "Introduction", *A Wild Flight of Gordons* (London: Weidenfeld and Nicolson, 1985), p. 12.
2. Ibid., p. 193 and ff.
3. Rosebery to IA, 23 Sept. 1922, HH Coll.
4. Pentland, p. 200.
5. Ralph Connor, *Postscript to Adventure, Part IV,* p. 173.
6. Ibid., p. 174.
7. John Sinclair, Lord Pentland, to the author, New York, June 1979.
8. Archie Gordon, 5th Marquess of Aberdeen, to the author, London, 21 July 1977.
9. Pentland, p. 209.
10. Archie Gordon, p. 199.
11. Pentland, p. 136.
12. Ibid., p. 137.
13. ICW, *Women in a Changing World*, p. 44.
14. Pentland, p. 141.
15. A Norwegian delegate to Lord Aberdeen, 1920 [?]. Quoted in Pentland, p. 142.
16. IA, "Notes on the real significance of the I.C.W. to me in my inner life", HH Coll.
17. W.L. Mackenzie King to IA, 16 Dec. 1919, Aberdeen Papers, vol. 2, PAC.
18. W.L. Mackenzie King to IA, 16 Dec. 1919, Aberdeen Papers, vol 2.
19. King to IA, 21 Aug. 1929, Aberdeen Papers, vol. 2.
20. King to IA, 30 Jan. 1933, Aberdeen Papers, vol 2.
21. IA to King, 30 July 1929, King Papers, PAC.
22. King to IA, 30 Jan. 1933, Aberdeen Papers, vol 2.
23. King to IA, 8 April 1934, Aberdeen Papers, vol. 2.

24.   King to IA, 10 Aug. 1936, Aberdeen Papers.
25.   IA to King, 2 Feb. 1937, King Papers, PAC.
26.   IA to King, 24 May 1937, King Papers.
27.   IA to King, 12 June 1937, King Papers.
28.   King "Diary", 18 June 1937, PAC.
29.   C.P. Stacey, "The Divine Mission: Mackenzie King and Hitler", *Canadian Historical Review*, vol. 61, no. 4, p. 504.
30.   King *Diary*, 1 Oct. 1936.
31.   IA to King, Memo, 19 June 1937, King Papers.
32.   King "Diary", 20 June 1937.
33.   King to IA, 31 July 1937, King Papers.
34.   IA to King, 21 June 1937, King Papers.
35.   Stacey, p. 505.
36.   King, "Diary", 23 June 1937.
37.   King, "Diary", 29 June 1937.
38.   King to IA, 23 May 1938, King Papers.
39.   King to IA, 29 Sept. 1938, King Papers.
40.   IA to King, 2 Feb. 1939, King Papers.
41.   IA to King, 2 Feb. 1939, King Papers.
42.   Quoted in Pentland, p. 231.
43.   Pentland, p. 232.

SOURCES

Bibliography

I. MATERIAL RELATING TO LORD AND LADY ABERDEEN

1. manuscripts

Aberdeen, Countess (later Marchioness) of Aberdeen (and Temair). [Ishbel Maria Marjoribanks Gordon]
    (a) "Journals" 1870 to 1884, (approximately), Haddo House Collection (HH Coll.), Aberdeenshire, Scotland.
    (b) "Letters from Canada, 1890", HH Coll.
    (c) "Letters from Canada and the U.S.A. 1891 to H.D. and J.S.", HH Coll.
    (d) "Canadian Journals, 1893-98". Public Archives of Canada (PAC), Ottawa.
——. "The difference between Anger and Affection", (aged 7), HH Coll.
——. "Farewell Address as President, ICW", Dubrovnik, Oct. 1936, Mackenzie King Papers, PAC Ottawa.
——. "Notes on the real significance of the ICW to me in my inner life", HH Coll.
"An Index Inventory of Family Papers and Charters from Haddo House, presented to H.M. General Register House by the Earl of Haddo Sept. 1926, to remain among the Public Records of Scotland in all time coming". HH Coll.
Family wills: Edward Marjoribanks 1 Dec. 1868; Second Lord Tweedmouth 1909; Rt. Hon. Dudley Coutts Marjoribanks, Baron Tweedmouth, 1894, at Somerset House, London. John Campbell Gordon, First Marquess Aberdeen and Temair, 1925, at Haddo House.
Haddo House Guest Book, 1877-1904. HH Coll.
Pentland, Marjorie. "Notes on the Marjoribanks family", personal papers, Mary Rothenburg.
Services of Heirs 1830 and ff., Register of Sesines, Edinburgh.

2. printed publications

Aberdeen, Countess (later Marchioness) of Aberdeen (and Temair). [Ishbel Maria Marjoribanks Gordon] . "My Stage Fright as a Debutante", "My Wonderful Years in the Highlands", "Why I Love Rotten Row", "My Honeymoon Adventure", "A Great Day in My Life", "A Ticklish Job for Lord Aberdeen", "My Greatest Friend", "The Perfect Marriage", "My Brother and Lady Fanny", in *Sunday Post,* Feb.-March 1935.
——. *Musings of a Scottish Granny.* London: Heath, Cranton, 1936.
——. *Onward and Upward.* James Drummond (ed.). Extracts (1891-96) from the magazine of the Onward and Upward Association founded by Lady Aberdeen for the Material, Mental and Moral Elevation of Women. Selected and introduced by James Drummond. Aberdeen: University Press, 1983.
——. "Summer in the Okanagan" *Okanagan Historical Society 18th Report,* 1954.
—— . *The Canadian Journal of Lady Aberdeen 1893-1898.* John T. Saywell (ed.). Toronto: Champlain Society, 1960, with introduction and notes.
——. *The Journal of Lady Aberdeen: The Okanagan Valley in the Nineties.* R.M. Middleton (ed.). Victoria, B.C.: Morriss, 1896.
—— . *Through Canada with a Kodak.* Edinburgh: W.H. White, 1893.
—— . *What is the Use of the Victorian Order of Nurses in Canada?* Ottawa: Mortimer, 1900.
——. "Why I Am A Politician", *The Gentlewoman,* 13 Aug. 1892
——. *Women's Liberal Federation,* pamphlet, 1927.
—— . ed., (prob.) *Archie Gordon,* a memorial volume, printed privately, December 1910.
—— . ed., (probably) *A Memorial Book to the Memory of Edward Marjoribanks, Lord Tweedmouth,* K.T. 1910 printed privately.

——. (ed.) *Our Lady of the Sunshine and Her International Visitors*. London: Constable, 1909.

——. and Lord Aberdeen. *We Twa. Reminiscences of Lord and Lady Aberdeen.* 2 vols. London: Collins, 1925.

Aberdeen, Earl of (later Marquess) of Aberdeen (and Temair). [John Campbell Hamilton Gordon]. *Jokes Cracked by Lord Aberdeen*. Dundee and London: Valentine, 1929.

Alexander, William M. *Place Names of Aberdeenshire*. Aberdeen: Third Spalding Club, 1952.

Benson, E.F. *The Kaiser and English Relations*. London: Longmans, Green, 1936.

Bulloch, John Malcolm. *The Gay Gordons: Some Strange Adventures of a Famous Scots Family.* London: Chapman and Hall, 1908.

Burke's Peerage 1970.

Collard, Elizabeth. *Nineteenth Century Pottery and Porcelain in Canada.* Montreal: McGill University Press, 1967.

Debrett's Peerage 1940.

Dictionary of National Biography (various dates).

Elwood, Marie. "The State Dinner Service of Canada 1898", paper prepared for the Nova Scotia Museum, Halifax, in *Material History Bulletin 3*. Ottawa: National Museum of Man, 1977.

Friedland, Martin L. *The Case of Valentine Shortis*. Toronto: University of Toronto Press, 1986.

Gordon of Ellon, Cosmo. *A Souvenir of Haddo House*. Turrif, Scotland: W. Peters, 1958.

Gordon, Archie, Fifth Marquess of Aberdeen. *A Wild Flight of Gordons: Odd and Able Members of the Gordon Families*. London: Weidenfeld and Nicholson, 1985.

Gordon, Archie, Fifth Earl of Aberdeen *Memoranda of the Life of Lord Haddo, Fifth Earl of Aberdeen*. E.B. Elliot (ed.), London: printed for private circulation, 1865.

"The Grosvenor Estate in Mayfair", in *Survey of London XXXIV*. London: University of London, Athlone Press, 1977.

Gwyn, Sandra. *The Private Capital, Ambition and Love in the Age of Macdonald and Laurier*. Toronto: McClelland and Stewart, 1984.

Historical Fancy Dress Ball, Ottawa, February 17, 1896. Ottawa: John Durie and Son, 1896 (introduction, by John Bourinot).

Hogg, Quinten, Lord Hailsham. *The Door Wherein I Went*. London: Collins, 1975.

Hubbard, R.H. *Rideau Hall*. Ottawa: Queen's Printer, 1967.

Hussey, Christopher. "Haddo House, Aberdeenshire," *Country Life,* 18, 25 August 1966.

Iremonger, Lucille. *Lord Aberdeen. A Biography of the Fourth Earl of Aberdeen, Prime Minister 1852-55.* London: Collins, 1978.

Lord Provosts of Edinburgh 1296 -1932. Edinburgh: University of Edinburgh Press, 1932.

Maguire, J.B. *Dublin Castle, Historical Background and Guide*. Dublin: Public Works for Ireland, 1975.

Memorial Book of the Victorian Era Ball, Given in Toronto 28 December 1897. Privately printed.

Pentland, Marjorie. *A Bonnie Fechter*. London: B.T. Batsford, 1952.

Piper, David. "Chapter Five. Mayfair and Perimeter", *The Companion Guide to London*. London: Fontana-Collins, 1964.

Schull, Joseph, "Lady Aberdeen, Stormy Petrel in Government House" *Weekend Magazine,* No. 37, 1964.

Taylor, A.J.P. "Two Contrasting Wars" *The Listener*, London, July 1977.

Thompson, David, and Victor G. Hopwood (ed.). *David Thompson: Travels in Western North America 1784-1812*. Toronto: Macmillan, 1971.

Toward, Lilias M. *Mabel Bell: Alexander's Silent Partner*. Toronto: Methuen, 1984.

Whitakers Peerage, Baronetage, Knightage and Companionage,

Who Was Who? (various dates).

Who's Who 1977.

Wilson, Sir James. *Old Scotch Songs and Ballads*. Oxford: Oxford University Press, 1927.

II. INTERVIEWS WITH FAMILY MEMBERS BY THE AUTHOR

Gordon, Archibald, Fifth Marquess of Aberdeen. London, 21 July 1977 (grandson).
Gordon, Lady June, dowager Marchioness of Aberdeen, London, 1 August 1977 (grandson's widow).
Rothenburg, Mary, New York, 12 June 1979 (great-granddaughter).
Sinclair, John, Lord Pentland, New York, 12 June 1979 (grandson).
Surtees, John C. and Ursula, Kelowna, B.C., 1 May 1979 (grand-nephew and wife).

III. ASSOCIATIONS RELATING TO THE CAREER OF LADY ABERDEEN

1. printed publications

Aberdeen Association for the Distribution of Literature to Settlers of the North-West. *Annual Reports* (various dates, 1896-1901-2)
Cleverdon, Catherine Lyle. *The Woman Suffrage Movement in Canada*. Toronto: University of Toronto Press, 1950.
Gibbon, John Murray. *The Victorian Order of Nurses for Canada: 50th Anniversary, 1897-1947*. Montreal: Southam Press, 1947.
International Council of Women, The. *Report of Transactions of the Fourth Quinquennial Meeting Held at Toronto, Canada, June 1909*. London: Constable, 1910.
Reid, Diane et al. *A Bridge to the Future. A History of the Council of Women of Ottawa and Area*. Ottawa: Regional Municipality of Ottawa-Carleton, 1976.
Shaw, Rosa L. *Proud Heritage. A History of the National Council of Women of Canada*. Toronto: Ryerson Press, 1957.
Victorian Order of Nurses. *Annual Reports* 1898-1980.
Women in a Changing World. The Dynamic Story of the International Council of Women since 1888. Foreword by Marie Helene Lefaucheux, president ICW. London: Routledge and Kegan Paul, 1966.

IV. HENRY DRUMMOND

1. manuscript

Drummond papers, National Library, Edinburgh.

2. printed publications

Dictionary of National Biography.
Drummond, Henry. *The Greatest Thing in the World*. Stirling, Scotland: Stirling Tract Enterprise, 7th edition.
Smith, Sir George Adam *The Life of Henry Drummond*, London: Hodder and Stoughton, 1899.
Who Was Who 1897-1916.

V. ASSOCIATES IN BRITAIN

1. manuscripts

Asquith, Herbert (HH Coll.)
Birrell, Auguste (HH Coll.)
Bryce, James (PAC)
Campbell-Bannerman, Henry (HH Coll.)

Chamberlain, Joseph (U. of Birmingham Library)
Gladstone, William Ewart (HH Coll.)
Jamieson, George (HH Coll.)
Lloyd George, David (HH Coll., House of Lords archival records)
Morley, John (HH Coll.)
Nathan, Matthew (Bodeleian Library Oxford)
Rosebery, Lord, Alfred Primrose (HH Coll., National Library of Canada)

2. printed publications

Baylen, Joseph O. "W.T. Stead and the Boer War: The Irony of Imperialism", *Canadian Historical Review*, vol 40, no 4, 1959.

Birrell, Francis. *Gladstone*. New York: Collier Books, 1962.

Cecil, Algernon. *Victoria and Her Prime Ministers*. London: Eyre and Spottiswoode, 1953.

de Mendelssohn, Peter. *The Age of Churchill, Vol. 1: Heritage and Adventure, 1874-1911*. London: Thames and Hudson, 1961.

Healey, Edna. *Lady Unknown, The Life of Angela Burdett-Coutts*. London: Sedgwick and Jackson, 1978.

Marlow, Joyce. *The Oak and the Ivy, An Intimate Biography of William and Catherine Gladstone*. New York: Doubleday, 1977.

O'Mahoney, Charles. *The Viceroys of Ireland*. London: Harper and Bros., 1904.

Ponsonbury, Lord "William Ewart Gladstone", *The Great Victorians*, Freeport, N.Y.: Books for Libraries Press, 1971.

VI. GENERAL

Begg, Alexander. *History of British Columbia*. Toronto: Ryerson, 1894.

Brault, Lucien. *Ottawa Old and New*. Ottawa: Ottawa Historical Information Institute, 1946.

Brown, R. Craig. "Goldwin Smith and Anti-Imperialism", *Canadian Historical Review*, vol. 43, no. 1, 1962.

Canadian Parliamentary Companion, 18 Feb. 1897.

Careless, J.M.S. and R. Craig Brown (eds.). *The Canadians, 1867-1967*, Toronto: Macmillan, 1967.

Careless, J.M.S. *Canada, A Story of Challenge*, Toronto: Macmillan, 1965.

Clark, Kenneth. *The Romantic Rebellion. Romantic versus Classic Art,* New York: Harper and Row, 1973.

Clark, Lowell C. "The Conservative Party in the 1890s", *Canadian Historical Association Report*, 1961.

Cochrane, Rev. Wm. D.D. *The Canadian Album. Men of Canada; or Success by Example*, Vols. I to IV, Brantford, Ontario: Bradley, Garretson, 1891-95.

Creighton, Donald. *The Story of Canada*. Toronto: Macmillan, 1959.

Dawson, R. MacGregor. *The Government of Canada*. Toronto: University of Toronto Press, 1947.

Debates of the [Canadian] *House of Commons*, various dates.

Duncan, Bingham. "A Letter on the Fur Seal in Canadian-American Diplomacy" (Wm. Stead to I.A.), *Canadian Historical Review*, vol. 43, no. 1, 1962.

Duncan, Sara Jeannette. *The Imperialist*. Toronto: Copp Clark, 1900.

Easterbrook,W.T. and Hugh G.J. Aitken. *Canadian Economic History*. Toronto: Macmillan, 1956.

Eggleston, Wilfrid. *The Queen's Choice*. Ottawa: Queen's Printer,1961.

Ferguson, Sir James. *The Sixteen Peers of Scotland*. Oxford: Oxford University Press, 1960.

French, Doris. *Faith, Sweat and Politics. A Story of Early Trade Unions in Canada*. Toronto: McClelland and Stewart, 1967.

Galbraith, John Kenneth. *The Age of Uncertainty*. Boston: Houghton Mifflin, 1977.

Gard, Anson A. *The Hub and the Spokes. The Capital and its Environs*. Ottawa and New York: Emerson Press, 1904.

Gay, Peter. *The Bourgeois Experience, Victoria to Freud. Vol.I: Education of the Senses.* Oxford: Oxford University Press, 1984.

Gilbert, G.M. (ed.). *Edinburgh in the 19th Century.* Edinburgh: J. and R. Allan, 1901.

Gloag, John. *Victorian Comfort. A Social History of Design from 1830-1900.* London: Adam and Charles Black, 1961.

Gray, Art. "Kelowna: Tales of Bygone Days", *Kelowna Daily Courier,* 1962-63.

Guillet, Edwin C. *Pioneer Inns and Taverns.* Vol.II. Toronto: Ontario Publishing, 1956.

Harrison, J.F.C. *Robert Owen and the Owenites in Britain and America.* London: Routledge and Kegan Paul, 1969.

Hobsbawn, E.J. *Industry and Empire.* London: Penguin, 1968.

Hopkins, J. Castell. *Progress of Canada in the Century.* London: Linscott, 1900.

Hubbard, R.H. *Rideau Hall, An Illustrated History of Government House, Ottawa.* Ottawa: The Queen's Printer, 1967.

Hurst, Theresa. *An Illustrated History of Vernon and District.* Okanagan Historical Society, 1967.

——. *Kelowna B.C., A Pictorial History.* Kelowna, B.C.: Regatta City Press, 1975.

Hutchinson, Bruce. *Mr. Prime Minister, 1867-1964.* Toronto: Longmans Green, 1964.

Jackson, Holbrook. *The Eighteen Nineties.* Edinburgh: J. and R. Allan, 1913.

Kelvin, Norman,"Afterword", to George Merideth. *The Ordeal of Richard Feverel.* New York: Signet, 1961.

Leslie, Anita. *Edwardians in Love.* London: Arrow, 1974.

Levitt, Joseph. *A Vision Beyond Reach. A Century of Images of Canadian Destiny.* Ottawa: Deneau, 1985.

Lower, Arthur R.M. *Canadians in the Making.* Toronto: Longmans Green, 1958.

——. *Colony to Nation. A History of Canada.* Toronto: Longmans Green,1946.

Mackenzie, Hugh. "The City of Aberdeen", *The Third Statistical Account of Scotland,* Edinburgh.

MacQuarrie, Heath. *The Conservative Party.* Toronto: McClelland and Stewart, 1965.

Macrae, Marian and Anthony Adamson. *The Ancestral Roof.* Toronto: Clarke, Irwin, 1963.

Mallory, James R. *The Structure of Canadian Government.* Toronto: Gage, 1984.

Marriott, J.A.R. *Modern England, 1885-1945.* London: Methuen,1952.

Massingham, Hugh. "Introduction", *The Great Victorians.* Freeport, N.Y.: Books for Libraries Press, 1971.

McInnis, Edgar. *Canada, a Political and Social History.* New York: Rinehart, 1947.

Midleton, Lord. *Ireland — Dupe or Heroine?* London: Heineman,1932.

Minto, C.S. *Victorian and Edwardian Scotland.* London: B.T. Batsford, 1970.

Morgan, H. James. *Canadian Men and Women of the Times.* Toronto: W. Briggs, 1898.

Newman, Peter C. *The Establishment Man.* Toronto: McClelland and Stewart, 1982.

Okanagan Historical Society annual reports, 1954, 1955, 1958.

Ondaatje, Christopher and Donald Swainson. *The Prime Ministers of Canada,* Toronto: General, 1968.

Power, William. *Scotland and the Scots.* Edinburgh: Moray Press, 1934.

——. *Should Auld Acquaintence.* George G. Harrap and Co., 1937.

Priestley, J.B. *The Edwardians.* London: Heinemann, 1970

Ross, A.H.D. *Ottawa Past and Present.* Toronto: Musson,1927.

Saarinen, Aline B. *The Proud Possessors. The lives, times and tastes of some adventurous American art collectors.* New York: Random House, 1958.

Saywell, John T. "The Crown and the Politicians. The Canadian Succession Question 1891-96", *Canadian Historical Review,* vol. 37 no. 4, 1956.

Schuyer, Robert Livingston and Corinne Comstock Weston. *British Constitutional History since 1832.* Princeton, N.J.: Van Nostrand, 1957.

Sheehan, D.D. *Ireland since Parnell.* London, 1921.

Smout, T.C. *History of the Scottish People, 1560-1830.* London: Collins, 1969.

Stephen, James. *The Insurrection in Dublin.* New York: Macmillan, 1916.

Stewart, Gordon. "John A. Macdonald's Greatest Triumph", *Canadian Historical Review,* vol. 93, no. 1, 1982.

Swainson, Donald (ed.). *Oliver Mowat's Ontario.* Toronto: Macmillan, 1972.

Thompson, David. *England in the 19th Century.* London: Penguin, 1950.

Trevelyan, George Macauley. *Illustrated English Social History.* London: Longmans Green, 1950.

——. *A Shortened History of England.* New York: Longmans Green, 1942.

Tuchman, Barbara. *The Proud Tower, A Portrait of the World before the War: 1890-1914.* London: Macmillan, 1966.

Underhill, Frank R. *In Search of Canadian Liberalism.* Toronto: Macmillan, 1960.

——. *The Image of Confederation.* Toronto: University of Toronto Press, 1964.

Volpi, Charles P. de. *Ottawa, A Pictorial Record 1807-1882.* Montreal: Devsco Publications, 1964.

Walbank, F. Alan. *England, Yesterday and To-day, in the Works of the Novelists, 1837 to 1938.* London: B.T. Batsford, 1949.

Walker, Harry and Olive Walker. *Carleton Saga.* Ottawa: Runge Press, 1968.

Ward, Norman and Duff Spafford (eds.). *Politics in Saskatchewan.* Toronto: Longmans, 1968.

Webb, R.K. *Modern England from the 18th Century to the Present.* New York: Dodd, Mead, 1968.

Willson, Beckles. *The Life of Lord Strathcona.* London: Cassell, 1915.

Wilson, Edmund. *O Canada. An American's Notes on Canadian Culture.* New York: Farrar, Strauss and Giroux, 1965.

Young, Douglas. *Scotland.* London: Cassel, 1971.

VII. ASSOCIATES IN CANADA

1. manuscripts

Bowell, Mackenzie (PAC)

Edgar, Matilda (Public Archives of Ontario)

Edgar, Sir James (Public Archives of Ontario)

Foster, George E. (PAC)

King, William Lyon Mackenzie (PAC)

Minto, Lord (PAC)

Thompson, Sir John (PAC)

Tupper, C.H. (PAC)

Watt, Mrs. Alfred (to Henry Robertson, K.C.) (PAC)

2. printed publications

Creighton, Donald. *John A. Macdonald: The Old Chieftain.* Toronto: Macmillan, 1955.

Dafoe, J.W. *Laurier, A Study in Canadian Politics.* Toronto: McClelland and Stewart, Carleton Library, 1963.

Hopkins, J. Castell. *Life and Work of Sir John Thompson.* Toronto: United Publishing, 1898.

Koester, C.B. *Mr. Davin M.P.* Saskatoon: Western Producer Prairie Books, 1980.

Pope, Sir Joseph. Maurice Pope, (ed.). *Public Servant: The Memoirs of Sir Joseph Pope.* Oxford: Oxford University Press, 1960.

Reynolds, Louise. *Agnes,* Toronto: Samuel Stevens, 1979.

Schull, Joseph. *Edward Blake.* Toronto: Macmillan, 1976

——. *Laurier, the First Canadian.* Toronto: Macmillan, 1966.

Skelton, Oscar Douglas. *Life and Letters of Sir Wilfrid Laurier.* Toronto: McClelland and Stewart, Carleton Library, 1965.

Tupper, Sir Charles. *Recollections of Sixty Years in Canada.* London: Cassell, 1914.

Waite, P.B. *Macdonald, His Life and World.* Toronto: McGraw-Hill Ryerson, 1975.

——. *The Man from Halifax, Sir John Thompson, Prime Minister.* Toronto: University of Toronto Press, 1985.

Willison, Sir John. *Reminiscences, Political and Personal*. Toronto: McClelland and Stewart, 1919.

IX. NEWSPAPERS

Aberdeen *Journal*, 1748, 1752, 1760, 1771, 1778, 1781, 1789, 1791, 1792, 1805, 1864.
Brockville *Times*, 1898.
Buffalo *Enquirer*, 1898.
Buffalo *Express*, 1897.
Chicago *Record*, 1898.
Chicago *Times-Herald*, 1898.
Edinburgh *Scotsman*, 1977.
Hamilton *Spectator*, 1896, 1919
Inverness *Courier*, 1904, 1906.
Kelowna *Daily Courier*, 1962, 1963.
London *Advocate*, 1898.
London *Times*, 1886, 1906, 1908, 1914, 1978.
Manchester *Guardian*, 1912.
Montreal *Daily Star*, various dates, 1893-1903.
Montreal *Daily Witness*, various dates, 1893-1898.
Montreal *Gazette*, 1894, 1898.
Montreal *Herald*, various dates, 1894-1898.
New York *Tribune*, 1899.
Ottawa *Citizen*, 1898, 1979.
Ottawa *Daily Free Press*, various dates, 1893-1898.
Ottawa *Evening Journal*, 1893-1895.
Ottawa *Journal*, 1979.
Perth *Courier*, 1984.
Providence *Journal*, 1898.
Quebec *Daily Telegraph*, 1893.
Quebec *Mercury*, 1898.
Rochester *Chronicle*, 1898.
Toronto *Empire*, 1893.
Toronto *Evening Telegraph*, 1902, 1903.
Toronto *Globe*, various dates, 1893-1898.
Toronto *Maclean's*, 1984.
Toronto *Mail*, various dates, 1896-1898.
Toronto *Monetary Times*, 1893.
Toronto *News*, 1898.
Toronto *Star*, 1895, 1979.
Toronto *Week*, 1898.
Vancouver *Province*, 1974, 1977.
Vancouver *World*, 1903.
Vernon *News*, 1905.
Victoria *Colonist*, 1894.
Washington *Post*, 1893.

X. Periodicals

Philadelphia *Ladies Home Journal*, 1894.
Toronto *Canadian Magazine*, 1893.
Toronto *Saturday Night*, various dates, 1897.

List of Illustrations

Front cover: Portrait of Ishbel, Lady Aberdeen, hanging in Rideau Hall, Ottawa. Courtesy: Rideau Hall
Back cover: Dinner at Haddo House. Lady Aberdeen is in the centre with William Gladstone seated on her right and Lord Rosebery on her left. Courtesy: National Portrait Gallery.

INDEX

Individuals having more than a single title are indexed under the most commonly used appellation.

Gordon, Dudley Gladstone, 4th Marquess of Aberdeen and Temair, 55, 273, 297, 299.
Gordon, The Honourable Ian Archibald, 55, 69, 221, 273, 278-80.
Guisachan, Canada, 120-21.
Guisachan, Scotland, 17-18.

Haddo House, Aberdeenshire, 50-52, 300, 304.
Haddo, Lord, George Gordon, 2nd Marquess of Aberdeen and Temair, 55, 95, 206, 245-46, 272-73, 299, 303.
Haggart, J.C., 163-67, 173, 175-76, 197.
Hitler, Adolph, 315-17.
Hockey, 134.
Hogg, Quintin, 23, 68.
Holland, Francis, 30, 37, 40, 46.
Holmes, Oliver Wendell, 115.

Illegitimacy, 149-50.
Immigrants, domestic servants, 99, 100, 149; ethnic background, 148.
Imperialism, 92, 97, 116-17, 266-67.
International Council of Women, 152, 182, 229, 264-65, 300, 303, 305-08.
Irish Home Rule Bill, first, 79-81, 91.
Irish Home Rule, 128, 275-76, 291-94, 297-98.

Joly de Lotbinière, Henri Gustave, 172, 216, 217.

King, William Lyon Mackenzie, 308-10, 312-18.

Langevin, Sir Hector, 110.
Laurier, Sir Wilfrid, 115, 160, 161, 170, 172-75, 187, 190, 200-04, 208-11, 215, 217-22, 223, 229, 258, 260-61, 262.

Macdonald, Lady Agnes, 111-13, 143.
Macdonald, Sir John A., 98, 109.
Mackenzie, Dr. Tait, 206.
MacLeod, Charlotte, 236, 239, 255.
Marjoribanks, The, 13-14.
Marjoribanks, Archibald, 19, 29, 179, 224-25, 271.
Marjoribanks, Coutts, 19, 29, 55, 100, 118 and ff., 271.
Marjoribanks, Sir Dudley Coutts, Lord Tweedmouth, 12-17, 22, 25, 81, 141.
Marjoribanks, Edward, 2nd. Lord Tweedmouth, 19, 29, 245, 276-78.
Marjoribanks, Lady, Isabella (Hogg), Lady Tweedmouth, 15, 16, 25, 27, 87-89, 273, 276.
May Court Club, 213, 252-53, 254.
Mercier, Honoré, 93, 110.
Minto, Lord, 242-43, 256-57.
Moody, Dwight L. and Sankey, Ira D., 38, 66, 68, 83, 108.
Mowat, Oliver, 96, 215, 247.

National Council of Women in Canada, 152, 154-58, 182-83, 223, 255-58.
Native Indians, 149.

Okanagan Ranches, 118-22, 124-26.
Onward and Upward Association, 53-54.
Osler, (Dr.) Sir William, 237-38, 285-86.

Palmer, Mrs. Berthe Honore, 114, 208.
Pentland, Lady, Marjorie (Gordon) Sinclair, 22, 55, 95, 107, 115, 224-25, 271-72, 309.

Quebec Chapel, 30, 36.